Parthian Stranger

Parthian Stranger

The Order

Stewart N. Johnson

Order this book online at www.trafford.com
or email orders@trafford.com

Most Trafford titles are also available at major online book retailers.

Printed in the United States of America.

ISBN: 978-1-4269-5435-1 (sc)
ISBN: 978-1-4269-5436-8 (hc)
ISBN: 978-1-4269-5437-5 (e)

Library of Congress Control Number: 2011900112

Trafford rev. 01/12/2011

 www.trafford.com

North America & International
toll-free: 1 888 232 4444 (USA & Canada)
phone: 250 383 6864 ✦ fax: 812 355 4082

CH 1

The Escape

"COLD WAR OVER "
"BERUIT BOMBERS CAPTURED"
"THE WALLS OF RUSSIA BROKEN"

This was a time of peace, the dirty infighting between the three superpowers was over, but for some that were caught in the crossfire, well they sit and wait, some in isolation, others, like Jack, well just do not know why he is being held.

For Jack, the days of intelligence gathering and learning of his countries most valued secrets has landed him in a U S Prison, or so it seems, the real story as Jack remembers it is that the US was a neutral country, so when he was captured, by the East German secret police, for having the information, that lead to the bringing down of the Berlin wall and arresting those behind the nations divide.

The US steps in, in all matters relating to world peace, so he turned all the information over to them in exchange for freedom and a new life, or so he thought, what he really did was make a deal with the devil. He did get away to another country that protected him, that is what they do, incarcerate all the foreign spies. He knows he is from Germany, but he couldn't tell them his real name, or what region he comes from.

You see the US has a way for you to talk, or so it seems, he was defied, lied too, and he believed deep down he was and always be a German citizen.

They had other plans, the US is a controlling country, if you live in its borders, and you must conform to their beliefs. Like walk the walk and talk the talk, and suppress and thing you knew of your

1

past country, like believing in Hitler. He felt he was truly a great man. Some thought it was for the revenge he took on the Jews, some people thought it was a personal grudge, he had against their race, or the culture they represented, but he and the rest of his countrymen knew the real answer.

For those of us that do, well, just like him, he sits in a prison, with no hopes of parole, and this is where they will live their last days. A lot of forgiveness has happen over the years, they say time heals all wounds, for him, he has been somewhat forgotten, not of course to his fellow inmates, who have somewhat given him a name, for they call him the PARTHIAN STRANGER. He was given that name for the way he fought in close. Then when he was out in the yard he stood larger than life. You see being in here is all about reputations and history, for him, he quickly gained a reputation for killing another inmate with his thumbs, did it happen of course it did, he is no pansy, he knows deep down he has a backbone of a warrior. He just wishes he could remember who he was. He chose the name of Jack, because it's cool, not like John or, well who cares. He once saw an elder, who had that name and realized I like it, and took it.

So all in all a reputation was born, and grew, as he deliberately, paid in cigarettes to spread all the lies and deceptions he might have caused, to the point that they needed to assign a group of guards just for him, ultimately it was his demise, so when the chance came to be released, no one from the state department came to tell them to release him, so now he sits here in isolation, all by himself, over the years he has seen his share of prison's, but most of his time he spent, was at Leavenworth, in Kansas. It was hot and humid summer days, and then he began a friendship with a guard, who told him that he would help him get out.

The guard's name was Marquis White, he tried everything, the press, women visitors, back then it wasn't popular to marry an inmate, it was a wrong time for him, then something happen a few month's ago, a older man came and saw him, he said his name was Jim and that , I'd get a transfer notice, which usually means when you get those, it meant either a hanging or a firing squad, but this move was different, everything about this was different the way he talked with me, to the treatment, he did mention something about me helping him, but I don't know about that, so the big day came and instead of the leggings they use to place on me, and a deep internal search, they just handcuffed me in the front, and said I was off to some minimum security prison.

It was along the coast, so I thought, finally a change of pace, the ride was long, we stopped along the way, to eat in a diner, slept in a nice motel, I guess they felt I would not run, I even watched T V, as we traveled to the deeper south, the temperatures soared, and the humidity was even worse, we got out onto a road that over looked the ocean, they called it the Gulf of Mexico, their was a sign that said "Welcome to Mississippi, the hurricane alley.

The drive went up and over rolling hills, to what appeared to be a fortress, Jim and his partner, got out, and a gate opened, Jack was led in, a brief good bye to the old man, Jack proceeded, into the warden's office, an older man stood up to say "Welcome to our Mobile Prison, says here you are soon to be released, and that your in here for aggravated assault, well, I hope your reputation doesn't get you into trouble.

My friend Jim Bannister, assures me that your reformed, and need some time to get acquainted with the real world, so I'm here to tell you that you pretty much will have a wing to yourself and in two months you will be free".

"Guard take Jack, that is your name right"

"Yes sir" said a grinning Jack, as he waves goodbye to his old man"

"To his wing" said the warden with a smile.

"I'll see you soon," said Jim Bannister.

Jack stepped into a night and day scenario, the warmness was instantly gone, to a dark and damp, even wet place, as they took off his cuffs, he was led into a wing, and the door was closed, that was the last he would see anyone.

He walked into a kitchen, that was off to the right, and a lounge on the left, he quickly went through it, to find meals in a pouch, and a bulk of it was dried beef and crackers, he went a ways to see two cells one opposite each other, and a door, at the end, it was mid day, so he tried it was unlocked, so he went through, to a yard on the left and a open field on the right, quickly he thought, "I could escape", as he began to run, he realized "Stop, this is a test, " and turned around, he saw no one, and went back inside, as the rain, began to come down, it began to leak into the building, he went into the kitchen, and had dinner, days became nights and a month went by, no voices nothing.

Jack spent a lot of his time in his room; he grabbed a box of crackers and a box of beef, and sat on his bunk thinking one more month and he would be free.

On a cold and breezy day, he awoke, his eyes open, it was just like any other day, he swung his legs around to sit up on his cot. To face a huge rat that was at his grasp, he lunged for it, slipped and the doors slammed shut, he heard a clank, and then tried to pull on the door, it was locked.

For the next few days, he just sat there staring at the door, and no one was coming to check on him, "what was going on?" he thought.

Outside a group of men placed a large sign on the building, it said, "Condemned for Destruction, Do Not Enter"

Left behind was Jack, or so it seemed. Jack stood, and countless times tried to pull that door open, using all of his six foot frame. His weight varies from around 160 pounds, with sandy blonde hair and green eyes, as he looks in a half cracked mirror.

He sits back down on his cot and looks around at his 10 x 10 confined spaces. Now he was in confinement by himself forever. There seem to be a change in the weather; a warmer feel was in the air, the rains still came in the afternoon, as he ate his meal, which consists of a cracker and some dried beef.

After a quick workout of pushups and sit-ups, he would run in place for a good hour and then plunge into a warm water bath that he would replenish every day. The tub was once connected to a water source, which has not works in a month. Therefore, Jack rigged up a hollow pole from his bed supports and tapped into the gutter system and into the tub. He would wash his clothes, towels, and bed sheets with the last remaining bar of soap. After his chores he would reminisces while lying in the bed with his head on a pillow.

The first thing that comes to mind is how to escape the situation he is in. The crowing of several large black birds, were outside his window. Then the rains would come, the visibility was zero and last, a few minutes to all-day and night. On this day it was over before it started, next to his bed was the toilet, which is where the rats live. It is a hole lined in bricks and covered in adobe, he knows this because he felt he could dig his way out, unfortunately someone forgot to tell him it was a closed pit. The guards use to put limestone and sand down there, but those days are long gone. As he knows this from Leavenworth.

The rest of the day is consumed by trying to escape, at first, he was using a metal knife on the iron bars, and then next by digging out the mortar only to find more vertical and horizontal bars, he tried to pull the bars. He just realized he must be there all by himself. He doesn't care the more mortar he takes out of the wall, the more exposed he is to the cold wind, now with half the wall gone, he is working on a specific hole between several rods, trying to bend the ones to fit through it, it is almost big enough to get his head in, the work is slow and tedious. After a while, he gives up and lies back down.

The days are filled with some anxiety as he knows that two month has had come and gone, now what is going to happen; first? Die of starvation or finally escape, he looked up and saw a stick of metal rebar, with some excitement, he stood up, it must be a hallucinations, he picked up the bar and with all his mite he tried to put it out it broke free from the rust and proudly held it up, then a look of seriousness occurred, he pulled his bed away from the wall and began to ram the bar into the already damp wall.

Jack was consumed with zealous; he continued to prod the wall with the stick. Little by little, chunks of adobe came out, he continued to do this for the next several days, to finally show a wall of rebar and he cleaned up the adobe chunks by throwing them inside. Each hour was the same, the wall was now completely exposed, with careful examination he found where a place two bars left a gap, using a sheet tore he wrapped his hands.

Jack began to pull the bars away to expose a hole the size of his head. With each passing hour, the hole became bigger; to eventuality, he realized he could actually get through there. He put his head through the bars and realized his shoulder was stuck. Looking around he thought to himself

"Where are the guards?"

He looked back and forth in the courtyard; he could see the sun lit up the courtyard.

Although, not a single soul was around.

"What is going on?" said Jack out loud, expecting to hear a response, he admitted to himself that it had been quite quiet lately, still he was hoping for some sort of life, nothing with the exception of the birds and occasionally a big gust of wind, it was quiet., the day was turning colder, the storm was coming in, the day turned into a nightmare through the night. The rain was getting Jack wet. He even moved his bed to the inside bars, the rain flew in and everything was getting wet including his food. Jack waddled up the food, and then bunched up the sheets to cover them.

Hours had passed, the temperature was cold, then warm, then cold, and then warm, it was raining something fierce. When it rained and pours, his once dry bed was a sopping wet there was water everywhere. He began to shake and shiver, as it was unseasonably cold. This time it was coming sooner than later, he pulled the blanket over his head, the winds picked up, now with the rain and lightning and thunder noises going off, there was definitely a change in the air, he cuddled into the fetal position with his food by his stomach and went to sleep.

The next morning broke with a continual of rain, he was lying in a bed of wetness and water, he could feel the rat crawling on his side, the smell of wastes near him, he threw the blanket off and sprung up, he immediately saw, a huge opening in the bars, immediately he dove through the opening.

He stood up in knee deep water, he turned to see the roof was bent down and leaning, he could hear the sound of creaking, he began to back pedal in the water, only to see the building he called home, collapse as the water raced off the roof and cascaded in with him. The weight of the roof broke apart and came to rest.

Moments later, Jack realized he would have been crushed under that rubble, he stood up, walked back to the roof, and began to climb up out of the water and on to the roof sections; with his worn shoes on, he climbed to the top of the structure he once lived. Quickly he looked around, saw no one, and realized it was time for a break. Standing on the structure, it was moving under him. The closest thing to him was a big 20-foot wall, so he scrambled on top of the remaining roof and as close to the edge and without thinking he began to sprint to the wall, he began to dodge the debris and gained quick speed and at the last possible moment, he reached out and leaped. His forward momentum carried him to the fence, with his fingers outstretched, his tips caught the ledge and just missing the braided constaine wire, he caught it with both hands as his body hit and crashed against it. It took a moment to stop the swinging, he pulled himself up and just in time as he sat in a sitting position, he could feel the wind on his face, he rested, then stood up and saw a bridge he could leap to which he sprung off the fence and landed easily on the bridge. He got up, feeling the few cuts he just received, he looked around, nothing , then he quickly walked to a door, he tried it was locked.

"Darn it, now what" said Jack as he wiped his brow of excess rain.

He looked around to see another bridge that led to the front the looked down and saw two sets of at least ten-foot high chain-link fences with a razor sharp Constantine wire. He decided to lower himself to the ground, he went for it, first sliding his legs out and facing the wall he lowered himself as far as he could go without letting himself go, holding on by his fingertips.

He began to count off.............

"Three, two, and one" he said and let go.

The fall seemed like an eternity, he hit the soft sandy soil and did a quick roll to absorb the impact; he came to a rest next to the fence, which he came to a rest next to the fence, which he could not remember if it was electrified.

"Wait what is going on here, maybe the storm knocked out the power"

He stood up and began to walk the walls perimeter to find the easiest way out. After walking around, he went back to the front and waited until dark to make his next move. He stood still and waited for the guards to come....

The sun began to set, he slowly climbed the first fence he got to the top in one motion he swung his leg out and onto the sharp wire. A stinging sensation was felt.

Jack carefully worked his way down the middle fence and slowly he put one foot down onto a sharp object, it went right through his shoe. A scream was building within his lungs that never surfaced quickly he lifted his foot back up and began to climb backup

"Damn them they put those steel stakes in the ground, Damn them." he cried to himself

Now looking back over his shoulder, he said to himself;

"I'm going to have to jump and hope it's not too bad."

In one instant he leaped off the fence and turning in mid flight to face the next fence only to hit it face first trying to catch the fence with his hands and missing he fell to the ground with his feet first, the left first and the same absorbing the sharp stick this time going into the foot, quick enough Jack clung to the fence and pulled up his foot and leg which was cut as well, blood flowed fast. Jack made his way up this fence fast and in one movement when he reached the top he swung over the sharp wire and without thinking he lost his grip and fell back to the ground, he landed on a slope slid around and the exhaustion and the impact put him out. His body went limp.

The next morning he awoke with a rush of blood to his head he tried to get up only to have his legs come over the top of his head. He turned around to the sitting position and felt his foot and leg was numb, he looked down at his leg to see that the wounds were superficial. Slowly he rose up, feeling his right foot was still throbbing he began to walk a little ways to the next fence. However he had two options this time either climb this last fence or dig at the base, he looked over to see a small rabbit hole, he made his choice and began to climb this last fence, he got to the top, he was at the tree level, he could see cars and a highway as the cars whizzed by.

Jack would duck down, and continued to watch the cars then decided to go for it, he moved and swung his legs over and in one motion he cleared the fence and freedom he didn't care and simply let go, he fell forward covering his face with his arm as he hit some sticky bushes before he came to a stop he rolled over on his back looked up to see he was surrounded by blueberries.

Jack picked one, smelled it and placed it in his mouth. Began to consume it, they became addictive eating till he was full. He stood up, looking over his arms and legs were scratches, his clothes were ripped to shreds, he continued to forage the blueberries, nightfall was coming soon, and so was the rain. He slowly made his way down to the highway then he began to slid down into a stream, he paused to take a drink, he followed the steam down to a large drainage pipe, along the side of a large bridge. He quickly made his way in and the sounds of cars and trucks died down, he continued into the pipe. He paused at a high place where a tee section was and it was higher, enough for him to lie down, to rest, lying on his side he rested his head on his arm. And fell fast asleep.

The sound of rushing water awoke him; he opened his eyes to see a large rat in his face he tried to grab it, only to see it slip though his hands. He rose up on his knees and followed the rushing water, down the tube, till the light grew brighter, he got closer to the end, the light opened up to a hazy day, as he hit the cool sand.

A fury of raindrops abound, rather large drops began to pelt his face, then the beach was getting hammered, in one quick moment, freedom was in his mind, he began to run on the beach, his momentum caused him to stumble and he went face first into the sand. He rolled around and began to dig in the sand, the rain came down and he was soaked a bit of a chill overcame him.

"Hey you" yelled a voice on the bridge

Jack stopped what he was doing, looked up and gave the guy a silent stare, then went back to what he was doing.

"Do you need help?" yelled the voice

Jack stopped what he was doing, stood up, looked towards the bridge, and then ran into the ocean, the first few steps were wet, and then a wave of warmth hit him as he dove in face first, instantly he felt the warm water.

Quickly a stinging sensation turned to a good burn was happened to his body, but he knew it felt good, he began to swim, it was a fond memory and he knew he loved it. The water was warm, not to cold, he continued to stay under, holding his breathe; occasionally he popped his head up to see if that guy was gone. Jack followed the beach and the current as it took him into an inlet channel sort of a cove.

The water turned cold, just as something brushed by him. He stood up in knee deep water, looking down to see a large fin, he grabbed at it, only to miss the slimy fish, but determination, Jack dove on it and grabbed it by the front gill and hauled it up to reveal a large catfish, in one motion he threw it up and on the grass, he worked his way out of the water and lifted himself out and on the grass, He saw the fish flapping on the grass, Jack went over and hooked the fish by its gill, he looked around and saw the large house on a small hill, so Jack went up the hill to a small clearing, once on the flat level of the hill he saw the oversized pool and a stainless steel grill, as he approached the grill he noticed the house, looked empty. He did not care it had been too long to enjoy a cooked fish; He opened the new grill and placed the still alive fish on the grill and shut the lid. He turned on the gas, turned the switch and with a flick the grill was lit, he placed it on medium heat, after a moment, the banging noise was gone as the hot flames put the fish to rest.

Jack began his search for what ever he could find, it started with the cabinet next to the grill where he found a salt, and peppershaker and some spices, he could smell the fish cooking. He opened the lid and with the salt, pepper, and spices he seasoned the fish on one side, then lifted the whole fish by the gill, and turned it over. He then closed the lid. He continued the search and made a discovery a long knife in a sheath, which he put in his shredded pants pocket. He found a spatula and a platter.

Jack turned the flame down and opened the lid; he rolled the fish over and began to cut the fish into sections with his new knife. He cut off the fins, tail and the head and placed them on the platter along with the rear section of the fish. With his fingers, he devoured the fish only to pause to remove the bones.

"That was good I think I will have another piece," he said to himself.

With the spatula in hand Jack divided the fish up and he had seven large steaks, which he divided and then seasoned each side.

Each was finishing cooking, as the grill cooled, he plated them and cut them up removing the bones. He thought that consuming this fish was the best meal he has had in a while.

Jack felt that meat is so great tasting. After a while, Jack grew restless, it was time to go, maybe search this house it was mid-morning. Jack tried the rear door and it was locked, but he looked up and saw a window open, Jack made his way up the stairs to the second floor deck; Jack peaked in to see it was a kitchen window, with his hand he pulled the window fully open and slowly climbed in.

Standing in the kitchen nothing jumped out at him, so he went room to room first he came onto a Child's room, then the master bedroom, it opened up into a small sitting room and off of it was a office, quickly he went through the drawers and found nothing, then he saw a bookshelf that looked out of place or a bit odd to him, so he began to touch all of the books when it triggered a big book to open to reveal a safe. Jack tried the handle and it clicked open, he swung the door open.

"Who in there right mind would leave a safe unlocked," said Jack to himself shaking his head in disbelief.

Jack looked in and saw a stack of girlie magazines, two stacks of paper sealed hundreds and some vials of fluid.

"Jackpot" said Jack aloud.

Quickly, he pulled the cash out and placed it on the desk, then stopped, he was silent and still he thought he heard a noise, and then he placed each bundle in each of his pockets and then closed the safe door, and repositioned the book when a clear voice said

"Honey lets begin this," said a sweet voice

Jack heard a man's voice say, "I can't believe you seduced my best friend for your sexual desires, you bitch"

"What are you saying, while I was with him you slept with his wife" said the girl

"So what, I can and you can't," said the guy

Jack repositioned his stance and pulled the knife and held it in a strike pose, just behind the door, which he pulled it a little bit more to hear better.

"You're a jerk, Ben" said the girl and adds, "If I hadn't caught you with her and her sister, we wouldn't be in this mess.

"Hey come here sweetie," said Ben

Whack, Jack heard the girl get punched, as she went down. She hit with such, a loud force that she began to sob violently, Jack was ready to move when he heard

"Ben please leaves me alone," said the girl desperately

"Leave you alone, you bitch, I'm going to mess you up. No one cheats on me and gets away with it."

Jack was already moving, with knife ready. Jack opened the door to see the guy on top of the girl throwing fist clenching punches at her face, in a instant, Jack used his free arm and placed it under Ben throat and pulled him up

"Quiet" said Jack as he placed the knife to his throat.

"Get up miss" said Jack in a command voice, Jack and Ben watched the girl slowly get up her face was bloodied and tears were streaming down her face.

"Please mister, we don't want any trouble," she said in between sobs.

"Are you with the mob?" said Ben

"Shut up, or I will cut your throat, you got that tough boy" said Jack to his ear.

The girl began to calm down a bit enough to say" Please mister do not hurt my husband, I love him.

"Sit down miss" said Jack and looks at her to say;

"Did he hurt you?"

"Yeah, but what's new, honestly this guy isn't even my husband" she said

"Shut up you whore" said Ben

Jack firmed up the knife against his neck and said" Another word out of you and you will be dead.

Jack looked at the girl who was looking at him as she spoke in a calm collected voice, she stood to say" Look mister, this guy has a safe in the next room, how about you and I split the money if you let me cap his ass." she was slowly moving to a dresser as both Jack and Ben watched

"No bitch, leave my gun alone" said Ben, Jack kept his word and sliced him from below the cheek to the other side only to see the girl turn with a gun.

She held it firm in her hands and pointed the gun at Jack and pulled the trigger, Jack jumped out of the way as the two bullets hit Ben true and in the chest. Jack peered over the table to see the girl drop the weapon.

"Alright let's go" she said
Jack looked at her in disbelief and said "What's going on here"

"Look this prick owes me and my boss some money and I was here to collect it" she said as she walked into the office to discover the money was missing.

"Hey mister, do you have the money" she yells to Jack
She turns to see Jack holding the gun on her as he says;

"Yeah I got my money"

"Let's go" she said in a rush

"Where" said Jack

"My cars outside and I can take back to my place and I will show you a real good time"

"What does that mean?" said Jack

"I will invite a few of my friends over and we will have a fucky sucky party and you're the guest of honor." said the girl with a coy smile.
Jack backed up to let her out and turned his head long enough for her to grab a syringe, she led the way as Jack followed keeping the gun pointed on her.
Out the front door he went to see her slid into the driver's seat and fire up the car, it sat idling while Jack pondered his next move, the passenger door opened as the girl leaned over to say;

"Come on get in, the cops are on their way"
In the distance, a siren could be heard and it was getting louder by the minute.
Jack made his move, got in, and shut the door. The car sped off and down a dirt road over a wooden bridge and onto a side street only to pass a police car going the other direction.

"That was close, you like to live on the dangerous side" said the girl as she took a bite out of his ear, but Jack pulled it away before she drew blood. He pushed her away.

"Thanks for saving my life, if you hadn't been there it would have been the same ole thing, he beats me up for a while and then screws me until I'm sore then finds another hole until I'm numb then calls over his friends and when it is all over with he throws me out." she said complaining to him, Jack just sat in silence keeping the gun on this new challenge.

The drive was short as she drove through the marina and drove towards a large building, where she took a sharp right turn and down a driveway, she hit a remote button and the large door opened, she drove down with a few turns she came to a stop.

"How about a kiss, "she said leaning her face to his, Jack backed away and said "No."

"Come on" she said coyly and adds" Come on up to my apartment looks like you could use a shower and a shave."

"Listen honey,, I will invite over a few girlfriends and I will cook you a steak and potatoes dinner." "How's that, and then if you want you can leave at any time?"

Jack slowly responded "Alright"

"What's your name mister?" said the girl

"Jack" said Jack, leaving the car behind he followed her a few steps behind, she turned to say "My name is Jennifer, but you can call me Jen" she lead the way to the elevator hit the call button and turned around to see Jack still had the gun on her.

"Come on Jack, you can put the gun away I won't hurt you, you have it all and in a little while you'll have Me." she said with authority.

Jack let down his guard, and placed the gun on safety and placed the gun in his back pocket.

"You know Jack, you did me such a big favor, thank you" as she reached out and hugged him as the elevator doors opened and several large men stepped out. Jack heard one man say;

"She's at it again"

The two broke their kiss and embrace, she led the way to the elevator, and Jack stood with his back against the sidewall. He watched as she pushed the button. They stood on opposite ends of the car as it traveled upward. He watched her in silence. The elevator came to a stop, she got off first, Jack followed her, and she led the way to a door just off the elevator.

She opened the door and said "Come on in, I won't bite you? Yet! "

Jack walked in, the room opened up to a kitchen right by the door and a large living room.

"Do you want to take a shower?" she said.

He nodded in agreement, as she led him to the bathroom to show him, the towels and soap. To add, "You can undress in my room, and then go into the master bathroom"

He watched her leave, closed the door and he locked it.

He finally felt relief, he sat down for a moment to relax and collect his thoughts.

Meanwhile Jen was on the phone to her two girlfriends and let them know it was a party. She went ahead to start working on that dinner she had promised Jack, by putting the potatoes in the microwave and some vegetables on the stove, next she marinated the meat with a spice rub blend and let it sit. She heard the shower come on; she just continued to work in preparing the meal.

Jack finished the shower and had a quick shave, he found some perfume and put some of that on, a knock on the door. Jack opened the door to see Jen holding some white briefs in her hand.

"This is for you to wear, they should fit" she hands them to him. His look caught her off guard and said "Wow you cleanup well" with a smile as he closed the door on her.

Jack could smell the now cooked food. Jack stepped out of the bathroom with his shorts and he was barefooted. He walked into the living room to see Jen had a nice place setting.

"Jack come over and have a seat and help yourself" said Jen

Jack nodded his head in acknowledgement then took a seat across from her and did not wait for her as he devoured his steak and loaded potato, he slowed so that she can catch up him.

"This was good, thank you" said Jack sincerely

"So you are a proper and sincere man, most guys I know take take take, without a simple thank you, its refreshing, I knew the moment I laid eyes on you, you were different, from now on, this is only the beginning, what I have in store for you, your gonna need your strength for and I hope you have enough stamina to go all night" she said defiantly.

"Sure" said Jack finishing his plate of food. You could cut the tension with a knife. When finally Jen spoke up and said "Take a seat on the sofa".

"Now that were finished with dinner let's go have some fun."

Jen got up first and adds "How bout I take off my clothes" and with that she began to slowly undress in front of Jack first was her top to reveal a creamy white tight bra which in one instant she popped off much to Jack's surprise, now topless all Jack could do was to stare at those breasts. She moved over towards him, placing her breasts near his face as she says   "Go ahead and touch them"

Jack slowly obliged her wishes and began to slowly touch.

He was slow and she sensed it, to reassure him with her own hands. He continued to go slow, taking his time, touching and how she felt and her baby smooth skin.

"Use your tongue, that's it, ooh yeah now that feels good" said Jen.

Jack quickly was getting a handle on this as his own excitement level was increasing as well. Jack continued just to focus on her breasts when Jen said

"Why don't you go down a little lower?"

Jack turned in the sofa and now faced her to watch her undo her pants, which she wiggled out of slowly and to her own beat, leaving her transparent g-string for Jack to remove

"Go ahead big boy, pull them down and begin to satisfy my needs"

Jack hesitated this was unknown terroritory it had been so long and the only pleasure he knew was for himself.

"Don't be shy, let me lead the way for you, with that in one fatal swoop, she stepped back and with one hand pulled off her thin panties and tossed them at Jack, who let them fall to the floor. Jen was now nude with the exception of her socks, moves in and says

"It's time for a lesson, now look up"

Jen moved forward and planted her crotch right in his face and said;

"Now lick me with your tongue, until I'm wet all over"

There was no more hesitation or delay's, Jack was forced to do it. He began with zeal and brought her, to her first climax, then another, and another, it was no longer work it was easy and pleasurable and with ease.

He was enjoying himself immensely until finally she had enough and it all came to a crashing halt.

"Ooh my god, your such a stud" remarked Jen falling back to the floor, followed by Jack who was now a animal in heat, he was pulling his shorts down to show her his manhood, he fell in between her legs and spread them wider, eager Jack entered her rock hard and ready body, his fast simulations indicated he was wild.

"Whoa tiger, slow down this is no race, take your time and make every stroke count"

Jack slowed his pace, even though he was ready to erupt now, all of a sudden Jen put on the brakes and began to hold off his climax, as she clamped down on his member.

"In the Kama Sutras, this is called fore -shadowing".

"I'll let you know when and where you can drop your load" Said Jen with the authority.

Jack followed suit and slowed to a gut wrenching pace and began to feel each stroke, and with each wave, Jen put on the brakes and showed she was in control.

Both of there bodies were sweaty and building up a lot of energy, she was very well lubricated and Jack was ready to unleash his fury.

"Now, I know your ready Jack, so what I want you to do is, pull it out and bring it to me"

Jack slowly withdrew, it ached him to leave the hot surroundings and got up and knelt in front of her face. Not knowing what to expect, Jen took him into her mouth and began to start the process and release twenty years of pent up emotions, Jack let loose, the build up was so fierce Jen began to gag and spit up and Jack had to get a hold of that fire hose, which he held on while it squirted all over her breasts, the build up was so strong, it just kept going and going till it ache and Jack fell on top of Jen. As they calmed, they both rested. Jen held him in her arms.

A loud buzz went off, Jen rolled out from under Jack to get up and go to the door.

Jack lay on his back with his flagpole still climbing to erect. With his eyes closed, Jack rested his head on the floor.

Jen opened the door just slightly to let her girlfriends in and said "Good you brought some beer."

"And some party favors" said one of the girls

The two girls smiled at Jen as she said "Let me introduce you guys to my new friend"

Both girls followed Jen as she locked and dead bolted the door, to the living room to see a well-hung man on the floor.

"Looks like you need some help" said one girl

"Jack, Jack, these are my two closest friends Tiffany the brunette and Clarisse the red-head."

Jack looked up to see one girl was young and the other was older, at a point Jack did not care anymore he was in heaven. He just smiled up to them.

"What shall we do first some smack or get this guy laid" said the older Clarisse

"You girls choose, Jack and I already went round one" said Jen popping the cap on a couple of beers.

She carried them to the living room and adds "Jack here's a beer for you honey" Jen hands it to him and he says

" Thanks, it looks like you girls are a little over dressed for the occasion."

The response was well received by both girls as Clarisse spoke first "I guess Jack made up our minds" and with that both undressed in a flash, Tiffany was first to mount an attack and continued to stroke the flagpole while Clarisse lowered herself down on Jack's face.

"Watch out Clarisse, your in for the ride of your life." said Jen who sat back watching the two girls have some fun, but it was short lived, after finishing off the beer, she was ready to go again and take advantage of Jack. Arms and legs were all over as one crotch leaves another replaces it and the face sucking of his manhood became another wild ride as Jen lowered herself back on him this time in a sitting position, and with the help from her friends was able to enjoy another full body explosion and saturation climax to drench Jack in her fluids, before getting up Jack made a deposit he so wanted to do earlier, as he finished with Jen, came the very young Tiffany who was so tight it hurt at first for Jack, but after a few strokes she lubricated up well and it was tight but well deserving as he felt more staying power and control as each stroke he took and the satisfaction Tiffany had from what Jack was doing and enjoying himself.

Jack was losing himself in the wave of euphoria. Last was Clarisse, Jack's least favorite of the bunch, she was a lot older and much looser, she grind down on him and at times he was losing his staying power. Jack's tongue was going a mile a minute, tasting the sweet juices from Tiffany as she lowered herself onto his mouth, He did his magic, which kept his mind off of the older woman who was on her own ride. The ride was over before it began; Jack was tiring of this event with Clarisse and wished for it to be over soon. Jack's inability to keep it strong forced Clarisse to stop and slid off. She got up and walked over to Jen who was in the kitchen washing up the dishes.

"Whatcha doing?" asked Clarisse

"Oh just finishing up the dishes" said Jen

"You got any smack?" said Clarisse

"Yeah I got a needle in my purse" said Jen she watched her comb through her things to find the needle and in that moment stuck it in and pushed it down, extracted it and threw it away.

"Thanks for leaving me some" said Jen who went back to doing her thing, while Clarisse made her way back to the couch to take a seat and watch Jack enjoy himself with Tiffany.

Tiffany had repositioned herself from Jack's face down to his groin, and brought him back to life.

A loud knock on the door, sent Jen to her room to put on a robe, as the knocking continued and it became louder, until Jen opened the door, with the deadbolt chain still on and said ; "What"

"You don't answer my calls, you have a John in there or what?" and adds "You better not be keeping a secret from me or I will beat you down you whore" said the guy on the outside looking in, do you have the money, the boss wants it now"

"Keep quite Vinnie you'll disturb my friend, he is no john, so go away and leave us alone" said Jen

"You got two hours then I'm coming in and you better have my money, from your lover boy." said Vinnie.

"You'll get it all, so leave me alone" said Jen closing the door and locking it shut. Her mood changed, and her demeanor.

Jack and Tiffany finished another session, leaving Jack to lie on the floor to rest while Tiffany went to the kitchen, saw Jen, and said;

"Can I have a beer for Jack and me?"

"Sure help yourself" said Jen

Tiffany walked past Jen to notice she was doing something a bit odd and said "Who's that for" pointing to the counter

"Shss, it's a secret" said Jen breaking up some white pills with the back edge of a spoon, and leaving a nice line of powder.

"You won't need that, cause Clarisse and I plan on keeping him busy for a while and if you give that to him, he'll be out, and we'd like to enjoy him a bit longer, besides he seems harmless and when's the last time you had a hunk over for us to share, you owe us." said Tiffany carrying two beers.

"Yeah your right" said Jen and adds "Hand me your beers and I will pop the tops"

Tiffany placed the bottles on the counter and said "I'm going to use the little girl's room" and walks off. Jen quickly popped each top and put a scoop of powder in each of the bottles.

She then takes them into the living room, standing over Jack she said;

"Jack here is something to drink"

Jack opened his eyes, reached up to rub the inside of Jen's leg pulling her closer to him with enough force she fell to her knees and sat down on his crotch, and parted her robe, which opened and Jack was ready for another challenge, Jen handed a beer to Jack who took a big swig and continued to fondle her breasts at the same time. Jen moved around a bit and found what she was looking for, she lifted up and with her free hand guided it in to herself and sat down, this time she was doing all the work, but her mind was elsewhere, as Tiffany came out of the bathroom having refreshed herself and took the beer out of Jen's hand and drank it down, as Clarisse took the beer from Jack to drink it down, while watching Jen and Jack work out to another climax together, feeling a bit left out.

Tiffany set down her beer and joined in the fun by lowering herself down on Jack's face, while facing Jen. The two both grind down on Jack, until Jack let out a huge muffled sound and his body quivered and went still.

Both girls stopped the grinding and stood up.

They moved next to each other to look him over, looking down at him, Tiffany said "You couldn't leave well enough alone, could you." Jack had a smile on his face yet it appeared he was dead. Jen knelt down and could here him breathing and said" At least he's alive" and adds "Lets get him to my room, can you go into the walk-in closet and get me a sheet" said Jen.

Tiffany then looks over at Clarisse whom was passed out on the couch as she laid on her side.

Tiffany returned with a sheet and saw Jen pulling Jack onto the bed, herself as both Tiffany and Jen covered him up.

"I didn't know you were so strong, you lifted Jack all by yourself"

"Look at him he is skin and bones, it was like he was in prison for twenty years"

"I guess the parties over" said Tiffany, "You lied to me, you did drug them both, maybe I should go?"

"Wait, why don't you spend the night" said Jen, "have a seat on the couch"

"You know I am kind of feeling sick to my stomach" said Tiffany, got up, and went into the bathroom.

Jen waited for her to leave, to decide what to do next.

"Great" said Jen to herself, "I got one passed out and the other sick, and Vinnie on my ass "said Jen to herself, she began to dress and then went through Jack's shirt and found the money, the gun and a knife only to pick up the money and grabbed her keys and went out the door and closed it shut and locked it down..

Tiffany came out of the bathroom having finished removing the white stuff from her stomach as she was allergic to them and found the apartment empty and called out to Jen;

" Where's you at, you bitch"

"Come on, Jen where are you at?" Tiffany said as she pulled her own gun out. then she quickly turned her attention on Jack, she lifted the sheet, to see his manhood in full display, Tiffany went back to work on Jack, by using some new techniques and to her surprise he came back to life although he still seemed passed out. Tiffany lowered herself on him and did all the work, Clarisse had revived herself and got up go get something to drink, and a bit woozy to walk she stumbled to the kitchen.

Clarisse saw a line of powder which she took her time and snorted it all down, then drunk a beer down. Then went back into the living room only to fall down and pass out.

Tiffany continued on and on for several more hours, until she heard noises, she looked back and saw a bunch of guys ruined her morning, unbeknownst to Tiffany the room was filled with macho men watching her get off; quickly she pulled the sheet over herself and Jack. The guy who appeared to be the leader, looked over Jack and said;

" You crazy bitch, this guy is passed out", the guy then used his fist and hit Tiffany in the head, she fell off of Jack, her head bloodied scrambled to get up, then fell flat down to a thud.

"Whatcha shoot her for you idiot" yelled up to the guy by the boss

"Sorry Vinnie, my bad"

"You're a jackass we could have had our way with her" said another

"Let's clean up this mess, get the coke whore and dump her in the dumpster and lets take the cute girl to the ocean and dump her body"

"What's about the guy?"

"Lets leave him here, maybe Jen will come back for her lover.

"We will wait for her return, so let's go" and adds "Will someone please cover up the guy and give him some respect".

Meeting Sara Sanders

Jack opened his eyes, a wave of warmth he could feel, both his legs and stomach was wet, he got up, still feeling a bit fatigued and pulled the sheet from over his body, slowly he made his way up. He made his way to the bathroom. Jack did his business and took a shower and shaved, he noticed how swollen his member was and made his way into Jen's room, he found some men's clothing in one drawer and some business slacks in the closet with a matching sports jacket, a bit big for him, but still fit anyway, a pair of socks and a pair of tight fitting dress shoes, he went out to the living room to find the place empty and then went back into the room, to see his pants on the side of the bed, inside he found the knife, he put into his coat pocket.

"What just happened?" was I drugged, "said Jack looking over the place to see a few blood stains. Then an idea came over him, and in a blaze Jack began to dismantle the room and into her bedroom. He began to emptying every drawer, turned the mattress and wrecked the closet, on his mass destruction tour he knocked off a shoe box and its contents fell to the floor, literally in going in all directions were twenties, he scrabbled to pick them up and stuff them into his coat jacket pocket. After a final search, he opened the apartment door, and looked out to see if it was clear, he was now cautious, he pulled the apartment door shut and went down to the elevator, but chose the stairs first, Jack took two stairs at a time to reaching the lobby. Jack opened the door, he moved slowly then picked up the pace, the coast was clear, he did a fast walk, when out of the corner of his eye he saw something and ducked, it was a bat as it swung over his head.

Jack knelt down and delivered a gut shot to the attacker, off balanced the guy dropped to the floor. In a split second Jack knew he could run or fight. Jack picked up the discarded bat and hit a homerun using the guy's head as the ball. A quick search, he found a wallet and a side arm, in a shoulder holster, which he removed from the dead guy. Jack took off his jacket and put on the shoulder holster, and then he put the jacket back on. Jack also found an ammo clip and a shoe knife which he put in his pocket. Jack was on the move, and positioned himself next to a wall when he heard a voice cry out;

"Frankie, you find that guy yet?"

"Yeah, I'm your man" said Jack stepping out from behind the wall, with a smile.

"Look mister we want no trouble all we want is your money and tell us where Jen is at." said the guy from behind another wall.

"I don't know where she is at and I don't care, if you want my money, then you come and take it from me" said Jack.
Jack was walking to that voice, he pulled his weapon, took it off the safety and held it up, ready for use. Jack continued to the spot where the guy was. And said "I can't hear you, didn't you say you wanted my money?"

"You aint the guy" said a weak voice

"I aint who's guy? I'm a guy the guy whose is gonna kill you." said Jack, standing right by the worried guy.

"Listen mister, we got it all wrong, you can go and we won't follow you"

"I, know, cause you aint gonna be round anymore." said Jack, stepping out and seeing the guy running away, Jack pulled off a shot, the guy fell forward. Jack moved in, and saw his work and was starting to remember who he used to be. Looking down the quick urination was the answer, a quick search found a wallet, a better gun which he put into his pocket and a silencer which he screwed on to the gun and much to Jack's surprise a right side shoulder holster to match the one he already had. Jack also found a wad of cash and a book of business cards, Jack turned to catch a glimpse of Jen at the elevator, Jack put on the other holster and tied them to together in the back, replaced the coat. Jack was on the move, through the stair's door and two to three stairs at a time; he stumbled and hit his knee. Jack came to a stop as the pain was intense, minutes went by, then he got up and walked normal, there was no more need to rush, he exited on her floor and knocked on Jen's apartment door while having his back up against the wall.

"This is Paulie, I got the guy" said Jack who holstered his weapon and pulled his fillet knife. The door opened to see a guy's face, in a quick move Jack was behind the guy and held the knife to his throat and walked him in. Jack walked in holding the guy with his free hand and arm and keeping pressure with his other hand on the knife.

"Hold on, mister, let Jimmy go and "the guy stopped in mid-sentence to look at Jack and speaks to Jen "This isn't your lover, so who is this guy?"

"Let the girl go" said Jack.
Both Jen and the others began to laugh, "This smuck don't know, does he" said the boss

"You can let Jimmy go" said a voice behind Jack "or I will kill you"
Jack made his move in a instant and slit Jimmie throat and turned to stab the guy in the chest, but not before getting off a couple of shots which Jack avoided, he turned to reveal both his weapons and face both the boss and Jen. Jack was eager to pull the trigger when Jen spoke up;

"Listen up boys, were not here to kill each other"

"Jack this is Johnny he runs the south crew, I told them about how you helped me and they want to hire you"

"Who's they" said Jack still holding his weapons out and on the ready

"Were the Russell family and we control most of Mississippi and Florida and a bit of Georgia. That's who" said Johnnie still holding a gun to Jack.
Jack still was looking back and forth, in his mind, he knew, he could care less, but held to Jen's wishes and shoulders each weapon. Johnnie still had his weapon on Jack

"Johnnie" screamed Jen "put the gun down."

"It aint over till I get revenge for Jimmy's, Frankie and Paulie death."
Jack waited no more, and pulled his gun and shot Johnnie. The bullet lodged in his neck, Johnnie was going down, and began to pull the trigger the gun was pointed at Jen, the first one hit her in the shoulder, the a second one , then a third one, Jen fell back and was dead before she hit the ground. Jack walked over to Johnnie still alive and said;

"I always work alone" then he ended his life. Jack did a quick survey to see the other two were dead or dying as well, then Jack did a quick search of the bodies collecting up there wallets and a few money clips and several sets of keys with keyless entry and on the table was a bag, on the table was the two money sets he originally had, he picked them up and tossed them in the bag. Jack then put the keys into.

Jack walked out of the room with bag in hand and several more ammo clips for his new small 9mm berretta and his primary weapon his 45cal combat colt commander, it will be his in close fighting weapon, he was on the move, he made his way to the stairs, he went down to see that the lobby was still empty, a wail of sirens was coming closer and more of them joined in. Jack paused thinking either go out the front, but as time was ticking off, he had to go now.

Jack crossed the lobby and exited into the courtyard to see a pool and walked past that to a gate, he went through that to a dead end, off to the left was a metal gate, he tried it was locked.

The sirens were close now, Jack decided to climb, up the wire fence and up to the second floor, hopping down onto the landing, and then up to the third level, it appeared that these apartments was the building next to the hotel. Jack knocked on the first door, waited, then, the next door and knocked on it to, a guy standing in the door way and said;   "Who the hell are you?"

"Wrong door" said Jack seeing the guy close the door and the first door open to an older lady who says "whats'a want mister"

"Wrong door " said Jack on his way down to two more doors, which he knocked on the third door.

Jack wasn't waiting for a response and knocked on the fourth, the door opened, Jack could see police was now present in the courtyard, so when the door opened he forced his way in, much to his surprise, a very pretty girl, was driven back into her living room, Jack pulled his colt commander and pointed it at her and said "Sit down miss and I wont hurt you."

She kept her mouth shut and nervously sat down. Jack waited by the window, with gun ready

"I can get you out?" said the girl

"Shut up, let me think a minute, your right, your gonna get me out" said Jack reholstering the gun, and adds "Take off your clothes"

She just looked at him as if he was crazy. She shook her head "No" and mouthed it to him.

Jack pulled his weapon safety off, as she heard it click.

"Whoa, Mister, wait a minute I don't want to die" she rose, she was shaking, as she pulled off her top, and slipped out of her pants.

"Everything" said Jack.

"I believe your not gonna shoot me, cause the cops will her it, just like when I start screaming" said a now defiant girl.

Jack pulled out a tube from his jacket, screwed it on the end and pointed it at her and fired a shot just jerking it away at the last moment to hit the wall all she heard was a thud noise.

"Alright, I get the point." then she turned and popped off her bra and slowly slipped off her panties.

"Come over here" said Jack now putting the weapon downward but still holding it firm, she turned to face him.

Then with one hand hiding her crotch and the other arm and hand hiding her small breasts. She slowly moved towards him. She was trembling and says "Are you gonna rape me?"

"Shut up" said Jack and adds "Go into the kitchen and wet you're her hair down, matter-of-fact why don't you wet your entire body down." He watched as she had her back to him, first she did as she was told, then her next instinct was to reach for a cooking knife, thinking back to when she refused to take a self defense course instead of just going to the beach.

"You grab that knife and I will drill you where you stand" said Jack
This time she felt no shame as she turned to face Jack with her hands to her side, her trembling stopped, now the excitement was kicking in as she says "What do you want to do with me now mister?"

"Go find a towel, and cover yourself up" said Jack, he watched her walk past him, like she was flirting with him and says;

"You might have to follow me" she winked at him as she pasted by, for her to say" I'll run the shower"
Jack kept his distance just to see her stop at a closet, open the door and bend over, slowly lifting up and holding a towel in her hand and says "Do you want to put this on me?"

"Nah, I think you can do it yourself, imagine that you just got out of the shower and hurry up" said a calm Jack, as he watched her put the towel around her top part covering herself up and another towel around her hair, she stepped into the bathroom, to run the shower, then turned it off.

"Now come here, I want you close to me" she moved as a few moments passed, she was standing in her living room, looking at him and said "What's your name?" she started to tease him by adjusting her towel.

"Jack" he said

"Is that your real name or are you lying to me?"

"Nah, its just Jack"

"My name is Sara, are you a hit man?"

"Nah, why do you want to know?"

"You're tough and rough and a guy like that can come in handy when"
A knock on the door "It's the police open up", Jack pulled his weapon up and motioned for her to come close, Jack dropped the bag and with his left hand Jack pulled her to him.
And whispered "Answer the police and if you scream you're dead as well as him and any of his friends, you got that?"
She nodded in acknowledgement and spoke loudly "I'll be there in a minute"
Jack let her go, as she turned the handle and opened the door to see a pair of officers

"Sorry miss, we hate to bother you, but were looking for a man, who some people had said they saw knocking on doors, did someone knock on your door?"

"No, not that I know of, I was in the shower"

"O Kay, would it be alright if we did a quick search of your apartment anyway?"

Jack placed the gun in the lower of her back.

"I'd rather you not please, my house is a mess, but if you must, go ahead" she stepped back and held the door up against Jack hiding him from there view.

"Go ahead I have nothing to hid" using her hand as a wand, the first officer went in, did a quick search, in the bedrooms and bathroom and said "You keep a pretty clean bathroom, there was sure a lot of water on the floor" said the officer seeing it was clear he said;   "Here is my card and my name is John, John Henderson, so if you hear or see any suspicious persons around give me a call" Sara just smiled at him as he continued, to talk;

"I will come personally to help you out "said the now flirting officer. Jack relaxed a bit while waiting for the cop to leave. The door swung shut and Sara locked it and dead bolted it. Sara turned to face Jack "Now what" said Sara.

"Thanks for the help, but I'm getting out of here" said Jack

"You can't go now, the police are all over this place, and you're going to have to wait at least till dark. This happens all the time over here."

"What happens all the time" said Jack

"The police, and the hotel next door houses the cities most famous criminals, so if you want to get out alive, I can help you."

"Fair enough and why do you want to help me out" said Jack

"I like you first and second I think you could help me out."

"What can I do for you?" said Jack he began to disassemble his silencer and placed it in his pocket and then reholstered his weapon.

"Have a seat if you want", said a sweet Sara who was helping Jack to a chair, next to it was a odd looking picture with some writing on it, Jack read it "To Sara, I will love you forever and know one else will have you, signed Steve" and adds "Who's the nut job, your husband?" said Jack.

"Nah, he is my problem, he stalks me day and night, we had a mistake one night and has become my worst nightmare, please Jack will you help me?," and adds " I'll do anything you'll like or I can even pay you some money, I don't have much, but my family is rich.

"Sure, call him up." said Jack in a flood of emotions she rushed him, hugged him and began to kiss him on the lips and then work down the neck, she opened his jacket to expose the two guns, and began to unbutton his dress shirt and lift up his t-shirt and she says;

"Ooh you smell so good" and with her hands she unbuttoned his dress pants and pulls his pants down to his knees.
Sara kneels down and discards both towels and says "these shoes seem pretty tight on you'

"Yeah, they really don't fit" said Jack relaxing in the chair while Sara did all the work. She took off his shoes and socks and had him stand up and as she pulled off his pants. Sara went back in opening his legs, she knelt down and with her hands began to work over his already swollen manhood, she used her mouth and hands to get him hard, enough for her to feel it as she stood and climbed up on the chair and lowered herself onto his manhood, she did all the work and went up and down while Jack was sucking on her breasts, he rubbed her body with his hands.
She said " Don't cum inside of me, O Kay" said Sara "I usually have the guy wear a condom"

"So you've done this before?" asked Jack

"Sure at least a couple of times a week, or you know when a girl can find a stud she likes"

"So I'm a stud" said Jack with a smile on his face.

"That and much more, "said Sara, repositioning herself for him. To add she says" It seems, I'm more attracted to the rough and dangerous ones more than the wimps"

"Then why didn't you have me wear a condom?" said Jack

"You're not the condom wearing type of guy," besides at this point, I don't care, you just shut up and fuck me already, I want pleasure." said Sara

"If you want pleasure, then let's go and get into your bed, because I've got some licking to do."
Sara stopped what she was doing momentarily, enough for Jack to lift her up in his arms, still inside of her, they stood up she wrapped her legs around him he walked her to the bedroom and over to the bed. He laid her down on the edge and started drilling her, till she reached her first orgasm. Then he turned her over and took her from behind, till she had another orgasm. Jack was still super hard, he began to undress and take off the holsters and placed a gun by the night stand, then got on the bed and laid next to her, she climbed up on him, and placed him inside of her and said "Oh Jack, please cum inside of me, I want to feel your love." With that Jack let loose and released his load much to Sara's surprise, she folded up, and laid on him, as he put his arms around her and the two went fast to sleep. `
The telephone kept ringing, which awoke Jack and nudged Sara and said "Who's that your mom?, "She knows your getting in trouble".

"Funny, you know it's not my mom, I'm what they call an out cast, but if you only knew her, you would like to meet her, I can make the arrangements" said Sara

"Whoa wait a minute here, this is a one time only deal, when this blows over I'm outta here" said Jack as he watched her get up. She arched her back and said "Now that was the best sex I've ever had."
Jack looked at her to say "There was some first's for me too"

"Really from that performance I would have never known" said Sara to add "That was something I could get used to."
Jack looked at her, and then placed his hand back on one of his guns.
She didn't respond to Jack's action, but went out into the living room. Jack sat up on the edge of the bed, waited for Sara to come back when he heard her say "Honey do you want something to drink?"

"Sure, and can you turn off that phone its driving me crazy."
Jack had his head in-between his hands, she came to the door, Jack

looked up to admire the view, and he produced a smile, much to Sara's happiness' she smiled too. And said "Here is your drink."

"I turned down the ringer so it won't bother you, so where were we at?"

"Come closer so that I may go another round" said Jack
Sara didn't hesitate, and did as she was told, she surrendered herself, mentally, physically and emotionally as the two of them went at it for the rest of the evening and well into the next day to the next morning, an alarm clock struck six a.m.
Sara awoke, being held in Jack's arms. She said to him, "Finally a guy, who is tough and a real bad boy, one I can take home and have him defend me". She loses her train of thought as Jack moves over to her and begins to go again, Sara says, "Wait, honey I need to call my Job and let them know I won't be in today"
Jack stops what he is doing to look at her and says "What type of work do you do?"

"I work part time at a clothing store at the mall, usually all day today, tomorrow and on the weekend."

"What day is it anyhow" said Jack playing with her, with his fingers.
Sara helped him along by guiding his fingers to where she really wanted him to play, and said to him;

"Thursday, do you want me to stay here with you or do you want to go to the mall, and let me work a bit and later have dinner with my parents." said Sara getting more excited than ever.

"If it were me, I would just lye here in this bed for the rest of my life and that would make me happy." said Jack as he got back up on her and continued to make the magic work, after awhile it was over. Jack was done, he couldn't take it any longer, and laid down beside her as the two kissed, a deep passionate one, long lasting. Sara gave him a two handed huggy, she looked at him to say, "Tell me now, should I stay or should I go"

"Its wise you probably should follow your routine, if someone is watching the apartment, then I'll leave before night"

"That solves it, I will stay with you"

"What about work?"

"Who cares about work, when I have you in my bed?"

"In case someone is watching the place" said Jack trying to get rid of her now.

"Alright, I'll go if you promise to be here, when I get back." Jack looked at her, her eyes as big as saucers, pouty lips and was going to say something when she said "Listen darling I will call a girlfriend of mine to keep you company, while I'm away."

Jack looked at her to say "Alright, just tonight, then I'm on my way"

"Fine, now come here and give me a big fat kiss" said Sara beaming.

Jack went to back to the bed, to rest his eyes, one hand on his gun and the other eye open. Sara went and took a long hot shower; blow dried her hair, which woke Jack up. He looked up at her, she was very pretty, and a bit of an excitement , he watched her get dressed, slowly of course, occasionally she would look back at him and smile, Jack slowly got up and made it to the end of the bed, and said;

"I hope your girlfriend is as hot as you are."

"Don't worry about her, she and I are exclusive, she is my lesbian lover, her name is Leslie" Said Sara.

"O Kay " said Jack, a little bit disappointed, gets up and walks past Sara who swatted him on the butt and says " I'm gonna call my mom and tell her I'm bringing over my boyfriend, to meet her and the family, after work today."

"How did I go from acquaintance to full blown boyfriend"

"Because I think I met the man, I'm going to spend the rest of my life with"

"Look at us, I'm twice your age"

"Age doesn't matter to me, never has, never will"

"Well then that's fine with me" said Jack

That put a smile on Sara's face, as she went to him to embrace him to say" Trust me, I won't disappoint you". Sara finished dressing and was putting on her lipstick only to see Jack staring at her.

She turned to face him and said "Come here and give your new girlfriend a hug and kiss."

Jack moved in held her and kissed her lips absorbing some of her red polish, the two looked at each other, Sara wiped off the lipstick on Jack's lips, and let him go. Jack went into the living room to get dressed, he put the two guns into a gym bag with the holsters and all of the ammo, and opened a hall closet and placed the bag under several blankets, he took out a wad of cash from the bag he was carrying and placed it in there too.

Jack was dressed in the dress slacks and tight shoes, a dress shirt and the jacket and sat down to begin to look at all of the wallets that bulged his jacket pockets, one by one he would look at the near empty wallets except the fake I. D's and driver's licenses and some had credit cards, one had some pictures, and one had a thief's pick pocket set.

"I'm ready to go, are you coming with me? I'll need to check my phone" Sara went to her phone and adjusted the ringer and hit the replay button and a voiced chimed

"Twenty-two messages, if you would like to hear your messages press one."

"Message one," "Sara this is Steve, I thought you were coming over to take care of me and my friends"

"You're such a slut" said Jack.

Sara hit the pause button and looked at him and said "Yeah only your slut now."

She let the tape go "message deleted, next message," "You bitch, you have thirty minutes to get over here or were coming over to see you", "message deleted, next message," "That's it bitch, were coming over to mess you up" "message deleted"

"That's nasty" said Jack.

"Next message," " Were outside your building, but I saw some tough looking guy go into your apartment, are you O Kay I don't know who he is, hey there are cops all over this place, we better get out of here, ssh, I'm on the phone with my girlfriend, lets tell the cops some guy is in there with her and then she will see that I'm a nice guy, beep," "End of messages, if you would like to erase this message, message deleted."

"Sounds like this guy loves you, maybe you shouldn't discount his feeling for you. Said Jack.

"Fat chance, I have you now". Said Sara looking at him for a response".

"I don't care about these boys anymore, besides he likes himself and sharing me with his friends" said Sara with her finger on the pause button.

"Now that's kinky, Sara I had no idea you did that" said Jack finding something of interest and became more absorbed in a wallet.

"Not any more, only for you Jack" said Sara
Jack looks up at her and says "You know it almost sounds like you're a call girl"

"Your right Jack, I'am, that's how I paid for school and that's how I have extra cash and the job I do at the mall is a cover up for my parents' sake."

"So this guy, Steve, is really a heart-broken John" said Jack and adds "That's even better"

"You approve then?" said Sara

"Sure I don't care how you make a living, I just pictured you as this all-innocent girl, who was being forced to do these things against her will, which is not cool, for that I would have seeked revenge for your honor" and adds "It almost sounds like I was the best thing to happen to you in a while."

"Your right, you are Jack, and I will do whatever it takes to get this guy out of my life."

"Come here" said Jack rising up to embrace her and the two kissed intimately she had her eyes closed, Jack just looked at her. She lingered with the kiss as Jack broke the kiss and said;

"Don't worry all your troubles will be ending soon."
Sara looked at him and said "What are you thinking about"

"Oh, just a way to get rid of the boy who seem to not want to let you go."

"Good from now on I'm all yours Jack" said Sara
Jack opened the door, to allow Sara out first, she came back to say;   "Where are you going we had a deal, you would stay here, and wait till I get back, and for that Leslie would come over and service you"

"Change of plans, I like this whole mall thing, besides I need some new shoes"

She agreed, as the two walked out to a warm sunny day, Jack shut the door as Sara dead bolted the lock.

"That's to keep your guns safe, you will need them for Steve" said Sara

"Nah, I can probably use my bare hands." said Jack, showing her, the two laughed.

Jack held the door open at every stage, all the way to the parking lot, where a big black SUV was parked, instantly four young men got out.

Jack shook his head in disbelief, knowing his guns were in the bag, he reached in to his pocket to feel the knife, he placed his hands on it to hear "Hold on Sara, what is going on" said Steve, who introduced himself, to say is that your father?", to add "Hello Mister Sanders, I'm Sara's boyfriend, I heard that there was some trouble here a couple of nights ago."

"So you're just responding now" said Jack wisely to him.

"Nah, I was here two nights ago, but there was this guy who looked a lot like you go inside, and my recollection was that, that person is just now leaving, so what's the truth?" asked Steve holding them up.

The three others had a half moon around Jack and Sara.

Jack spoke "When my daughter called me we were suppose to have dinner together, and then the police came and locked us down"

"Yeah, right, prove it" said Steve

Jack fumbled around in his pocket, to find the thing he was looking for, a card, he pulled it out and handed it to Steve, to say "Give him a call, he took a real interest to Sara, I think they maybe they will be going out soon"

The others had to hold Steve back as he began to curse and swear, and throw his arms, as Jack and Sara stepped back. Jack was calm, even though he was holding onto his knife with the other hand, not liking his position, he was still amped up, but Sara's hand on his arm indicated it was time to back down.

She said "Look Steve, me and my father need to get going, I need to go to work, and can I see you later?"

"Sure, you promise, you will take care of me and my boys"

"Steve, I can't believe you're saying that in front of my father"
Steve calmed down, enough for his friends to let him go, as the group followed them to her car, she unlocked the passenger side, as Jack waited for Sara, to get to the driver's side door, she slid into her seat to hear   "Alright I will see you tonight, can you come to the clubhouse."

"Yes Steve I will" she yelled from the car.
Sara closed the car door, tears rolling down her face, as she cried. Jack watched as the bullies got in their SUV and sped off, backwards, then did a quick turn and sped off. Jack sat down next to her to say   "Let me see your keys"

"Don't worry, I'll go with you, I don't feel like going to work today" said Sara, as they both got out of the car.
Sara led Jack back up, to the apartment, she unlocked her door, the two went in as Jack closed the door, she let out a cry, Jack went to his bag, as he pulled off his Jacket, he slid on the two holster's, then his jacket to say "Alright where is this clubhouse, its time I had some fun"
Sara wiped her tears away, to face him she had mascara and blush, running, for Jack to say; "Looks like you could get cleaned up."

"I will darling" said Sara and ads "But first I want to say, from this point on, I will never refer to you as my father ever again"

"That's alright, it was a good way of diffusing some violence, but that's gonna be short lived, because I'm going to the clubhouse to exact some revenge for your honor"

"That's what I like to hear, finally someone who will stand up for me"

"What about your father, had you asked him for his help."

"I have in the past, but he has referred it out to some of acquaintances, and look at me now, believe me, I found an angel, when you stepped into my life"

"In a few hours you won't have anything to worry about"
As Jack was heading to the door.

"Whoa where do you think you are going?"

"Out to do the job"

"Not without me your not, besides, they see some guy dressed in all black brandishing two guns is sure to stir up some trouble, let me drive you in, and you beat them all up, I could give you a list, there is about ten in their gang."

"Really that many, Alright, but I want you to stay behind, I'll handle this" said Jack at the door, as he saw that she had changed, and was wearing something provocative and very revealing, as she lifted her skirt to show that she wore no underwear.

"What do you think?."

"My heart rate has jumped a beat, come on, do you have to wear that"

"Now you are sounding like my dad, hush, I'll wear what I want"

"Really now, I would think if I were your boyfriend, I'd have a say to what you wear"

"Does that mean you'll stay longer, if you do that I'll wear whatever you want me too?"

"Fine" said Jack coming to her.
For her to say "Is that fine you'll stay or fine, you will be my boyfriend"

"What is your obsession with me being something in your life?"

"Listen Jack, this is a small city, there is only a small amount of eligible men to choose from, and the gathering place is college"

"So, I guess if it means that much to you, fine you can call me your boyfriend, now lets go in and change you" said Jack, as he led her in to her bedroom, as she stood on one side, waiting for him to choose, he went through her, underwear drawer, to pull up a pair of hi-cut panties, he tosses them to her to hear her say "Grandma panties, come on Jack get with the times, we all wear thongs or nothing else, nothing like this"

"I can see that, now put them on"
Sara slid them on, and then adjusted her skirt.

"Now the top" said Jack, motioning for her to throw it to him, which she pulled off to reveal she wore no bra, as he fished through her drawers, he pulled up a red bra, he shows her to see she is

shaking her head no to say "It depends on what top you want me to wear"
Jack saw what he was looking for, pulled it up proudly, to show her a white tank top"
"Pull out a white bra, please "she said to him
Jack tosses it to her a white bra, she puts it on, then the tank top, then in a lower drawer he finds a pair of green shorts, she comes over and takes them away to say "You are old fashioned aren't you."
Jack waited till she was dressed and for her to change her shoes, to lead the way out.
Jack was confident, now that he had protection, he followed her out, as she led him to her car, he choose to sit in the passenger seat and said;   "What's this clubhouse like"
"Oh you'll see, it's just like a regular house. She said with a smile.
He looked at her as she drove to the location, up a hill and back down.

" with one exception, its heavily armed, it sits by the old docks" she said while she continued to drive her old little four door compact car, as she turned off, she came to a gate, she stopped, went out, while Jack watched, she opened the gate, she came back to look at him, then got in, and drove up the hill, then down, into what looked like abandoned fishing village, a huge house, was in the middle.
They both got out together, for Jack to say "You stay here, matter-of-fact, turn around and drive back up that hill, and park, off the main road, go" said Jack who stood watching her turn the car around and take it back up the road, then turned his attention on this huge structure, a bit apprehensive, Jack went up the stairs, to knock on the door, no answer, he peered in from a side window, still nothing.
Jack followed the wrap around patio to the back, where a pair of jet skis were making waves in the cove, Jack turned his attention to the door that was open, so Jack went in, instantly encountering a

half awake guy, who was coming down stairs to say "Who are you dude?"

"Looking for Steve, is he around?" asked Jack

"Don't know dude, lets go see, follow me", as the guy led Jack through the lower part of the house, including where Steve slept, as the door opened, it was evident, someone needed to stop this Steve guy, all over his walls were pictures of Sara in all positions and in all forms nude, semi-nude, clothed, and then there was the poster of her sex acts ranked 1st to 10th, for all to see.

Jack thought "Should I stay here or "

"Dude, you can see he isn't here, come upstairs I have someone who would like to meet you, said the guy with an ugly look on his face. Jack followed, the dude up the stairs, as he reached the top step, someone from the wall slipped behind him and pushed him all the way in.

Jack stood up to see it was a barrack type set up, with boys and girls in some twin beds, he noticed he was way out numbered, as the punches started to fly, Jack ducked the first few, but it was the sheer numbers against him, then he changed, as he saw red, blood from a gash, as his head hit the bed frame, and it was as if he reverted back to spy training, instead of going for the head and body.

Jack went for the legs, and then one by one, cries of agony were heard, as Jack gained an advantage, as the momentum swung, in his favor, by first taking down ten boys and then the remaining four girls went down screaming. Jack stood by the door, didn't know what to say, he didn't even know who these people were, let alone, as he counted the bunks, realized, he would be quickly out numbered, when they returned, so he quickly exited.

Jack went down the stairs, and out the door, he was on the beach, he wiped his brow, he ran across the beach.

On the other side, Jack saw a barrel of gas and a refueling depot, so Jack turned over a sealed barrel, and pushed it along the sand towards the house, taking his knife, he stabbed a hole in the side to see the fluid spray towards the house.

"Hey what are you doing "said a voice behind him.

Jack turned around to see the two young men looking at him, as Jack continued to let the gas continue to spew out. As the two boys came at Jack only to stop midway to see Jack pull out his Colt Combat Commander.

The two boys took off like a scared rabbits, only to stop, and hop on their jet skis, look back, then sped off.

Jack stood there, watching, then , walked away, a short distance, then took a shot at the barrel, waited, then took another shot, he felt like he missed so he opened up the whole gun, and still nothing happen, so he turned, and as he walked up the hill he heard a noise, as a black SUV came over the hill, side swiped Jack as he tried to get out of the way, the vehicle, hit his leg and threw him into the bushes.

The SUV, went down the hill to the house, stopped, as all four men got out, then the screaming started, Jack got up and was on the move, his leg hurt a bit, Jack looked back to still see nothing had happened, but was still moving, as he was able to get to Sara's half hidden car, he opened the door, for him to say "Lets get going."

Jack eased into his seat, as the door closed as she sped the little car out, on the road, she slowed to see that the once open gate was closed and a lock and chain was on. Sara pulled the car to a stop, as Jack remembered seeing a pair of tools in a small case, he picked up, and he stepped out, and ran to the gate.

Jack pulled the case out, to extract a pick and a wedge, he inserted them, turned them, it clicked open, thinking back, it must have been the training, and he puts them in his pocket, undoes the chain, and opens the gate.

Sara drives through, and then Jack, pulls the gate closed, rewraps the chain, and then locks it again, as he left it as he found it. Jack takes a few steps back then lunges for the fence, catches it, swings his body up and over and in one motion, he was running, got into her car and as it sped off.

Sara looked at him to say "I should take you to the hospital, your bleeding."

"No back to your house, drive" he said

She piloted the car back to her apartment, she parked, in her parking spot, only something different was going on, two police cruisers were parked, on opposite ends. An ambulance pulls up, then a fire truck, all the while, Jack crotches down in his seat, as the emergency vehicles blocked them in.

"Come on lets go inside, you'll be fine, this happens at least once a week" said Sara, getting out of the car. Sara got out, to see John the cute police officer, come towards her. He approached her with a grin on his face, to say "Hi Miss, you remember me" said the officer.

"Yes I do, what is going on here, will me and my father, be able to get in there, have you caught that person you were looking for?"

"whoa wait Miss, to answer all your questions, there was a lady on the third floor, had a heart attack, and yes you may go on up, and actually no, but the detectives think he is probably gone back to Atlanta or some place like that", said John, trying to look at her, and at the car, then to her, to say "Will you need a personal escort up?"

"Nah, my father will walk with me, then he and I are going shopping, just stopped by to pick up a few things"
The officer felt satisfied, left, to say "Take the north entrance, and have a good day, said officer John, as he left.
Sara, motioned for Jack to come, Jack got out, and hobbled with her to north entrance away from the scene, then using her key, she let them in, she led, as Jack brought up the rear, up the stairs they went, on to the third floor.
Sara was in the front, to see all the people, fire fighters, and then her police officer, who saw her and was heading their way when he was called back, long enough, to have Sara help Jack up the stairs, and as fast as her key was inserted and Jack fell into the living room, she tried to close the door, there was a knock on her door, then a voice;

"This is Officer John, do you have a moment."
Sara stood at the door, and waited till Jack crawled into the bedroom, then as she was about to open the door, she saw Jack crawl to the bathroom, and close the door.
Sara opened the door to see John, all handsome and dashing in his blue uniform to say "How can I be of a service to you, John"

"Well I wanted to know your name".
"It's Sara, without the H"

"Nice, is there any chance you would go out with me?"
Sara hesitated to think what to say to get rid of this creep, to say
"Sure what did you have in mind?"
"Really, well that would be great, there is a police officers ball tomorrow night"
Sara looked at him, from halfway behind the door, and then she almost leaped forward as Jack had his hands on the other side, touching her un-exposed breast, to where she started to laugh, to say "Alright, shall I meet you there"
"No, can I pick you up?"
Jack whispered in her ear "Say yes"
"Yes that would be fine, what shall I wear?"
Jack said "Nothing" as she shooed him away, with her unseen hand, as he was on his knees reaching up in her shorts, which she spread her legs apart for him.
"Something to match my blue uniform, would be a compliment" said John.
"I might have a full length Navy dress with white trim, and black pumps"
Sara was closing the door to hear him say "What time can I pick you up?"
"What time is the event?" she countered, this game.
"Starts at 6 PM, that is dinner, then the ceremony"
Sara thought a moment, to remember she had to work late, to say" alright 6 PM is fine."
Sara forced the door closed, as John had his foot in the door, blocking her attempt. While Jack was undressing her; John said;
"Can I pick you up at 5:30 PM"
She kicked John's foot, to say "Fine, see you then" and slammed the door shut, and dead bolted it, only to step out of her shorts and underwear, Jack pulled her down onto his face, she pulled off her tank top and bra, to say "I never wear a bra, look at my tits, they stay up right, she stood up and turned around to undo his pants. Jack was shirtless and cleaned up as she sat back down, letting Jack do what he does best, she herself found what she liked, when all of a sudden her phone rang, and rang, eventually she got up off of him,

went to her phone and turned it off, after she saw who called her, this time it was to sit on what Jack had to offer.

Sara sat on his manhood, to place her hands on his chest to say "You're not jealous of me going out with the officer?"

"No, why should I be?"

"Well, I'm your girl"

"Yeah, that doesn't mean I own you"

"That's refreshing to hear, all my life I've had guys who want me to themselves, and you know exclusively, you know like husband and wife"

"That's where you got me all wrong, I promised you I'd stay another day"

"Wait a minute, your not jealous because, when I go out with Officer John, you'll hit the road"

"Something like that"

"No, that's not our deal" said Sara, to add as she tries to get up off of him and he holds her in position, to say "Oh I get it now, your O' Kay with sticking that into me, but not to see if we can have a relationship, if you don't decide now, I'll walk out that door and tell Officer John."

Jack lets her go, and uses his hands to motion for her to go, as she gets up to say "Don't test me Jack I'll do it" she said standing by the door."

"Alright you win, can you come back over here, I'm sorry I was just testing you."

Sara smiles, then walked back to him, spread her legs, she lowered herself on top of his manhood, to say "Most couples have ground rules, but I don't.

Jack looked up at her, as she again smiled to say "All I want from you is that you stay here in Mobile, and give us a chance to see if this will work out, fair enough? and in return you can have me as often as you want and any other girl you see fit, in addition I have a girlfriend, who would sure like to share in this fun, she's a brunette, and her name is Leslie"

Jack looked up at her, to see she had wiped away some loose tears, to say "Fair enough, I'll give it one week"

"I guess that's the best I can hope for, shall we spend it in bed the whole week"

Jack looks at her, to let loose, for her to say "Whoa this wasn't part of the deal"

Jack closed his eyes to enjoy himself, as she said "Hey you don't get to cum before me, Mister."

CH 3

Danger, Danger its Steve.

Jack followed Sara, as she led the way; she was dressed in jean pants and a white blouse. She came to the locked gate, opened up the door, and said, "Let me hold the door open for you dear." She was acting somewhat silly to Jack, who was serious and stern, but did not say a word. He hobbled along, feeling the pain in his leg. She led the way to her small car, he see a few people mulling around.

"There always around" said Sara.

"Yeah just like the police"

Jack follows her and sees her to the driver's door to say;

"Do you wanna drive?"

"Nah, you go ahead, it's your car.," said Jack who gets into the passenger side. He sat down. She got in, then fired the car up, backed up from out under the carport, and then sped down to the end of the parking lot. She turned left and got out onto the busy street, Jack saw the ocean and the port and said, "The water seem stormy"

"Yeah, you just missed, a hurricane that had wiped out most of New Orleans and some of Mississippi, but we were spared," said Sara.

"Really" said Jack

The rest of the drive was silent until her cell phone rang; Sara said, "Should I answer it?"

"It's your phone, I don't care" said Jack

"It's him," said Sara

"Yeah, tell him you met someone new and it's serious and tell him to get lost."

She did as she was told and said, "Yes, what do you want?"

"You bitch, where have you been?" said Steve

"With my mobster boyfriend"

"What boyfriend, you're a lesbian"

"Yep, he just got into town, he is a boss and I told him all about you, so if I were you I'd leave me alone."

"Ha, fat chance, Sara why are you lying to me, who in there right mind would be with a stank like you, your not even pretty."
Jack took the phone away from Sara and said, "Hello, this is" Click, the phone went dead.

"I guess he didn't want to talk with me," said Jack
He handed the phone back to Sara and it rang again, and again, then Sara answered the phone and said "Hi" a bit hesitant, then with enthusiasm said, "Hi, mom, I'm fine, just hanging out with a friend, do you mind if I bring him by for dinner tonight?" In addition, adds, "Yes he is a guy, actually he is a lot older, your age or more."
Then says, "I know but you know me and how I'm more attracted to older men, rather than to younger boys." Then waits, and then says;

"It was just the spur of the moment and it just was right, so I'd like to bring him home to meet you both." Then waits, and adds, "He is a salesman and his name is Jack. Okay I'll see you tonight, I love you, good bye." said Sara.
The ride was quiet, yet Sara, turned up the radio, to listen to some music, off to the left was a gigantic building that had all kinds of names, noticed Jack, to read a large sign that said
SOUTHEAST MALL
Sara pulled the car to a stop and said, "Were here, do you want my keys, in case you want to go any where"

"Nah, what time do you want me to meet you back here?" said Jack

"First off you're not wearing a watch, and second I hope you come by and buy some clothes at my store and then take me out for a lunch." She smiled at him, then leaned into him and gave him a kiss, while he caressed her left breast and followed up her with a kiss on her neck.

"Stop you're going to get me started again." said Sara.

Jack stopped, and said "You better get going; I'll walk in with you."
She had parked a good two hundred yards away from the entrance
as Jack said, "Why did you park so far away"

"It's the people at the mall said to, besides, it's good to
walk."
Jack got to the Mall door first and held it open for Sara and then out
of the corner of his eye, he noticed someone looking at them, and
then he looked away, to allow Sara to pass in front of him.

"Thanks Jack, you're such a gentleman I like that," she
said.
She pasted him with a lingering smile, he followed her in. a whole
world of opportunity opened up to him, everything and anything was
available for sale, he thought.

"Jack, my store is over on the left, so I guess I'll see you
later?" and then comes to him and gives him a quick kiss. And
adds, "I'll see you soon, have fun."
Jack watches her leave for a moment and then his attention is
directed to the shoes he is wearing, and begins to walk the other
direction from her to see a sport shoe store. He then walks in to see
anything and everything to wear, a lovely saleswoman comes up to
him and says, and "Is there something I can do for you?" she said
with a smile

"You seem happy and fun," said Jack

"Why I 'am and would love to help you sir"

"Well I got some borrowed shoes and I need, well some
sport, maybe able to run in them and a pair to match what I'm
wearing now."

"I can help you with the sport and running shoes."
She looks him up and down to say, "But you're going to have to go
to a dress store for the shoes."

"Lets see what you can offer me?" said Jack looking
around.
She looked him over and said "I think this and that pair will work for
you."
Jack shook his head in acknowledgement.

"Have a seat and let me take your foot's measurements."

Jack took a seat and let her do her thing; she removed his shoes and checked his foot and then the other one, and said, "Just as I thought."

He watched as she moved quickly to get him his shoes. She then came back, knelt down, then placed a good-looking shoe on his foot and asks him to stand. Jack stood up to feel the room and the comfort and it felt good to him, to say" I'll take these."

Jack then sits down so she can put on another pair, this time these are sleek brown in color and a waffle tread on the bottom.

"The insert is arch supporting to make your feet feel fantastic after standing all day".

Jack slipped his feet in them, they had no laces and they were a brand name and she was right they felt good and he stood, then walked in them, then said "I'd like to wear these out" said Jack.

"Yes Sir, will that be all?" said the sales girl

"Let's make it happen," said Jack

"How will you pay for this sir?"

Jack fumbled in his jacket pocket, to pull out cash, as she took the gold credit card, she ran it and said, "I just need you signature, Mister Giogorio's." she said with a smile.

Jack looked at her like he was guilty, and that it wasn't his card, for her to say " From now on all you say you're here shopping for your boss, and we usually ring it up differently "

Jack signed J G and left the store with his first purchase.

"Oh Mr. Giogorio, do you want your old shoes?" said the young lady behind him.

"Nah just keep um," said Jack already out the door, with a pair of new shoes and a bag in hand.

Jack strolled down a ways, saw a cooking store, and went in, immediately a salesgirl approached him and said;

"Hi, how can I help you sir"

"I'm shopping for a young lady's parents, what do you think, I can give them for a gift?"

"I think it could be nice if you give some cookware and the most expensive we have is five hundred dollars."

"That's fine; can you wrap it up for me?"

"Sure it will cost you a little more"

"That's fine if you don't mind if I use my boss's credit card?"

"Can I see your card?"

Jack hands her Mr. Giogorio's credit card, she takes it and says; "Anything else do you want to add to this."

"Nah, I'm good."

Jack, stood waiting, finally the package was wrapped up and given to him with Mr. Giogorio's credit card. He walked out with the heavy package and next to the cookware store was a jewelry store, which Jack walked in and looked around and then saw it a large diamond necklace in a display.

"I'd like to see that necklace, my boss sent me down here to buy something for his wife." The girl behind the counter smiled, then pulls it out of the case and holds it up to show Jack.

"Can you put it on so that I may see what it looks like on a beautiful girl" said Jack smiling at her. She did so with Jack's help. Both of them looked at the guy who appeared to be the manager by giving her his disapproving look.

"He is just jealous, don't worry about it."

Jack watched as she modeled it for him and it fit well, then he said, "Can you wrap it up?"

"Sure, how will you pay for it, with my bosses card, Jack hands her the card.

A little while goes by, the girl comes out and says, "At first I couldn't get it approved, but I called the credit card company and they approved the purchase, so if you could sign off for it, you can take it."

She handed the card to Jack, and the receipt, which Jack looked at and paused, at the total, $25,000 dollars, then signed the initials of J G. She handed him a copy and the wrapped gift and said, "You're going to make your boss a very happy man and his wife will be wearing a one of a kind. She then said "I took the liberty of adding some insurance on this piece, which is this paperwork" she shows him. "Just have your boss fill it out and send it in".

"Thanks I will do that," said Jack as he left the store, with a smile on his face and saw a trash can, and placed Mr.Giogorio's card in it. The next store he came upon was a greeting card store which he walked in, looked around and found a card for Sara, he went to the counter and said" Can I borrow a pen?." He picked up one, when a clerk said, "No, it will cost you two bucks. " Jack set down his purchases and said, "I'll take one pen and I'm going to leave my packages here"

Jack went back to the card he liked and opened up and took it to the counter then wrote how he felt about Sara and signed it with love. Jack gave the clerk the card; she rang it up and Jack paid cash, and put the card in a envelope and licked it and sealed the card up. He put it in with the jewelry bag.

Jack left the store and nearly ran into a guy and his three friends; nearly knocking Jack over, he was forced into the glass wall by one of the guys.

The big guy holding Jack heard another one say "Sorry Mister, we didn't see you old man, ha ha", laughed the others.

The apparent leader said "Let the old man walk. Let's go visit my girl and see if we can bang her in the dressing room."

Jack was caught off-guard, his mind was elsewhere, as he tried to regain, the high he was on. He began to think what just happened. He walked a ways and saw a nice men's store with ties and accessories.

Jack walked in and set his packages down and saw a blue tie that matched his Jacket and then added a yellow one when a sales woman spoke from behind him and said" Their three for ten dollars."

"Then I will take this black one, Jack turns to see this very tall gorgeous woman in a low cut dress smiling back at him. She says; "Anything else?"

"Now that you mention it, I would like a suit, but a little more roomer," said Jack

"Absolutely sir, I'm a tailor, what did you have in mind?"

"Well something with a little gap under the arms, but not to show, and something similar to what I'm wearing now, with a pair of dress shoes, and   can I have it by six tonight?" said Jack

"Sure but it will cost you"

"Fine, how much? "

"Oh I'd say thousand dollars," said the cute tailor.

"Let's get it done," said Jack

"Follow me in the back," said the woman
Jack picked up his packages and followed the sexy woman in the back, to a room. Jack walked in and then laid his packages down.

"Take off your clothes, down to your underwear please. I'll be back in a moment"
Jack took off his jacket and then his dress shirt and then his dress pants down to his underwear. He waited until she came back in. she got very close to him, rubbing her breasts upon him and bending over for Jack's advantage, she finished by rubbing his manhood, trying to stimulate his action.

"It helps if you remove your clothes." said Jack with a smile, although she was way ahead of him, on her knees, working on his manhood.
He helped her get up, as she stepped back, Jack realized he was going to get a show, as this dark haired big-breasted woman, un-zipped her tight dress, she went over, and locked the door. She came back to Jack and dropped her dress, and popped her bra, to let her huge breasts free, to move and show them to Jack.
Jack reached out and touched them; she went back down on her knees. Then slid down his white under pants to his ankles and went back to lengthen Jack's manhood. It did not take long for her to get him fully erect. Enough for her to say;

"Take me from behind." she demanded.
She hands Jack a condom and says, "Put this on"

"You want it, you put it on" said Jack. She did as she was told and placed it on, then turned around to say "Take me from behind, I like it that way, the best"
Jack stuck it in and the pressure of the condom increased the pressure as he went back and forth, she was loose and Jack could feel something totally different, as the pressure was, increasing then he let loose.
It was over before it began, both of them were panting as she had a slight orgasm to follow his, when he really felt her lock him up with her convulsion's and another discovery was the gush of fluid on him and it was running down his legs.

"Whoa, that was unexpected," said Jack surprised by what happened.

"I'm sorry I don't do that too often only when a guy really turns me on"

Jack finally pulled out to get another wave of fluid, showering him, he pulled off the condom and tossed it in the trash, while the saleslady was at a sink washing up, then she said, "In a moment I will come and clean you up."

Jack watched and waited watching her clean up her privates and her hairy legs, then she came to him in the nude, she knelt down and washed him off good.

"That should take care of you," she said with a smile and ads "Maybe we can do this again later"

"Yeah, maybe another day another time" said Jack.

He quickly pulled his wet drawers up, then down and said "Can you get me another pair of shorts and a new t-shirt?"

"Sure" said the sales girl who was back in her dress, unlocked the door and went out and came back in a flash with a new pair of white under shorts and a new pair of t-shirts.

Then with each trip, some new clothes, a new blue silk shirt, and the tie Jack liked, it was black, and she brought him a pair of black dress pants and a loose fitting black jacket. Jack put his knife in the pocket and the rest of the credit cards, Jack hands her another card that says Johnny Cantrell.

"Do you have any dress shoes that will match this out fit?" said Jack

"Sure what size do you wear?"

"I think it's eleven," said Jack

She went out and returned, to hand him a pair of new shoes and socks, from which he slipped them on.

Jack felt good, walking in them, when she came back and said "anything else Mr. Cantrell?"

"Yeah, I need a good watch"

"I'll add that to your charge," she said and in a moment came back with an all blue faceplate with a metal band. She slid it on his left wrist and snapped it in place. And said "Here is a pair of cuff-links with the initials of J C", she puts then on and adds, "All you need is a hat"

Jack walked out with his packages in hand, leaving the mess behind.

"Don't worry I'll clean that up"

Jack followed her back into the shop to see her lifting off a white full brimmed hat with a feather in the side. She placed it on his head, stepped back and said "Wow, now that's a statement"

"You like that" said Jack, looking at her, with a surprising smile she returns the look and hands Jack the credit card receipt, Jack looks at the total in excess of ten thousand dollars. So he signed it J C. She handed him a copy and said "I'll have it ready before six p.m. tonight or sooner." and adds "It was well worth the experience we had earlier and thanks"

"I should be thanking you; you gave me an experience worth several." Jack lost his train of thought and said, "I got to go, thanks".

Jack, walked out of the store feeling like a million bucks, but a rude awakening occurred as he stepped out into the flow of disguised looks, and sneer comments, Jack was absolved with his self as he strolled back to Sara's shop with gifts in hand. People were shaking their heads in disbelief at him, all the while Jack had a smile on his face, and he started to sing a tune he heard earlier, in the car. He got close to the store that Sara worked at.

From his view was the store he thought Sara went into, but was not sure, he walked in and everyone stopped what they were doing and just stared at Jack. Jack spoke up and said, "Hi, how are you doing, to a young lady who fled out of the store. Behind a curtain one girl said to the other "Look at this pimp daddy who just walked in"

"Yeah, this guy has flash; I wouldn't mind him being my sugar daddy".

Sara had just finished crying, from receiving a visit from Steve who harassed and nearly raped her, until security dragged him out. She heard the two girls talking, so she came over to them and said;

"Who are you talking about?" She looked out to see Jack.

"Oh my god, that's my new boy-friend Jack"

"Where was he when you were attacked by your old-boy-friend?" said one girl.

"Looks like he went shopping" said another girl

Sara led the girls out to face Jack and they met him in the middle of the store as Sara said "So I see you did a little shopping, so do you want to go out for lunch now?"

"Sure if you're ready, how do you like the outfit?" said Jack to Sara.

"Everything looks sharp except the hat." said Sara and ads "The secret is to take off the hat while indoors." Quickly Jack pulled it off.

"Much better" said Sara, and turns to say nothing as her two friends were gone, and says "I was gonna introduce you to my friends, but their gone, oh well, lets go." Sara wraps her arm around Jack. Sara holds his hand as the two walk together. She was feeling safe again, and says, "Do you want to take those packages out to my car?"

"O Kay" said Jack

Sara led Jack out to her car, she unlocked the trunk, and Jack unloaded the packages, except one and carried to the front after closing the trunk.

He opened her door, and then went around getting in and sitting beside her. Then he said, "Now close your eyes hold out your hands." Jack placed the card, box in her hand, and said, "Open your eyes" Slowly, and with hesitation, she looked down to see and feel the weight of the box and the card and said, "You didn't have to do that, what happen to you were just leaving" she first opened the card slowly and read it, to the point of drawing a tear, she began to cry.

"Stop" said Jack

"This is a cry of joy, my love, that was so sweet what the card said and then what you wrote, you touched my heart, thanks." she swung in close and gave him a kiss on the lips and pushing his hat back on his head. "We also take off our hats in the car"

She then pulled away and started to open her well-wrapped box and finally she opened the contents to discover the diamond necklace. She literally began to shake, she dropped it, opened up the car door and vomited, after several heaves, and she calmed down, wiped her mouth, and then closed the door. Started the car. Jack looked at her in amazement and said "I'll never get you another gift again."

She sped out of the parking lot, raced down the street, faster than before, and back to her apartment, and parked the car. She turned to him and said "You just spent twenty-five thousand dollars on a necklace I have admired for over one year", she looked at him with a smile to say;

"And now you have come into my life and bought me a gift no man has ever considered of buying me". She turned in her seat, to face him with a smile, then a stern look to say;

"So where do we start, do you want to get married, have a lot of kids, I know I would want at least ten, lets go upstairs and start working on number one or two."
Jack sat in wonder as he spoke occasionally nodding yes and agreeing with her, then he helps her put on the necklace, and the two get out simultaneously as Sara says "Lets go, I'm taking you upstairs and gonna fulfill every fantasy you might have, you got any?"
Jack adjusts his hat and says "It would be fun with a friend, who's that brunette you know, does she have a large chest?"

"You got it boy" said Sara, quickly she was on her phone.
Sara had calmed down long enough to tell her friend "Hey can you come over now, I have a friend, who wants to meet you", and the two talked about what Jack just gave her. Jack followed Sara up to her apartment; she opened the door, and went straight into the apartment, as Jack was right behind her, she went into the bathroom. Jack shut and locked the door, and went into the living room thinking, about his last encounter. He had, he saw Sara come from the bathroom, for him to say "While we wait for your friend, I'm taking a shower, can you make me a sandwich? "

"Sure anything you would like, tuna fish alright"

"Yeah, sure" said Jack going into the bathroom, and closing the door.
She was happy, as she prepared his and her sandwiches, a thought occurred to her, and "This is what I've always wanted, a guy like my father, but one a little more exciting and dangerous, but in a nice way, not the scary way, like Steve"

Jack emerged from the bathroom, hair still wet, wearing only a towel, to sit in his favorite chair. Sara brought a plate of food to him, as the two ate together,   Sara turned on the Television.

The two watched and ate and waited, and began to watch the news, it switched over to the weather and the devastating hurricane and then the mob killings and in another incident, a prominent attorney was killed. As of yet no suspects were arrested.

"Headline news, said Jack to himself adjusting his towel, as his excitement was growing. Sara got up to take their plates, and went into the kitchen, then pasted through the living room, to the bedroom, a few moments passed and out walked Sara, wearing nothing except her diamond necklace and said "How do you like me now?"

"Fine, now come on over and sit on my lap.' said Jack, Sara walked slowly and then started to ask questions, "What do you want Jack, my boy-friend, kids, another girl or several more, which is it Jack".

"Well Sara, I hadn't really thought about it, but I can tell you this I like everything about you."

"You're the perfect girl any guy would want, in addition to your attitude, and the fact your so damn sexy". To add "and for the time being, I will stay and see if this all works out. In the meantime, I like to see you in nothing as much as possible".

"Get rid of Steve and you'll have me for the rest of your life"

Then there was a knock on the door, Sara got up and went to the door.

Sara looked through the peephole, she saw. Sara opened the door, for her friend.   Quickly another girl appeared, Jack took notice quickly, she was near perfect, with a flawless face, curly brown hair and striking blue eyes.

She had a smile that lit up a room, she had ample breasts barely covered by her almost see through top, she was hot, Jack rose, and his manhood came to attention.

"Jack this is my close friend I told you about, her and I share everything, her name is Leslie and she is here to help fulfill our dreams"

"I' am" she said hesitantly, looking at her friend.

Sara grabs her arm and led her into her bedroom, as Jack watches in amazement. He begins to change channels to find a music station and turns to hear some voices and some giggling. Jack goes in to investigate. Jack sees first Leslie, minus her pants, led by Sara, who comes over to Jack and the two of them pull on his towel, while Leslie begins to pleasure Jack with her mouth. He felt her tight mouth suck on his knob, he strained under the pressure. Next, it was Sara, who helped Jack to sit back on the bed. She stood up on the bed, and then knelt down so Jack may pleasure her pelvis.

As Jack licked in between, he could feel her heave and sway, for him to say "I hope you not going to vomit again"

"I don't know, I'd never really felt so overwhelmed before, maybe its you."

"Or its love" said Leslie. To add "I did that once, it's a girl thing"

Jack continued to satisfy Sara, while Leslie was doing her job, to the point that she could no longer, hold out and pulled off her panties, and sat down on Jack's manhood. Jack felt that she was extremely tight. And then the wetness occurred, wave after wave. Jack was wet. Then it was gush after gush Jack was feeling the waves, and so was Leslie who easily got off and continued to flood Jack's lower body. Jack's privates were saturated, to the point of which Jack let loose inside of Leslie who also clamped down on his manhood and rode it out till she was finished. Sara let loose as well to Jack licking her privates, to orgasm.

Afterwards, Leslie resurrected Jack's manhood back to full erection. Leslie stood up and announced "Look kids I got to go back to school, call me, let's get to together any time it was fun." Jack was busy kissing Sara on the lips, parting them with his tongue.

She lowered herself on his manhood, and the two went slowly for several more minutes, all the while, she rode him to several more orgasms. Finally, Jack came again.

Jack was exhausted and this time he went flat. Their two hot sweaty bodies intertwined and as they kept kissing each other,

Then Jack said "I got to go" and Sara got up off him and then followed him into the bathroom.

Both of them took a shower together, as Jack was feeling that urge again, and grabbed Sara's arm, and pulled in behind her, she let out a yell "That hurts, Jack, stop it", as he tried to put it in from behind. Jack let go and said "What' s wrong with you", she turned to face him, with tears, and said "Jack , Steve and his friends came and saw me at work today, he got rough with me, and that's what he does with me"

Jack let her go, and was deflated, as she saw to say "I'm sorry Jack, I was gonna tell you, but with this gift and all."

Jack pulled her in tight, the two embraced, he kissed her, then pulled back and said" Lets go back to the mall, Ill take care of this Steve today."

"Finally, I'd never thought you would say that, I thought you were suppose to protect your girlfriend from leeches like him" said Sara jokingly to Jack

"I'm working on it, but from now on you'll be protected."

"You really mean that, or are you just playing with me"

"I don't know I'd been thinking about it, I am going to be there for you".

The two finished the shower and Sara blow dried her hair, while Jack, put on his suit and his hat and stood by the door to see Sara, had changed into a pair of Jeans and a tank top and came in to model for Jack " What do you think?" asks Sara

"You look perfect, now that's the outfit I like" said Jack

He led her out, he knew he was getting close to her now and he liked this feeling, at every stage. Jack was first to the gate and opened it, and then down to her car, he held the door open for her.

"Thanks darling, you're such a gentleman, later I'm going to take care of you" she said with a smile. Jack noticed a marina on the right this time, instantly got an idea.

Sara parked the car closer to the entrance, this time she turned to face him and said "Here are my keys, and my cell phone" she opened it up the door to say" You can speed dial me just hold down number 2, my mom is 3 and if you want to reach Steve well it's the last number received. "

She hands them to Jack, leans in and gives him along lasting kiss, then says "I love you Jack, my darling, my protector".

She got up and left the car, she slammed the door shut. Jack also got up and out of the car; he locked it and then began to walk the other direction, to the Mobile city docks, which were a good half a mile away. He felt fine; he had a plan now it was time to execute it. He got to the dock to see a long like H in formation dock and a information booth with a gate. There stood a old man

"How can I help you son"

"I was looking to rent a boat, Mister" said Jack

"There are four purposes to rent a boat, for pleasure, business, and fishing and to live on one, which is yours, Mister" said the old guy.

"Well first off my name is Jack" the two shake hands and the old man says "I'm Guy, said the old man, to add "I "m a volunteer to which I run the gate from morning till night, after five it's locked"

"That's good to know "said Jack, looking at him weirdly.

"Your dressed to the ten's "said Guy

"Yeah I like to be the best I can be at all times" said Jack honestly

"So, I guess it's for pleasure" said Guy

"Yeah, a little of this and a little of that, but for the most part," said Jack as he looked up to say "I like that big boat"

"That one over there". Said Guy. "I could show you it."

"That would be fine with me "said Jack

"Let me lock up the shack, have you had lunch?" said Guy

"Nah, I guess I have been to busy" said Jack watching Guy picking up the clipboards and putting them away.

Guy turned and locked the door.

"Today's your lucky day, on the other side of this dock, is the best crab and slaw sandwich in the city and it will be my treat." said Guy. Guy led Jack down to the dock, as a large crowd gathered. The two walked to the entrance to the marina, on both sides of the street stood two-food shack's one was busy the other not so.

"Jack, wait here" said Guy, who went behind the busy Crab shack.

Jack was standing besides a vacant building, that had a for sale sign on it.

Moments later Guy remerged with two plates and handing one to Jack.

"Here you go old boy"

The two made there way through the parking lot to a picnic table.

"This is known as the city park" said Guy and the two sat down and began to eat the juiciest fabulous sandwich, dill pickle and drank a small container of milk.

"So Guy do you know the city" said Jack finishing off his plate

"Oh yeah, been here over thirty years, and a commercial fisherman for most of that time"

"Really, do you have a boat?"

"Yeah, it's the big one you showed interest in, I am trying to sell it so, I can retire" said Guy

"How bout you rent it out to me?"

"Nah, I can't, it doesn't run, but I have a friend who will let you take his out, the one next to it, you see"

"That small one"

"Yeah, its fifty footer crab boat"

"How much you want for your boat?"

The two finished lunch when Guy said "Let me show you it and then you can offer me a price"

"I don't know what a going price is for a boat" said Jack

"Well I can tell you this, new ones are about a million or so, I'll sell you mine for a tenth of that."

"Sounds good" said Jack.

Who remembers seeing the boats go out to sea from his prison cell when he was on the east coast, and always dreamt of being on a ship?   Jack followed Guy down the dock to his boat.

"It stands thirty feet tall and is one hundred feet long; it has two engines and the capacity to hold one hundred thousand pounds of crab or fish. The boat has four bunk rooms, a galley and a wheel house in front is the captain's room, right now I use it for storage." Guy led Jack around showing him, the rundown dirty boat which Jack actually liked. As the two stood in the wheelhouse, Jack saw a large bed, and bathroom, on the same floor, to say "that is nice"

"Yeah I put that in; it was storage, before I remodeled it."

"No I like it, but what's up with all the rocking?'

"Something you have to get use too, so are you still interested?"

"Yeah, so if I give you ten percent down, can I buy it from you?" said Jack standing in the wheel house and looking out and onto the view, and then at the bed, with large windows"

"Sure, but it still doesn't run" said Guy

"That's fine; can you help me fix it?"

"I can do that, first off I'd recommend putting it in dry dock, for a month, have the bottom reconditioned, rebuild the engines and any remodeling you may want to do, I can write all this down, if you like" said Guy.

"Nah, you just take charge, and see if you can do it all for let's say one hundred thousand, and I'll pay you extra to see that it is taken care of".

"I guess I work for you now" said Guy, with a smile, to say "I got a friend who could help us out"

"That's fine, hire him too"

"Now we need to talk, with you about the fees and the rights" said Guy.

"What do you mean?" asked Jack

"You know I told you I fished, well as long as I have this boat I have fishing rights".

Guy paused as he saw Jack sit on the master bed, to look at him, for which Guy said "Which I can sell to you."

"Sure, what do I need them for?"

"That's what will make you the real money, you see having a fishing boat's is one thing, but its real purpose is to fish". "Any where you go, but in the gulf waters, they (the government) requires you to have fishing permits". "Today they are worth about one hundred thousand dollars each, and I have thirty two fish rights".

"Think of it as a state fishing license. You are given a certain amount of fish or crab to catch". "The ones I have are of about thirty-two different kinds".

Jack looked up at the ceiling not really listening.

"From that, I need to catch two hundred thousand pounds of."

Jack sat up to say "So now I need to go fishing"

"No, you can leave it the same as I have it now; I have them rented to my friends" Said Guy to add "In turn, they will pay you roughly one dollar for each pound, per each season and we have four seasons so you could make eight hundred thousand dollars a year"

"Wow really, so why would you sell then"

"Because, its time for me to retire, and someone needs to either work them or I lose them and then the government will take them away"

"I see now, you need someone to work your share"

"That's right Jack, if you went out you could double or triple that amount. " "Yourself."

Jack looked at the old guy and thinking and saying out loud;

"Wow I hit the jackpot"

"Not really, it may sound good to you, but it will take millions of dollars, to turn this into a money maker, let alone managing all those rights, actually your gonna to need help, then you need to update them and ensure you quota is being caught." said Guy looking at him.   Jack laid back to look at the ceiling to say "How is the lights stay on?"

"By a bank of batteries, and a generator, that is recharged by the engines"

"Wow this all sounds so interesting, could someone live on here"

"Sure, that's why I put the bed in, up here and have the crew down stairs"

"So what do you think it would take to live on this boat?"

"Some one who has a lot of money, you see Jack, me trying to sell my boat, is difficult especially trying to find someone who has cash to buy it.

"Why someone with cash?"

"Because there is no bank that will lend you the money, so Jack are you still interested in buying my boat?"

"Yep, how much for the rights and fees and such?" said Jack pulling out a wad of cash.

"I like you Jack, I'll sell you my rights for 2.5 million dollars and my boat for 100 thousand dollars and but you have to make sure the boat gets a major facelift and overhaul."
Jack counts out seventy five thousand dollars, in wads of money he remembers taken from the dead mob guys, and gave hands it to Guy, and said "Can you give me a couple of days to get the rest?"

"Jack you can take your time, give me some time to get everything in order, and I will oversee the fixing of the boat, do you have a name in mind" said Guy

"What do you mean?" asked Jack.

"You now own a boat and you need to name it"

"What's wrong with the name on it?"

"That's mine, and I'm keeping it my families name The Phoenix, you need to come up with something that sparks interest and shows your masculine side"

"O Kay call mine the Sara's Trust"

"That sounds like a girls name, is she a girl you admire, be reasonable"

"Alright, how about the Parthian Stranger"
The old man looked at Jack and said "O Kay, I will do that any specific color you want the hull"

"how bout blue and with white trim" said Jack he had cleaned out his pockets of cash, all he had was the knife and a set of keys and Sara's cell phone and the rest of the credit cards, thought about offering them , but chose against it, and said to Guy

"What about that boat next to us, do you think that I can rent it for tomorrow? Can you introduce me to your friend?"

"I'll do you one better, I have his keys and I'll let you borrow his boat, come follow me"
Jack followed Guy who led him to the next boat over. It was a bit smaller, but it was a crab boat as well and Jack saw those crab pots and got a great idea.

"How far do those go down" pointing at the crab pots.
Jack thought to himself, they could easily hold several bodies.

"Oh one hundred feet or so, but you can't fish those they are by permit only"

"You don't say" and ads "What do you have for me to fish with"

Guy pulls out some large poles from a cabinet and shows Jack the bait box to say "You place fresh ice and boxes of herring in here".

"affix a fish to the line and throw it out, keep the boat slowly moving and you'll catch some fish, I'd recommend you get out of those clothes, or you'll ruin them."

"Alright give me, an hour and I'll be back with my friends" said Jack

"I don't mean today, maybe tomorrow, it will give me time to register your departure, and you will have to go shopping for bait and groceries, by tomorrow, I'll have the fishing poles ready, a boat log issued and a permit for a small party of people. So say 10 AM tomorrow" said Guy.

"Yeah, let me go check with my girl, to see if it's alright, can you wait till I get back"

"As long as it's before five" said Guy as he watched Jack walk the dock and out through the gate. Jack crossed the street to the mall, he quickens the pace, and he made it to the mall.

The air-conditioned felt refreshing as he made it past some shops to stand at Sara's store and saw her, he walked in. Sara saw him and left her customer and went up to him and said "Ooh you smell like fish." Jack pushes his hands up to her face; she backed away and said; "You take care of Steve yet?"

"Nah, but I'm working on it, I need a change of clothes" said Jack

"Finally deciding to get out of the suit, for more practical clothing, how about some jeans and a tank top, then we can match" said Sara, leading Jack to the Jean section, Sara pulled out a tailor's tape and measured and touched him.

"Don't get me started, or"

"Or what take me in the back and"

"Just stop it lets be serious" said Jack a bit annoyed with her

She found the pair he liked and a large tank top, she led him to the changing room, where she left Jack alone to be.

He undressed and changed into a new pair of jeans and put on the tank top, and he stepped out to show Sara.

"Much better Jack, now I like that look"

"Yeah, but my pants are falling down"

"Here is a belt, try it on" said Sara she watched him fix his pants and tuck in his shirt.

"I need a jacket now" he pointed down to his knife, which he had on his pants but moved it to the belt, she hands him a green medium jacket and instead of his white hat she gives him a ball cap green which he slid on his head.

"So how will you be paying for all of this Jack" said Sara, he hands her Johnny's credit card. And says to him" Letting someone else buy these for you?"

"Yeah you could say that, hurry up I'm in a hurry and can you put ten pairs of different outfits together while I'm gone and then charge it to the card."

Yes sir" said Sara, "What about me?"

"Buy whatever you like, I don't care" said Jack and ads;

"Give your boyfriend a call"

"What do you mean, your right in front of me, you mean down there?"

"No" he said and shakes his head, to say "I mean Steve". Jack hands her phone and says" Have him meet you down on the docks slip twelve C next to the end boat on the Far East side for tomorrow morning at 11 AM sharp. Then we will spend a day of deep sea fishing." "And bring his friends the more the merrier and most important have they bring a lot of cash; this will be a day they will not forget."

She looked at him to say "You're not going deep sea fishing without me, and you want Steve, instead of me, are you crazy?"

"Just make the call and have him meet me down there" said Jack waiting for her to do this.

Sara did as she was told and rang up Steve and began to apologized to him, and say "Steve I was wrong to scream and put up a fight with you, can you let me make it up to you. She paused to listen to his garb to say ", I and my girlfriends are going out on a boat tomorrow morning can you meet me there say around eleven sharp."

There was a pause, then he said "You got me in trouble I will only if you promise me that you'll have the ship full of your hot girlfriends" Sara looked at Jack, who shook his head "Yes",

"Of course, I will make it up to you, and your friends, you know I realized how wrong I was, and thought that about the ocean and how I like to be naked, so me and my girl friends decided to skip work tomorrow and take out a friend's boat."
He countered by saying "You really owe me, I want your closest friends to be there, like the young Leslie, Erica and Rachel, and to make sure their on board I want a call from them personally"
Sara looked at Jack who shook his head "Yes"

"Listen, you know I can't get them to call you, but I can assure you that I will service your every need while we deep sea fish."

"How does that sound". She paused to listen to his bullshit and then she said "Where?" looking at Jack for help he mouthed the words" Mobile City Docks, twelve C, that sounds good I can't wait to do you either, but I can't see you tonight, tomorrow. "Oh, yes and one more thing, if you want Leslie, Erica and Rachel, it will cost you."

"Yes, meaning cold hard cash, and lots of it"
"This shouldn't cost us a thing," he countered.

"We need some help in paying for the renting of the boat, the food and bait"
"Alright"

"Now that will impress the girls, thanks, bye." Sara closed up the phone and handed back to Jack who was standing in front of her and said "How was that, was that convincing enough, now I want to go"

"Well see" said Jack holding her phone in his hand."
She looked at him, to say "What is your plan, when they see that neither I, nor, Erica, Leslie or Rachel, is there, do you think that you all are gonna get along, listen Jack they could care less about fishing all they want to do is get off, so you need me." she said, looking him over to say "What your just going to lure them out there and toss them over."

"Hush up, what I do will be a lot of work, and maybe some fun" said Jack.

"It's not fair you get to have all the fun without me"

"Believe me its no fun and I don't want something to happen to you, let me think about it, I guess it depends on how you behave"

Jack kissed Sara on the cheek and said "I'll see you later and call me when you get off?"

"In about two hours then were going to my mother's and fathers house."

"Fine I'll pick you up soon"

Jack left, and headed back to the tailor's shop, to see her, she said; "Not ready yet"

He continued. Thinking back, that his watch said "it was about 4:45 PM and Guy said the docks closed at five, so Jack left the mall, through a side door, and hi-tailed it over across the street, to the docks, as it was still a little light, as he saw a lone figure on the dock by the boat, as Jack raced towards him, to come to a stop, half out of breath, hands on his knees, to look up, to hear " So I got all the details worked out, you have the boat, all day tomorrow, in the wheel house is a map, if you like you can drop a few crab pots, in the designated area's I marked, you place some bait in each one, if you like I could go with you"

"Nah, you know it's me and my girlfriend, and we would like some privacy".

"Alright, so it's just you and a girl" said Guy as he jotted it down on a piece of paper.

"What are you writing down" asked Jack looking at him.

"What you said, there will be two of you on the boat"

Jack looked at him as he looked back at him to say;

"You said something about using those crab pots"

"Yes, see that crane, the controls are over there, you pick it up and then move it to the rail, lay it on its side, open it up, grab a bait can, hang it in the middle, drop the gate and tie it off, then release the crane line and then release the launcher." said Guy pointing to everything.

"The most important thing is that you'll need to go shopping"

"For what" said Jack in a inquisitive way?

"look its for staples like, potatoes and some fresh vegetables, get a pot going in the galley, the aroma will help you to recover from sea sickness" laughed Guy, to Jack,

'Who is going to cook that? "

"Well that could be me or maybe your girl"

"Alright something to think about"

Guy said "Here is the key, to the gate and to the boat, I'll be off tomorrow then, I'll see you on Saturday and thank you again"

"What for"

"For buying the Phoenix, oh I mean the Parthian Stranger, cool name, I like it, see you"

The two walked together, to the end, as Guy closed the gate, inserted his key and locked it and Guy said "Can I drive you somewhere?"

"Nah, I'm going back to the mall" said Jack as he was in sprint mode, he felt good in his jeans, which became a full run, over the small hill and across a designated sidewalk, into the parking lot of the mall, looking at his watch it was a little past five, he made his way back in and saw that the mall was near empty, as Jack made it to the tailors shop, the light was on, but the steel door was down, Jack tapped on it, until he saw a head pop up, and saw her face, she smiled at him, came over, turned a key, and the grate went up, Jack stepped in, and followed her, back to where she was at as she said "Almost finished", she stood up with pants and jacket in hand, to say "Can you try them on now"

"Here?"

"No silly in the back, come follow me" she lead him back, once in the back she came to him, began to rub his thing, as he said   "Whoa wait a minute, can I get my pants off first" as she was grabbing to help him out when a loud guy's voice said "Cassandra, are you in the back?"

"Who is that" said Jack.

"Don't worry about him, it's only my jealous husband" she said, as she turned to say "Just try it on, I'll go out and get rid of him"

She left, and closed the door, Jack went to the door, opened it and saw a similar situation, he was in, a younger woman and a very older man, he looked old and graying, big full beard, and somewhat a robust man, he tried to kiss her, she turned her face, as she was pushing him out of the store, to hear her say "Alright, be back in thirty minutes, I have a customer in the back"

"This is my store, and I'm staying right here"

"Fine let me continue the fitting and then I'll be ready"
She turned, as Jack took a few steps back, to slip on the pants, and then the jacket, to hear her knock, and say "Mister, its, Cassandra, are you ready for me?"

"Yeah, I'm dressed" said Jack
She pushed the door open, to see him, to say "Oh, that isn't right, she took out her marker, to make some marks, to say "Listen, my old man, is here, I was wondering if you and I could meet up at a hotel room, here is my card, and let me write my cell number on it, she leaned in to say   "You drive my wild"

"What about the old man"

"He is harmless, if you know what I mean"

"No, not really" said Jack pulling off the jacket and dropping his pants, to show what he had for her, as she stroked it a few times, to hear in the other room "Come on Cassandra lock up already, and lets go".

"Don't mind him all he is, is a sugar daddy"

"What is that" said Jack getting dressed, as she helped him.

"Its when a very older gentleman, has money to spend, on a young girl like me, and for those efforts, he bought me this store and bankrolled my inventory, and for all that I get to live in his big house, drive his cars and have my own room"

"That's nice for you"

"True, true, but I like you in a bad, bad way; I hope we can spend some quality time together"

"Perhaps, I too must be going"

"Call me"

"How about you call me when the suit is done" said Jack as he exited, and saw the guy hunched over the counter, as he went out into the mall, as it was nearly empty, he went down to Sara's store and saw Sara with a load of bags and a her co-worker smiled at Jack, as she pasted by, for him to say "Let me help you out with some of those bags, looks like you have been busy."

She smiled to say "Do you want to take me home now or just go to my mom's house"

"We can just go to your mom's house"

"Sounds like your tired", she said as she winked at him.

CH 4 ---

Swimming Pool

S ara drove the way to the large house on top of the flat hill and parked, Leslie was right behind her, she came for support only. Both Sara and Leslie walked hand in hand while Jack took up the rear; he was carrying the package he had bought as a house-warming gift for her parents.

Jack saw Sara and Leslie walked into the garage first they met up with her brother, a strapping young man who was tall, he was working on his off-road motorcycle, next to it was another one.

"Tim, I want you to meet my new boy-friend Jack" said Sara, turning to grab Jack's arm.

Tim stood up and held out his hand, Jack extended his in return, both men looked each other over and Tim was the first to say something "How long you know my sister" said Tim, trying to get a read on Jack. Jack responded, "Oh I don't know a couple of days."

"She must think highly of you, she usually doesn't bring anyone by at all, she is a very private person, so Jack what do you do to support her?"

"Odd jobs at best, I'm not one to have a job for to long" said Jack.

"That's cool man, that's what I do too, you know handyman jobs, for lonely house wives, you should try that racket, they pay you and you get the fringe benefits, hey just don't tell my sis, she'll flip out, she is such, a nicety, nice girl. You know man, I gota hand it to you, to hold out for her." said Tim

"What do you mean?" asked Jack

"She is waiting for marriage, if you know what I mean bro," said Tim.

Jack walked past Tim with a weird look and up some stairs and opened a door to see a lot of people, Jack handed Sara, the present which in turn she spoke up loudly and said proudly,

"Here is my boy-friend his name is Jack"

Everyone comes at Jack, first was her Dad who looked a little older than him, who said his name was "Hi, I'm Sara's father, my name is Doctor Gregory and I'm a vascular surgeon, that's my wife Doctor Heidi, she is a OBY-GN, and here is my eldest daughter, Doctor Kate, who is has a pediatrics practice, I've been trying to get all the family together for a family practice, you met my son, Tim, is just finishing High school and he will go into the Navy. To study medicine, so Jack what do you do?" as the Dad pat is his hand on Jack's shoulder.

"Oh you know, just odd jobs, to make ends meet" said Jack

"Come on you can tell me, you look like a tough guy"

"Now I can see why my daughter is attracted to you, but really what do you do?"

Jack paused, and wondered himself and before he spoke, what should he say he was a killer or what, Sara, said nothing about what I should say so I guess its o Kay or is it, then he speaks

"Well I'm from Germany, and after High school I joined the elite Army and" Jack paused, that was supposed to be suppressed or is it, thought Jack. Jack moved away from her dad and into the living room where a beautiful girl sat.

"Hi who are you?" said Jack holding his hand out.

She turns to face him and says, "My name is Debbie but you can call me Deb, I'm Kate's girl friend."

"That's nice don't think I've meet her"

"Are you Kate's Dad friend?" said Miss Debbie who now stood up and faced him, there eyes met and an instant connection was made.

"No, not really, I just met Greg, he seems nice but that's it," said Jack turning to see his love interest come to him and say;

"Deb, have you met my boy-friend?" she said mockingly. Jack saw that she was mocking her and getting away with it. Debbie said, "It was nice to meet you, have fun with Sara."

"She seemed a bit upset" said Jack to Sara

"She has some problems of her own, she is in love with my sister and the two is trying to keep their relationship a secret."

"There relationship, you mean like yours and Leslie," said Jack

"Ssh, it's a secret and you're the only one that knows, but mister I will tell you this, Leslie told me that she really likes you in that way and from now on our relationship will be equal, we will both share you equally and say at a later day you want to spice it up, were both game for it, that means were not going to tie you down."
Jack looked at her oddly, for her to say "What I mean is you can still have other girls"
Jack shook his head, "Yes "then walked away from her.

"That's cool" said Jack as he sees a huge model boat that sat in a sewing room.
Sara followed him to say "Do you know what that means? "

"Actually, I really don't care, what's up with your Dad."

"I think he is actually excited to know I have a boyfriend and I think he hopes I get married and have a boat load of kids, interested"

"No, with this model"

"You're not listening to me, I just gave you freedom to have sex with any other woman you want, what do you think?"

"Sure why not, we are our own persons".

"So why wouldn't I go out and have sex with other girls"

"You don't get it, some girls would get jealous"

"Your not some girl, you're my girl, I like you and I think I will do anything for you, so why not give you a couple of kids if that is what you really want.

"That's what I would love to hear" said Dr Greg, who came in and gave his daughter a hug and says "If this is the guy, then you know I approve of anything you do, if I can't get you back into Med School, then extending our family with Jack is all that I could hope for, so come on out to the patio, dinner is ready, your Mom is worried".
Jack followed Sara and her Dad, through a small dining room and out onto the patio, it was lit up, in the middle was a pool, big and on one end was a slide and next to it was a diving board.

"Sweet, "said Jack

They came to a large table off to the left was Sara's family on the close left was Sara's sister Kate, next to her was her girl-friend Debbie and next to her was Tim and on the end was Sara's mom, Heidi and next to her on the left was Leslie and Sara took a seat next to her, while Jack was checking out the pool.

"Nice pool you have" said Jack who sat on next to Sara's left, next to her Dad.

Jack helped push Sara's chair in before he got comfortable.

"Thanks Jack," said Sara as everyone was watching, as he adjusted in his seat.

Everyone was loading up their plates and began passing around in a clockwise motion, Jack had the littlest portion and it was first Sara to notice it.

Jack took far less than she did, but it was her dad who said something first;   "Are you not hungry, Jack" said Greg

"I wish I could eat more, it just seems to go right through Me." said Jack quietly.

"Why don't you have Sara bring you by my office tomorrow and I'll do a battery of test's to determine what's wrong how that does that sound?"

"Fine, do you take cash?" said Jack, they all laughed

Sara watched how her Dad was interacting with Jack, it was something special, and with that, she wrapped her arm around his, squeezed, and then kissed him on the cheek. Jack ate slowly, occasionally looking at Kate across from him, but more importantly, it was Debbie who was staring at him, Jack returned the favor, she was similar to Leslie in the way her face looked, and her body was just like that of Sara's he thought to himself "Maybe she has the best of both girl's bodies", but said "Nah, I'd better leave her alone" Nevertheless, it was the brunette and straight hair.

Which was a turn-on to Jack? Dinner was over, and Jack got up and said to Sara "I got to go to the bathroom" everyone looked at him, as Sara said "Let me show you the way"; she saw everyone's faces, of concern.

She held his hand and led him into the house and down the hall; she opened the door and turned on the light.

Jack went in and lifted up the lid and started going as she was watching, immediately, she closed the door when she saw her Mom

"Sara, is Jack alright?"

"Yeah mom" said Sara, wiping away a tear and as she said; "Dad seems to like Jack"

"This one is likable, I even like him, even though he is our age, I see your father might have a new friend, is that what your thinking,"

"I don't know yet, right now he is my friend, who knows I might find some one closer to my age, but right now, he is it"

"You know me, I'd rather you find someone closer to your age" said Heidi

Sara, who stormed out, past her Mom, leaving her to go to the kitchen, to cut the pie, she turned to see Jack.

"Do you need any help" said Jack holding out his hand, Heidi set the two different kinds of pies in Jack's hands, Jack carried them out to the table where everyone was sitting Sara and Leslie were holding hands and sitting very close together, Jack looked at them as if it was a show or a act. Across from them was Kate and her friend Debbie, while Jack sat back by Greg and the questions began to flow and not what anyone was thinking either

"Do you play golf?"

"I don't know if I do or not, I don't think I really have played it."

"What have you been doing all your life?"

"Oh, you know odd stuff; I was in the Army for the longest time."

"What do you like to do?" said Greg

Everyone was holding their breathes especially Sara and Leslie, when Jack said, "I love the water, and your pool look's inviting.

"Go ahead and get in, I think I have a suit for you to wear" said Greg.

And ads "Follow me after we get some of this good pie, you know my wife is the pie cook." Greg ads "I like you Jack and I think you will be a positive influence on my daughter"

"Thanks Greg I like you too." said Jack as he received a slice from both pies, one being lemon meringue and the other pecan. Jack slowly tasted both and liked the lemon one better but finished them both off, with a little more speed this time.

Jack even thought about having seconds, when he could feel his stomach rumblings so he picked up his plate and Sara's and Leslie's and went into the house, having deposited the plates in the sink, he turned to hear Greg.

"I have two that might fit you"

"Which ever one, it doesn't matter to me," said Jack

"What's your favorite color?" asked Greg

"Red, I'll take the red one" said Jack receiving the swim trunks in the air.

"Come with me, and I'll show you a place to change"
Greg led him to the sewing room, and said "Change in here, you stuff will be safe"

"O Kay thanks Greg, I'll see you soon."
Jack quickly undressed, while he looked at the boat model.
He left the door open, much to Debbie's happiness, she stopped and began to watch, peeking and seeing Jack, nude, he turned to give her a full show, then slipped on the swim trunks, and came her way. Debbie stepped away just to accidentally run into Jack and when she did, she brushed up on him, first with her hand and then leaned into him with her breast's and then nearly kissed his neck, as Jack stopped and held onto her so he didn't knock her over.

"Sorry, I didn't see you," said Jack really meaning it

"That's alright, it was my fault," she said with a smile, she batted her eyelids as he walked pasted her.
Jack took a few steps and gained momentum, then saw the path was clear so he went for the door, just as Tim was doing the same thing, Tim made it first, and Jack second, Tim hit the water in a style to make a loud splash and tried to get his sister and Leslie wet, Jack on the other hand dove in face first, and felt the chloride water, which stung his eyes, he quickly closed them and glided under the water, he liked this and went to the bottom and then quickly up as he expelled the rest of his air, he reached the surface and blew out the remaining air.

Jack, sat on a perch in the water, the cool of the night, felt good, but the warmth of the water felt even better, Jack watched as Tim went of the diving board, several times, when Tim stopped and said;

"Come on Jack do you want to give it a try?"

"Yeah, Jack" said Greg, who climbed the ladder and stood at least twenty feet up on the slide, Jack turned and stepped out of the water and by the fence was a ball so he picked it up, held on to it, it was spongee in feel.

"Soak that ball in the water, and then try to throw it at me," said Greg.

Jack did as he was told, and dropped the ball into the water, letting it get wet; a sinister look came over Jack.

Jack thinks to himself, "Now was the time to get Greg."

And he retrieved the ball from the water and waited.

"Here I go Jack"

Jack watched, for Greg to swing his legs out and push off, Jack readied and then aimed and threw it, the ball hit the diving board easily missing Greg who was long gone and in the water.

Greg resurfaced and said" You missed me".

"It's your turn, but first throw me the ball, before you climb up." said Greg now standing on the side of the pool.

All four girls were standing together, watching when Heidi, re-emerged from the house to say;

"Come on girls, look your Dad is having a fun time, let's go join in."

Heidi had a couple of towels, she put down on the table, and then she entered the pool wearing a little bikini herself.

Jack slid down the wet slide, and in the middle didn't react fast enough and the ball hit his head, knocking him back against the slide he dropped into the pool, with a little splash., quickly he swam to the side, pulled himself up and said " That was fun" with a smile on his face.

Heidi tosses Jack the wet ball, which he catches, and squeezes it out a bit enough to get a grip, realizing he needs to aim lower this time. He watched Greg on top of the slide say "Ready"

"Yeah" said Jack.

Greg jumped off with authority and Jack did the same and nailed Greg as soon as his head was visible, Jack raised his hands and arms in the air to celebrate, when Sara who had changed into her small string bikini said, "That's not the object of the game"
Jack went and picked up the ball and threw it at her, hard, he missed her and Leslie picked it up and tossed it to Sara, who waited for Jack to get to the top

"Jack the object of this game is for you to catch the ball and we as a team score a point, if I hit you and you don't catch it then the other teams gets a point, if I miss you altogether then no one gets a point, do you understand this?" yelled Sara

"Yeah I got you, " said Jack who launched himself off the top and face first down the slid, catching Sara off guard and she threw it way off as Jack dove in and swam half way down the length of the pool. He came to the top, to see Tim reach out and help Jack up out of the water.

"I guess were teammates "said Tim
Jack and Tim walked over to the others, and heard Sara talking and she was saying "Alright then, if Kate and Debbie are a team, then why not you, and Mom, be a team, Leslie and I will be the other and Tim and Jack."

"Fine "said Greg

"We'll go first, first to five wins," said Sara
Jack said to Tim "What are we playing for"

"Oh this is just to have fun, this is the first time in I don't know how long my Dad and Mom, has had so much fun, so lets run with it." said Tim.
First up was Leslie, she went down and missed the catch but Sara hit her anyway, next or following them was Kate who said, "Thanks Sara for the point", Kate watched as Debbie slid and the two connected with a successful throw and catch. Jack watched and now saw what to do.

"Dude, I'll throw "said Tim to Jack

"Sure" said Jack moving around to the line, behind Leslie.
As Greg was next, Heidi was throwing for their team, she threw it to Greg and he caught it. Then it was Leslie's turn to shine, she went down and caught it, then Jack went to the top, then much to his

surprise, he heard Sara, Leslie, and Debbie cheer him on. He left slowly and mid way easily caught the ball from Tim, swimming back to the side, he hands Sara the ball, and she bends down to take it from him.

"Come on Leslie we need this to stay in the game, after the first round, Kate and Debbie are in the lead, with two points and you all have one each, except us, we have none, ready"
Leslie left the top, Sara threw it, and she missed. And said;

"Ops I'm sorry dear"

"Maybe you should of changed and let Leslie throw it "said Tim, who was laughing at his sister, Jack followed in as well.

"Stop it you guys," said Sara
Next to throw was Debbie as Kate tried the slid and the two connected.

"Nice throw" said Jack

"Thanks "said Debbie with a smile to Jack
Kate threw the ball to her father from the water, Heidi, went down and the two connected.

"Score another point for our team," said Greg
Heidi threw the ball from the water at Jack who caught it with authority, he waited for Tim, saw, he was ready and waited until the last possible moment and connect just as Tim was near the bottom.

"Cheater" yelled Sara
Jack just looked at her and walked by her, he went over to the side of the pool, next to Debbie who said, "I'm sure by now you have seen her competitive side, and she can sure get vicious."
Jack helped Tim up out of the water, and said, "Thanks bro that was close"
The score after this last round is Kate and Debbie are in the lead with three points, the rest of you have two and we have none." said Sara.
Sara, who again was throwing. Both Tim and Jack were laughing together, for good reason, Leslie slid and Sara threw a good ball, Leslie tried to catch it, but it just bounced out of her hands.
Sara went to retrieve the ball, and threw it back to her sister.
Kate said, "Looks like we can seal up a easy win with this throw"

Kate readied herself, waited for Debbie who was halfway and the two connected for a easy win.

"Now that we won, we want you and your girl-friend Leslie to take off your swim suits and give us five laps of the pool," said Kate and Debbie who were standing by each other laughing

"Fat chance, we will swim, but were not getting undressed, besides if we were to do that you both would have to do the same, the four girls were looking at each other, while Jack, Tim Heidi and Greg walked back to the table to take a seat. When Greg spoke up

"Jack you can stay the night if you would like to. I can set up a cot in the sewing room, then tomorrow morning you can ride with me to the hospital, how does that sound?'

"Whatever Sara wants to do, I 'm fine with that," said Jack Both Greg and Jack got up. "It's getting late, I need to go to bed "said Heidi

"I'll be with you in a minute," said Greg

"Wow, really, alright then" said Heidi and ads "Jack you can stay over as much as you would like"
Greg led Jack and Tim into the house as Tim spoke up and said;

"I'll get the cot from the garage"

"I will get the pillow and sheets," said Heidi

"Jack, feel free to get anything out of the refrigerator you want, I need to leave here tomorrow around 7: 30 a.m. and I'll get you up around six."

"Thanks Greg, and tell Heidi thanks for a nice dinner and dessert," said Jack

"Go back outside and enjoy the pool, I know the girls are going to get crazy and their gonna need your help."
Jack and Greg shook hands and parted ways, Greg eagerly went down the hall, and Heidi came from the laundry room with a pillow, some sheets and a light blanket. She didn't speak a word but handed them to Jack who said "Thanks"

"You got them going," said Tim bringing in the cot and he quickly set it up for Jack.

"Thanks Tim," said Jack putting on the sheets with Tim's help.

"Would you like to go dirt bike riding sometime?"

"Sure it sounds fun," said Jack

"Saturday, I and a couple of friends are going to the water park, do you want to go?"

"I don't see why not, let me check it out with Sara and I'll have her call you."

"Thanks Jack" said Tim who shook Jack's hand and left. Jack did, as well, back to the pool and to a big surprise; standing toe to toe was four naked girls, yelling at each other.

"Whoa" said Jack what are you guys doing?"
They turned their attention on Jack; first, it was Sara who began to chase him. Then it was by Debbie, Leslie followed as well. Kate decided she had enough and put a towel around her body and went in.

"Stop it "said Jack holding his ground enough for Sara to hold one arm and Debbie the other and Leslie pulled his shorts down. They all laughed except Jack who but couldn't help to look at all three girls, especially Debbie, who possess a rock solid body, perfect breasts and exceptional legs, that came to a point which showed a well groomed brown hair patch.

"Come on lets play another round" said Sara
Jack was getting turned on, which it showed, Sara led Jack to the side of the pool and said" Jack you and Debbie be a team and Leslie and I will be the other and this time lets play for something good."

"What do you have in mind" said Debbie

"It has to be something with Jack," said Sara

"Leave me out of this, said Jack.

"If Debbie and I win, you have to take us to the water park on Saturday," said Jack

"And that includes lunch and dinner" said Debbie who was holding onto Jack's arm, Jack slid his free hand down her butt, to get a feel. He began to rub her lower back.

"And if we win, Leslie and I get you Jack in our bed tonight" said Sara with a wink

"That's not fair for Debbie, you left her out, what can she do for you guys" said Jack

"She can clean up this mess," says Sara

"'Well if she does that, then I will be doing that too she's my partner and you know Sara how much I help my partner" said Jack

"That's sweet of you, Jack," said Debbie

"Alright do we have a deal?" said Sara

"Yeah we agree," said Jack as Debbie nodded in agreement, still holding onto Jack and liking it, with a smile.

"You guys can go first, were playing to ten, Leslie come here" said Sara

Jack led off while Debbie was the thrower, Jack watched Sara and Leslie talk and went for it, he easily caught Debbie's throw, he did much of the catching and Leslie did most of the missing and even though they didn't make it to ten, they all ended up in the pool.

Where they played a couple of games of catfight and of course the team of Jack and Debbie ruled, he would lift her up on his shoulder's with his head between her legs, she was having a fun time, laughing, when it all of a sudden came to a end when Leslie said;

" I got to go to school, look its one a.m"

"Are you spending the night?" said Sara

"Of course let's go to bed" said Leslie, taking Sara's hand and led Sara out of the pool.

Sara waved to Jack and went inside.

"I guess you're just a front?" said Debbie

"What do you mean?" said Jack doing a light stroke to the deep end.

"You don't know do you, both girls are lesbians" said Debbie, who was closing in on Jack

"So what." I don't care" said Jack who rests on the perch, feeling the cold of the night

"It's getting cold out here do you want to get into the hot tub?" said Debbie lifting herself out of the pool.

"Say what?" Jack followed to see Debbie pulled off the cover, turned on the jets, and said, "Come on in the water is hot and so am I"

Jack trotted over to her and took it one foot at a time and slowly settled in, looking around he saw the tub was hidden on two sides one by the wall and bushes on the other side in front of them was the ocean, which the full moon highlighted, when Debbie made the first move and slid next to Jack, placed her hand on his manhood and said "You know I like you so why are you with Sara, who has only had women as friends and dislikes men?"

"That might be true, but I scarred her into liking me and for that I get the reward of another women's company."

"Why don't you sit on the edge and I will show you what you're missing," said Debbie who was now more than ever excited. Jack gets up and Debbie parts his legs as Jack sits on the edge, she begins to fully erect his manhood and it was stiff, she was right it was different, to the point that Jack was feeling ready to erupt, and Debbie felt it to and said "Go ahead I don't mind let me have it I want to taste what you have to offer, Jack obliged her and let loose his load, which she swallowed and then licked her lips and said "Now its my turn". She sat on the edge, spread her legs wide, parted her lips, and said,   "Now big boy finish me off and lick me between my legs."
Jack went in tongue ready and worked her over, so that she let out a small scream she bite her hand holding back the pleasure Jack was giving to her, on he her last orgasm, Jack took charge and stood up and in a instant, he put himself inside her with out warning, and began to drill her.

"Whoa, I don't let any guy in there without a condom"
Jack continued to drill her and then started to tease her and pulled it out and played with it,

"Please put it back in, but, don't come inside of me."
She guided him as she held onto it and turned around and said,

"Now stick it into me"
Jack with her help slid it in and it was tighter and it felt good, he put his hands on her hips and went a long time enough for her to have come four times and building one last one when Jack said " I'm ready where do you want it"

"Quickly here in my mouth, as she let out a loud cry of joy, Jack pulled out and gave it to Debbie who then sucked him dry.
She got up and said" I got to go, but why don't you come by and see me at the hospital and I will take good care of you from now on."

Jack got out and watched as Debbie put the top back on and then led the way, to her clothes, which he watched her get dressed. She then helps put on Jack's swim trunks which were now dry.

Then Debbie came up to Jack and gave him a long lingering kiss and said "Goodbye for now and I will see you later"

Jack picked up the remaining plates, and blew out the candles, and went inside deposited the plates, heard a few noises, then went slowly to the sewing room, he found his cot, and lay down and went to sleep.

"Jack, wake up its six AM" said Heidi, who wore her scrubs, she bent down, to say "Your like a breath of fresh air, last night you set a fire in my husband that has been missing for a while, so whatever your doing with Sara, I approve" she knelt over and gave him a kiss on the cheek.

Jack opened his eyes, to see her leave, as he followed her, only to find the bathroom, he turned on the water and got in, and pulled the curtain closed, as he showered, someone came in, he waited, then he thought it was Sara, that he pulled the curtain open, only to see Kate, her legs spread, doing her business, she looked up to see his face, then down to see what he had to offer, slowly she closed her legs, to say "Sorry"

Jack pulled the curtain back, and finished showering, he turned off the water, pulled the curtain back to see no one only to hear Sara's voice, she came in, shut the door. She faced Jack drying off, to say;

"Listen we need to talk"

Jack finished drying off; he placed the towel around his waist.

"I don't know what's going on here, but everyone in my family loves you, this is my greatest dream realized" come here and give me a hug, then she kissed him on the cheek.

Jack looked at her, to say "I've changed my mind, why don't you call your girlfriends over and we will all go out on the boat today"

"Really great, thanks"

"Later I and my friends will show you our gratitude".

"Why don't you and your friends go shopping for say some soup and some drinks and meet me down by the docks around 10:30, this morning?"

"Alright what are you doing?"

"I guess your mom is taking me to the hospital to get checked out"

Jack went past her, he left her standing, he went in to his room, closed the door, quickly changed, and opened the door; he went to the kitchen, to see Heidi and Greg.

"Jack, have a seat" said Heidi

Jack looked over at the smorgasbord of food; Jack took several pieces of bacon, hash browns and biscuits"

Next to him sat Kate, who said "Let me help you with that", she took some gravy, split the biscuits and poured it on, for her to say;

"Are you not going to get any grits?"

Jack shakes his head "No," then says "I don't think I ever had that"

"Its good, here let me serve you" said Kate, who herself, looked around the table, to say "This is nice, isn't it?"

Jack nodded, but ate, then Greg spoke "Usually we have patients fast before they have their blood tested, but for you we will find a baseline first, then determine at a later time if we need more blood"

Jack looked around, as he ate, to say "Who's going to do it?"

"I will" said Heidi, and "I will take you in with me, Greg you and Kate will go together"

"Yes Mom" said Kate, who was getting comfortable next to Jack, only to have a hand on her shoulder, to hear "Sis, can you scoot over, to give me and Leslie some room"

She moved to allow Sara in, next to Jack, and then Leslie, sat down. Jack stood up he was finished as he announced, with a half eaten plate, which Sara slid to her, to finish it off, as Kate watched to hear Sara say "Who's going to check out Jack?"

"Just think you could, if only you"

"Knock it off Kate" said Greg

"Yes father, it will be Mom" said Kate getting up.

She saw Jack sitting in the living room.

She came to him, to say" I want to apologize for this morning; I hope you can forgive me"

Jack stood to say "Yeah sure, it was an honest mistake, I was just hoping you were going to get in" catching her off guard, she looked

at him and smiled, then Kate, left him, in a hurry, as Jack laughed.
To see Heidi was ready, to say "Shall we go Jack"
Jack saw Timmy to say "Later, we will see you there Saturday"
"Really great, say what are you doing today"
"Ah, not much", as Jack leans in to say" Your sister and I
have a little business to take care of, if you know what I mean"
"Yeah I get cha" said Timmy
Jack pasted him and went out into the garage, to see Heidi uncover
her car, and she pulled it out, Jack got in sat in the passenger seat,
only to see Sara come out into the garage with her hands up, as
Jack did the same thing back at her. As the car sped off.
"You know she is playing with your heart, now my oldest
daughter may fit with you perfectly"
"How so" said Jack looking at how nice the car's trim was.
"Well she is a doctor, her life is set, and now is looking for
love, how did you meet Sara?"
"At the mall, she was so helpful with picking out my outfit"
"Really, how do you like the car?"
"Yeah it's nice, what kind is it?"
"It's called a Mercedes, SLR"
"That's nice", said Jack as the car, came to a stop, right by
the hospital; she pulled into her parking spot. They both got out
together, towards the entrance, for her to say "This is the doctor's
entrance, on the north side is the emergency room, where we all
take turns on that type of medicine, we have a clinic for us" as she
led him to a small room, where she took his blood, his weight and
height, to say "Your right at your size, but you may need to eat more
healthier"
"Yes I know, I guess I will with Sara's cooking"
Heidi began to laugh, to say "I'm sorry to tell you, she can't cook,
if you're looking for someone to cook for you well you may choose
another family"
Jack just looked at her, for her to say "Like all rich families, we have
ourselves a cook"
'That's nice" said Jack, as she handed him a cup. Jack just
looked at her.

"Go over to the stall, and fill it up, don't worry I won't look, I'm a doctor"

Jack did as he was told, and filled it up, and let the excess go, he turned and handed her the wet cup. She took it and wiped it off, to say; "All done, we will let Sara know the results, do you need a ride somewhere?"

""No thanks, the Marina's just around the bend, I'll walk"

"Bye for now"

Jack walked out of the hospital, cross the street, down a side street, before he stopped to think , "Oh shit now they will know who I am", said Jack as he looked up at the hospital, then decided to carry out his plan, and ran off.

Jack made his way back to the boat dock on foot.

With key in hand, he saw Guy, standing on the dock with a phone in one hand, signaling to an in coming tugboat.

"Jack I'm putting the plan in action, the tugboat will tow my boat to the ship yard and work will begin tomorrow, when you get back I will have all the details, come on aboard and let me show you what I have done and by the way you look more like a fisherman."

Jack followed Guy onto the next boat the two of them watched as a couple of men boarded the Phoenix and roped it up and in an instant, the Phoenix was moving out of the dock area.

"Jack come into the wheelhouse and let me show you around," said Guy who gave Jack a quick tour of the boat and then showed him how to use the radio and the satellite phone and some of the deep-sea gauges and then how to run and operate the boat.

"Now what time do you think you might be back?"

"Oh, I imagine in a couple of hours, say around five p.m.," said Jack

"That's fine then, I'll see you later buddy," said Guy and the two shook hands. Jack watched as Guy left the boat. Then on the pier near the crab shack, he saw first victims, coming his way and said, to himself "right on time" he sees four pretty girls all in little bikini's, carrying groceries in hand, Jack checked the bait box, he opened it up to see the once empty to a now full of bait and ice. Jack thinks to himself "that Guy is a nice guy".

The girls stood on the deck to say "Captain May we come aboard?"

Jack popped his head up to say "Yes you may", one by one each girl jumped in, but it was Sara, who went up to Jack and pulled him aside as a red-head say "I'll put the bags in the galley for you Sara", "come girls lets leave them be". Said Leslie

"Listen I don't know what's going on here, but you left without kissing me or anything" as she began to cry.
Jack consoled her to say "I don't know about all this, your sister said you were only using me"

"What, what are you saying, listen my sister is jealous, as is my step-mom, remember I told you, it was you and I forever"

"Fine what happen last night, which was you and her?"

"And we thought it was you"

"I didn't even know where you went"

'To my room, her and I played, and while we were doing that, we had to stop, to watch you and Debbie go at it, believe me it was hot, but we were both were waiting for you to come and take care of us, believe me, just ask Leslie, she knows she is second to you and from this day forward it will only be you, she was right you know, I am in love with you"
Jack held her face in his hand, to say;

"Are you one hundred percent positive?"

"Yes my dear, from this day forward, consider me you loyal and loving servant"

"Hey, hey, hey bitch Whatcha a doing with my girl?" said Steve
Jack turned to see an ugly dude and his band of idiots, he slid his cap down to shield his face to say "You slept with that guy", and went up to the landing at the wheelhouse, where Leslie stood, to say "You know your wrong about her, I've never seen her like this, you're a lucky man, besides, I don't think those boys know what there in store for either."

"Get aboard and cast off the lines" yelled Jack.
Steve and the others looked up at Jack, and then Steve barked out orders.
The boat came to life as Jack fired it up, then he slid the window open and said "Take the girls forward, and get naked for the boys".

"Yes Captain as you wish" said Sara with a smile

Jack yelled out, on more time "Men can you untie us and get on, Sara's waiting for you, are you or one of you Steve?"

"Yeah, I am "said the tall handsome one

"Great, then you must be the leader?"

"Yeah, that's right old man," said Steve

The other men got on board while one undid the mooring lines and two others rolled them up and set them on deck, while Steve went up to see the captain.

"Yo, old man" yelled a disrespectful man

Jack lifted up the throttle and turned the wheel and lurched the boat forward, he saw on the map where he wanted to go and entered into the coordinates, then set the auto-pilot, as it hit the harbor in stride, coming up to see Jack was Steve, saying;

"Yo, old man you know where my bitch is"

Jack readied himself as soon as he saw Steve. To say "Look out front, there they are", to add "Hey over here" said Jack getting his attention, to say "She told me to collect all the money you have or she won't come out of her cabin, which is there." "She said to have you all strip naked and one by one she will see you, you being I guess Steve." Steve pulled out a wad of cash and handed to Jack, who did a quick count, it totaled five thousand dollars.

"That should make her happy "said Jack

"What's you say old man" said Steve getting in Jack's face.

"Nothing" said Jack, with his hand firmly on a metal bar, he could not resist, so in one swing Jack nailed Steve in the back of the head, and he fell down. Jack jumped up and put the bar away and carried Steve into the front cabin, onto the bunk, then using some rope he tied Steve up. The gulf waters were visible now, as the boat was on course.

Jack had picked up his pipe went down below to the galley to see one white Guy and two black guys, one large and one medium build.

"Hey guys I'm the captain named Jack, and Sara asked me to collect all the money you brought for her and give it to me to hold"

"When do we get to see her?" said one guy.

"Well I believe Steve is with her now," said Jack

"Oh yeah, that's cool" said another.

"So in the meantime I laid out four poles and lets go out on to the deck and I will show you the bait" said Jack leading them down through the bunk rooms and onto the deck, each man came up to Jack and gave them their share all in all it totaled ten thousand dollars.

Which Jack put in his pocket? Each man grabbed a pole, a herring from the bait box, and affixed on the line. Then each of them went to the stern, climbed up on the bridge, then casted out their lines. Jack came back out with three chairs and a message;

"Steve said one by one come in to the forward cabin and take off all your clothes and have a condom ready, because you'll all get the four girls all at once, rather than each of you has one to begin with." said Jack

"Aw man, let's do rock, paper, scissors," said one of them; they did that, to determine the going order.

Jack turned to face the guy's and said, "I'll call you one by one, and to come up to the wheel house and from there you'll go down to the main cabin"

Jack went back in to the galley, picked up his metal pipe, and went up to the wheelhouse to check on Steve, who was still out and not moving. Jack closed the hatch back down to hide his body.

Jack checked his heading, to see the girls were all laid out taking in the sun.

He checked that he was still on course; that Guy had mentioned to him that these were shark-infested waters. Jack was ready it was about noon and about half way there when he called on his next victim, Jack switch on the intercom and said" Will the next gentleman please come up to the wheel house, please", Jack looked out the front window, down to the girls, who laid out in the nude, taking in the sun.

The first person to come up was the biggest black person who was hung like a horse.

"Come in I won't bite, there down in the front hold, through that door, which Jack opened up for the guy and the guy ducked his head and said "What the hell" clunk the metal pipe struck his head and the black guy went down, Jack followed him in, quickly closed the door and thought to himself, maybe I ought to call all of them up here now and get it over with.

Jack quickly tied and duct taped the big black guy.

Two down, two to go. Jack came out of the cabin to see it was Sara.

"What are you doing lover"

"Just taking care of your problems, why don't you go up to the front and lie out with the rest of the girls, when I'm done I will come up and see you" said Jack, leading her out front, down onto the Bow, then turned to see the medium built one, who was behind him.

"Instantly Jack saw in his in his eyes and for a split second Jack knew what was coming but could not do anything about it, the guy began to scream, saying " Help me Rob" and Jack stepped into it and swung his fist for a gut shot, driving the man back, into the wheel house, he saw a man scrambling down the bridge to get to help his friend, so Jack took the metal pipe, he used it like a bat, the pipe hit with such force nearly taking his head off. The medium built guy fell to the floor and blood was literally just pouring out of his now lifeless and dead body, the smell of urine filled the cabin. In raced Rob who was caught off guard as Jack went head hunting catching him at eye level and dropping him backwards, back down the stairs and into the galley, he was a bleeder too. Jack tossed the weapon aside and pulled his knife and with one hand drug Rob's body out onto the deck, where he began to filet his victim and cut him up. Jack got over to the crane controls and moved attached crab pot, over to the railing, then opened up the pot and rolled him in. seeing he might have only room for maybe one or two more, Jack went back in to get the young black man, whose head was dangling by his broken spine, Jack picked him up and took him on deck and cut off his head and then stuffed the rest of the body in the crab pot.

The deck had blood all over it, Jack went back inside and up to the wheel house with only his knife in hand to see something, swoop over his head as he lunged out and stabbed the tall black man in the heart, as the man fell on Jack, Jack pulled it out and stabbed him several times over, to see the life of the guy. Jack grabbed the guy's long nappy hair and pulled him up and out onto the deck, as the boat slowed to a stop and idled at the position, it was suppose to be at. Jack cut up the tall black person with his sharp fillet knife. And stuffed him into the full crab pot closed the large door and tied it shut.

Jack raced over to the controls, and released the launcher and off it went, into the ocean, where they were at was the shark infestated waters.

Jack's attention was diverted when he saw his arch nemesis, Steve who was now loose and yelling;

"I'm gonna get you bastard, I'm gonna kill you, he held up the pipe and was on the upper deck, why don't you come up for your turn old man" said Steve and ads "I got something for you"

Jack was on the move, quickly coming at him and in a surprise move, Steve evaded Jack and went down below, Jack searched and found nothing, thinking I should have had that gun, so Jack went room by room and finally the engine compartment, which Steve was trying to sabotage with cutting the fuel lines and using a hammer on the heads and knocking out the exhaust manifold until Jack stuck him with his blade in the back, rapid times until Steve turned around and squarely hit Jack in the side with a hammer, knocking Jack down, losing the knife, under the engine, Jack got up and tackled Steve and began to hit his kidneys with such force, causing Steve to vomit blood, but Steve retaliated and kicked Jack in the face and Jack let go.

Steve worked his way up to the wheel house and grabbed the key and shut off the engines Jack quickly made his way up to the wheel house to see the key was gone as was Steve out on the deck he heard Steve calling out his friend's names. No one answered then Jack arrived and with a grabbling hook stabbed Steve in the upper back above the shoulder and with his hand strikes Steve in the jaw knocking him to the deck. Jack tied the rope from the grappling hook to the crane and lifted him up off the ground. Then he swung him to the seaside.

"You bastard, you tricked me and my friends; you will pay, when I get down from here."

Jack pondered his next move, how can I kill this guy, then a though crossed his mind, get the sharks in a frenzy and drop him off in the middle. Therefore, Jack took a box of frozen herring and tossed it over board, nothing happened.

" Ah, the blood, so Jack began to work and mop up all the blood, with each bucket he dumped over board, and much to Jack's surprise, finally a few sharks appeared, after the final cleanup, Jack decided to dump the bucket and then drop Steve into the water.
Jack then broke out the boat's fire hose and began to wash off the deck of visible blood; only to look up and see Steve was gone.
No trace of him any where except pieces of his flesh on the hook when Jack, retrieved it.

"Damn it "and ads "Now what" and began to look, then he saw Sara in Steve's hands, he yelled out to Jack "Yo old man, where are my bro's"
Jack looked up at Steve, thinking of the other girls, to say;

"You don't want to do this man"

"I know you dude, you're the one who was at her apartment, and you're the one who tried to blow up our house, but what you didn't know was it was kerosene, but I got you back sucka, when we struck you with the SUV, yeah I knew it was you, you know what I tried to check you out and you know what your off the grid, so that means your either a FBI or some spook, so who are you"
Sara used all her mite and pushed the unsuspecting Steve.
Away from her, who lost his balance as Sara pushed him overboard, to the waiting sharks, to hear "He is my boyfriend" she yelled at him as the sharks were enjoying their meal.
In a instant she was on the deck in his arms as he said "It is over now, let me steer the boat back to the harbor, thanks"

"Your welcome, did I prove my love to you now"

"Yes you did, now listen, strong and defiant one, can you clean up the wheelhouse and the galley, of the blood, while I go down to see if I can fix the damages" while he looked at her rather naked body.
Jack went down to the engine compartment and fixed the fuel lines and the exhaust manifold and its connections, then saw on the wall a remote start switch, he went to it and turned the switch and hit the button, then he held it down for a minute it fired right up. Jack worked his way back up to the wheel house, he looked out to see no

sign of Steve, then set a course back to the harbor, and off the boat went, while Jack went back down to the galley to see Sara covered in blood, he looked around and then went out and on deck took all of their clothes and separated their wallets and placed them all in a large black bag. He saw a fishing weight; he placed that in the bag, tied it up and tossed it overboard. Jack found Sara cleaning.
Jack helped out and broke out the bleach to say "Where is the food at? "

"What food, didn't I tell you that I couldn't cook, so I brought the bleach and vinegar, instead?" Jack just looked at her to say;

"That was premeditated murder"

"It was, and when you got the idea of using a boat, well I thought, here is my chance, to secure a man forever, you see now I have something on you, so if you think that this relationship won't last, your wrong, your stuck with me forever" she said defiantly, they both went back to cleaning. Jack went through the paper sacks to break out the vinegar he poured it on the floors, while Sara scrubbed the floors and the walls and together they cleaned the front hold area, to make it look and smell clean, they spent the rest of the time making sure everything was clean, later Sara cleaned up herself, Jack was sitting in the captain's chair, Sara and Jack had lunch together, eating some baloney and cheese sandwiches, and watching the calm sea's and the three other girls, had amazing tan's and then later the three went down into the cabin to sleep abit. He enterer the harbor and took it off autopilot and slowed to one third, the dock was calm not a person in sight, actually Jack could see the gate was closed, he slowed the boat as he approached the dock and threw it in neutral, he let the boat coast in and quickly made his way to the deck and took a mooring rope and tied the boat up. Securing it to the dock.
Next he went to the other side and secured the other rope, then he jumped back on and climbed the ladder to the wheel house and down into the front cabin to the engine room. He then hit the switch and shut the engines down.
Jack worked his way back up and out on the deck. He spotted Sara gathering her girlfriends, she waved goodbye to Jack as she and the girlfriends left. Jack rechecked everything out, then made his way

off the boat, with some keys in hand he made it to the parking lot, clicked on the unlock sign and the big black SUV, unlocked itself, Jack started the SUV, the music blared, he turned it down, to off, he backed up, and threw it into drive, and took off, he drove the speed limit, up and around the bend, to the clubhouse, he got to their road, he busted through the gate, and picked up speed, as the two left side tires came off the ground as he made the final turn, the place seemed empty, he held out till the last minute then jumped out as the cruise control was set for seventy, it went up the stairs and through the front windows, Jack stood up and waited, then he could hear some rumblings, and then Jack took off.
Jack was halfway up the hill as the house exploded, sending shrapnel. Jack was literally climbing the hill, he stood at the top to see the house burning, cries of agony, could be heard, as well as the siren's, knowing that he couldn't make the gate, he went further east, over the ridge, he saw amusement park sign, he saw a fence, and went up to climb it, when he lost balance and fell back, into a drainage ditch..

CH 5

The Boat

J ack awoke to the sound of the phone, that rang in his pocket, slowly he pulled it out, to hit talk, as Sara was screaming on the phone to say,   "Is this Jack, who is this? "
Jack sat up, looked at the phone to say, "Yes it's me"

"Thank god, why didn't you answer me" asked Sara, to say;   "Where are you, you wouldn't believe what happen to me yesterday" as Jack held the phone out away from his ear, as he sat under the huge willow tree, the sun was coming up, to hear ;

"Where are you at, I'll come and get cha".
Jack finally said "Out by the clubhouse"

"Really, on the news they said the house burned up, along with the largest amount of pot, they found in the basement"

"That's nice," said Jack as he got up, to say, "look I'll meet you at your parents house, it's still early"

"Yeah good idea, they don't get up for an hour or so, see you there"
Jack closed the phone up, took a running start, to the south, past the sharp willow fronds, and hiked over the fence easily, over the hill, down the bank, to the street. A short hike down, he followed it around, then back up, he saw her parents road, thinking "They have this whole property", quickly making it to the flat part.   The garages were closed; he walked around to the gate on the east side. Jack discovered it to be unlocked.   He went into the back yard; he saw the gazebo, and then went to the sliding glass door. He tried it, it was unlocked, and he went in, down the hall, to the sewing room. He saw that the cot was still made up; he quickly stripped down, and slipped under the covers and went to sleep.

The smell of bacon cooking and fresh coffee brewing, he held his eyes closed to prolong the dream he was finish in, up.   Jack was thinking how great this is and how this family liked him so, and for the first time that really felt safe, both physically and mentally. He lay on his back, still wearing his white underwear and held the light sheet tightly around his neck; he had a smile on his face.

Standing at the doorway was Sara.

She came in slowly and in one move, straddled him, to take a seat and say   "How was you evening, Jack?" trying to pull down the sheet.

Jack opened his eyes, to see her, he offered no response, and she on the other hand spoke

"My dad sure likes you and you won over the rest of my family."

"I want to first offer my apologize for not giving you a proper good night kiss" with that she bent down, parted her lips and began to kiss his lips. Then with her tongue she probed his and passionately began to kiss him, which lasted all but a quick minute when she heard her Dad say, "Yo, Jack are you up?"

Sara stopped the kissing to look over her shoulder to see her Dad looking at her and responded

"I can see why he can't answer, are you going to give him a break" said her Dad.

"I will, when I'm finished talking to him," said Sara.

"Fine, breakfast will be in about thirty minutes," said her Dad

"Now where was I at, oh yes, I hope you forgive me for being so selfish with you, I know what you did last night, but let me tell you what happen to me, I took the girls back to my apartment and guess who was there"

"Steve"

"No silly, it was John"

"Whose John, your new guy, it's hard enough trying to keep up with all the guys in your life, I swear."

"Hush up Mister, you are still my boy-friend and no John or anyone will change that," said Sara acting weird.

"Sure, I have no worries with you, and you will be mine, I get that, so tell me about this John, did your night go well'"

"Let me tell you, it is Officer John, you know the one who wanted to take me out"

Jack began to laugh, to say, "Right on, did you guys make out?"

"Hush your mouth, and no we did not, I spent half the night worrying about you, I thought about you and I called you, at least over twenty five times, I thought we would go back to my apartment and have make up sex"

"Why do we need make up sex, what did I do?" asked Jack.

Quickly Sara turned her head to see her sister standing at the door, with a smile on her face, to say, "Jack are you O Kay my sister is a lesbian?"

"I see no problems with it, you are your own person, you're free to make your own decisions and I'm just grateful to have met her and your family."

Kate quickly left the doorway to see Greg had filled it to say;

"I think you can get off of him now Sara", she slowly pulled herself off of him, to say "Were not finished talking" as she left. Jack got up and followed Greg, only to see on his left was Kate, coming out of the bathroom, having just finished a shower.

"Don't forget to put the seat down when you are finished." said Kate, with a smile, as Jack pasted her, to go inside.

Jack looked back at her and lifted the seat and did his business, flushed and looked at it for a moment then laid it back down, he turned to see Sara in the doorway who said "From now on Jack, I want you to close the door, so you may have some privacy for yourself and especially for others"

"O Kay" said Jack and ads "Alright" and drops his shorts, turns on the water and steps in.

"Oh, you're such a bad man," said Sara, who was turned on by Jack like no other man she has ever known, he is tough and likes to play games. For that, she thought, I now know what I want to do with my life, that is, to take of this man who has set me free, as she, herself closes the door and took off her robe and stepped into the shower with him.

Jack and Sara finished a long hot shower, with Sara washing his back and front thoroughly, Jack put on his underwear and Sara with her robe, it was quiet, Jack made his way to his room changed and dressed back into his dirty clothes.

"Life was good," said Jack walking out into the kitchen, to see Greg was ready

"I guess Sara said she will to drive you, you don't have a car?" said Greg

"Nah, just a boat?"

"How's that?" said Greg

"I told you that I'm a fisherman and I have a boat that I live on and right now it's in dry docks getting the engines repaired." Greg interrupted him and said, "I don't remember you said you had a boat, let alone be a fisherman?"

"Yeah, maybe some time you and Heidi can come out on the boat"

"Heck yes, that would be fun, maybe some other time, I gotta go in for some rounds today, hey why don't you come and have lunch with me at the cafeteria, I must leave now or I will be late, I'll see you soon, help yourself".

Jack saw the cooked bacon, eggs and hash browns, made a plate for himself, then poured two cups of coffee and made his way to the table, and began to eat. Half way finished, he saw a dressed Sara wearing his new favorite outfit on her; a white tank top with green shorts.

"You like my outfit" says Sara

"Yes that makes you look so sexy, have a seat."

"I'm not really hungry, but I'll have some coffee"

"If she won't eat it I will," said Kate

"Go ahead, I don't care" said Jack looking at this girl in her Doctor whites.

"Do you like how I dress too" said Kate teasing him.

"At first I didn't know to much about you but as last evening wore on I think I like you better and I know Debbie really likes you, so if she likes you, you must not be half bad." said Kate with a smile.

Jack just continued to eat, while the sister's went at it.

"Leave Jack alone" said Sara

"Why don't you both come visit me at the hospital, what are your plans for today? "

"Well Sis I have to go to work and Jack well I don't know what he plans to do"

"So Jack why don't you come see me at the hospital and I will buy you lunch, you do eat something, don't you" said Kate.

"Well see I have to be at work at eleven o' clock, I guess I could call in sick" said Sara.

"Nah, the best thing you could do is just work, I'll come visit you Kate" said Jack

"You know Jack, that was a nice thing you did for our parents," said Kate to him quietly

"Just trying to be a nice guy and make a good impression" said Jack finishing his food.

"I just hope they liked it," said Jack clearing up his plate and taking hers.

"I'm off, I'll see you kids at the hospital; try not to get into too much trouble."

"Are you ready to go?" said Sara

"Yeah, can we stop by your apartment and then I need to go to the docks," said Jack

"Sure, but first I have a present for you, she pulls a small package from her pocket, she hands him a wrapped gift. Jack takes it and slowly begins to open it up, to reveal a box, he lifted it off to see a flat piece of ivory with symbols engraved in it in black, a leather cord was circled around it and says, "Thanks, what is it"

"It's a necklace silly, here let me put it on you, I had it made for you at the mall, you know when, after you overwhelmed me I felt the need to return the gift giving."
Sara pulled it out and tied it at his neck "It means you're a very bad man who is nice to women or something like that or so it says in Chinese" and ads "I hope you like it"

"Yes, thank you, I will cherish it forever," said Jack

"Wait, I have one more thing, sorry I didn't know you would get so excited about opening a gift, I would have wrapped this one as well" she handed him a new cell phone. "And I took the liberty of programming everyone in this family phone number and I also put in them in speed dial, like I'm number two, hit that and you reach my cell phone, number three is my work, number four is this house number." "Five is Kate, number six is Tim, seven is my Dad and eight is my Mom and even Debbie wanted to be in your phone so she is number nine. You can program up to one hundred names and numbers. To talk press the talk button, to end the call hit the end button."

"Thanks "said Jack, closing it up and putting it in his pocket, as he pulls out hers and hands it to her, when an older lady came in to say "Leave the dishes I'll take care of them".

The two walked out together and got into her car, Jack thought what is next, should I get a car or no maybe a truck, yeah a truck, whoa what about a driver's license and what is my last name.

"I don't know" what it is, thinks Jack to himself, to add;

"Can I make one up?"

Jack felt around in his pocket, he had been thinking about it awhile now. Sanders, I like that, Jack Sanders, or what about Money. "I know Jack Money, no that sounds weird, how about Cash, can I call myself Jack Cash."

Jack continued to be silent, during the drive, and started to think about this whole driving thing.

Sara parked the car, Jack awoke, together they walked up through the gate and up to her apartment, and she opened the door and said, "I'll have a key for you, made today."

Quickly Jack went to the closet and found his bag, looking inside to see all that cash, then the wallet's and the set's of keys and had an idea, how to convert all these items to cash and pay for the boat and put some away for later.

"I'm ready," said Sara

Jack looked down at his guns, then decided to close the closet door and said" Lets go, wait," realizing maybe he should think this out first, then decides to go into the bathroom, passing Sara in her room, he walks in and closes the door, shut and sets the bag on the counter and begins to count out twenty-five thousand dollars for Guy, for the purchase of his boat.

Then he counted out another ten thousand for hiring him to help and lastly counts out ten thousand for a truck. Wads up the money, folds it over, and puts it in his pockets separately. He closes up the bag to hear

"Jack are you alright, can I come in said Sara and ads "What I meant was close the door when your at other peoples houses and outside but here in our place you can leave the door open"
He opened the door to say "Sorry."

"You're acting like someone who has been isolated for years and now it is my job to retrain you," said Sara and ads "Is that true?"

"Your right I have been out to sea all my life."

"And now have decided to spend some time on land, can you help me," said Jack putting the bag back in the closet. And closes the door.

"Let's go I'm ready now, on to the pier, I need to pay for that boat," he said to himself.
Sara led the way and Jack followed, as the two walked, down below the courtyard was buzzing with ugly looking men in black suits and Jack though it would be nice to come back and mingle with this group and find out what is going on, he thinks to himself "They have money and how can I take it from them" Jack takes his spot in the passenger seat, while Sara drives, she says "When are you going to drive me around"

"When I get me my own truck"

"Your getting a truck, cool, when?"

"Later today, I thought I would ask Tim to help me out?"

"Really, my brother, he would love that, he usually gets out of school around three," said Sara, excited.

"Today is Saturday he is already off

"Oh, sorry, yeah I knew that", then she thought "Jack is making an effort to getting to know my family, and maybe I should find out a little about his, but first I may began to contemplate my own sexual preferences, like my sister Kate". "She seems to have a keen interest in him and when that happens I usually lose out, so maybe I should call it quits with Leslie and tell Jack I'm all his."
Sara says to Jack " I've been thinking about us, and what do you think about me stop seeing Leslie as a couple and spend all my time with you, cause I think I have some stronger feeling for you

than I have had with her and we have been together for over six month's."

"There is the turn off," said Jack and ads "It's your life and I don't care if Leslie is your partner, lover or whatever, I'm just happy to have a chance to be with you," said Jack "Park over by the booth.
Jack got out first to see his new friend, Guy who was putting up a sign that said Hiring Inside

"I'm looking for a job" said Jack the two shook hands and then turned to say "Guy this is my girl-friend Sara, the two shook hands as he said, "Wow, she is young, good for you."
Sara held onto Jack's arm as the three of them walked the dock.

"Looks like you had some trouble" said Guy
Jack looks at him funny, and then says, "What do you mean?"

"The captain's sleep hole has some damage on the latch," said Guy

"Anything else you notice?" said Jack

"No, and I went over it with a fine tooth comb, do you have the key?"

"Well about that I lost it, some where and had to go down and remotely start the engines"

"That's alright; I may have a spare at the house".

"I will make a replacement, other than that, I can fix the latch, now I can see how it broke." they both looked at Sara.

"What, it wasn't me" said Sara acting innocently

"So Guy, wait, I have this for you, this is the rest for your boat" and hands him the rest of the money. "And this is for helping me out, this is only to get you started."
Just as Jack was remembering the kids money he had in his other pocket, he pulls it out and hands that to Guy and says "This should get you started on paying for the repairs on the boat".
The two talked quietly to each other while Sara roamed around;

"And you know what I was thinking, how about you and I run this boat out for weekend fishing trips and charge oh I don't know, what do you think?"

"Yeah, we can try it, until we get your boat up and running" and ads "I know a few good fishing holes, like around sharks cove and endless valley, to name a few, oh and as far as your boat, there painting it this morning" said Guy..

"In addition they will be bringing a crane in and lifting both engines out to take them to their shop, so far they think it may just cost around twenty-five thousand," said Guy

"Alright, I'll leave it into your hands, oh let me get your phone number" said Jack

Guy tells Jack his phone number, which he programs into his phone and says "Do you know the number to the ship yard and how to get there I want to show my girl-friend" said Jack.

Guy tells him that number and gives him directions to the dry docks. The two shake hands and say "Good bye till later and I'll pay for any thing I damaged" said Jack

"Don't worry about that, I'll take care of that, and get the word out we will charter the boat for weekend tours" said Guy with a laugh.

"Sara come on, we have to get going, and I want to show you our boat"

Sara came down from the second level and on to the fish deck passing Guy and waving him "Good bye for now" and says to Jack;

"I really like that boat "

"Then you'll like my boat, because that's where we are going now"

He pulled her along by the arm, it was getting late, Jack looked at his watch and said "Don't you have to be at work at eleven."

"Yes but who cares, I may quit that job, and go back to Medical school, like my Dad wants me to and thanks to you."

"It was you that gave me some focus, besides I really don't need that job anyway, my Dad, pays for my apartment and all my bills and gives me an allowance".

"O Kay, but really you gave the store your commitment to work this weekend and I think you should keep your word, then if you want to quit, do so next week.," said Jack

Sara sat in silence and looked at him then said "You sound like my father, but I like it, from now on, I want you to tell me what to do and I will do it without challenging it" said Sara, gaining a new found respect for her boy-friend.

"Take the road onto the right," said Jack. They rolled past her parents house on the major highway south and said, "Now take the ship yard exit to the right" she did that, Jack looked at his watch and saw he had only thirty more minutes with her. On the right, the sign said Dry Docks.

"Go to the right" said Jack, Sara drove and did as she was told.

"Now park over to the very right" said Jack who saw his magnificent boat it was out of the water and Guy was right it was freshly painted Navy Blue in color and the back letters were painted White that read PARTHIAN STRANGER. The car stopped, first to get out was Jack who said, "Come on Sara" she followed a bit back and says to her "Here it is, what do you think"
Sara stood at the end of the boat looking at the stern, in amazement. The boat stood at least forty feet high to her, the twin propellers looking at her, were a brilliant copper and new in looks and then someone appeared from beside it and said, "How can I help you"

"I'm Jack and this is my girl-friend Sara, were here to see my boat"

"Oh, yeah, Guy gave me a call and said you might be stopping by, what do you think of the color"

"Looks great, can we go inside and see the rest," said Jack

"Absolutely, let me show you the way." said the security guy.
He was first to lead them to the left side next to another boat and said "Watch your step and hold onto the railing", then behind him was Sara and bringing up the rear was Jack. Sara got to the top platform and looked out onto the fish deck or main level; she walked aboard.
The security guy said, "Later we are installing a security booth at the end of the road, you must have picture ID to get in" as the guy looked at both of them. No one responded, and then said;

"Be careful, the backend is removed and there are people in the cabin area's cleaning it out"
Jack led Sara around the boat, showing her the engine hold.
They both looked down at the rear of the boat, then went and turned around and went into the first level on the right they looked in to

see a wet room and shower area, and directly on the left was the maintenance room and stairs going down to the engines.

"Nice layout " said Jack, as Sara found the galley, Jack walked in to see the table was gone off the left and her standing in the kitchen, they continued onward and found two more room on both sides and then Jack opened the far north door to reveal a large storage room and said;

"This will be our bedroom," said Jack

"Looks like a storage closet" said Sara

They turn and went back up a flight of stairs to the galley and then Jack led her up the stairs into the wheelhouse. Jack stood at the edge to show Sara the bed and how big that cabin was around it. She said, "Wow, this is nice, I could put up some curtains"

"Sure but why, this will be where we will be at, and if we fish we will have the crew down below"

"Oh, O Kay, I see"

Then Jack led Sara outside along the catwalk holding onto the railing, to the front or the Bow. Sara who said "I could lay out here and get a tan", she walked around to where the dual anchors sat, they both tip-toed over both of them, then went back around, back up to the wheel house, where the controls were at, the window was open and saw her man Jack and said "Hi stranger", then walked around and through the door.

"This is big and look" she pointed to a hatch and ads;

"What's that area?"

"It's the captain's bunk and stateroom," said Jack showing her the room.

"This is just like the other boat, lets make this our bedroom, and we can put a skylight in to see the stars, look how roomy it is" Jack thought about it to say "Yeah, we could, I guess use this room for our place", then began to think to himself "Maybe a trap door to the next level".

Jack continued the tour, back out, into the wheelhouse, then through a open door, past the large smoke stacks, on the other side was the solid windows of the big bed, they both walked out onto the platform. Jack said to himself "You could land a helicopter on here", for her to say,   "What are those racks for?"

"The portable boats and other equipment, like the ships generator, and other things"

"Interesting "said Sara, off to her right was a crane and further back by the middle was another crane

"Look honey you need to get going,"

"Or you'll be late for work," said Jack looking at his watch. Sara sighs and says "Alright are you sure you don't want me to stay here and christen the boat together" said a grabby Sara.

"Nah, I'll be fine I have to work out some details with the workers, I'll stop by and take you out for your dinner break."

"I'll count on that" said Sara, she gave him a kiss on the mouth as he hugged her tight, the smell of her was intoxicating, she broke away and said "Your right, I'll go to work and on Monday I'm going to re-enroll in Medical school, at University hospital, oh by the way, you told my dad you would stop by for a visit, don't let him down, or me."

"I won't, I'll go visit him". said Jack.

"Well you'll need a car, why don't you take me to work, and then you can have a way to get around"

"Nah, I won't need it, you take it, I'll be fine, now you get going and I will call you just before dinner"

He watched her leave and he sat down to rest, it was a moment until the phone in his pocket rang.

"Hi, this is Jack"

"This is Debbie, I hope I wasn't bothering you, I got your phone number from Sara, this morning and wanted to know what you are doing for lunch."

"Nothing right now, I'm actually sitting on my boat," said Jack   "Looking out on to the harbor and of the slips along the bank and of all the trees.

"Boat, you have a boat," said the astonished voice on the other line

"Yeah, I live on a boat," said Jack calmly

"Can I come down and visit you on your boat and take you out to lunch, I know a great seafood restaurant in the harbor" said Debbie

"Yeah, sure, do you know how to get here?"

"Yes I do, are you in the public harbor or the private one?"

"Right now I'm in the dry docks getting repairs done on my boat, you can't miss it its blue"

"What's the name of your boat?" said an excited Debbie

"It's called the PARTHIAN STRANGER"

"Wow, that's cool name, what does that mean?"

"I'm a miss-understood stranger," said Jack

"Not to me your not, I know where the dry docks are and I'll see you in fifteen minutes," said Debbie.

"Alright bye" said Jack who hit the end button. And put the phone back into his pocket.

Just then, a worker came in and saw Jack and said, "Hi my name is Dan and I'm the one in charge of remodeling your boat"

"So you're a friend of Guy's, him and I go way back".

"If you have any questions, here is my card and give me a call."

"I have one, can I land a helicopter, on the roof of that level"

"It would be tricky, but we could extent the platform out a ways, it would interfere with the crab launcher, and the crew's work below, but if you were to outfit the boat to long line and place the drum on the end, you could get rid of the launcher and then you would have enough space to land a small two seated., we did that to a similar boat and it worked fine"

"What do you think the cost would be?"

"oh, I'd say we could put the platform in around ten and install the long-line drum for ten and swap you out the launcher for the drum on a swap". "Then we could exchange some crap pots, how about ten thousand for all of it and Ill throw the paint in as well, you know because you're a friend of Guy's and your buying his boat, I'm doing this as a favor,"

"Thanks that's nice of you" said Jack and ads "If you extend the platform out in the back can it go out to the sides as well rather than just onto the deck?"

"Interesting, what do you have in mind?"

"Say I wanted to add a smaller boat, like a couple of shore boats"

"Yeah, we can do that and it will also give the boat, some strength and additional weight, not to mention you could put a couple of jet skies on the back, I got a pair of semi-new ones for sale if you want them."

"Where are they at?" and what do they look like," asked Jack

"Tomorrow I will bring them by and If you like I'll show you how to operate them, their made for salt water application, but also can be used in fresh water. "

"O Kay, sounds good, I guess, sees you tomorrow," said Jack

Jack considered how much he was spending and now how was he going to get money. He stood on the rear deck looking into the engine compartments when Dan said" Jack I think you have a guest"

Jack went to the stern, to look over to hear "Jack, its Debbie"

Jack sees her dressed in all white and looking hot. He said, "Up here, take the stairs up"

Debbie went up the stairs to the top platform, to see Dan passing her, to say "Hi Ma'am".

"When you said you lived on a boat, I didn't realize you meant a yacht, this thing is huge and must have cost-ed you a fortune."

"Yeah, it has, how are you, you look good" said Jack, who stood beside her but on the boat. She came to him.

She stepped onto the boat to give him a big hug, then a kiss on the cheek, he returned the gesture by kissing her on the lips, which she let linger and started to probe his tongue, with zeal and excitement. Jack broke away when the grinding started to begin.

"Ready" said Jack taking her by the hand, and leading her off the boat. The two stepped down to see her car; the shiny new silver two door was classy and looked extremely expensive.

"Do you want to drive me" said Debbie flirting with him.

"Nah, it's your car, you're the one who wanted, to take me out remember"

"Yeah, most guys can't stand to let a woman take control"

"I'm not most guy's I'm me, so drive me around" said Jack following her and ended up on the passenger side. Her car fired to life, her car had that new car smell, and he asked;

"How much was this?"

"Oh about four hundred a month" said Debbie

"How's that?" said Jack

"I went down to the dealership and picked this car out and with my credit I paid nothing and drive it around for just a monthly payment, it's called a lease."

"Really, what do I have to do?"

"I know this car salesman who will give you a great deal, how's your credit?" said Debbie.

"I don't know" pause to say, "What that is even" said Jack.

"Interesting" said Debbie who kept quite for the rest of the trip, Jack realized he might have made a mistake, not knowing what this credit is and how you get it, I know about credit cards, yes, let me use that credit card to pay for lunch he thought about the ones he has, not his but what the hell," he thought.. She stopped the car and was a bit different to him; he made the move and opened the door for her. But she said nothing to him and just walked in, followed by Jack, she was sure different to him now; they waited in the lobby of the classy fish place. Debbie stood away from Jack, a hostess led them to their seats, she sat first, and the hostess blocked Jack from helping Debbie out.

Jack took the seat across from her; she had her head buried in the menu. As Jack spoke up and said" Did I do something to upset you?"

"No not really, but you have that big boat and you don't know what credit is? That's weird"

"I'm sorry about that, this credit thing; I don't really know what you meant"

Jack waits for a response from her, she says, "So I have to pay then"

"No I will pay for lunch, I usually just pay cash for everything and don't owe any one any thing, is this credit important, cause I do have these"

Jack shows her ten or more credit cards fanned out like a deck of cards. "I use these only in emergencies"

A smile reformed on Debbie's mouth, realizing maybe its all in the translation and says "Where were we at, I'm sorry, I guess I was little miss-understanding when I mentioned credit and it looks like you have that, great, who's buying now"

Jack looked at her, saw a change, and did not like her now, she ordered the most expensive meal on the menu and even was excessive on all those diet cokes, Jack ordered a small plate of shrimp and a potato au gratin and drank milk. She left half her plate to say, "I'm full" as the waiter brought the bill to say, "Shall I wrap that up for you miss?" And handed the bill to Jack.

"Sorry, it's for the lady, it's her treat"

"Jack, you're the gentleman, you have to pay, I asked you out to lunch, so I may see you again, and after you pay, I will take care of your every need." she said with a wink

Jack handed the waiter one of the cards, and the waiter left.

"See Jack that wasn't so bad, from now on if we go out to lunch or dinner, you'll pay for everything or you won't get anything else" said Debbie

Jack ads "then who pays, when Kate and you go out"

"She does of course; I'm the lady, for you and her"

"Really, now I can see that"

The waiter returned and handed the bill to Jack "Here you go sir" said the waiter

Jack signed it and set a tip on it, then set it down and said "Ready to go" to Debbie, who he saw her in a new light.

Jack led Debbie out of the restaurant and realized more and more Sara was right for him, he also saw the waiter was watching him for no apparent reason.

"So Jack do you want to go back to your boat or do you want to go to my place"

"Neither, can you drive me to the hospital, I'm not feeling so great?" said Jack.

Jack was holding his stomach.

"Is there anything I can do?"

"Nah, just leave me alone "and ads "Just drive, hurry"

Jack, pretended to be doubled over, she sped up and in a instant, she was at the emergency entrance, whereas Jack got out ands stumbled inside, as Debbie said "Wait there, I'll go park the car", Jack slammed the door shut, watched the car move, stood up and walked normal over to a directory and saw Dr. Gregory Sanders name and that he was on the second floor, Jack took the stairs up to his floor, jumping one at a time, then up to two as he gained momentum.

Jack's stomach was feeling fine, but his mind was stuck in thirty years ago. He reached Greg's floor, walked up to the door, saw a waiting room full of people, and went up to the reception nurse and said,

"I'm here to see Doctor Sanders"

"Which one" said a nurse?

"Greg" said Jack

"Why don't you have a seat, can I ask what your name is?"

"Tell him it's Jack"

Jack took a seat and saw a magazine that read University Class catalog, picked it up and began to look at the pages, then he came across a special section called The Emergency Medical Services and its fellow components.

"Hi" said a voice

Jack looks up to see Kate, and smiles, she smiles back at him and says;

"Jack, I'll be your Doctor, Dad is busy and he asked me to help you." and ads "Come with me and I will take care of you."

Jack looked at her strangely and took the catalog with him, and followed Kate back and into a room.

"Have a seat on the table."

Jack sat and watched as Kate administered a blood pressure test, then took his heart pulse and finally took out her stethoscope and said;

" I want you to take deep breathes, please" she continued to check his breathing. She then finished, when she pulled out a needle, found an vein on his arm and stuck it in, then using different vials, she extracted four tubes and said, "That's it.

Jack looked at her to say, "What is it with your family, first your mom, remember yesterday she took blood and urine, now you". "I was actually here to see your father for lunch and that was it, are you finished".

"'yes I am, sorry, will you forgive me?"

"Sure, I like you; I think you're very nice"

"Really, what makes me so different from my sister?"

"Oh you know, you make me a little weak at the knees when I'm in the presents of a beautiful woman," said Jack looking up at her.

"You think I'm beautiful."

"Sure, you and your sister are exceptional"

"So Jack did you still want to go out to lunch?"

"Sure, what about Greg?"

"Greg, my father asked me to take good care of you and told me he was to busy to get away". "And great news for us is that Sara called us to say she is going back to school and all that thanks to you, what made her change her mind?"

"Maybe it was divine intervention" said Jack.

"I doubt I had any thing to do with it, it was her time to realize life is short and "
She cut him off and saw his necklace and said" Cool necklace when you got that?"

"It was a present from Sara"

"Is it alright if we go down to the cafeteria?"

"Sure, I'm right behind you"
Jack followed, instead of walking beside her, down to the basement, or the lower first floor and to an elaborate kitchen, there were at least five different stations and two salad bars and a meat station.

"This is how it works" Kate said to Jack "Go get plate of anything you want and put it on a platter, then go to the drink station and get a glass of something its unlimited drink, if you get a carton of something then that's it, so do you understand ?"
She turned to see that he wasn't behind her, she looked around to see Jack had cut the line and was over at the pizza station, then over to the salad bar and grabbed a couple of containers of milk, one whole and one chocolate.
Jack went to the checkout line, and a lady said "That will be eight dollars, please"
Jack hands her a twenty-dollar bill and says, "I'll pay for this and I'm buying Doctor Kate Sanders lunch, do you know her?"

"Yes, I'll give her the change, thank you sir"

Jack found a empty table with two chairs and took a seat, he first tried the pizza, it tasted different but it was good, next was the different thing he found at the salad bar, except it wasn't salad, like this red sour tasting something and then it looked like corn but it was tiny, and some yellow type of round beans all this was topped with a salad dressing called House. Overall it was good and he enjoyed it all, till he was full, he still had a little of everything on his plate, when Kate made it to the table.

"Thanks for lunch, I was going to take you out, here is your change"
Kate takes a seat across from him in this crowded place and says, "How do you like the food?"

"Its good I may eat here every day this is fun"

"Its palatable, but your right it is healthy and it is better than fast food"
Jack focused more on eating as he nibbled while she ate, rather than looking at Kate who was trying to get a read on him when in between bites says" So what do you plan on doing with my sister?"

"I don't know, it's really up to her."

"She seems infatuated with you, are you concerned?"

"Nah, I think she likes the danger aspect of my life."
Kate looked at him funny and said, "What does that mean?"

"You know my job as a commercial fisherman"

"Oh that job, I see now, and what do you plan on doing?"

"it all depends on Sara, if she wants us to continue as a couple or she may chose to continue her relationship with Leslie, I don't know, it will be all up to her." "I told her she should get back into Medical school and follow in the family business, looks like you guys are doing well for yourselves"

"Do you think your age might be a factor on how she decides?" asked Kate.

"like I said before, she is the one who chose me, if I had it my way I'd been gone long ago and away from here, but I think something happened when we first met that changed both of our lives forever, and it doesn't really matter that she has a girl friend or that she shares her with me, I'm just happy having the chance to be with her."

"That's nice of you to say, I wish I could find some one like you," she said in a desperate voice.

"That's your problem," said Jack, finishing off his plate and licking his lips

"What's my problem?"

"the searching part, if you live your life based on how others will interpret the way you feel then you're the one who has the problem, besides you have a great girl in Debbie, I like her, she is funny, bright and pretty, so why are you so down?"

"She cheats on me?"

"What does that mean?" questioned Jack, looking at her.

"Every chance she gets she is all over any one new, like you for example, she was saying Jack this and Jack that and how much she wanted you Jack, to make her feel special, and that's all I want is to feel special and to have someone to come and sweep me off my feet just like what you did with Sara, she loves you Jack and now I know why and honestly I'm a bit jealous, but really I do like you Jack and especially my parents, my mom is just stunned you came into Sara's life and turned her in a complete opposite direction, did you know she was leaving to go to Atlanta with Leslie to move out of this city and get away from all of us, no Jack it was all about you and don't tell her I said this but I imagine if your happy then she will make you the happiest man on this earth and marry you." she paused to say;

"You know she wants lots of kids and a great big family, Leslie, I feel was a rebound from a guy who broke her heart when he joined the military and left her behind and didn't want anything to do with her, Jack she has been hurt in the past but I feel she is in a safe place now".

Kate paused to take a breath and waited for Jack to respond.

Then he said, "So do you think I should propose to her and tell her that I want to take her name and to have a large family?"

"Yes Jack, she will say yes, yes do that, you want our name?"

"Sure why not"

"Well that is quite special, usually it's the woman who changes her name to suit the man, but you will actually change your last name to hers, which is amazing"

Jack looked at her in disbelief and then thought maybe I should get away from this weird girl"

His phone rang quite noisily, he answered it "Hello, this is Jack how can I help you?"

"Really I wasn't aware of that, but if it must be fixed than go ahead, lets keep it at ten thousand any more give me a call, thanks" said Jack closing up the phone

"Who was that?" asked Kate, Jack looked at her and was starting to get annoyed with her, when he said "I got to go and check out a problem with the boat, but it was nice having lunch with you" said Jack and gets up, to take his platter to the end, thinking, "Yes this is my new place to visit and ads "What a weird girl and she thinks Debbie is the one who is messed up, not like this whack job, trying to steal her sister's man, shame on her.

Jack walks out of the hospital, at the doctor's entrance, to see a familiar face that was on a smoke break, sitting outside on a bench, this time Jack decides to go on the offense and sees her before she sees him and says ;

"Hey Debbie thanks for the lift, what are you doing now?"

She looks up at him taking along drag on her cigarette, exhaled;

"Oh, just burning time before I must see some patients, what about you how does your stomach feel?"

"Oh, better now that I ate in the cafeteria," said Jack taking a seat next to her.

"You ate that stuff in there, gross"

"If you have time I'd love to see your office," said Jack

"really" she finished half of her cigarette and stamped out the rest and stood up and looked at Jack and said," Come let me show you the way".

She led the way back in as the two walked together, Jack liked this girl, she was sexy and had a major attitude, not to mention a killer body that he would like to get back inside of.

The walk was short; she opened an unmarked door and led Jack in. She closed it and locked it down; she turns to him and says,

"How much more do you want to see" a playful Debbie said

"Take it off, slowly" said Jack, Jack walked past her to take a seat on a two seat sofa; she went past him and pulled the blinds shut.

Debbie turned, and then on the front door of her office, she pulled those blinds shut as well.

"I'm waiting," said Jack

"Hold you horses, if I had to wait this long, then so do you. Said Debbie who stood in front of him, slowly she unbuttoned her coat and then she let it fall, next she began to unbutton her blouse, which she let fall exposing a black pushup bra. She then unzipped her skirt and stepped out of it, she was getting ready to pop her bra when Jack said   "Hold it, can you turn to the right and now bend over, she did as she was told, Jack was liking this and it began to turn him on to see her do anything he commanded of her, she moved around like a cat and then said "Come Jack are we going to."

She was interrupted by a knock on her door, reality came crashing back to her, and she scrambled to get redressed, missing a button here and there, while Jack was laughing on the couch.

"Ssh, what's so funny, ha ha" she said and put her coat back on and buttoned it up then unlocked the door and opened it up to see a dynamic young Korean girl with short hair and a small chest and pretty brown eyes, step in and see Jack to say "Sorry to bother you Doctor Connors, but your two afternoon patients cancelled and you have one at five, do you want me to call them up and reschedule for another day so". Looking at Jack

She was cut off by Debbie who said   "I'll keep that appointment thank you, Denise, page me if you need to talk to me again"

"But I did already" said Denise who was staring at Jack inventively.

"That will be enough, go get out please, I'm with a client" Debbie closed the door, locked it, and said, "So Jack are you going to bend me over that sofa or would you rather I just do posing all day long?"

"I'm thinking I like to see you without any clothing on and then put your lab coat back on" said Jack settling in for the upcoming show, as she did as she was instructed, quickly taking off her clothes and then slowly she popped off her bra, she turned to show him and then in one motion she pulled off her semi-wet panties and said;

"Do you want them"

"Yeah, sure" said Jack she then tossed them to him to smell and sample.

Jack was admiring, just looking at her move around in the nude. Her moves were exceptional, especially in those stockings and high heels she wore, she bent over several times when another knock on the door, this time it was a familiar voice saying "Debbie this is Kate are you in there, I just talked with your assistant Denise and she told me that you have a tall dark, and handsome gentleman"

"You said you were alone, You have no one scheduled, and who is he?" "Could you please open up your office door, I hope this isn't true."

Jack stood and shook his head and said, "This girl is whack, why can't she leave me alone for half a second", Jack watched as Debbie just put on her lab coat and placed her clothes under her desk, as Jack went to unlocked the door and opened it up.

She saw him, then Jack said "Come on Kate, I've been trying to talk with Debbie to tell her how you really feel, if you must talk with her now it will only ruin what I have already stated, why don't you give us say thirty minutes and I guarantee she will be receptive to what ever you were thinking about doing."

"O Kay" said Kate, Jack watched her walk away; Jack put on a smile and pulled the door shut and relocked it.

"So lets see now, oh yes why don't you come over and sit down on the sofa" said Jack She did as she was told, " now spread your legs " said Jack, who knelt down to view, he closed his eyes and went in face first, the aroma was intoxicating as his fingers and tongue did all the work, she pulled off a quick orgasm, he then had her turn around and continued to do what was already working and brought her to another orgasm, this time she flooded his face, Jack, fell back with astonishment and Debbie stopped as embarrassment surrounded her face and said

"Oh my god, I've never done that before, it was where you licked that triggered that response, we must do this again and again, every day, can you teach Kate how to do that that was incredible, do you want me to finish you up" she said.

"Nah, your going to need some time to clean this up, I got to go visit Tim and get over and pick up Sara, how about you give me a call tomorrow and we will pick up where we left off and if you know any other girls who would like to participate let them know I'm available." said Jack, who left Debbie, unlocked the door and walked out and closed the door, thinking like he accomplished something today.

CH 6

Samantha the Great

J ack walked out to the street, in front of the Hospital and noticed a Bus stop; several people were waiting for the bus and off to the left was a girl in a wheelchair. She was dressed in a short pink dress, beautiful flowing black hair and amazing arms, her low plunging neckline showed amazing assets needing immediate attention. Jack walked over to her and stood right by her, looking at her red lips, red fingernails and bare legs, he even saw she had painted her toenails red, she looked and smelled hot, she spoke first "What are you staring at?"

Jack looked down at her and said, "I was just wondering when the last time you had an earth shuddering orgasm was?"

There was a long pause from her and played coy and said, "When my boy-friend gave me one? " And ads "Why do you ask?"

"Oh no reason, except I have this talent to make a woman release herself in oblivion and beyond" said Jack still standing a staring at her.

"What makes you think I'm interested at all?"

"Your eyes, the moment our eyes met I knew you were interested," said Jack seeing the bus coming.

"I might, but I live with my mother, how you suppose that will help me"

"Oh, there are many ways, like say the women's bathroom inside the hospital"

"Nah, that too dirty"

"Or, say a motel," said Jack playing with her, she was playing along, and teasing him back.

"How about my place, except I would have to carry you up three flights of stairs and then down two"

"And what and where is that?" she said interested as the bus came to a stop, Jack watched as a platform came out she rolled onto it and took her up near the rear, Jack got on the front and paid two dollars and said " How far to the mall", " another stop and another bus down south. Jack took a seat near the front, forgetting about the rival, the bus was hesitant to move when the bus driver said," Miss, will you stay stationary please."

Jack turned in his seat, to see her coming up to him. She, stopped and blocked the isle way, near the driver, who turned and said "You can't stay there, your blocking the isle way"

"I'll go back only if you tell my boy-friend, he has to move back there with me"

"You heard her, go back there will you, so we can get going, I'm late as it is already"

Jack stood and said, "I'm right behind you honey."

Jack followed her back, to the designated area for her as Jack said,   "Talk about segregation."

Jack takes a seat beside her.

She speaks first and says, "You're the first guy, who has tried to hit on me since my accident two years ago"

"That's a shame, what happened to you"

"The worse part of it all, was I had no control over the situation"

"Please tell me what happen," said Jack interested in spreading those useless legs.

"It all happened the night of our graduation, my girlfriend and I were drinking and she drove and another drunk driver hit us and killed her and put me into this wheelchair."

"Wow, your so pretty and now what do you do" said Jack

"I go see Doctor Sanders Monday, Wednesday's and Friday's and Saturday mornings for physical therapy and the rest of the time I live at home with my mom, I get no visitors and my last boy-friend left me for a girl who can walk and now I meet you, a older guy, who before the accident I would have never talked to and here we are you talking about wanting to please me and I don't know if my equipment even works."

"When you were in the accident did they take anything out?"

"No, they said I broke my pelvis and fractured my spine, but you know I have been getting some feeling down there, I guess I could go with you for awhile is your place close by?"

"I think it's the next stop"

Jack stood up and pulled on the cord as he watched others before him do and at the next stop, the bus came to a halt at the gate to the private pier, which stood a guard, who has a golf cart nearby. Jack waits for the young lady to get off the bus and Jack falls behind her and begins to push her, she lets him, as he pushes her up to the guard.

"How can I help you Mister?" said the gate guard

"I'd like to get in and go to my boat?" said Jack, looking at the guard.

"Can you tell me what the name of your boat is sir."

"I am in the dry docks, my name is Jack, and the boat's name is the PARTHIAN STRANGER.

"Oh you're the new guy, I'm sorry sir to hold you up , can I give you and the misses a ride over on my cart" said the guard showing Jack a lot of respect, another guard appeared and said " Hi"

Neither Jack nor the girl said anything, as a white golf cart came up with the security guard driving it. And says, "Mister you can take our cart if you would like, we can send someone after it later, if you like to."

"No, that's alright why you drive us." "Here, let me pick you up," said Jack moving in and lifting her up.

She placed her arm around his neck and Jack placed her in the front seat of the covered cart and said, "I'll hold onto your wheelchair."

Jack sat down on the back, lifted the wheelchair with ease, and laid it on its side. The cart took off and zipped along a walking path. The cart traveled around the outside of the docks to where Jack's boat sat, standing all mighty and powerful, the cart came to a stop, Jack jumped off and set the wheelchair down.

"Thank you sir for the ride" said the girl.

"Your welcome Miss." and ads "I'll probably be seeing more of you what's your name?"

"My name is Samantha Smith and what is yours "

"My name is Harvey". The two shook their hands.

Jack heard her name, began to use it, and said "ready Samantha, sorry Harvey we got to go."

Jack picks up her, pulls her in close, she puts her arm around his neck, and says, "This is your boat, and it is sure big,"

"Yeah, it's alright, ready to go aboard"

Jack didn't wait for an answer, and took a stair at a time, he paused half way when she said "you sure working hard to get into my panties, but I can assure you it will be well worth it"

He continued to struggle but made it all the way on to the deck and sets her down on a large box. Then Jack says, "I'm going back down to get your wheel chair"

"I'll be waiting here for you"

Jack made it back down with ease, hoisted the wheel chair on his right shoulder, and took the stairs with ease. He saw her still sitting there he could have sworn the saw her move her legs, but did not say a thing. He pushed the chair towards her and says, "Do you want me to put you in there"

"Not really, I'd like for you to make me feel good and take me to your bed"

Jack nodded his head and came over and picked her up and carried her in and up the stairs of the ship to the wheelhouse, turned and up the small steps of the bunk and laid her down on his bed a stained sheet and a pillow. He looked down at her.

"Do you want to undress me?" she offered.

Jack looked at her and was a bit hesitant.

"What's wrong are you having second thought, I'm here in your bed for the taking you can do anything and everything you want to do to me"

That was enough of an invitation, Jack knelt down an slowly pulled up her dress, to see a pair of red panties, and he picked up each leg separately to spread her legs a little wider.

"Aw that hurts, I don't think I've had my legs that far apart before,"

Jack was hesitant, and slipped his fingers on the lip of her panties and pulled them down quickly, and off her body, he looked down to see a very hairy forest. Next he took the pillow and placed it under her pelvis and then each leg he bent upward and let it rest on the wall together and noticed something by her side, then goes back down and sees a worker, and then goes out to talk with them and then comes back in and sees the cushion from the galley and grabs two of the vinyl bolsters and back up to the wheelhouse, and up to the bunk, he then placed a bolster on each side against the wall, then re-spread's her legs wide, then decided to go in and smell that forest, with his tongue and mouth and fingers, he worked on it, after the normal time, nothing.

She just laid there and said, "I don't feel a thing, but go ahead and when you give it to me, can you wear a condom, please"

"I don't have one," said Jack in a statement.

"you're the one who came on to me and you don't carry a condom, you know I might actually have one in my purse, here can you look, she hands him her purse that was around her neck, Jack opened the purse and a quick search found a small package, it dropped on her stomach, Jack reached down to see a tube and said "what is that "

"It's my colostomy bag, for my urine, so that I don't have accidents any more"

Jack was a bit confused, he did not know if he wanted to continue or just give up, then got an idea.

"I'll be back in a minute," said Jack leaving her, while she wiggled out of he dress and then undid her bra to lie naked on the bed, she lifted her arms above her head and waited.

Jack was in the galley, looking through every drawer and then found what he was looking for a jar of olive oil. He then headed back and up to the bed to see she was laid out nude, from her pretty face down to her pelvis she was near perfect, in beauty.

"Where have you been, I've been waiting, are you going to put this on and take care of me or what"

"Hold on, I got things under control now "

125

Jack poured a little on his hands and began to lube her up, creating some friction, by using his hands and fingers, occasionally touching her breasts, it was weird that she was just lying there it was a bit of a turn on. Thinks Jack.

Jack slipped out of his tank top shirt and pants and then stripped down to nothing to show her how hard he was.

"Come here, I want to feel it" said Samantha.

Jack crawled over her, and knelt down by her head, and she went to work on him and he could feel how excited she really was , he felt up her breasts, while she worked on him, using her hands skillfully, to a point of Jack was ready to release and said "Hold on I'm about to come".

"That's alright, I want to feel it so let it go, and Jack shuddered and then erupted in her mouth, and she took all of it and much more as she kept on going to re-arouse him.

She stopped and said" Your not an old man, your like a young buck, now go down there and get yourself off inside of me.

Jack looked down to see the covering on his manhood, she slid it on.

He went back around, to get off the bed, he positioned himself and mounted her and slowly, stuck it in. It was super tight and he went slowly and in and out when she said "Oh my god, I feel that, do you feel that, oh your so big and large, my god, I feel that, Jack looked down to see blood and says;

"I think something is wrong, there is blood down here"

"No, no you have just popped my cherry; I'm not a virgin, anymore".

She said with a smile and ads "Oh I feel that, and it feels so good, don't stop, oh my god, please don't stop. Jack continued to drill her as wave after wave overcame her, each time soaking him with her pent up fluids and saturating and the bed began to smell, finally Jack said "I'm ready to come again."

"Go ahead and let me have it" said Samantha

Jack let loose and exploded, and then collapsed on her, her body was sweaty and so was his she put her arms around him and finally the two kissed, and kissed, and kept going to well into the later afternoon hours as Jack awakes to hear his phone go off.

He breaks their embrace and gets up to smell and see his body is covered in blood across his stomach as well as hers, she looked more worse than him. Jack gets to his phone and answers it by saying; "Hello" and ads" What's going on, really I'll right, hold on, I will be there to pick you up around six p.m. bye" said Jack, to Samantha to say "I got to go. "

"Not before you clean me up, you had your fun with me, now you must wash me and re-dress me, and then I'll let you go," said Samantha.

"Alright, hold on," said Jack, who went down to the galley and retrieved a bucket and found a wash cloth and a jug of water, which he found a bowl and put the bowl of water in the microwave and heated the water, he then combined the hot water with the cold water and it became warm and went up. He first pulled out both bolsters and set them aside and began to give her a bath, carefully cleaning off her front side, then rolled her on her side and handed her colostomy bag and worked on her side and back up to her neck, then he lifted her up and into a sitting position resting near the wall.

"You don't have to worry about my panties"
Jack watched her put on her bra and lifted her dress above her head.
Jack watched how well she was doing this.
Samantha, pulled it down, to cover her body, meanwhile Jack washed his front side, then turned and she said, "I'll wash you off"
He knelt down so she could reach his neck, then he stood up and she did his butt and lower legs.
Jack dressed quickly and saw the time was coming close and said,

"Are you ready?"
"Yeah, but looks like I ruined your bed."
"It sure looks like someone died there." and ads "I hope that cleaned you out of all that gunk inside of you", said Jack.

"Yes, I think you saved my life, I was feeling a build up that I just had to relieve and you did it, and I have no one to help me like you did, thanks Jack and By the way do you even know my name?"

"Yeah, its Samantha"

"No its not, you can call me Sam, only my boy-friend calls me Sam everyone else calls me Samantha, you got that Jack" said Sam.

"Whatever you say Sam, now I got to go, as he picked her up and carried her down the stairs and onto the dark deck and down the lighted stairs to the stern of the boat.

"You don't have a car, are you going to call a cab?"

Jack looked at her weirdly and then she said;

"I have a cab, who knows me, do you want me to call. Jack went back up to get her wheel chair and came back down to see Sam on her cell phone.

"I talked to my cabbie friend and he told me he could be here in five minutes.

That gave Jack time to go back up and dump the water and pull that mattress out and he tossed it into a large roll off dumpster, sheet and all, then he hears a car with bright lights on.

Jack made his way down to the stern of the boat and on the ground and went to Sam and helped her into the cab as the cabbie put the wheel chair in the trunk as he folded it down much to Jack's surprise, then slid Jack slid in the seat next to Sam.

"Where to Sam "said the cabbie.

"On to the mall first, and I will pay for her trip home," said Jack.

She snuggled in close to Jack and said, "That was fun can I see you soon?"

"Sure what are you doing tomorrow?"

"Just spending time with my mom, at home doing nothing"

"Before the accident, what were you planning on doing?"

"Well after high school, I want to go into business management, and become a office manager; I do well on the phones and love to market a business.

"Really "said Jack, beginning to think and then said,

"You know I have a friend and I are starting a charter business and really need a person to help us"

"Do you think you might be interested in helping me out?"

"Maybe, why don't you let me see your phone?"

Jack hands her his phone. Quickly she programmed her phone number in and then said" I put my cell phone in, so your girl-friend won't know who this number is and I added my phone number at my house, so call me tomorrow and come by and visit my mom and me and we will talk about this job and how much you will pay me and how much I will do for you" she said with a wink.

The taxicab came to a stop at the mall.

"How much will I owe you?" said Jack giving Sam a kiss to say;   "Goodbye for now"

"Twenty will do it, plus a little tip "she says, "Thanks"

Jack hands the driver a twenty and turned to see Sara coming to him. As the taxi speeds off.

"Oh my Jack, we need to go to a bail bonds man and get my Brother out of jail, thanks for going with me, I need to go downtown, that part of town scares me, come on get in"

Jack sat down next to her as she drove wildly and with determination, into a dark part of town, by the city jail.

A bright neon flashing light that said BAIL BONDS.

Sara parked the car and Jack led Sara by holding her hand to the door. Jack was getting a good feel for this as he led her up the stairs and opens the door to see a great big guy sitting behind a desk in the middle of the room.

"Have a seat and I'll be with you in a moment," said the guy

Jack stood and began to look at a bulletin board and on it was a sheet of over two hundred plus names and said "What's this list for?" said Jack.

"Sir, I'll be with you in a moment"

He finished up with a young lady and got up as Jack turned to see this hulking figure with a gun, hanging down.

"What do you do, to wear a gun?" asked Jack

"I'm a bounty hunter," said the guy

"What's that mean?"

The guy just looked at him and said" I'm a Federal Bounty Hunter and can go anywhere I want to catch and apprehend criminals."

"I like that job, is it hard to join," said Jack looking at him.

"No, not really, what I usually do is take a guy with me the first time and try to get one and sees how well they do."

"Sounds interesting, can you sign me up?"

"Really you want to do it, you look like a guy about my age, I have to warn you there will be some violence and you may have to carry a gun".

"I have two, and the upside is," said Jack

"For a evening of work or less you'll make a grand."

"That sounds great, when can I start." asked Jack.

"How about tomorrow night, come as if your going to beat up someone like how your dressed now, dirty, as he got a good whiff of Jack to say "You stink, I like that, is that fish or something like that, don't worry about carrying a gun I'll take care of that, just be ready to run and do some fighting, so was that the main purpose of your visit?"

"Were here to bail out my brother, Timothy Sanders," said the very pretty Sara.

He turned his attention on her, and then looked at Jack to carefully place his words.

"Oh yes, the kid who was charged with grand theft auto and possession of a controlled narcotic, the bail is set for ten thousand dollars, so I need to see a proof of I D and a social security card and cash or money order for the amount of say thirteen percent".

"But, if your boyfriend joins us, well its usually fifteen and he joins us then I'll cut the rate, so thirteen hundred for the kid"

Jack pulled out a wad and counted out the cash. And the guy swoops it up and gives them a release form to sign, which Sara did and showed him her two forms of I D."

"Stay right here, I need to make a call and he will be released in a hour".

The guy gets on the telephone and makes the call, and then he says;

"Come with me" he led them outside, to which he locks the door and says "Over here, I will go in and get him, do you want to come?"

"Nah, that's alright" seeing the Jail was enough to possibly reconsider this line of work.

And ads "I'll stay here and wait for you"

"Whatcha a wash" said Red, "Come on let me show you what a true bounty hunter does"

Jack followed Red as he made his way to the entrance. Red knocks on the door with his fist, yells "Open up its Red and one" Red turns, and says, "Pull out your I D to show the sheriff's deputy. Jack just looks at Red in disbelief belief and replies, "I don't have it on me."

"Then you can't go in, so stay outside and wait for me, while I get Tim released."

Jack stood by the curb only to see Sara come up to him and embrace and then kiss him on the cheek and said, "How am I suppose to keep this a secret"

"You'll just have to wait and see how all this plays out," said Jack, still holding her and feeling the embrace, and then lets her go. They both turn to hear Red's voice.

"Jack" said Tim

The two-shook hands as Sara hug her brother as he spoke;

"It is all a big misunderstanding," said Tim

"Lets go get in the car," said Jack leading the two to Sara's car as Jack says, "I'll see you tomorrow and I'll be ready to go"

"Great if you do, just wear something more in the work type of clothes like jeans, steel toed boots a dark shirt and be ready to work, say around eight p.m"

"Yeah that's fine," said Jack, while getting in the passenger seat, while Tim takes a seat in the back. Sara drove the car; the music was low as Jack decided to turn it up, to listen to a certain song. Tim spoke up over the music "Sis, can I spend the night with you guys."

Sara looks over at Jack, who is still engrossed in the song, with his eyes closed, mouthing the pretend words.

Sara immediately turns the radio down to get Jack's attention. Jack looks up to see Sara and says, "I don't care, does he spend the night with you often"

"Some times, if he stays late at school, I pick him up and it's almost eleven o'clock"

"Then let the kid stay with us, but you better call your mom and let her know what is going on" said Jack.

"Your right Jack, and I'd been thinking about you lately "
Jack nodded his head, in acknowledgement to her.
The rest of the ride was quiet. Sara parked the car. everyone got out
as Sara handed Jack her keys and dialed up her mom, she trailed
the two of them as Jack opened the doors up to her apartment once
on the railing Jack heard several loud voices down in the courtyard,
where Jack paused to listen to them talk and say "What do you mean
just disappeared, I want you to overturn every stone and scour this
city, talk to your contacts and lets find this killer, hell this guy might
be living here in this hotel." "I want revenge for my son's death."
Jack opened up the door and held it open for Sara who just finished
her conversation with her mom. Sara kissed Jack on her way by
him on the cheek.
Jack smiled as Sara said, "There will be more of that later"
        "I'm hungry "said Tim.
Jack closed the door and locked it down.
        "Jack do you want me to fix you something to eat" said
Sara
        "Sure, I'm going to take a shower, do have those clothes,
which you picked out for me from your store?"
        "Oh I forgot, I'll send Tim down to the car and get them for
you"
        "Tim is already in the bathroom." So said Jack to say,
        "I think he is busy; I'll go do it", toss me your keys."
Jack went out, closed the door, to slowly hear two men talking, to the
amount of "One hundred thousand and a million more if he is alive"
said the other guy.
Jack smiled, and went to her car, to the trunk, retrieved the packages,
he returned up the stairs.
This time, he walked slowly, trying to hear them, when all of a sudden
he heard "Hey you on the third level balcony, you eye me again, I'll
come up there and kill you myself."
Jack entered the apartment, and closed the door, Sara was in the
kitchen, on the phone with her mom, while Tim was lounging on
the sofa watching T V, Jack went to the bedroom, placed the bags
down, looked through the bags for underwear, pants and tank top,
and then went into the bathroom, closed the door, and locked it,

then shredding his shirt and pants and hopped into the shower, and began to wash off the remaining dried blood, he washed up.

Jack stepped out of the shower, to hear a knock on the door; Jack opened the door to see Sara holding a plate with a sandwich in hand, chips and a pickle. And said, "Tim's lying on the sofa and he wanted to tell you thanks for what you did." said Sara "and I'm here to thank you personally." she set the plate down and closed the door, then began to kiss his neck as Jack took a bite of the sandwich. She began to undress with her free hands, as Jack was ready; quickly he turned her around and mounted her from behind. He said;

"You know you brother still thinks you're a virgin" as he worked her from behind until she was ready to let go and Jack pulled out and Sara finished him off, she licked her lips dry and with a smile said, "What he doesn't know won't hurt him, lets just keep this our secret and I hope that was a good start to show my appreciation"

"Yes it was" said Jack finishing drying off and put on a new pair of underwear, but liked the T-shirt, he wore he thought about it.

"No, no, no you don't" said Sara and ads "You might live on a boat, Mister, but you need to put those in the dirty clothes hamper and put on a new pair. Jack watched as Sara picked up his dirty clothes and deposits them. She unlocked the door, and pulled him into her bedroom, where stacks of new clothes were all laid out for him. Jack looked through the pile and saw a new pair of pants and a green tank top t-shirt.

"Is that going to be your choices, now look over here I've cleaned out this side of the drawers for your clothes and I will place them in here neatly and the rest of your clothes is hanging up in the closet." Jack watched as Sara put his clothes away and showed him the closet and she even pulled the covers down on the left side of the bed and said "This is your side of the bed, is there anything I can get for you?"

"When's Leslie coming over?" said Jack as he prepared and slid into the bed.

He propped up his two fluffy pillows and laid his head back to look at her.

"She's not, not with my brother here" said Sara leaving the room.

Jack saw a remote by his nightstand and hit the power button, which turned on the television, which was large, and flat and mounted to the wall, he used the arrow keys to scroll though a set of different channels to stop on a sexy movie it appeared and began to watch it.

Sara came in with a glass of ice water and a plate. She sets the plate and glass of water by him on his nightstand and says,

"I thought you might want to finish the sandwich"

"You didn't answer me," said Jack

"Its over" said Sara getting up on the bed as she pulled off her white robe she was wearing and laid up on Jack's side and placed her head on Jack's chest.

"That's a shame, just when I was getting use to her being around."

"Don't worry there will be others and besides Leslie doesn't even like you, so I told her its over between us because Jack, you of course are my boyfriend and lover and the man I want to spend the rest of my life with, how does that sound" as she hugged him with her hand and kissed his chest.

"Sounds great to me, you know I really like this idea of working as a bounty hunter and I really like the idea of you going back to medical school and becoming a doctor and my wife"

"You want me to be your wife," she said with enthusiasm and excitement as she moved up to give him a kiss.

"Yep" said Jack and ads, "I like your whole family and most of all I like you."

They kissed and she said, "You may like me Jack, but I love you and yes I will marry you"

"I guess I love you too."

The two kissed and played around Sara turned off the television as Jack was sound asleep, she gave him a kiss on the lips and pulled the covers over him and looked over him, to watch him sleep soundly she said to herself "Jack I'm you guardian Angel and will do anything and everything you want of me, for I have never loved anyone more than I will love you, good night my love and I will be with you forever.

The next morning awoke both Sara and Jack with Tim knocking on their door.

First up was Sara who put on her robe and went to the door and opened it and said "Calm down what's wrong"

"I got to go to baseball practice can you drive me home."

"Drive the kid home," said Jack who was sitting on the bed naked

"Go sit down I will get dressed and run you home" said Sara she closed the door and took off her robe, Jack looked up to watch her get dressed, first putting on her bra then a set of matching panties and blouse, she did that to get Jack's approval.

She held up a white tank top, Jack smiled and shook his head Yes motion; he showed his expression with a smile. Which she put on and then slipped into a pair of tight fitting jeans, a pair of socks and some flat shoes, she bent down to kiss Jack and he pulled her down on the bed and began to play with her breasts by placing his hands under her tank top and into her bra she let him do it and began to enjoy it when she heard her brother's voice again and said "I'll be there in a moment and we can pick back up." she said. Sara got up to look at her man, he being fully erect and looking at her with his saucer eyes and that big wide smile. She was melting in his presence and knew she needed to leave and right now. She stood up and adjusted herself and then bent down and gave him another kiss and left.

Jack lied on the bed for a while then got up and looked through his clothes, he finished off the rest of the sandwich from last night and thought about the food at the hospital, he dressed in a green tank top and jeans and put on a pair of shoes, he went out into the living room to retrieve the bag and saw all the keys and other wallets he began to count the money when he heard a knock at the door.

Jack quickly puts the cash away back into the bag and into the closet, he goes to the window and looks out from behind the curtain to see it was Leslie, so Jack slowly unlocks the door and opens it up while still standing behind it, Leslie steps in and says "Sara it's me Les"

Jack slams the door shut and smiles at her she looks at him and says; "Oh hi Jack"

"Sara's gone, what do you want?" said Jack staring at her flimsy top and short pants

"I just came by to apologize to her about last night"

"So I heard, so you don't like me, why's that?"

"First off it's not like that at all, I do like you but you just met her". "Her and I have been dating for over six month's and all I said to her was, I think your not in it for the long run and your just like every other guy out there only wanting one thing from her and that's it"

"Which is what?" said Jack

"You know putting you dick inside of her as much as you can and when some other girl comes along you'll leave her for a new one and I told her, I didn't want to be a part of that triangle how do you feel about that?"

"I think its sad, you hot and the two of you are in love so why break it off, enjoy the moment and enjoy each other." said Jack passing her and went back into the bedroom.

"Is there anything I can do for you, to help me convince Sara to take me back?"

"Sure, undress, let me see what you have" Jack takes a seat on the edge of the bed and looks up at her. She was hesitant to move and said, "Its not like you haven't seen this before" said Leslie.
Leslie begin to strip.

"Hold on, I want you to go slowly" said Jack watching with his eyes.

"O Kay, let me put on some music, Jack watched as she turned on a box and out came some music, Leslie began to dance to the music and slowly and in motion pulled off her top and then slipped out of her shorts, then popped her bra and threw it at him, to show those lovely big breasts, flopping around, she turned and pulled down her panties, turned and threw them at him. And said "Now what, I'm naked and you not, with a giggle she jumped on the bed and helped Jack out of his pants and she sat down on him, inserting him into her and saying "That feels really good, come on Jack give it to me I want your full and entire load, Jack was getting a handle on this control issue and really liked the variety of different positions, which he practiced with Leslie he had her every which way and in the end he finished between her breasts and dropping his load on her. He got up still leaving her panting for more.

"Jack come back for more," said an eager Leslie
Jack heard his phone, went to pick it up from the laundry basket, and answered it

"Hello, yes this is Jack, yeah, that's fine, I'll be down there later today I'll call you when I get there, call Guy and let him know, thanks, bye" said Jack closing the phone up.
He went back into the bedroom and began to get dressed.

"Get up and get dressed, Sara should be back anytime soon, why don't you give me your phone number, Jack hands her the phone, she quickly programs her number in his phone and says "If you plan on keeping me a secret from her, I'm fine with that". "I just love when you give me the personal attention I really need, now I know why Sara wants you over me and I'm fine with that."

"Its not like that at all, she will know, I will tell her your back in the game"
Jack watched her get dressed; she saw him and said, "That really turns you on doesn't it"

"Sure so far, it's a highlight" said Jack

"The next time you convince Sara to have me over, I will have a surprise for you," she said as she walked past him and opened the door and walked out.
Jack went back to his bag, picked up a wallet, saw the I. D card, and said to himself "I'll use this one and pulled out some cash and stuffed it into the new wallet. He looked over the stacks of cash and really liked it. He put the bag away and thought of the boat and the near completion of the deck and then he thought of Samantha, and said "I'll call her and was about to dial when the door opened and he saw Sara and quickly put the phone away.
Jack saw she was carrying some groceries and he went and helped her with them.

"Thanks Jack" said Sara
He placed them on the counter as Sara begins to unpack them. Jack watches her pull out food and then a bouquet of flowers.

"What's that for?" said Jack.

"Their for me, they make me happy, and I was out and about so I thought I would buy some for us."

"Interesting, oh by the way your old girlfriend stopped by and said she was sorry and would like to know if the three of us can make up"

"It's up to you, what do you think?" said Sara

"I'm O Kay with the two of you getting together, just as long as I can watch"

"Oh your not going to watch, you'll will be the main attraction.
I will only do it, if you so want"

"How about tonight after you get off work we all go out and have dinner," said Jack, she moved in and gave him a kiss on the lips and said "Do you want to pick up where we left off earlier"

"Sure" said Jack, as Sara led Jack into the bedroom, she stopped and looked at the bed the sheets that were on the floor and in the middle of the bed was a giant wet spot.

"You've been a naughty boy, haven't you?"
Jack just looked at her and said, "What do you mean"

"I know that wet spot anywhere you and Leslie had makeup sex, now that's not fair, I hope you have enough for me" she said with a smile, Jack undressed as fast as Sara did and he did things with her like or as he did with Leslie, but it seemed to be different with Sara, it was like more heart felt and she liked to touch him more especially when it came to kissing, touching and warmth. She was hot to touch and very wet and Jack felt at ease with her and when he finished with her he came inside of her exactly where she wanted it and said;

"From now on, I want it there all the time and I want to have your baby"
Jack finished up and began to dress, he watched her strip the bed and pull out new sheets and a blanket and remade the bed, in the end Jack helped.
Sara went in to take a shower, while Jack waited on the bed, she came out wearing a towel, which she dropped it and slowly began to dress, making sure Jack saw everything and she was beginning to enjoy dressing in front of him and said to him," What are your plans today"

"Oh I need to meet up with Guy and finish up our fish business and then over to the hospital for lunch and then later I'll spend it with you and Leslie and then out with Red and do some Bounty hunting"

"Sounds like your going to be a busy boy"

"If you want you can come visit me at work later."

"I may just do that "said Jack holding the door open for her and looking down into the courtyard to see the convention of people.

"Oh before I forget, here is a set of my keys; for my car, this apartment and my parent's place." she hands them to Jack who accepts them and sees that they are on a hook.

"Clip that to your pants loop" she showed him, he opened the doors for her all the way to the car and she said "Do you want to drive?"

"No, its your car"

"From now on its our car," said Sara

Jack kept his tongue and the ride was quiet to the mall. She parked the car close by the entrance and began to make out with Jack. Sara stopped abruptly and said "If we keep this up, you'll want to make me miss work and go back home and"

Jack cut her off and said, "We don't want you late, go ahead run along, maybe your right I'll use the car to get around"

"O Kay then "she took her keys out of the ignition and gave Jack a long satisfying kiss on the mouth and said;

"Until tonight my love."

Jack watched her leave and decided it was long enough having other people drive him around, so he slid over behind the wheel, started the car and put it into drive the car slowly went off he practiced turning and parking and just getting an overall feel for the car, long enough to realize he could do this with some authority, all this thinking, it wasn't like the SUV, where it was all about the instincts, so he put on his turn signal and made a left turn at the light just as Sara had done and drove a short ways adhering to the speed limit and being very cautious, he saw the sign for the hospital and turned in parked the car, locked it up and went inside.

CH 7

Jet Skis

The hospital was buzzing, the ambulance was screaming, people were mulling around as Jack calmly went down a flight of stairs to see paradise. Jack read the sign that stated the hours of this phenomenal buffet, quickly he picked up a platter and a plate and began to load up on various types of meats, cheeses and baked dishes and then he saw something familiar to him what looked like a bowl of fried corn mush, using a spoon he tried it.

"Oh that is good" said Jack to himself and took the whole bowl. He finished at the drink station with two glasses of milk, one chocolate the other whole milk. He paid for the meal, sat down by himself, and began to consume the rather large portions.

"Hi Jack "said a sweet voice.

Jack looked up to see Kate; she spoke first "Mind if I sit down?"

"Nah, go ahead" said Jack, continuing to eat.

"So I heard the good news, your going to be my brother-in-law," said Kate arranging her food on her plate. Jack continued to eat and ignored her in the process.

"I guess word travels fast" Jack tried to keep it on the down low, with much difficulty.

"I just love the food; it's a great place to eat"

"I'm glad someone likes the food, but let me tell you, that last night I had, a young woman, came in suffering from internal bleeding and I guess she and her boyfriend had sex and opened her up and if it weren't for that encounter, she would probably have died last night."

Jack looks up at her, stops eating and says, "You don't say, what's her name" "her name is Samantha, she was the one who was severely injured in that car accident a couple of years ago, it was in all the papers, she is my patient, you know what's sad, is she just recently lost her Dad and "

Jack cut her off and said, "How about I go up and cheer her up with a bouquet of flowers"

"That would be nice, Jack, normally we don't allow visitors up to the I.C.U., but I will make an exception to you," said Kate finishing her plate. Jack was done and full.

"Oh by the way I got your tests results back and you have low blood sugar and may be a candidate for type two diabetes, does your family have a history of diabetes?"

"Not that I'm aware of, but who's to say their not" said Jack. Jack stopped by the florist and picking up a dozen long stemmed red roses, paid for them with cash and caught back up with Kate. Kate led him up the stairs to the elevator. Jack stood in the back, holding himself at the railing. He waited then watched Kate get off on the eight floor, and Jack followed her, down a hallway to Sam's room.

Jack stood at the door only to see two older women and a older man about half out of it, and in the middle was Samantha propped up on some pillows with a breathing tube in her mouth.

"A friend of our family, named Jack heard about Samantha and decided to buy her a bouquet of flowers" Jack moved in past the two old ladies and saw Samantha flutter her eyelids and try to smile as Jack set the roses down, then turned and walked past everyone and out the door.

"Jack" said Kate

Jack turned to see Kate and said "Yes"

"The family, said if you want to come back later, when Samantha has her breathing tube out, so she can thank you herself"

"Sure, what time"

"Around three would be a good time, just come to my office and I will escort you up," said Kate.

Jack made it to the elevator and rode it down to the main floor. Jack was on the move only to hear his name called by another girl, Jack turned to see it was Debbie. He stopped, to turn and say;

"My don't you look spectacular today"

"I want to show you something new, and I have another Doctor who might be interested in playing our games"

"Really, set it up and then give me a call," said Jack as he waved to her, while he went out the back door. She watched and waved back, as he got into Sara's car, looked at her and drove off. The ride to the dry docks was short, he pulled off and saw a line had formed to get in, slowly one by one, cars and trucks were allowed in a gate guard was looking at something.

One by one, the cars started to move. Jack eased the car up to the gate guard.

"What's going on here?" said Jack

"Someone found a bloody mattress in one of the dumpsters, now there is police all over this place looking for a body and I was told no one is getting in without proper I.D and a place for which they are going, so what is your name"

Jack thought about it and then decided to be honest.

He said his name was "Jack, and I own the Parthian Stranger."

"Oh the blue boat" said the guard, "So show me some form of I.D and I will let you in" Jack searched his pockets and then said;

"I must have left it on the boat"

"O Kay is there someone who can vouch for you"

"Do you know Guy the fisherman" said Jack.

Jack found his name and dialed him up

"No I don't know any Guy, but if you say so" Jack hands the phone to the gate guard, who talks with Guy. Then when he was through, he hands the phone back to Jack, to say, "Go ahead this time, but next time, you make sure you have some sort of Identification on you at all times". Jack drove through and waved to the gate guard, then parked down by the top of the ramp to where his boat was.

A swam of police officers, and a familiar one, came up to him to say,   "Sorry sir you can't park here"

Jack looked at his nametag that read "Officer John Henderson", which he was the only one in that area. Jack stated, "May I drive on down to the lower docks, on the left"

"That's where the crime scene is"

'That's where my boat is"

"Let me call down there to see if its alright" said Officer John.

Jack looked him up and down, to say "Not bad choice Sara" to himself.

"Alright, they will let you down there, proceed slowly, try not to make any sudden moves, carry on", said Officer John, as Jack watched him as he drove by, down to the bottom of the hill. On the left was a massive crane, as it lifted a platform onto his boat. Standing awaiting Jack, was a police officer, Jack got out of the car.

Jack watched the platform go into place. The police officer who was already talking and repeated himself. Trying to talk over the loud crane's noise.

He came closer to Jack to say, "Officer John informs me that you're the owner of this boat". Then the police officer says, "My name is detective Shawn Gates" and said "Looks like there was a murder on this boat, do you have any idea who might have been on it?"

"Yes sir, it wasn't a murder, my girlfriend had an infection and began to bleed, she is at University Hospital her name is Samantha Smith, she is on the eight floor, I just came back from seeing her, she made such a mess that I wasn't thinking and threw out the mattress."

"Well I don't know about that, but we can check out that lead, in the meantime I want you to stay in the city, here is my card," said the detective. His suspicious eye was raised.

"Why are you here, then if she is in the hospital?"

"I'm supposed to meet, my remodeled, ah there he is, his name is Dan"

The officer looks at Dan as he passes them, to say "The great Dan Davidson, the famous ship builder"

"I guess, really I don't know"

Dan parked his truck and trailer, to see Jack and say, "Wow what happen here"

"It's a private matter Mister Davidson."

"Its really a big miss-understanding." said Jack

"What is your business here?" asked the detective.

"I'm remodeling Jack's boat, as you can see from my crane, its lifting a platform on it"

"Yes but there is blood all over the place, it is a crime scene"

"Really to me, it looks like a commercial fishing vessel, of course its going to have blood all over it"

The officer looked dumb founded, to the point to say, "Hold on."

Jack and Dan followed the officer and up the stairs to see a crime scene of over twenty people, mulling around, Jack watched as they combed through everything and took blood samples, then Jack thought back to the boat he took out and to the ones he killed the others on.

The large platform was set in place on the deck, and what a difference that made, a flat deck, along the crane side, to its end.

"That changes everything "said Dan

"See how you can land a small helicopter on the edge, over there, and on the ends you can have a pair of shore boats." he then turned to Jack to say "I know what your doing here, your making this a pleasure cruise ship. That is a brilliant idea, by taking a solid steel hull, gutting it, updating it, your going to have remarkable vessel that can circumnutates the entire earth"

Jack just looked at him, then said, "Can I still commercial fish"

"You could, lets uncover the forward and aft holding tanks to see if the platform, doesn't hinder the brailer, for off loads."

The detective came back to say "We checked out your story, it was true, sorry about that, I'm happy to hear, that she is alive and made it through surgery"

Jack looked around, inside the wheelhouse, thinking "He should do something more for her, he was right she is lucky"

Seeing this investigative team at work. Jack knew now, he had to be careful in the future and decide on how he will do it in the future. He went to the platform, to see the crane lift out each engine separately,

for Dan to say, "One engine is pretty good still while the other has some bottom end noise, we lifted off the two holding plates, the first one barely clears, but aft is wide open"
Jack watched as the police officer were packing up and leaving.

"That was close huh," said Dan, to Jack, for him to say;
"What do you mean?"
"Well she isn't the one who drives the Mercedes is it?"
"No, why do you ask"
"Well for a guy our age, you get around, I've seen three different girls here in one day, and to me that's a record in anyone's book"
"What are you saying" said Jack.
"I can't have friends over to see the boat" asked Jack
"Don't get me wrong, but in all my years, I've never seen young and hot girls attract them, like you do, let alone willing to do whatever you want them to do, I know you asked us to leave, so my guess was you were doing something that you wanted it to be a secret"
"Yeah so what, what is this of any of your business"
"I was just saying, it was close, that's all"
Jack just looks at him to say, "Any leads on how I can get that those two shore boats?"
"Not yet but I do have your two Jet Skis, do you want to come down and I'll show you how they work" said Dan. Trying to change the subject quite quickly.
Jack left the railing and past the remaining police workers and followed Dan. Jack walked with him to see saw the sleek little crafts.
"They are the state of the art, in Jet Skies." said Dan to add;   "Think of being on the water, either in the ocean or in fresh water, the versatile of these machines will amaze you, you can turn on a dime and do flips and all sort of tricks, are you ready to go?"
"What do you mean?" asked Jack, looking at him, not fully understanding what Dan was asking him about.
"Do you remember me telling you that I can put two Jet Skies on you boat for say five grand and I'm here to show you how"

"Sounds fair," said Jack, "Just use that crane to hoist them up"

"No it doesn't work like that, I want to show you how to have fun on them and take you out for a test drive, would you buy a car without first test driving it?"
Jack thought about it to say to himself "Yes I would."

"Hop in and I'll give you a ride down to the inlet Harbor." said Dan.
Jack looked at him, to finally move and get into Dan's truck and immediately liked the larger vehicle. The two rode a brief ways and came to the boat ramp, in one turn Dan was backing it into the water, put the truck in park and jumped out into the water.

"Come on Jack, help me out"
Jack opened the door and carefully stepped out into the water, it was warm by feel, as he was quickly getting his shoes and lower pants wet, he slowly walked back to see Dan. Dan unhooked the first one and slid it off the trailer, as he held onto the rope that was attached to the front and guided it around to the dock, to tie it off.

"It's just like a motorcycle, hop on that one and I'll unlatch you."
Jack lifted himself out of the water and on to the railing of the trailer, to sit on the skies; he then put his hands on the control handles.
Dan stood in front of him and said, "Before I release you, you must know a little about safety;
First off, in the harbor the speed limit is the first notch down and no horsing around. It is only when we get to open water will we open it up.
Think of it like driving a boat, take it easy around other boats and people and always stay to the right."
Dan released the strap from inside the cargo hold to affix ate to Jack's wrist. And said, "This is for when you lose control and is thrown off the ski, it is a kill switch. The ski will right itself and then just get back on and go again, do you have a wallet, cell phone or your keys," said Dan.

"Yes"-said Jack
Dan hands Jack a orange bag, and then he opens it up and says, "Put all you valuables inside, it will keep them dry and safe."

"But if the ski sinks then, you'll lose them, if I were you, I'd put them in my truck for safe keeping."

Jack hands over his keys, cash, wallet and cell phone to Dan, who reattaches the front panel and then says, "In a minute I will push you away, as you float, hold down that red button for a few seconds and the Jet Ski will fire up, leave your right grip alone, you will sit on idle."

"Do you see this button here, is a selector switch for reverse and click the next one is the first of four gears." As Dan was ready to push Jack off he says "In the event you kill the ski when you tip over then it will reset back to neutral, understand?"

"Seems easy enough" said Jack who waited, then Dan pushed him off, Jack cruised a bit, trying to find a balance, and then hit the switch, and it fired his ski up.

He sat idling as Dan got into his truck and pulled the truck up the ramp to park. He came down to the dock, got on his and un-hooked it from the rope.

Jack floated a bit and but gave it some fuel as it propelled the ski forward.

Dan waited for Jack to turn around his ski. Dan waited until Jack was next to his before, he clicked it forward, the ski sat flat in the water and it was going smoothly for both of them. Jack positioned the ski behind Dan's., Jack held onto his, as he slowly went, that was until Dan throttled down.

The huge wall of water sprayed Jack down, to the point of him rolling to one side.

Jack lost his balance and into the bay water. While Dan was in full throttle mode.

Jack hoisted himself back up on the craft. The other Jet Ski was jumping the water, while he tested the throttle and could feel the instant response under him.

The sun was blinding his eyes.

Jack squinted his eyes, only to see Dan come back up to him, providing a wave for him to ride out.

"Sorry about that, stop being a sissy, step on it and have some fun, I want to see you smiling before the day is through"

Jack fired his up. It came to life and in an instant did a quick circle around Dan.

"Be careful not to lean one way or the other, you'll tip over, come follow me" said a screaming Dan. The Jet Ski took off and shot a tall rooster tail, which put a smile on Jack's face. Jack turned down the handle and it jerked forward. Jack cruised at a slow pace for a while testing it out and eventually catching up with Dan. They hit the large inlet, where there were boats all over the place, Dan and Jack kept to the right side of the inlet. They followed it around to see the cities public boating dock. Jack saw the boat he borrowed and then Dan took off down what looked like a waterway a narrow strip of water. Jack followed and started to shift gears the wind at his face felt exhilarating. Up ahead he saw Dan turn at the dam and shot back past Jack. Jack tried to turn and when he did, he found himself upside down and drinking water as it all came to a sudden end. The ski was off as Jack pulled himself back up, re-attached the strap and fired the ski up. The Jet Ski was now facing away from the dam and off he went.

Jack picked up momentum only to see Dan come screaming past him, causing a wave as Jack crashed, and was back into the water; Jack was back on the ski and realized he needs to lean into the waves and be more flexible.

He knew he needed to gather himself, instead of just falling over at any time. Jack was back on the ski, fired it up, re-tightened the loose strap and just let the throttle go he did a few "s" type maneuvers and lost control and dumped it again. This time he got out of the water to see Dan was laughing at him and said "Jack your trying too hard, just let it flow, let the ski go and find the balance of a little control and let it do its own thing, really your on it for the ride, so enjoy it."

Dan took off, spraying Jack with his rooster tail.

Jack re-fired the ski and did as he was told and he then started to have some fun, as he took it slow, moving side to side to get the steering down and back into the inlet, the water was calm.

Jack tore through the water, with such ease as the minutes turned into an hour.

Jack was enjoying himself; he dumped it once or twice more, but for the most part found a new toy to play on.

Dan came close to Jack, while Jack was just idling after a fun spill to say, "You ready to go back in and purchase these two Skies"

"Yeah, I'll buy'em" said Jack.

Jack took a head start and pasted Dan with full throttle open, but that lasted a mere minute as the more experienced Dan surged past Jack and into the lead, Jack slipped behind Dan and followed him into the bay and back to where they once started.

Dan had already tied up his ski and was after the truck as Jack arrived; he idled it down and waited until Dan had the trailer in the water, before Jack moved it into position. Jack leaned forward; he clipped the ski in place. Jack then hit the on/off switch and saw Dan unhook his and with the rope, he threw it at Jack who caught it. Jack then pulled the other ski onto the trailer, clipping it to the eyehook and unclipping the rope. In one motion, Dan pulled the rope back and curled it back in place and in the back of his truck. Dan then ran around and said;

"I'll pull you up and into the parking lot, then get off"

Jack sat still on the ski as the truck pulled the trailer up and out of the water; the sensation was cool to Jack as the two Jet Skies settled into position as the truck made its way up the boat ramp.

Dan parked the truck off to the side, Jack got off his and stood on the ground to watch Dan secure the Jet Skies in the rear and latch them down.

Dan also took out both rubber keys and put them in his pocket and said, "Ready to go back, get in, I put a towel down for you to sit on"

Jack got in, realizing his pants were still wet, he saw the orange bag next to him, he opened it up to see his cash and everything else he had.

"Go ahead it's your bag, keep all your stuff in it while you dry off, and here are your two keys, for the Jet skies."

Dan drove the truck back in front of his boat.

Dan said to Jack "Do you want new racks made for the Jet Skies or simply modify the trailer for them to fit on the platform?"

"They seem to weigh something; can you modify a frame on each side of the two shore boats?"

"Yea sure, I see what your trying to do, let me park these next to your boat" and then backed them in next to the boat.

Jack counted out five grand and gave it to Dan and said;

"Here you go, thanks that was a fun time"

"Let me get a receipt for the sale of these and "said Dan Jack cut him off and said "What about this truck how much you want for it"

"Its not for sale, I need it for work and besides I still owe money on it"

Jack sat in disbelief and was ready to get out when Dan handed him a written receipt and said "Here you can take this to the Department of Motor Vehicles and register them, and if you interested in buying a truck, I know a friend who has an old truck he might sell you".

"Or you know what you could do, if you have ten grand down you could get a brand new truck" said Dan getting out, Jack followed, out his side; he looked at his watch to see it was nearly three o'clock.

Jack watched as Dan unhitched the trailer from the truck and attached a wheel underneath it and began to spin a handle to lift the trailer up and off the truck. Dan then un-did the lights and said "That's it; I should have both your engines done on Tuesday of next week and a frame in place for a small boats and the jet skies." How do you like the platform?"

"Great, you did a nice job, but I prefer you stay out of my personal business." said Jack watching Dan get into his truck and drive away.

Jack went up on to his empty boat and began to strip down to his underwear and shoes; he laid out all his clothes on the platform to dry. Jack went back into the wheelhouse to see the drawings of circles of blood splatter and the smell was still nauseous. Jack took off his shoes and socks, set them on the platform by the door, and realized he needed to make a place more secure and be more careful on what he does in the future. Jack's phone began to ring, several times; he got the orange bag to it finally and answered it "hello" in a horse voice.

Samantha said, "Thank you for saving my life and those roses are so beautiful, I told my mom what you did for me and she wants to meet you."

Jack paused then said, "I can come up to see you soon, are you alright"

"I'll tell you, when I see you, but you saved my life, and I feel so much better, thanks, bye Jack"

He was still listening to the phone when it went dead.

He looked down at the phone to see it said, "You missed three calls"

Sara programmed the phone to show him how to use it, retrieve messages and how to send them.

Jack went to retrieve the messages he remembers how to do it from her.

"Message one, yeah Jack this is Guy, I lined up several people for a charter for this next weekend, with our split you'll make about six grand, call me."

"Message two, hi Jack this is Debbie I hope you come visit me at work, I'm all dressed up and I'm ready to take it off for you, and I have a friend who will join us, bye"

"Maybe it's the hot Korean girl "he thinks.

"Message three, Hi Jack this is Kate, just wanted to let you know how kind and respectful man you are and I welcome you into our family and would like to spend some time with you, when you have the time, from your soon to be sister-in-law, bye Jack"

Jack closed up the phone and went back outside to turn the clothes over and check on his shoes, then came back in and decided to go down into the galley, looking around he saw a door half open, but first he saw a refrigerator and opened it to see several cans of soda, he grabbed one it was cold, un-did it and took a sip of it and said;

"Oh that was good".

He read the can to say "Crème soda" and then he continued to look around and opened the door to show a full size washer and a dryer.

Jack took off his wet underwear and threw them in to the dryer and turned it on, he finished his drink and went back up to the platform to pick up his clothes which he first slipped on his shoes, that steel platform was hot as was his near dry clothes, which the warmth felt good, so he went inside and put on the pants and the tank top, and then sat down on the bench.

Jack pulled on the socks and retied his shoes. He grabbed his orange bag and took out his keys, wallet and cash, then placed his cell phone in his pocket, he noticed a lock on the handle as he closed the door, and he went down the stairs to see the workers returning with Dan.

"Do you have any keys to the locks on the boat?" asked Jack

"I don't, but maybe Guy does and if he doesn't I can have them re-keyed.

When the boat is ready to turn back over to you, I will have a set for you." to add "look I want to apologize for my behavior, I was wrong, you're my employer and I need to respect you"

"Thanks" said Jack in passing, to say "Oh by the way, Dan"

"You said something about if I had ten thousand to put down, that I could get a brand new truck?"" asked Jack.

"Yes I have a friend who has a dealership, you give him ten grand, and he will get you a new truck and make payments of about 400 a month."

"Do you know what a brand new one runs?"

"Oh about thirty grand"

"That sounds even better, make it happen"

"Yes sir" said Dan

Jack pasted by him to get into the little car, started it up backed it up and pulled forward, past the gate guard and up to the highway, a left hand turn and west he went back to the hospital, the ride was short and getting easier.

Immediately he knew the time was running out and would have to skip seeing Debbie, and her new friend, he was walking into the main entrance and there she was.

"Hi Jack did you get my message " said Debbie, looking extremely sexy, catching Jack off guard, he saw her break from her associate and come up to Jack, inches away from his face.

"I'm here," said Jack, to say "Where is your associate going?"

"Oh, no she isn't the one, the one that is interested is on the fifth floor, her name is Mary, and she is a internalist Doctor.

"Really, then call her up and have her meet us in your office.

"Wow what's that smell is that you smell like the ocean?" said Debbie.

Debbie was leading Jack to her office.

"I went Jet Skiing, and then I bought two of them"

"Oh I just love to Jet Ski, have a seat I'll call up Mary.

Jack sat on his favorite sofa while Debbie was on the phone with Mary, to say "She will be down here in a minute. "

"In the meantime, I will stand over here, let me show you what I have on, you know yesterday was so exciting that it just gets me so wet, just thinking of undressing in front of you."

Jack didn't say a word and waited. Meanwhile Debbie was at her desk, reviewing papers. Jack just sat and watched her work. And finally, a knock on her door, moments later, a tall, beautiful girl, who had short blonde hair, a huge rack, and disguising eyes.

Debbie got up and went to the door, locked her door and closed up the blinds as the two both began to dance around closer to Jack and as Debbie spoke "Your such a dirty boy, and that's what I like about you", she and Mary took off their lab coats to show a magnificent looking dress with black nylons and jet black pumps, for Debbie, and Mary wore a white Tank top and khaki pants. Together slowly they unbuttoned her top and let it fall to show her sheer black bra, which she couldn't wait to show him and popped her bra, letting him see her two beautiful breasts, next was Mary's turn, to pull off her tank top, and her white bra, to show her massive melons. Debbie then unzipped her skirt and let it fall to reveal a black garter belt with strap.

While Mary unbuttoned her pants, to step out of them, only to show him that she wore no underwear.

Debbie moved closer to him and said "Why don't you unbutton them"

Jack was eager to help; he was being turned on by both of these girls and their creative display.

Jack helped her undo the front, then she turned around and he did the back, she bent over and pulled down her wet panties, Jack reached in with his fingers and began to play with her, adding to the excitement, Mary followed suit and allowed him to do the same for her.. Jack was ready to go when a knock on the door ended the moment. Debbie stopped as Mary continued.
For her to say, "Who is it, I'm busy can it wait "
"Your patient's need you; the Chief of Medicine is doing rounds".
"Doctor Gregory Sanders will be here in just a minute."
There was a long pause, to hear "Doctor Sanders is here and would like your presence." said the voice outside of her door." who sounded a lot like her assistant.
"I'll be there in a moment," she yelled and ads while getting dressed "I'm sorry Jack, I must go, let's do this later, and I get off around six, .but Imagine Mary can stay"
"Yes Jack, while she has to leave, all you'll have is me to stick that into" Mary said with a smile.
Jack watched how fast Debbie was dressed and back into her lab coat, she unlocked the door and then closed it shut.
Jack stood up, his pants at his ankles, he stuck it in to Mary's tight space, as she was bent over, Jack did all the work, till he heard voices out side the door, and pulled out of Mary, who quickly got dressed, and stood, in the closet, Jack closed the door on her, he was dressed to turn to see.
Gregory Sanders with Debbie come in to say "Hey Jack funny meeting you here"
"Yeah, I stopped by to see Debbie, and she gave me some work to fill out", he held up some papers, to show him.
Jack followed them out into the hallway, where a team of young physicians waited and Doctor Greg Sanders. Said "Well at least your making us proud to getting those checkup, and doing follow-up work, stay with Debbie and she will get you back on track"
"Yes, I plan on doing that for a long time to come" said Jack with a smile.
"So what has my future son in law been up to this day? "

"You know getting a second opinion for my low blood sugar and eating at that wonderful place down below"

"That's a good choice, you know I had Debbie herself, design that, and as well as being a doctor she is a board certified nutrientist".

Jack watched as they left to walk down the hall and Jack went the other way towards Kate's office, he went to the receptionist and asked for Kate.

"She said to tell you go back and her office is the first one on the left."

Jack knocked on the door that read "Dr. Katherine Sanders"

"Come in" said the voice

Jack opened the door and saw Kate sitting at her desk;

"Jack come in and shut the door". Said Kate, looking up at him, to add "Have a seat across from me"

Jack pulled out a large leather armed chair and plopped down.

"I'll be with you in a moment "said Kate finishing up some paperwork.

Jack sat; he noticed her desk was made of clear glass.

As he looked, he saw Kate's skirt was hiked up and her legs were spread apart with her feet resting beside the chair, to show a pair of white panties, very visible, Jack continued to stare.

"Shall I take them off so you can get a better look?" said Kate.

She was looking at him now as she closed her legs, to get his attention.

"Sure if you want to, It isn't like I haven't seen it before" said Jack with a smile on his face.

"I was kidding; you're my sister's finance and wouldn't want to spoil it for her"

"What does that mean?" asked Jack

"It means in the past I have taken other men from her, and for that she doesn't appreciate that, and she doesn't like to share either."

"Says who, I share her with Leslie and she brings her over so we can both share her together, I'm sure she would make an exception if she brought you in, besides I've already saw you naked"

"Yes, about that, it was unexpected and I get crazy when I drink, especially Debbie, who can't control herself, so if you saw me naked, then I guess it could be alright"

"I'll do one better, I'll convince Sara, that it would be what I wanted"

"You have that much power over her?"

"I guess so, so what do you say" asked Jack, to ad "Come over here, and stand before me"

Kate stood up and came around to the desk to stand by Jack, close enough for Jack to take his hand and move it up and under her skirt to reach her already wet panties.

"What is it about you that I'm so attracted to you; you have this way about you, oh"

Jack found her wet spot and worked his fingers in. A smile was on Kate's face as she said "It's been so long since a man has touched me in that way and"

She was interrupted by a knock at her door. "Honey, can I have a word with you" the door opened and Kate stepped away from Jack, to see her father "Dad can't you see I'm with Jack, give me a minute".

"He sure gets around" said Greg who waved at Jack.

The door closes and Kate goes over and locks it shut and says;

"Now where were we at".

She sees Jack get up and slide the chair back in place, then goes over to her and say "Can you take me up to visit that miracle girl"

"Yes, but what about me?" pointing down to where he had worked earlier.

"How about another time, when were not interrupted" said Jack.

Jack passed her and opening the door for her, as she said;

"It's not over between you and I, mister." She led the way, then evading her dad's group and onto the elevator they all went, they got off at the next floor, which left Kate and Jack alone, just as the doors closed, she came to him, his finger found her spot, then the doors reopened, and others got on, all the way up to the recovery floor, it stopped, Kate got out first followed by Jack as they went to Samantha's room.

Jack was hesitant to walk in, but it was Kate's introduction that led everyone to say hi and welcome Jack in, Jack saw Samantha with a beautiful smile on her face, her long flowing brown hair off to one side, she mouth the words "Hi"

"How is she doing?" asked Jack

"Well she is the miracle girl, not only did we find a leak, but she has sensation in her legs, soon she may walk again" said Kate.

"I'll leave you alone to get better acquainted"

"How do you know our grand daughter?" said the Grand pa

"I plan on hiring her to help out my business"

"So you're the one, she is talking about, you could be as old as her father, you old bastard, you better leave my daughter alone or I will call the cops, sicko" screamed her mom right in Jack's face.

"Enough Mom leaves Jack and I alone, he saved my life, so please leave."

Jack watched as the older people filed out of the room, Jack came to her bedside.

"Thanks for coming, let me tell you what you did, first off I can't have sex for at least six weeks, so I may heal, second all of my stuff works. Whereas the doctors though it was dead and from my waist down I have a greater sensation of feeling in my legs and in my left big toe."

Jack comforted her, by touching her arm, as she looked up at him, to say   "It was the hormones that did it, I had felt this bloating feeling for the last couple of days."

The Doctors said "It was the size of a pin tip, that the blood was leaking out into my uterus and because, I was still a virgin, the skin held it in like a dam, ready to burst."

"I'm glad I could save your life" said Jack

"If I had not met you, the dam would have burst probably in my sleep and I would have died, said Doctor Kate" said Sam to Jack. To add "But because, you did what you did and got me so stimulated, when you penetrated me it erupted, and I bleed out, the visceral fluids, cleaned out the uterus and because of the hormones the artery now has a tear, which they went into and repaired."

Jack began to stroke her pretty face.

Jack thought to himself, "Wow, she is so beautiful"

"The result of all this is that, I may even be able to walk soon." she smiled at him.

"All this, just because you liked me enough, to want to be with me".

She paused then said "For that I am grateful and from this day forward I will work for you, and help you with you charter business."

"That's great news, Thanks" said Jack

"In addition, you don't owe me anything, if you want to be in my life, that's fine, if all you want is sex from me, that's fine too"

Jack looked her over, as he pulled the sheet partway from her nude body, to expose a right firm breast.

"I know that you have a girl-friend, who your going to marry, its all over the hospital, so I will keep this our secret from now on"

"Did I hear something about sex?" said a nurse, from behind the curtain of her private room.

"Its time for your sponge bath, Sir you'll have to wait outside"

Jack was beginning to move and said "Sam, I will visit you tomorrow, get some sleep and rest"

"Say goodbye, to your father" said the stern nurse, beginning to pull her covers down to expose her breasts and everything else.

"He is not my father; he is my boy-friend. And he can stay if he wants to" said a smiling Samantha.

"Your going to have to wait in line honey, everyone want's that one" said the nurse.

Jack was already down the hall, and waited by the elevator.

The doors opened and Jack got in, he made his way out of the elevator, when it hit the lobby, he made it out of the hospital, without incident.

He started Sara's car, he drove the car like a professional, and went the speed limit and used his turn signals as he made his way back to the mall.

Jack went into the mall, to remember that suit he had made, and that phenomenal tailor, so he diverted his path to the tailor.

Jack stood at the door to see this beautiful, striking woman, much younger and very tall, and soft pillowy lips, with jet black hair.

She was helping another customer, when she looked up to see her one-day-stand, and said "Long time stranger, what happen to I'll be back tonight at six and I will pick up the suit"

Jack stepped in and came up to the counter and said "How much do I owe you?"

"Honey, you owe me nothing, as far as the suit goes well you can pay that back to me, as my little sex slave"

As several customers walked in, and said Hi to her.

Cassandra says, "John and Tom I'll be with you in a minute"

"Sounds good, do you want to go back in the room and go at it again"

"No, not here, why don't you come to my house later tonight, let me write my address down and my phone number, she hands it to him, can you come around ten p.m."

"That might work, I have a job tonight around eight o'clock and when I'm done I'll give you a call."

Jack picks up the suit from the garment hanger and walks out into the mall, but he was going east and away from Sara's store and seeing the different shops, then he comes to a phone store and walks in, literally all the walls were covered in phone accessories.

"Can I help you sir?" said a male voice from behind him.

Jack turned to see the very tall large person, his nametag said;

"Store manager"

"I was looking for something to get the phone out of my pocket." "Then place it on a belt or something or on my body somewhere," said Jack pulling the phone out of his pocket to show him.

"Well sir, there are several carriers to keep your phone safe".

The store manager leads Jack to an area on the wall that just has holsters, "How about this one" and hands Jack a rugged heavy-duty cloth case with a snap strap and a clip on the bottom. "You attach it to your belt".

The store manager showed Jack and placed the phone in the carrier and the clipped it to Jack's pant loop. To say "Normally it would hang off of a belt, Sir"

"I like it, can I have it"

"Sure come on over and let me ring it up"

Jack's mind was pre-occupied with seeing Sara today, he paid cash for the carrier, and left. Jack walked the mall's large aisle way noticing all the pretty girls, who were smiling back at him.

Several giggled at him, but Jack continued to walk towards his path to Sara's place of work.

Jack stood at the edge of the large door watching Sara work, how she was helping a young woman with some clothing.

"It's not nice to stare," said a voice behind him

Jack turns to see a very pretty girl, with curly hair and a short t-shirt and shorts, looking up at him and says, "It's not nice to sneak up on an old guy like me"

"Oh your not old, you're the right age for my friend Sara, you should of seen the loser she was dating before you, that guy was a freak and wouldn't leave her alone, now you your different, a lot more mature and have given our Sara the direction she needs."

"With your assistance and stability, she will get her life back on track and maybe away from her friend Leslie, so you go boy and get your girl"

"Kerrie what are you doing with my man" said Sara behind Jack.

"Oh you know Sara, girl stuff like seeing if he will take me out, and wine and dine me, so I too can fall in love with a guy like Jack. "Jack do you know any nice boys who would want a girl like me?"

Jack smiled with a stare at her, thinking of one "Dan", just to have Sara kiss Jack on the mouth, using both of her hands to hold his face, still holding his suit in one hand.

Finally she let go and said, "What gifts have you brought me"

"None, this is my suit, but you can wear it if you like" he hands it to her.

She takes it from him and says; "I may just do that, the color seems so striking."

Sara walks back into the store, with the suit, followed by Jack and Kerrie. Sara goes behind the counter, hangs up the suit, and says, "Have you too been formally introduced?"
Jack stands in front of Sara; next to him is Kerrie and then a woman with some clothes stands by them.

"You guys step aside, let the woman through, Kerrie take Jack out in the mall and let him know what we have planned.'
Kerrie took Jack's hand and with her, other hand held a drink.
She begins to pull Jack along only to hear Sara say;

"I'll be done here in a minute then we will all go".
Jack continue the resistance much to his liking, as Kerrie continued to pull Jack along, Jack had a smile on his face, they stopped out in the mall where Kerrie still had Jack's arm and was caressing it with her hand and says "Your one lucky guy."
Jack continued to smile and kept quiet, wondering who this girl was and how can he could get away, although looking at her beautiful face and what was under that tank top would be worth investigating.

"O Kay lets go" said Sara leading them with the suit in hand, both Jack and Kerrie followed, with Kerrie still holding onto his hand.
Sara held the door open for Jack who held the door open for Kerrie, who in turn walked past Jack. Both girls went hand in arm through the door. Jack took up behind them, watching the two of them sway their butt's for Jack's amusement as Sara said, "Did you tell Jack yet"

"Nah, I thought it would be a surprise," said Kerrie.

"Nice park job" said Sara kidding. The three of them stopped to admire the car taking up three spaces and parked at an angle.

"I was in a hurry and wanted to see you as soon as possible," Said Jack.
Jack went to the driver's door, unlocked the door and hit the unlock button.
He then realized what he needed to do. In an instant, he went around and opened both doors for the two ladies.
Jack stood watching them close their doors on him and then went back around, to get in behind the wheel, he fired the car up, and the radio was loud as Sara turned it down and said;

"You're partying it up"

"Yep, where to?"

"Where do you want to take two young hot girls?" said Sara with a wink

"To the hospital's buffet line"

"No silly, your going to take Kerrie, my bests friend in the whole wide world and me to the most expensive restaurant in the city called Lighthouse Resort, which over looks the harbor. "

"Just tell me where to go," said Jack now driving and watching the road.

Sara snuggled up next to Jack and said, "I told my friend Kerrie what we were doing and I think she likes you, after dinner I have a surprise for you".

Sara firmly grasp Jack's arm and places her head on it. She explains the directions to him and he drives safely and in control. The rest of the drive was uneventful, except the drive up the steep road to the top; to a sign that read "Welcome to Hilltop Lighthouse and Spa Resorts", the road opened up to, and a small city the large parking lot was in the middle.

"Drive up to the front, the valet will park the car, and give him five dollar bill" said Sara.

Jack drove up to what looked like a bridge, and drove underneath it, a man waited dressed in a red suit with fridges and a black cap, the door opened for Jack to hear "Welcome sir to the hilltop Lighthouse restaurant." Jack stood up and reached for his money, found a five-dollar bill and handed it to the guy. Jack stepped away towards Sara and Kerrie.

"Thanks sir" said the valet

Jack followed Sara and Kerrie in, and realized maybe he should have been wearing his new suit"

The two girls led him up the two sets of stairs to the upper dining room, a server was with Sara and Kerrie as Jack lagged behind, looking at a few people and another young couple and finally to their table where Sara and Kerrie sat already.

Jack took a seat on the end across from both girls.

The two were talking amongst themselves, laughing and giggling.

"Kerrie and I said if we ever find a man we were going to marry, then the first place we were going to go is to the Lighthouse., isn't the view spectacular? "

"Yes the view is nice," said Jack standing up to look at the harbor. The night was settling down, boats had their lights on and off in the distance, on the point was where his boat was.

Dinner had come and gone just as fast, Jack wasn't as excited as Sara or Kerrie was, even though the place was cool to look at and even seeing the harbor, the bill came and Sara handed it to Jack, who looked at it and began to calculate it then pulled out a wad of money and laid out two hundred and sixty dollars cash.

"Let's go," said Jack.

"What's the hurry?" said Sara, acting a bit weird, she places her hand on his arm and says, "We and I have a surprise for you, and don't you want dessert?" She said it with slur voice.

Jack helped her up, and put her arm around his neck as Kerrie said,   "She got you a room here, and I helped her out, follow me and I will take you there".

Jack helped Sara along until they got out of the restaurant then Jack hoisted her up and into his arms and carrying her was easier, they got to the room, Kerrie opened the door and let Jack in, Jack came into the room and placed a pasted out Sara on the bed.

Jack turned to see Kerrie standing there in the middle of the room. Jack pulled away from Sara to sit on the edge of the bed to watch her, to say,   "Go slowly I like a show".

Kerrie did a slow dance looking the other direction, just as she had pulled off her tank top. She turned to say;

"The surprise was for you to share me tonight"

"Be quiet, and do a little dance, slowly take it all off" said Jack now watching, this beauty do her thing, she wiggled out of her tight, tight shorts, then slowly the bra. She paused to turn around to hear the door click shut.

Houses on the Hill

J ack made his way to the hallway and out into the lobby, he pulled the ticket from his pocket and gave it to the valet. Jack waited until the car got there and as the guy got out Jack went in, and off he went.

"Hey mister, you didn't pay the"

Jack slammed the door shut and drove the car down the hill onto the highway and off the main street exit, down by the lights that said;

"Bail Bonds"

Jack's mind was racing, his adrenalin was running and now it was time for work. Jack knew later he could go back there and take care of the two girls.

Jack parked the car and went on up to the door, he tried the door, it was locked, he rang the buzzer, through the glass Jack could see a tall red headed guy, bare chested carrying two pistols and one in his belt, and came towards Jack, he unlocks the door.

"Didn't think I would see you tonight, just getting it on with my local slut's, come on back and join in if you like," said Red.

Jack followed Red back, and then Red opened a door to show two young girls. They were on the carpet floor taking care of each other, naked; while two other boys were sitting back watching. Jack took a seat, to watch, those two young girls devoured Red. He took care of both of them each, displaying to the boys and Jack how a real man gets the Job done. Afterwards Red said, "Who wants em"

Both girls sat eagerly in the middle ready to please, while Red toweled himself off and got dressed. Jack turned both girls down first, and then they went to the boys.

Jack rose and followed Red back into another room where he finished dressing and putting on his holsters.

"You know, you ought to enjoy the fruits of this work, those two girls were once bail jumpers now their my play things"
Jack took a seat, while Red finished dressing.

"You seem like your amped; now lets see your ID, did you bring one?" "No need to lie to me, either you have one or you don't".

"I don't have one"

"We can work with you on that, but here me out, never lie to me again, you only lie to women, when you want something and when you give something"

"I don't know what you're talking about," said Jack

"Well either you are an escaped prisoner or a harden criminal. Which both don't matter, I can still help you," said Red

"Well, I don't know, I've been on a boat, doing commercial fisherman work"

"So you're a merchant Marine, you still need a passport."

"Where is that?"

"I don't have that either"

"And a local driver's license, what country are you from?" asked Red.

"I think I'm from Germany," offers Jack

"Yo Johnny" yells Red.
A young nude man with his flagpole swinging appears.

"This dude needs a I D. and a passport" said Red with a puzzled look on his face and ads "Come to think about this, you know there was this dude who was brought here from Atlanta about two month's ago, and placed in the old prison, they say he was from Germany although it was classified as a International Criminal, are you that guy?"

"Nah, I'm not that guy," said Jack adamantly

"There you go lying to me again, oh yes you are, here is that clipping, showing Jack what was written, by a girl name Natasha Rogers, from the New Orleans Times.
Jack read the article, claiming it that he was an International Super spy, was coming here to live out his last days.

"The place I was at was deserted"

"You know that place is no prison, you were in has been closed for years, now all they do is shoot movies and run some drills out there, although it is not known, to the general public. But any way, she wrote you went to the new Super max, on the Inlet island, look if this works out, you and I could be one solid team, obviously someone wanted you out". Said Red, looking at Jack. And yells;

"Johnny get in here now" and ads "Have a seat Jack that's what you're calling yourself right? "

"I can help you, and I want to help you, hey what's in the past is in the past, lets live in the moment". Johnny appeared with a kit in hand and partly dressed, he then lays out the kit.

"Jack it is of extreme importance to have an I. D and to have roots and what Johnny will do for you is create a past and provide dates, a good cover is being a merchant Marine; you could be missing for over twenty years. Next, we will issue you a semi-fake passport, from Germany, Its only good for one year from this day, give or take a couple or so days to get it ratified by the German embassy. Red looks at him to say, "What we can do is list your name as Jack, we need a good German last name, do you have any idea's? "

"How about Money, I like that name," said Jack smiling

"Nah, it will throw up a red flag, you got any ideas Johnny?" who pulls out a name book.

And begin to go through a list of German names; "Allen, Boeckmann, Cash, Hoffman, Reichel, Schaaf, Talbott and Woodward".

"Choose one," says Johnny

Jack looks at the list to say "I like Cash, isn't that the same as Money?" to add   "It really is a true German name?"

"Yes, matter of fact, a friend of mine at a conference I attended, his name was John Cash, and he was one son of a bitch, so why not, I'm cool with that , Mister Jack Cash, what do you think Johnny Cash"

"What; come on, is that his name" asked Jack

"Nah, were just joshing you, Ha, Ha, Ha" they all laughed.
Johnny took Jack's hand and began the fingerprint process.

"What's that?" asked Jack

"It's fingerprinting and is required for all passports and I. D's don't worry Jack; Your, hold on Johnny" said Red and pulls out a exacto knife and say " Jack let me have your thumb and forefinger of one hand and your other fingers on your right, we need to disguise the databank, hold your palms up"
Red made some slight incisions to Jack's fingertips, in such a way that, he did not even bleed.

"Now what I did was to slow down the investigative process, and give you more time, but listen, you can either stand up and fight or be on the run, which do you prefer?"

"I'll stay and fight," said a renewed Jack

"Good that's nice to hear, its good to have you part of our team".

"I'll let you know at some point, but, your gonna have to fight, and listen Jack, me and my team will be by your side" said Red
Johnny administered the fingerprints; "The connected lines look real, .nice job Red" said Johnny and ads "Jack that should last you at least five years of protection"
Johnny was finished and sat down and began to type on a computer, and said, "Let's begin, shall we, what is your last name to be?"
Jack says "Cash, Jack Cash".

"Yeah alright, let me put it in here, what is your hair color, Brown, eyes Brown, now date of birth",

"Let's get the year right, and use April 4th"

"Sounds good, "said Jack

"Jack Cash" said Red and ads "It does sound like a cover name, you may need to change that as soon as possible, what about that girl you were with, when you bailed out her brother, what was her last name?"

"It is Sanders" said Jack

"Yeah your right, its right here, why don't you take that name" said Red

"O Kay, that's fine with me" said Jack agreeing with them

"Hold on its not that easy, I mean you should marry her."

"then take it as a legal name, in a documented ceremony and then have five or so kids to make it official, you know Jack the more events you can make legitimately, the greater the chances of your success. Then to get married and change your fake name to a real one, you must do in a public forum, will help to dissolve your past and fast forward your future." said Red.

"Sure, I will do it tomorrow," said Jack

"Lets be serious, you can't get married tomorrow, well I guess you could, but realistically you can't, tomorrow is Sunday, you need time, so that the public has a chance to get to know who you are and build a reputation"
Jack just looks at him with a glazed over look..

"Then if the chosen girl has strong roots in this community, like the Sanders name, well then it will take time, money and dedication, because it will be a major event" said Red.

"Where in Germany are you from" asked Johnny

"Lets pull out a map of Germany and let Jack decide, where he was from" said Red
Jack looked over at the map, to see the west from the east, to say;

"I think I'm from the west side" Jack places his finger down, they all look at it, it read "He is from Cologne and was born April 4th and the date was 1986." " What it means you were out to sea for 19 years, which makes you 38 years old, in a month you'll be 39 years old," said Red

"How do you know all of this" asked Jack.

"Well actually there is a school that teaches you all that stuff."

"Cool, how can I join? "

"By invitational only, there is a process and lots of money, now stands over by the wall and I will take your picture," said Red.
Jack stood up and positioned himself by the wall, Red pulled out a digital camera and took several shots and says " You know Jack I know of a way that could ensure your safety and keep you cover intact, I could send you to the academy." said Red

"What's that?" said Jack sitting back down by Johnny

"The Academy is run by the U S marshal's and certifies International Bounty or I guess they call themselves; International Fugitive Recovery Person's and it would give you a sense of direction and clarity, not to mention a ton of certificates and stature"

"What's the catch?"

"Well to be honest with you, your stuck, once a agent you will always be a agent, the upside is a steady paycheck, and lots of travel, and you become an American citizen, and then there is the wives program.", to add "I had a choice and I chose the adder, that is why I'm here, but you, I know you'll chose what they want, and that is why I know you'll be a good agent."

"Jack I ran your name through the FBI's CBI network, and it comes up, that you're a German citizen, your here on a one year working visa, you're a commercial fisherman. Here Jack is your I D card and your passport. I printed a soon to expire driver's license, you will need to renew it in the next couple of weeks. "Said Johnny. Johnny was packing up his stuff, to add "But by then, your ID will check out and you'll have no problems getting a real one" said Johnny. To add "Give it a couple of days before you try to use anything."

"Don't worry Jack, in the school, they will issue you a International I D card and a driver's license amendments, which you will learn to drive everything from a motorcycle to a semi-truck's".

"Now let's take a look at you" said Red and ads "Johnny bring Jack a belt"
Jack stood by the wall, looking at the rap sheets and wanted posters.

"Here you go," said Johnny and hands Jack a black belt, with suspenders.

"This is what I wear" said Jack

"Go ahead and put it on" said Red, stepped over and helped Jack with the belt and snapped it in place and said "On your left is a pocket for handcuffs, next to it is two clips of spare ammo clips. Which I will wait to give you a gun, till your tested".

"But next to it is a flashlight, on your left hip is a set of quick ties and another set of cuffs, they are military style." "Then on your right hip is a pocket pick, and a set of tools, next to that is an all-purpose tool." "Then this is your holster and in front of that is a place for your phone, which you put on silence and next to that is pepper spray"

"Where's the knife?" said Jack

"Oh you Germans, like that weapon that cuts instead of "said Red .

"You gotta go," said Johnny

"Come Jack, lets go", Red lead Jack.

They went through the back only to pause, in the back room for Johnny to show Jack a case of knives.   Jack picks up doubled edged titanium fighting knife and a sheath to put it in and clipped it to his belt, then followed Red out. They went into the backyard and through a gate where a large truck was running, Jack went to the passenger's side and in the back he saw a large boom and got in to say "What's that thing on the back?"

"Let's call it the equalizer," said Red who drove.

Red held onto a piece of paper and small light shone onto his dashboard, so he could see the letters.

Jack set back into the seat as the truck powered up a hill and as it crested, Red slowed the truck, going slowly on the descent he made a right hand turn and parked it, killed the lights and turned off the truck; Red looked over at Jack to see he was gone. Red scrambled to get out, only to see Jack was at the address, with knife ready, waiting.

"Are we ready to go in" said Jack

"You don't know, what he looks like," said Red

"Yeah I do, he will be the one running from us" said Jack with a smile.

"Listen to me, let me do all the talking, you're just too eager, it could get you killed" said Red.

"Kill or be killed," said Jack to himself.

Red knocked on the door, in a hesitant way only to move at the last second as a double barrel shotgun went off, putting two large holes in the front door, sending Red flying and down. Jack powered his way up and through the door and in and then tackled the shooter, like a pro and using his right forearm, Jack drove it into the guy's cheekbone and knocking the guy out. Jack then turned him over, and then used his handcuffs, Jack cuffed the guy down, and as if it was something, he did before.

Another shot rang out over Jack's head, whereas Jack rolled and threw his fighting knife it hit its mark and the guy let out a cry of

agony, Jack was already moving, he pulled the knife out from the guy's left arm and with his right hand clinched Jack drove it into the guy's solar plexus, thus doubling over the guy. Jack picked up the guy's weapon and moved back towards a room, whereas men were moving, girls were screaming and shots were being fired at Jack.
Jack returned the fire and with some accuracy, firing off the pistol in a controlled target pattern.
It ended as fast as it had begun.

"Stop firing "yelled a voice, as you could hear the sounds of cries of agony.
Red made his way next to Jack to say, "You got some massive cahuna's, my friend"

"Drop your weapons, we got you all surrounded" yelled Red back.
Weapons began to hit the floor as both Red and Jack rose with guns still out stretched.

"Whoa, it's only you two, where is the S W A T unit?"

"Who was laying down that accurate shooting?" asked one of the men.

"Who cares?" said Jack

"Up against the wall, all of you, Jack pat them down and check for weapons, use the zip ties, off your belt". One by one, Jack searched the men and then moved all the women onto the sofa.
Jack then used the zip ties to handcuff the men, overall it was five men un-hurt and two of them was hurt.
Red was on the phone calling the police and emergency crews.
While Jack had each girl get up, zip tie each one to say "We got one hurt" said Jack

"You'll have to take her in to the hospital, in the meantime take that bag over there and load it up with money, as fast as you can" motioned Red.
Jack looked around at all the stacks of money, bags of white looking powder, it was everywhere, and the girls were talking on the couch and telling them two; that their boyfriends were going to kill them.
Jack was on the floor grabbing stacks of money, wallets and stuffed it all in the medium sized bag. Jack then watched as Red began to collect the bundles of cash, and stuffed his own bag, he had swung

around his neck. Just as the first responders arrived, police swarmed the small house, with guns drawn. Jack dropped the gun he had and raised his hands.

"Were bounty hunters, him and I" said Red

The lead officer stepped forward and him and Red hugged and said "Red fancy seeing you out here, I thought you were confined to a desk, your too old to be doing this, your gonna have a heart attack"

"Yeah don't you know that, hey John I want you to meet my new recruit, his name is Jack, he is going to the academy soon."

"Hey, how are you doing, learning much from this old guy, you better take care of him?"

"You can count on that," said Jack

The officers finished the searching as one reported to John.

"We hit the mother load, John there must be over ten thousand pounds of cocaine, some heroin and an operating meth lab down stairs."

"Then on a table down stairs, we found a vault of over one hundred g's."

"Well you boys, you all just helped contribute to the policeman's fund, by eradicating some several well known drug dealers". "I'll let you both, take your two prisoners and here this is a present from the police department" John hands Jack the money bag and says "I think were off to a good start, here is my card, Jack read it said John Weston"

"If you ever need some back up or just to call and tell me what fugitive your picking up, I'll be there to assist your every need." looking at Jack with a stern look. Jack smiled back in a mocking way. John Weston says; "Now I know why Red is out from behind the desk, good luck to you and many happy arrests to come"

"Your welcome" said Jack, he bent down and picked up the weapon he took, to led and escort his female prisoner, while Red held onto the shotgun shooter. Jack led the girl out to the truck"

"No, no, no you're going to the hospital, I called a cab for you Jack, she needs medical attention immediately," said Red.

"What about the ambulance, why don't we let them handle her?" asked Jack.

"Once they get their hands on her, you lose your bounty, she is your charge now, and worth about 2500 dollars, so you remember once you make contact with a fugitive always secure them down or have them in your possession at all times. Red looked at Jack to say,   "And by the way you can have that bag of cash, use it for you tuition and some spending money, so take the cab to the hospital and get her treated and detoxed." "I'll drop off this guy and meet up with you a little later." said Red .

Jack held onto the girl with one hand and the bag of cash with the other,   Jack waited for the Cab, Jack realized, he better choose another way, so he called the cab driver, who Sam uses, and he arrived in minutes. Jack opened the door for her, and slid her in; he takes a seat next to her, to say "Please drive us to the hospital, but around the back"

Then Jack was on the phone, it rang for the longest time.

Finally she picked up to say "Who is this, restricted caller"

"It's me Jack, I need your help, can you, come by the hospital, and down to the doctor's clinic?"

"Yes, I'm already here, just working late, no particular place to go, Debbie seems preoccupied, with a new girl, some internist from the 5th floor, and I'm now officially single".

"Listen, I have a woman, who is injured in the lower leg, I need you to keep this quiet, I should be there in ten minutes, and can you detox her"

"Yes, I'm for here you my brother, but what does all this have to do with fishing"

"It doesn't, I'm working as a Bounty Hunter now" said Jack as she was quiet.

The cab sped along, as it pulled up to the back entrance of the hospital.

"Kill your light, I need you to stay here, I'll double your meter"

"Triple it and I will" said the cab driver.

"Fine" said Jack as he opened the door, to see Kate waiting, with a wheelchair, as Jack pulled her along, she began to scream, that is until Jack hit her in the stomach, so hard, she began to vomit, Jack held her away from him, to let her run her course, in the end, she continued to scream, and once again Jack punched her in the stomach, she slumped to the ground crying, and dry heaving, till Kate closed in on them to say "Stop it Jack, I've never seen this side of you. Kate helped the girl up, as she bit and held onto her arm, then Jack hit the girl in the face, which caused her to release Kate's arm, and went down, to hear Kate begin to scream, as she bled, to say;

"Oh my god, I hope she isn't HIV positive."

"Come help, her inside, said Kate.

Jack picked her up, and carried her in, and down into the doctors clinic. While Kate went to the ER, to get wrapped up, a shot taken, and a swab, to check for the HI-virus, then she came back down to the clinic, to see the girl laid out on a table, and Jack was looking through the bag, in addition to the money was ID's, and Keys.

"Jack do you know who this girl is?" said Kate looking at him.

"Nah, we raided a fugitive's house, and she came with him, he went to the Jail, and I was told to bring her here and get her leg patched up, then I will bring her to the jail"

"Alrighty then, help me with her pants."

"Her pants?"

"Yeah I need to remove them to work on her thigh, and to see if she has any other injuries", said Kate to Jack who went to her feet, slipped off her shoes, and yanked her pants.

"Are you alright" asked Jack. To Kate.

"I'll be fine, I just can't believe, you're a Bounty Hunter, of all the professions, you know what, you are really a bad man, and you know what, my sister, will so love this"

Kate un-did the girls pants, as Jack pulled them down, to see that she wore no underwear, he had them in his hands, when out of the pocket an ID, fell out.

Jack picked it up, to say "Her name is Tiffany West"

"That's why she looks so familiar; I went to school with her"

"Med school"

"No silly, high school, her and I graduated together, now look at her, she is a waste, and this is what drugs does to you, as Kate went to the computer screen, next to the bed, and typed her name and info in, she came up, HIV Negative, as of last month. "She came in for a miss- carriage", said Kate.

"Wow, too bad for her"

"The wound is superficial, who ever shot her knew how to aim, and the bullet went clean through, was that you Jack"

"No, it wasn't me, I'll I did was escort her here, it was Red.

"You mean Big Bad James Combs, also known as Red"

"Sounds like you know him"

"I do, he and I dated, after I got out of Med School and as I joined the practice here, about four years ago"

"What happen" asked Jack

"He cheated on me and with every other girl out there, that man is a pig"

"Really because from me, it sounds like, you still have some feeling for him"

"Doubtful, but its true, that after him, I swear off all men, and just dated girls"

"That's your problem, you want women."

"Just, look at yourself, hey how old are you, what your what 28, and your sister is what 22,"

"Try 23, and I'm 27, going on 28"

"Alright, how is it that you stole, most of the men away from your sister, when, oh Kay" Jack changed his thought, to say;

"Your four years apart"

"Well, she would bring them home and I'd put on my southern charm, and flash them my privates to lure them into my bed"

"There is another word for that"

"Actually there is, I'd prefer you not to use it, be respectful Jack"

"How is she Tiffany West doing?"

"Well I gave her a sedative, so she should be out for a while; I patched up her leg and gave her some anti-bionics, so now it's just you and I"

"Sorry to ruin that party, but I gotta go, take her to Jail, and spend the night with Sara" said Jack, pulling Tiffany's pants back on, and up, then snapped them back in place, replaced her shoes, and reached in to pick her up, to say "Thanks Kate, I hope you keep this our secret"

"Just as long as you come back and give me pleasure"

Jack walked out the door to say "Never in a million years"

The cab driver, opened up the back door, so Jack could set her in, for him to say "Why don't you sit in the front seat"" by the way my name is Leon, and your is "

"Jack", thinking about his cash bag,

Jack closed the back door, then went around, saying;

"Stay here, I gotta go back in"

"Will do" said the cabbie.

Jack went back in, to grab his bag and when he came out the cab was gone.

Jack's head was not in it, he mind was racing, as he walked the main street next to the hospital, then down the street a ways, only to see that same cab, nearly sideswipe him, he lowered the window, to say;

"Sorry man, I was running out of gas, I filled back up, I saw the way the two of you were looking at each other, and I know you're a player"

Jack sat next to him, and closed the door to say "On to the jail", then looks at him to say "How do you know that"

"Cause you're him"

"Who's that?"

"The mob is swarming, about a guy who killed the bosses' son.

You fit the bill, if I were you I get out of town for awhile till all of this blows over or there will be lots of blood shed"

"What will it take for you to keep your mouth shut?"

Jack digs into his bag, to pull out five, one hundred dollars in bills"

"That's a start"

"How about, I do what I've done to others, and stop this cab, and cap the two of you's." said Jack looking at him

Jack showed Leon his pistol..

"Whoa mister, you got me all wrong, five hundred is fine, your one bad dude, you don't have to worry about what I say, your reputation is growing with each passing moment"

"What reputation?" asked Jack?

"Oh the one, that you're a major player with the ladies, take for instance, that Doctor you saw, her name is Kate, her and her sister are the society of Mobile, and your all over that, then, you got little Miss Samantha Smith, on the hook, I'd love to tap that myself, but you know I ain't got the balls, and whoever else you might throwing it too, your dangerous and very unpredictable."

"True, true, thanks for the ride, oh one more question, and do you know where High-Gate Lane is?"

"Yeah, about a mile, due north of here, take Adams to West, then North, to a gated community, follow the road, around, and its about a few houses on the hill overlooking the city."

"Thanks, you want me to wait"

"Nah, you go, I'll be fine" said Jack, as he gets Tiffany out of the back, and carries her to the prisoner entrance, and touches the buzzer, the door opens, Jack walks in, to hear "State your name"

"Jack Cash, Bounty Hunter, here with Tiffany West fugitive"

"Place her on the bench, and I need to see your ID and papers"

Jack checked around and realized he had no papers, to see through the window.

The phone number to the bail bonds, and dialed it up, it rang and rang, and then at the last minute it was answered by a girl.

"Put Red on, It's Jack Cash"

Moments later, he answered, to say "Where are you at boy"

"At the Jail"

"No, no, no, bring her here, we need to fill out the paperwork, how is she?"

"Out of it"

"Great, come on by"

"Officer, we are stepping out", as Jack picked her lifeless body up, and was buzzed out. Jack walked next door, to see the door was open, and a smile on Red's face, who says "We got ourselves a natural born hunter, put her in the back"

Jack carried to a bed, and laid her down, then walked out, as Johnny closed the grated holding cell.

" So you're the real deal"

177

"Look Jack, we have a certain way we handle female prisoners, first we sober them up, from the detox drugs they give to them, then we have them checked for HIV and STD's, if they are clean, then we fuck them till there bowlegged, some may pled it out but not this one, a once beauty queen, will be another notch, in my belt" said Red.

"I guess she is all yours then"

"Whoa where are you going" asked Red

"I got some unfinished business I need to take care of"

"No your not, to be one of us, you get the first shot, and you'd better make it a good one" said Red, as Jack looked back at the passed out Tiffany to say "Alright, when she wakes up, give me a call", said Jack as he pulled off his harness, and his knife and hands it to Red. While he carried the money bag out.

Jack was out the door, only to turn back to see the startled looks on the rest of the guys.

"Hey what is your cell number" asked Jack as the two of them exchanged numbers, Jack said "But seriously I need to finish something, but the moment she wakes up, call me, and I will come back and do her, no one else is first right?"

"That's right Jack said Red, go have your fun, and while you're out can you bring us some beer and whiskey back"

"Absolutely Red" said Jack, as he left.

Red got up and closed the door and locked it down, to say;

"There is a true Bounty Hunter, the way he went in, he was fearless, Johnny, this guy may someday become a legend, you guys go in the back, and I need to make a private call"

Jack drove Sara's car with enthusiasm and zeal, as he took the cabbies advice, as it led him up to the gated community, he turned off, and parked on the street, he put his bag in the trunk, hopped over a fence, and quickly ran up the road, passing each house until he came to hers.

Jack checked the address, he saw hers then went around the huge mansion, to the lower level, and onto the covered patio, all was quiet, and so Jack stopped, sat down, and dialed her up.

Cassandra answered the phone to say "Hello, who is this"

"Jack, I'm out back, do you want to let me in"

"Of course, I'll slid the sliding glass open, you slip in"
Jack waited, then he saw the door, slid open, he stepped in, to the dark room, to hear" Please take off your shoes"
Jack closed the door, and took off the shoes, he saw her in the shadows, wearing very little, she motioned for him to come to her, they met at the doorway, and kissed, Jack's hands were all over her breasts, for Jack to say "Where's your old man?"

"He is out of town, to New Orleans for the rest of the weekend, but I will tell you this, your late, and now you'll have to make it up."

"In addition, I have a spy watching us, let me take you upstairs, and I will show you".
Jack followed her up, the lowly lighted rooms, to a room that had no windows, it was a closet, the light was on, he could really see through what she was wearing, for her to say "Your way late"

"Sorry I had some things I needed to do, but I'm here now"

"In the next room is the bathroom, I'll run a bath, then the pervert will be watching me, there is a telescope, in the next room, and its fixed on his position, as I slip in, see if you can catch him".

"Sure no problem" said Jack, he went into the other room.
Jack looked around the room, and then peered in through the scope, to see, a woman, half nude, doing something on a mat, she was graceful, and somewhat sexy, she was even hotter than Cassandra. Jack moved it around; he saw his intended target, staring through a telescope, back at him. Jack looked through the doorway to see Cassandra posing, nude, with her butt up against the glass, for Jack to say "Talk about egging him on, why you don't go down there and have a threesome with them"

"Cause there not married, she lives in one part and he lives in the other"

"So you've tried"

"No that guy, is a psycho, besides I have you tonight, come in here, and turn out the dimmer light, we can see with all of these candles" she said. To add "Did you see um?"

"Yeah who is it?" asked Jack.

"Well I could tell you and then you would have to beat him up, because he does this every night, just come in here and make love to me"

Jack entered the room, and turned down the lights way low, he pulled off his dirty tank top and undid his pants, he stood in front of her, he being this buff guy, with his taunt body.

For her to say "Come to me, with that beautiful body"

Jack eased into the tub, slowly, the hot water, felt good, as he slid in, looking at Cassandra wasn't half bad either, she looked amazing, without any clothes on, she sat on one end, across from him, he pulled up some of the bubbles, to his chest, then found the soap, and began to lather up his body.

Cassandra said "Why don't you come closer, and turn around, I'll wash your back"

Jack moved, turned, and eased up next to her, she had her legs spread, to allow him even closer.

she took out a luffa sponge, and began exfoliating his back and arms, her soft touch was incredible to feel, then Jack rested his head on her shoulder, as she worked over his chest.

Jack closed his eyes, and then for the first time in his life he felt safe.

She took her time with each stroke, and with her other hand, she touched him, it felt soft, secure, and non-evasive, she took her time, Jack thought "This is what a baby must feel, and I like it."

She began to lightly kiss his neck, then wrapped her arms around him.

She continued, then under his arms, down to his manhood, as things were heating up, she touched him first, and began to stroke it lightly, as quickly Jack was ready, she knew it to say "Turn around"

Jack did as he was told, and scooted back down to his side as the water was cooling, he eased his head back, only to feel Cassandra, ease on down, as she straddled him, taking all of him into her, she whispered "You know my policy is always a condom, but for tonight, its an exception, just don't come inside of me"

She grinded on him, and worked her magic as he was thinking of running in the fields, while she was getting off, and his mind was elsewhere, while she took advantage of him. Upon her last and final

climax, she rested on him to say "I can't believe you're still hard, you know I should call my friend Terri, to come over here"
Jack opened his eyes to look at her as she extracted herself off of him, she eased on out of the tub, to make the call, moments later the two were having a conversation, as Jack tried to hear.

"Sleeping beauty rests, come on over here, your man's out of town, I have a huge stud in my bath, who just satisfied me, and he needs more, so come on over, yes put your IUD in, and get over here, hey can you call Marci and see if she is interested as well'
Jack looked at her as she looked back at him to say "I know you must be almost double my age, but, your staying power has wore me out, I have a super hot girlfriend coming over, and she will probably bring her friend with her, don't worry, it won't be long, they live next door."

"Are they as hot as you are"

"Yeah, even hotter, Terri is this little thing barely 5-5, and her friend is tall like me, her name is Marci, both of them are sexually deprived, and wouldn't you know it, their husbands are all out of town, like mine is, come to think of it, they all said they had to go to New Orleans, separately of course, interesting "
Jack rested, while Cassandra, let the water out, and turned on the warm water, at the same time, she placed a towel by Jack's leg, as she turned on the hot water, for her to say, "Do you want to get out while I fix the tub"
Jack pulled himself up, then went over to the toilet to do his business.
Jack watched Cassandra, bent over, refilling the tub, he finished his business to flush, he got up, he was still ready to go , when he tried it sick it into her from behind, she was just holding on, when all of a sudden she was dry, and she said "Please stop, that hurts me Jack, pulled it out", to see Cassandra, turn to see, she was crying, quickly she turned her head away and wiped the tears away.
She was in tears as she said "you hit the wrong hole".

"Your water is ready, have fun with my friends, I need to go lay down, and rest."
Jack watched her leave, as he washed himself up, he turned to hear a noise, to say "Come on in, I won't bite"

There standing in a white robe, from what he could see was this adorable girl, who was very petite, step in to say "where's Cassandra?'

"She isn't feeling well, and went to bed,".
Her curiosity made her come forward, she saw him, to say;

"I've never done this before, but I'm so sexually frustrated, will you, be careful with me?"

"Absolutely, go ahead and take off that robe, let's see what you have under that thing"
She was hesitating, but went ahead, and undone the belt, she opened up to show him that she wore pajama's, a cute top and full bottoms.

"Go ahead, and remove those"

"Well I never have undressed, in front of anyone before"

"If you're going to get in the bath, you're going to have to take off something, or it will get wet"

"True, but can I turn around?"

"Nah, come closer, I want to touch you" said Jack, as she slowly moved towards him, until he could touch her leg, he took his left hand and placed it on her thigh to say "Now pull off you top"
She began to shake, but slowly, pulled off her pajama top, for him to see, she had a white bra on.

"Come closer" said Jack to add "Now take off your bottoms, as he touched her breasts, she quickly pulled away.

"No your not, step closer, now take off your pants" demanded Jack, as she slowly pulled them down, to show off her white panties.

"Now off with your bra" said Jack
Slowly she reached around to the back and unfastened it.

"Now let it fall off"
She held her hand up, to cover them up as she pulled the bra off.

"Next is your panties, use both hands and pull them down, to your knees" said Jack, who was watching her every move, as she let her hand drop, he could see that her shaking was nearly gone, as a new confidence had come over her, as she did what she was told.

For him to say "Stop right there, leave them be, now turn around and grab your ankles"

She slowly turned around, bent over, as Jack slowly moved up, as she went down, he put his nose in between her, and smelled, then begin to lick her, to the point where she was leaning into him, to the point, Jack repositioned himself on the top stair, while Terri lowered herself onto his manhood. It was like an awakening for her, she was in control as she rode his stick.

Jack had her breasts in his hands, as her first orgasm, was heard throughout the house, she sprayed him all over, and stopped to say;

"Oh my god what did I do"

"Nothing, that is normal, now come back on here and ride it some more".

This time she didn't hesitate, she, said "I want you on the floor, mister"

"Names Jack"

"I don't care, face up" she demanded, Jack stood up, to see someone standing at the door was this tall gorgeous blonde who Jack said "Well hello."

"Take a number Marci, he is mine first" she commanded.

Jack lay down on the carpeted floor, with his head back as Terri, went over spread her legs, then knelt down and inserted it back inside of her, to take all of him and began to grind, while Jack played with her breasts. Then out of no where, she bent over and began to open mouth kiss Jack, their two tongues met in a match, while he continued to gyrate with her, building up another climax, she heighten up and began to scream, she let out, and it was over as she dumped another load of fluids on him, they were both sweated, and both of them looked up to see Marci playing with herself, watching them.

Terri pulled her strength together to say "This one isn't done yet Marci".

"This one still has a lot of fight left in him, she said as she extracted herself off of Jack to show her why, Jack's manhood was still at attention, for him to say "Next"

"Oh my god, look how big that thing is" said a gushing Marci to add "That's twice as big as my husband's"

"So what are you waiting for" said Terri, who saw the bath, was her next spot to visit, to freshen up.

"Its getting cold" said Jack looking up at Marci, who slid down her panties, to get ready to mount Jack when he said;

"Are you sure, you want to get that dress dirty, why don't you take it off"

She looked down at him with a smile, then unbuttoned it, and then pulled it off, to expose, her blonde patch, and white bra, which she just popped off, to let her beautiful breast's free, as she looked down at Jack to say "shall I just sit on it"

"Yeah go for it" yelled Terri.

"Shut up, the neighbors will hear us," said Marci, as she spread her legs, and slowly went down, to insert Jack into her, all the way down, she could feel him inside of her, she placed her hands on his chest to say" Your so, so big, your like a horse, you fill me in every way, can I just hold it in there"

"Sure, if I can kiss your lips and touch your breasts"

She leaned over, to allow him to caress her creamy soft natural breasts, to say "I've never kissed any other man before."

"That was our deal, your holding it inside of you for some kisses" said Jack

"A deal is a deal, she leaned over and her lips touched his lips, parted them and touched tongues, a kiss led to a half hour of lip locking, slow grinding, and several climaxes for her.

Jack's hands thoroughly worked over her breasts, pulling on her nipples, but what he discovered, was the contour of a woman's body, her waist, her arms, her neck, and her soft legs, as she laid back, for him to rise up and mount her, he entered her, he had her legs spread wide, as Jack's big manhood, was in a long stroke, out a long stroke, using his hands to take a long stroke.

Jack was beginning to like to touch other parts, and when the newly clean Terri came over to be part of the fun, well she lowered herself on Marci's mouth.

Jack played with her small breasts, she herself wanted to continue the kissing, so she initiated it with Jack and was pulling his face to hers, she too was kissing his neck, face and pulled away to say ;

"You need some moisturizer, I know a great spa, to exfoliate your face and body, and you're drilling the owner"

Jack continued what he was doing, it was sheer pleasure for him, which he decided it was time to let go, to say "I'm ready to let go"

"I want it " said Terri, who interrupted them, and his train of thought. To add "Do me from behind. As she got up, and positioned herself on the steps up to the bath, Jack got up and checked his position this time, and bent down, to slowly insert it to the very end when it stopped.

"That's it, you hit that spot and I'll explode" said Terri

Jack kept his pace as he went slowly at first, gauging the distance, while Marci had her arms wrapped around his chest and was kissing on his neck, he was gaining momentum, as her breathing was getting quicker, until she yelled out now, hit it now."

Jack touched it so ever so lightly, and the tapping was regular as it was what did it, as she let go, soaking him, several times more, to collapse on the steps of the bath with exhaustion, but he was still very hard. To say "It's your turn now" said Jack.

Marci moved in next to her neighbor, as Jack pulled out of Terri, who crawled into the tub, to put her flames out.

Jack repositioned himself behind the taller Marci, whose butt was in the air, he pulled it down, as he inserted into her, for her to say "You can drop that load off into me, if you like, I'm on the pill".

Jack went all the way in, to another stopping point, pulled back a ways, then began to stroke her, she was extremely wet,, and the slow grinding felt good to Jack thinking I could go all night, as he looked out, he saw the upper light of the house below go out, but the lower light was still on, as the young woman was naked as she stood in front of the glass. As Jack was stroking Marci he saw the girl, her perfect silhouette was evident as she danced. The two saw each other as Jack continued to take Marci from behind, till she let out a scream, "I'm coming."

Eruption, after eruption, she collapsed, as she pulled off of Jack. He still showed how very hard his manhood was.

For him to hear" Oh my god, your purple, you need to let that thing dump.

Terri said, to add "Help me out, she said to her friend, as she tried to get Jack's meat into her mouth, with no success, so she stroked it with her small petite hands, for her to say "Marci help me out"

"I can't I'm exhausted" she said as she lay back in the cool tub.

Jack heard his phone ring, so he left Terri, as she was not helping any, as he was swinging freely, to answering it" Yes"

"Hey this is Red, Tiffany's up, and wants some meat"

"Alright I'll be there in thirty"

Jack closed up the phone to see both girls were exhausted, for Jack to say "Come on ladies you're letting me down"

"Call us later and we will give you a rain check", then they both passed out.

Jack quickly got dressed, and thought about Cassandra, one more time, then went down stairs, slipped his shoes on, he was still so very hard, it was hard for him to walk, let alone run, as he decided to check out that nude girl, still dancing at two in the morning?.

Jack came, up to a short fence, to see that lower part of the house had a balcony, as Jack still saw she was still oblivious to his appearance, he tried the door, it was locked. So he knocked on her door, moments later, the door opened slightly, to say "Who are you"

"I'm the one you had been watching, from your window"

"It wasn't me, you must be talking about my husband"

"Why don't you let me in, it's cold out here"

"I can't because I have no clothes on"

"Why's that, why are you nude, now to me that's an invitation, to have someone come in there and screw you"

Jack couldn't wait any longer, as he pushed the door open, to see her standing there in the nude, her long flowing hair and her innocence, her fingers buried in her box to say " Your a man's man, that was hot, you slayed three women, all them rich, you turned me on so much, I just was hoping you'd come down here, come in and now take off you clothes, here let me help you" she pulled Jack's tank top off, and undid his pants, to see that purple thing pop out, to see her gush over it.

She went to her knees, to work on him, as her other hand was in her box.

It was some what exciting for Jack, but as she had trouble while it was in her mouth, the fun was over, and he took charge, and forced her down, inserted it into her, and stroked her out, finding her spot. Jack hit it several times till she released, but it was no use, he was in his head, as he continued to get her off, he still couldn't pull the trigger, he got off of her, leaving a pool of fluids under her, she waved goodbye, as he dressed, he left her house, and walked weirdly to Sara's car, he got in, to get stuck, and it hurted, he drove slowly back to the Bail Bonds place, he got out, up the stairs, he knocked, and Red, let him in.

"She is up and ready, coincidently she asked for you as well"

Jack went to her door, to see a totally different looking girl, Johnny unlocked the door, opened it, and Jack went in, maybe it was the light , but she looked hot, but instead of her, taking off her clothes it was Jack who turned into a madman, and began to rip off her clothes, as the rough sex began, she slapped him, as he ripped off her shirt and bra, and then it got all quiet as Jack had her pants off , his was down to his ankles, he noticed a stack of condoms, he took one, ripped it open, and peeled it on his swollen manhood. As he had her legs pinned down.

Jack with his manhood he surged in and out of her wet box, from the roughness turned soft to playful, Jack kept his distance as he continued the spearing, judging her distance, he hit her spot, as her fingernails dug into Jack's bare back, she let out a scream, and erupted, which drove Jack to do the same, and he pulled out, and with such force blew off the condom and sprayed the room down. She smiled at him, then used her feet and kicked him back, to say "I'm ready for the next guy".

Jack held the door open for Johnny, who was the next eager lad, only to say   "It's gross in here Red"

"Jack a moment of your time", was Red watching Jack dress.

"Yeah sure what's up"

"Well I called a friend of mine, and he said he could get you in on the next class at the academy, I guess something about how they need hunters immediately, I told him about you and he said you're in, so congrats man, The next class starts, this coming Monday."

"Really, cause I got a few things working now"

"The sooner the better for you, so what was your take , you know the bag you took"

"I don't know, I haven't counted it"

"What have you been doing then?"

"Satisfying a half of dozen girls tonight"

"Sure, " he said sarcastically, to add" So we will leave today around 6 pm, I'll drive you."

"I'll have to think about that one"

" Don't think too long, this is a once in a lifetime opportunity"

"Alright I'll see you, tonight then.

PART 1

The Attempted Breakup

J ack eased into the room, to see that it was quiet, on the bed was Sara past out, while Jack placed the bag, on the dresser, then went in and took a shower, cleaned up, stepped out and dried off, then placed the towel around his waist. Jack went out and picked up the bag, and set it on the table, then turned it over, he set out all the bundles of one hundreds, then fifties, then twenties, then tens, then fives, then ones., all in all, in there was one hundred thousand in 100's, and the rest all equaled, a quarter of a million dollars, lots of bills, stacked neatly, fit nicely, with some room to spare. Jack was winding down, so he pulled off his towel, and slipped into the sheets with his love goddess.

During the early morning, Jack was trying to sleep, but his mind was back with that damn sexy Marci, whose sexy and curvy body was a supreme turn on, she was fit and every part of her body gave Jack wood, that was the type of girl he wanted to be with, he thought. Then he moved closer to the sleeping Sara, her back was to his, he placed his cool hand on her warm hip, to run it up to her armpit, and then back down again, thinking of this as Marci and her spa, as Terri told him.

Jack continued down to her butt, he followed the rounds and then down to that place, where the thigh meets the butt, nothing, Jack felt nothing, unlike Marci, he had constant growing wood, and then there was that very sexy exhibitionist, for all to see, that girl had one killer body, the lines on her was incredible, he remembers touching her and running his hands down that well sculptured back, Jack could feel it rising, he stroked it himself a bit, to get that feel, as he moved closer to Sara, he lowered down, to stick it in, she move abit, to allow him access. She was wet with each stroke, he was limited on how far he could go, as his energy was also a factor, this was all totally different than, Cassandra, Terri, and then Marci, and above all Marci is the one who stands out, she was the tightest and most fulfilling. Sara continued to sleep through the encounter, but her juices told another story, as he worked, a puddle of her fluids, were spreading, to where he was working it out, as his mind was elsewhere, when he finally, concentrated on her, he let go, to drop another load, he could barely keep awake, to fall fast asleep.

It was early afternoon, on Sunday; Sara woke to have to feel something inside of her.

She reached back to feel it was her man, she knew they must have had a good time but she couldn't remember it, she lay in a pool of her fluids, she slowly pulled away from him.

Sara got up, and went into the bathroom, and took care of her business, she came out of there, to see the big bag on the table, next to it was a passport, and a license, and a phone. She pulled it up to her swollen eyes to read it said "Jack Cash, address, she really didn't know where that was, then she looked at his passport to see he was a German citizen, from Cologne, "interesting" she thought. She then looked up at the clock it read "1:26 PM".

"Wow I did over sleep; she looked at her man asleep, on the bed, to go back to the bag. Inside was money lots of it, she took out a bundle of 100's, and flipped with her hand.

She sat in silence, thinking "From now on I'll never need to work ever again, this man is a money making machine, I'd better go over there and wake him up"

Sara jumped on the bed, and then crawled onto Jack, as he rolled over, and she fell off the bed, she got back up and tried, to finally see he was awake, to say, "I know who you are now"

"Really "said Jack, to add, "Did you talk with your sister"

Sara looked at Jack to pause, to think what she was going to say and said, "Are you and her sleeping together?"

She waited for him to answer, and then she started to punch him in the face and body, she was crying then Jack backhanded her, sent her flying into the wall, she slumped down, in a daze, she looked at him, and then began to cry.

Jack looked at her, as he slid to the side of the bed, to say;

"I think it's over"

"Why because your fucking my sister?"

"No, I just want out"

She got up, went into the bathroom, and slammed the door shut.

Jack got up, started to get dressed, he went over to the table to see a loose bundle, of 100's he tossed back into the bag, he put his wallet and passport away, to slip on his shoes, he grabbed the bag, as he went to the door to hear "Wait, what have I done to cause this?"

"Nothing, as Jack turned the knob.

"Was it that I hit you?"

"You're getting warmer"

"Couples have fights all the time, listen come back here, let's talk" said Sara.

Jack stopped, to close the door; he turned around to see her do a dance, to say, "You like my body right?"

Jack watched her to say," Well that you mentioned it"

"What, come on, we just had sex, and you sure liked it then, so what has changed since then"

"You hitting me for no apparent reason, is a start"

"You slept with my sister, that slut steals all my guys".

"So yeah, I flew off a little bit, look I'm sorry, it will never happen again"

Jack just looked at her, wanting to go; maybe back to that hot girl he did this morning, and takes her away from her peeping tom husband, or that Marci, wow"

"What are you thinking about?"

"Leaving, you hit me once, you'll hit me twice"

"that is bullshit, Jack, I hit you and you hit me back, I think its even now, ever since we first met, you been wanting to go, well you can't, not like this, it has to be for a better reason than that, so lets go back to my apartment, you have your stuff their, we will talk this out and see if we can come up with amicable closure or we make up, stay here and I will get dressed, you can watch if you like, I know how that turns you on".

Sara sat in silence with her arms crossed and looking out the closed window as Jack drove, he kept speeding the car up.

"Is it something I said or did, to make you upset with me?" said Sara in a huff.

Jack was silent, as he drove faster.

"Why won't you answer me, are you sleeping with my slut of a sister of mine, you won't answer me on that, just what is it then?"

"I've decided to leave, its over between us," said Jack

"What, that's it, people just don't break up simple because one wants to leave, for what, is it travel, listen I don't care if you did sleep with her".

"I just need to know, I still want to marry you, hell I don't care if you sleep with the whole town, answer me did you sleep with my sister?"

"No", "I didn't, are you happy now"

"Then why did you ask me to ask her about you?"

"I don't know, but I don't think this is going to work out"

"Stop saying that, what is wrong with you, are you mad I passed out last night, cause I talked with Kerrie and she said;

"Nothing happened, that you left, listen whatever it is, I'll do for you, if you want ten girlfriends, then you can have them, what can I say or do to put this back in the place it was last night, tell me Jack and I will do it"

"No it's not about you," said Jack

"Then who is it about?", at least your talking to me, is it because I snooped through your stuff, I will tell you this, from now on I'll never ever do that again, tell me what I need to do to make this the same"

"Nothing, its just over, why can't you understand that, look you're a nice and pretty girl.

"With a rich background, you don't need a guy like me"

Jack pulled the car into the parking space at her apartment, and parked it, he handed her his keys, for her to say.

"Wait, I need to know what I did that was so bad, I need closure, alright I'll let you go Jack, but will you come up stairs with me, to talk this out, then I will feel better, when you leave my life for good"

Jack looked at her, to say, "Alright, lets go upstairs, and we will talk"

"Great, follow me, remember I have your keys now"

Jack followed Sara up the stairs, as down in the courtyard, there was an afternoon party in full swing, he felt tired and worn out, that park was really fun but was still pooped out and love to take a nap"

Sara unlocked the door, to say, "Do you want to change out of those clothes, they look dirty."

Jack went into the bedroom, while Sara went to the closet, Jack found another tank top, and jeans only to look up to see Sara at the door with a gun held on him.

"Now I want answers, who is she Jack?"

"What are you talking about?"

"The girl, or whoever she is, that's why men leave, either for that or something much more bigger than all of us, which is it, you know what I'm going to do the same thing you did to me, hold this gun on you till I get the answers, I think that are true"

Jack took a seat, to look at her, to say "fire away"

"I'm not going to shoot you, I love you, and there is no other person that I want to spend the rest of my life with"

"So I should rush you and then it will be over and I will leave"

"Don't try me Jack, I know I'd say I wouldn't shoot you, but test me and I might just end your life, then mine, you got that?"

"Alright I'll stay here, what do you want to know?"

"What happen last night to cause all of this?"

"Nothing really, it was this morning, actually when I found out that I was accepted to go to the e Bounty Hunter's Academy"

"So why would that change our relationship?"

"I don't know, I guess I'd be leaving, and didn't want to hurt you like that guy you were seeing, and he went into the service"

"so this is what this is all about, something my sister said to you and everyone else, that I had a boyfriend, that left me, to go into the service and never saw me again, is that it?"

"Yeah, sort of, something like that"

"Oh that bitch, she is gonna pay for lying to you, you see Jack it was her, who stoled him away from me, when she slept with him, the day before he left, to tell him that I wasn't interested in him anymore, but it wasn't true, Jack I want to tell you this, did you know that I was adopted by the Sanders."

"It was Grandpa Sanders that loved me as a child, when he pasted, Greg and Heidi adopted me, so that is why Kate is the way she is with me and the men in my life."

'Now that, that is out in the open, what's next, where are we at, do you still want to go, without me?"

"I don't know, Red says that for me to stay in this country I need to marry someone"

"Yes, yes, yes, you want to do it today, let's fly to Las Vegas, and we will be married, what do you say"

"That you have all the answers" said Jack, as he gets up, she waves the gun at him, to sit back down, for Jack to say "listen, I really don't know my background, or who my real name is, so most of my life is a lie"

"So that's it, that's why you want to run, let me tell you what I know, I know who you are, I looked you up on the internet, and found you, your what every young girl's dreams are made up of, you're a International Super Spy, yes I know about you, you see I know you need help, the moment we met, I knew I could trust you and I made sure that you could trust me, that is why I paraded all my friends in front of you for your taking.

"Jack Cash as you want to be called, that is fine with me, call me Sara Cash, I don't care, what's important to me is that you know that you have me for the rest of your life, also I do know that our country is in short supply of spies, and at some point I knew that you would leave, but here me out, I'll let you go, under one condition"

Jack looks up at her.

"That you marry me first, or if something happens where you find someone else first, then me second or third or so forth, anyway you look at it, I want to be one of your wives"

Jack looked at her to say "What are you talking about, I'll I'm doing is going to Bounty Hunters Academy"

"Now where are we at? Do you still despise me or can I put this gun down and have make up sex"

"Alright, your right I wanted to leave, because I do know that I was once a spy, true, but I didn't want you to get hurt" "Let me finish, the drive over here taught me that those you can trust you hold onto, those that are suspicious you eliminate, your one I can trust but before you come over to me, I want my own concessions."

"Name it and I will do it

First, I want your body to be as perfect as it can be"

"That easy enough, I'll go to the gym everyday. Any where in particular you want shaped up?"

"No, all over"

"Fine you got that, anything else"

Jack looked at her, to think, for her to say, "So this is what it is really all about, my body isn't it"

She looked at Jack who turned his head away from her, for her to say   "I know I've been lazy, letting myself get bigger, well that will all change, your right I will work out, while your gone and when you get back, I'll be back to my old self"

Jack looked at her to say, "I'm sorry, come over here"

Sara came to him, handed the gun to him, he placed it down and sat down as she sat on his lap to say, "I promise with all my heart, that you can trust me, I will be your loyal servant".

"From this day forward, I will do what ever you ask of me, and I will never ever get in your way or express any envy or jealousy, for the rest of my internal life, and I make the promise that, I will give you as many babies as you so desire, and I will start to make up for this miss-understanding right now, who do you want me to call to come over to further our pleasure"

"No one, I just want you" said Jack as the two kissed.

She broke the kiss to say "Really, I want to make it up to you, my dear, is there anyone you want me to call to invite over"

"How about Leslie, she seemed fun"

"Sorry I can't I broke up with her and she isn't talking to me"

"Give her a call anyway"

"O Kay dear, I will for you"

Jack was on his phone making a call to his new friend Red, while Sara dialed up her friend Leslie as Red answered.

Jack said, "Yeah Red, when do you want to go, really that soon, I think my girlfriend wants to go, really alright I will tell her, see you soon, bye."

Jack closes up the phone and waited to see her come back, wiping her face of tears, with the closet bag in hand, to say, "Here is you gun bag do you want to take it"

"Nah, it will stay here with you, as well as the guns, you know for protection".

"Red, said you can't go, he is going up to Montgomery to catch a bail jumper and thinks it may be too dangerous for you, I'm sorry"

"That's not the right answer, my question to you is am I going to be on of your wives or not"

"Yes, yes, you are "but, before Sara could react, Jack says, "What shall I tell Red"

"That I want the last few hours to be spent with my husband, we are getting married right"

"Absolutely, now come over here and kiss your husband."

"Gladly, I was being serious; who do you want me to call."

"How about Natasha Rogers" she stopped in her tracks, to look at him, for her to say, "You know her."

"her name is Nattie to us sorority girls, I met her in college, she was a slut, tramp, whatever, she did a story about you, and shared some of that information with the other sisters, that we actually tried to visit you up in Atlanta, but she found out much more than she told us, like you have a Mom and a sister who was trying to get you out of prison"

"Really how much more do you know, and what, if I wanted to break up with you in the future, you would have played that information, be truthful with me Sara"

"I will, I will never use anything against you ever, you're going to be my husband, if you want I will go find her and drag her to you"

"I like that, now were getting somewhere, so I have a sister and a Mom"

"Don't forget a soon to be wife, a conniving sister-in-law, a younger brother, and my parents, who like you immensely, actually you brought us all closer, so Jack don't be so hard on yourself, you have a family that we support you through thick and thin." " Let's get back to me, what is it you want from me? A child, one you can call your own," said Sara

"I don't know, I've been so alone most of my life, I know what I really like is the hospital's buffet line"

"So you're saying you want a great cook, you know my grandmother is a wonderful cook, maybe I should go and spend some time with her and learn how to cook the right way"

"Or I could send you to school"

"The only school, I'm going to is Med school to be a doctor, your gonna need someone to patch you up and to take care of you when you get older"

"I'll pay for that"

"No need to, it's already paid for, by my grandfather"

"So why haven't you been going"

"Like you I felt lost, alone, but all that has changed, you're my light as we passed in the night, but instead of going different directions, we will be separate for a while, but in the end we will reunite as one"

"I agree with that, we have a partnership for life, I guess there is a lot I need to tell you"

"Now you have to kiss me, first" said Sara waiting.
Jack leaned in and Sara grabbed at Jack's neck to pull him closer as she lifted herself up onto Jack's waist and straddled him with her legs by wrapping them around Jack's waist.
She said "Jack I love you, you're the best thing to come into my life and I will forever be yours" she kissed him on his neck.
Jack fumbled with her tank top.

"Do me Jack"

"First I want to talk with you, I want to be honest with you, other than being in prison, for who knows what reason, I did buy that boat, and do want to go fishing, in the mean time while I'm away, I want you and this other girl to watch over it and make sure it gets accomplished, while I'm away"

"Who is she?"

"Her name is Samantha Smith"

Sara looked at him to say, "How do you know her"

"Let's say we met"

"That was you, Oh my god, you are the one who inspired her, wow, and how did you know"

"Well she just turned me on and I went for it"

"What do you mean; Kate told me what you did for her, the flowers and the kindness"

"I was the other guy as well"

"get out, you're the one, who took her to bed and slayed her, well Jack I'm very surprised, I had no idea you had that kind of compassion, let alone the instincts to bed that one, I'm impressed, do you want her in our bed"

"Will you let me?"

"Of course, are you kidding she is gorgeous, I can see why you like her she is very pretty, this is getting me very wet"

"Well you know about Debbie"

"Yeah I saw you drill her in the hot tub, no big news their, except getting back at my sister, way to go, so far your choosing the right ones, tell me my sister"

"Nah, I just put my finger inside of her, then your dad walked in, but then I did do the internist on the 5th floor, I think her name is Mary, who Debbie is now in love with, enough of them.

"What I want you to do, is get to know Samantha, and she will formulate a plan to help us with the charter business, and take care of her other needs if you know what I mean"

"I do, you can count on me, and really I can call her and have her come over",

"She is still in the hospital, but I will consider it later, next I need you to secure a place for this charter business, there was a place for lease behind a crab shack, on the Public's Pier"

"I know of that place I eat there from time to time"

"Good, if you need money I will get it to you or take it out of this bag"

"Is that all sir",

"Turn around I want you from behind."

Sara did as she was told and turned, then bent over at the waist, as Jack slide down her loose fitting shorts, and mounted her and forced his way in, it easily penetrated, she was very wet and ready, Jack realized this was a fun position and held on to her hips and continued to ram it deeper, with each passing stroke. He then kept the momentum building within her as Jack could feel the urge to let go when Sara yelled out

"Jack I'm coming now"

Jack could feel her tighten up and then a wave of wetness exploded out.

Jack let go his load as well, she convused on his pulsating rod. Jack rode it out driving her down onto the new clothing bags, to collapse on top of her. Jack laid on her, pinning her down, she didn't move. Jack moved abit to hear "Are we over?"

Jack pulled out of her, as she turned to say" From now on, you do it anyway you want, in addition, I want to get pregnant and next time you see me I will be off birth control pills"

Jack got up to say, "Maybe I should take only what I need, in a couple of bags"

She laid in silence with her eyes open looking up at him.

Jack passed by her, only to see her scrambles up, preventing him to go to the bathroom.

Sara kissed Jack on the cheek and announced, "Thank you, thank you, thank you my darling, what shall I wear, oh no I must take a shower, but first let me give you my suitcase"

Jack watched her, pull out a huge suitcase, seeing him to shake his head "No", "Something smaller, I want to leave as much stuff here as possible"

"So were good now, were in it for the future"

"Yes were good now, and no I won't be leaving you, you will always be in my life, either now or in the future"

Jack saw that she had a smaller long bag; she put on the bed, as they both went to the dresser. Where he pulled out the drawer to see his underwear was nicely folded. He pulled one on and a neatly folded socks and put them on, then went to the closet to see his clothing all hung by what it was and color and thought to himself ;

"That is nice and organized"

Jack finds a pair of jeans and a tank top and puts them on; on the floor under his clothes was his shoes, and a pair of boots. He pulled out only to see Sara standing naked and wet looking at him and said,   "Which pair do you want to bring"

"The ones I'm wearing, maybe, or maybe the boots."

"Go ahead and put your clothes in the bag, which you think you need."

"I don't know what to take, I don't know what to expect"

"Well honey, I could pack you if you want"

"Sure go ahead, that would be great"

Jack moved away to see Sara move into action, without hesitation, he watched as she pulled some clothes from the closet and the transferred the long bag onto the bed. While she worked Jack watched her move, and he was getting hard again, came at her from behind.

Jack began to rub her bottom.

"Jack what are you doing, I thought you said you wanted to go"

Jack continued to press himself against her, then he reached down to feel her wetness, as he pulled down his underwear he placed it inside of her as he forced his way in.

"Ooh honey that feels good" said Sara who was bent over the long bag as Jack continued the stroking, while Sara tried to arrange the long bag, with each stroke, Jack gained momentum, he could feel her clamp down on him as he was ready to go and then they both came together.

Jack pulled out and pulled his underwear back up, whereas Sara went back to arranging the long bag, Jack went in to the living room and to the closet and found his money and keys on the floor, he counted out ten thousand dollars and placed it on the shelf and then closed the doors he turned to see Sara had his long bag in hand and was dressed.

Jack looked her over from top to bottom and said, "How did you get dressed so fast"

"That's what I do, I'm ready honey"

"I'll put on my choice, the boots and we will go"

"Do you want me to make you a sandwich, to take with you?"

"Sure that sounds good," said Jack watching her set down the long bag and go into the kitchen. Jack sat down by the chair and pulled on his boots. Then got up and went into the bedroom and found the other bag and placed it on the bed and opened it and began to count the bundles to total over fifty thousand dollars and placed them in a light green jacket, and put it on, to say "I like this job", he closed the bag up and saw Sara holding a bag and said, "I'm ready to go"

Jack picked up the small bag and went to the closet; he placed the two bags together,

For her to say, "After I get back, I will open a saving account and put that money away"

"Nah, don't do that, if anything, find a special place and bury it, in a protective box, I need to be able to get to that money when ever I want"

'You're the boss, I will do that".

"When you get back, I want you to meet my grandmother, she has a house in the country, you know she willed the house to me, only, cause I was Grandfather's Sanders special grand daughter."

"That's nice, he thought of you in that way."

"Well what's mine is yours and what's yours is yours". Said Sara, at the door.

At the last moment Jack decided to take the big handbag, along with his clothing bag and went to the door; she opened it for him and went out.

Jack opened the trunk, set the long bag and the bag inside, and closed the trunk, Sara was already in the car as he got in, and then Leslie drove up and parked next to them. Jack got in, fired up the car as Sara rolled the window down; Leslie did the same and leaned over.

"What do you want me to tell her?" asked Sara

"Tell her were going out and you'll be back soon"

"Hey les, Jack and I are getting something from my brother on Jack's boat and we will be back shortly"

"Should I wait?" asked Leslie

"yes" says Sara looking at Jack, nodding his head as he speeds out , then on to the highway.

"That was mean of you to lie to her"

"That's what I do, so, what is her deal anyway, how long do we have to wait, really that girl takes forever, when I want sex, I want it now, and I can't wait"

"I know honey, and from this day forward I will sense when you want it and I will have her on speed dial"

"That sounds good," said Jack to add "So are you two going to make up?" who was driving past the hospital and thinking to himself "Aah great food, boy am I going to miss it"

"Yes as soon as I get back". Thinks Jack.

In a flash, they were at the Bails Bonds place and Jack pulled the car to a stop only to see a big black SUV parked in front. Red emerged from his office with a cute short blonde-haired woman in tow.

Jack got out of the car, with Sara; it was Jack with his keys, in hand.

That opened the trunk and pulled the long bag out as Sara lifted the bag.

The two walked to the black SUV to see Red opening up the back and say   "Jack what's up bro"

"Not much same old same"

"You bring you ID and passport"

Jack felt around his pockets and came up short. Sara produced a wallet and handed them to Jack and said" Here honey, I got your wallet and here is your passport."

"Thanks "said Jack.

"What would you do, if you didn't have her here?' said Red putting that long bag in the back.

"What does that mean?" said Sara to herself, reaching for a door handle.

"Where do you think your going?" said Red to Sara

"She's with me; leave her alone, besides who's the girl you got?"

"Oh that's Kim, Kim meet Jack and his friend, what's your name?"

"Sara" the two shook hands; they both got into the back, sitting next to each other as Jack said,

"Her and I will sit in the back, why don't you ride up front with your old man"

"He isn't my old man, he asked me to come along, so that you can do whatever you wanted to me"

"Are you a pro? "

"No just a bored housewife, who's husband owed Red a favor"

"So you never have done this with anyone else"

"Yeah sure"

"Then go up with Red and sit with him," said Jack as he got in, to sit next to Sara.

Red fired the big vehicle up, the radio was blasting, he turned it down as Jack looked at Sara, to know instantly he made a mistake earlier, and for her to fight, knew he could trust her.

Red reached back to hand Jack 2500 in twenties and said,

"Here is your cut"

"Thanks" said Jack, taking the money, then hands it two Sara to say, "Here go pick out a ring "

She shakes her head at him "No", to add, "I don't think so". "When we go shopping for rings, it will be you and I, while you're gone, shall I plan our wedding"

"Yes that is fine with me, do you need any money to start it"

"I have it in my hand, besides my father is paying for our wedding" she said with a smile.

Jack reached over the seat to grab the bag, and he handed it to her.

Jack said, "Use all of this as well."

"I'm sure I'll be making more" said Jack

"oh yes, I know you will be, so you don't want saving accounts, how about, I put your name on all my credit cards, will you pay off the balances?"

"Yeah sure, use that money," said Jack who was using the time to rub her arm, at the elbow.

"You like to touch, don't you?"

"Yeah, I guess, you're so soft"

"Well you know I could be even softer?"

Jack looked at her, in a puzzled sort of way, as she said, "When you get back I will take you to this spa I use from time to time, and you will be as soft as I am"

'Alright, that sounds good"

"What colors do you like?"

"I don't know, I like white, especially on you, reds are nice, maybe even some blues"

"That gives me some ideas, what about foods, what do you want?"

"The hospital's buffet line"

"Really ,you like that food so much, to say that, I may have to visit it, you know it was Debbie and my father that created it, to cut down on everyone having take out, so why do you like it so much?"

"I guess they call it pizza and the corn mush"

"its called polenta or grits, you know your free to touch me anywhere else you like, how about my legs?", she pulled one up, so that Jack could feel how smooth it was, for him to ask;

" How do you keep it so smooth, he then thought of Sam's, hers were hairy, that was nice he thought.

"I shave them once or twice a week, along with this," she points to her box.

"Do you have to?" asked Jack

"No, why do you want me to grow it out" she looked at him to say, "You do, don't you, alright when you see me again, I'll be hairy, your one kinky man, but I like it, I love the way you think"

She leaned into him to kiss him, she looked up to see Red, was eye balling her in the mirror.

Jack stroked her thigh, behind her knee.

"Stop that you're tickling me, no I really meant, you getting me hot"

"Enough you too, stop that," said Red, kiddingly.

"Where do you want to get married?"

"Where ever you want," said Jack.

"How about where we almost broke up, the Lighthouse Resort"

"Fine with me" said Jack.

"Who will be your best man?"

"Oh I don't know, maybe Red"

"Red what "he said

"Do you want to be my best man?"

"Yeah, sure, we just met"

"That's alright, I chose you for the Bachelor party host"

"Oh that's not fair, but I like it" said Sara.

"Are you asking him, because of my sister and his connection?"

"Yep, to get her back for you, and one more twist were going to use her as the guess whore"

"Oh your bad, bad man, but I like it"

"Who is your bridesmaid?" asked Jack still stroking her leg.

"I have a dear friend her name is Tabby, short for Tabitha, she lives in Seattle Washington, the state, then we will have, Kerrie, Erica and Rachel, oh before I forget, in our family we have a tradition;

That you must sleep with all the bridesmaids, before you can marry the bride, are you willing to do that?"

"Sure if I have to?"

"Yes you have too"

"When do you want to have this wedding?"

"Why do you ask?" asked Sara

'So I know how long it will take me to bed them"

"No, its not like that, the design, is that, you bed, each and everyone of them, that night, then when you and I finally, consummate our marriage, you will not want, seek or desire another women ever again"

"All in one night, how many will there be,

"Well there will be four"

"That's it, what about Leslie, and Debbie, if I'm doing this lets do this and go out with a bang"

'Normally, there is eight, my grandfather had ten, my Dad had six, so it varies on who the brides friends are that want to take part in the tradition"

"Well you think this Tabby will do it"

"Probably, if not, I will chose the line up based on their order when you walk up, we take our vows, that will include, that stipulation, then you will have before midnight to accomplish this"

"Then let's have a morning wedding"

"Its gonna be an afternoon wedding, don't worry about it, its not something to fret about, just think of it as a fringe benefit, also, after we get married, you can still see Debbie, or whoever, just as long as they are healthy"

She lowered her leg, as Jack was lifting up her tank top, for her to say,   "I can pull it off for you"

"Nah come here, as the two kissed, till he could feel the SUV slowing, Jack pulled away from her to say, "I want to take your last name"

"What Sanders, no I don't want you too, I want Cash"

"It's made up"

"So what, our love is not, if you go by as Cash, so will I"

"But I thought I could honor your father."

"No, we have Timmy, he will carry on their name, no Jack, you chose the name, and I will choose it too,"

"But why" pleaded Jack.

"Hush up, your not changing you name to Sanders, and that's final"

Jack looked at her, to say, "Alright, we will keep, that name"

"If in the future you find out what your real name is, then we as a family will consider changing it to that, but right now, people all over town know you as Cash, you're already gaining a strong and powerful reputation, and I like that in a man"

Red slowed the SUV, at the gate, to the right to a big intersection to a sign that read; "Welcome to Fort John C Morgan, and the home of the U S Marshal's Academy. Red came to a stop at the gate, powered down his window and showed his credentials pass as the gate guard said,   "How many visitors besides yourself are you carrying"

"Three, I mean four"

"Let me see their ID's pleased, is any of them going to the Academy?"

"Only one, his name is Jack Cash" and ads "Okay lets pull out your ID's for the guard so we can get our passes."

The girls pull out theirs as Sara nudges Jack. Jack hands Sara his wallet, she leans over the seat gives Red his ID. Jack has his hands on her butt, and she waits, while Jack touches, the curve, for Jack, he found someone's who curve was so pronounced, as he liked it.

Red gives them to the gate guard. A few minutes passed and Red got the ID's back as the gate guard says, "Mr. Combs it's off to the left is the Academy, as you know". For Red to say "Will you sit back Sara?" The metal gate raises and Red drives through, off to the left and down a long straight road.

They drove a ways to a small parking lot, where it was lit up. A small shack stood.

"Here we are, you girls stay here while I check in Jack; then will go have fun"

Jack got out, as did Sara and the two met at the back where Red had the long bag in hand already.

"Say your goodbyes already," said Red

Jack took Sara in his arms as she placed her arms around him and gave him a kiss on the cheek and then said "Call me every day", she said "And take this bag of food I hope you like it, I made it with all my love and affection."

"I will try, I don't know what will happen" said Jack as the two finally kissed on the lips as Jack tried to feel her sides one more time, she said "Don't tempt me, and I'll take it all off right here."

Jack broke away with Sara.

Sara, she displayed her emotions as tears were streaming down her face.

"Stop that or your makeup will wash off your face" said Jack.

She looked at him to say "I hope you wear that necklace proud and I will wear mine when I go to bed every night, and I promise not to have too much fun while you're away, here is a card with my address and my parents address, so write me as often as you can, I will do the same"

Jack said "Alright" and puts it in his pocket, steps away from her to wave goodbye, turns and walk's through a mirrored door, it closes shut.

PART 2

The Academy

R ed was first followed by Jack, into a small room that had a
waiting area where several other people were sitting.

"Take a seat Jack, I'll get everything in order" said Red

Jack sat down with only a single bag in hand in hand, he wore his
light green jacket he checked the entrance money in all of its inside
pockets. Jack looked inside the brown bag, found a sandwich, and
began to eat one, part of the half, and it had chips, a drink, and a
fruit cup with a plastic spoon. He finished off the contents of the bag,
threw away the rest, and sat back down to see Red coming back
without his bag.

"Where is my Long bag?"

"I checked it in; you'll get it back after three days"

"What do you mean, what's in three days?"

"You'll find out, and that's the best to keep it a secret, so the
guy told me another shuttle is coming in five minutes, so sit tight,
listen I know you wanted to work with me, but I'm sorry, this is for
your own good"

Jack closed his eyes, still feeling a bit weary from the weekend, and
took a catnap, not thinking about the words, Red just said to him, or
that Sara was gone.

Jack felt his ribs being nudged and awoke.

"The bus is here, let's go"

Jack rose, and waited as others before him and Red filed through
a door to a waiting bus a guy dressed in camouflaged outfit was
calling out names and yelled " Cash, where you at?"

Jack responded by saying "Yeah here"

"Good, next time speak up"

Jack took a seat in the very back to hear the guy say;

"Mr. Combs good to see you again sir"

Jack watches Red come by him and take a seat.

The two sit in silence as the lights of the bus shine in the darkness, the ride was long, bumpy, with some twists, and turns, up over a large hill to a flat surface and they came to a stop. In the distance in front of them a jet was landing, it was loud; the bus took a right turn and drove a small distance, to park in front of a huge three-story building.

"All out, then go inside the building, to the right and sit in the chairs"

Red led, Jack followed out the bus and up some steps to the building, Red held the door open for Jack who was last to get off the bus. Jack stepped inside to reveal a huge hallway, where the others from the bus went into the first room; Red continued and said, "Follow me"

They came to a room that read Commander Michael Johnson.

Red knocked on the door, the door opened to a pretty lady, who said,   "How may I help you gentlemen?"

"Can you tell Commander Johnson, that Red Combs and a applicant is here to see him"

"Come in gentlemen and have a seat, I'll let Commander Johnson know your both here"

Red led and Jack followed in to take a seat, in a nicely padded chair, Red grabbed a magazine while Jack closed his eyes for a moment to hear.

"Red you old buzzard, how the hell are you, are you here to become a teacher or what, its nice to see you"

"Mike I'm here on official business, you know I called you last night about a recruit"

"Yeah and I told you, why don't you and your friend come into my office"

"Jack" said Red

Jack awoke and followed in, taking a seat. As they hear the door close shut,

"Alright fellows, why don't you tell me what is on your minds"

"As I said from last night, I have an applicant who is interested in going to the school"

Is it to become a US Marshal?" asked Commander Johnson

"No silly it is not to become a U S Marshal, Jack is here to attend the Bounty Hunter school" said Red.

"Oh yes that's right, as I remember you saying you had someone interested, but not 100 percent committed, well I can't leave an exemption on the table and not see you for six month's, I had to fill it almost immediately, listen Red, I like you a lot and I still remember you saving my life and for the fact that your name is on the top of all the records here, I would give you an exemption in a heart beat, but my hands are tied, hold on a minute." The Commander picks up the telephone.

He whispers into the phone to say, "Can you come into my office and give me an update on our recruits please"

"you know Red I needed a commitment, the I FR P is at least six month school reserved in advance, and now with the title seventeen act by Congress, we have to divide the school in half and we just don't let anyone through the door's and accept them." "This training has change since you went through, it is a little different then most, the applicants, can either choose to be a Bounty Hunter and or a U S Marshal or the both of them, we still have in place a class size of twenty and of them ten are exempt, the rest make up of a pool, of players who go through Hell Week and are voted on by a board of bureaucrats, to make the final selections.

A knock on the door, in came a well-dressed Chinese man, who comes up to the Commander and lays out some cards on the table.

"Gentlemen this is Hiro Osage from Japan, he is the martial Arts instructor and number two at the Academy"

"Hey" said Jack and then spoke up to say, "What's the big deal, I'm here to learn, I'll participate and if I don't get selected then it's no big deal"

"That's refreshing to hear, that's all Hiro, and I'll be with you and all the applicants in a moment".

Hiro leaves the room and closes the door.

"Red let me tell you what's going on, they gave me Hiro to keep an eye on me, but he knows the score and he is cool with that, we get applicants from all over the world, those from other countries are given diplomatic immunity and their tuition is paid for by the country sending them, that's why I limit ten exemptions a class. This is how it will work now, for the next three days, your friend"

"Jack"

"Jack will go through a series of tests to determine his mental, physical, emotional and spiritual wellbeing, all the while amassing points to qualify for the remaining nine spots, you'll go head to head with some pretty powerful people, afterwards a selection process will occur and the remaining finalist will join us for the rest of the program".

"If you fail at any one point or get injured along the way you will be disqualified, does that sound alright to you Jack?"

"Sure, when can we get started?"

"As soon as you pay our fee of 50,000 dollars"

Jack pulls out five stacks of ten thousand dollars each, places them on the desk, and pushes them towards the Commander.

The Commander takes one pile and flips through it and says, "Looks like we got a deal, Jack step through that door and down the hall to the assembly hall and take a seat, I'll be there in ten minutes or so"

Jack rises and says "thanks Red, I'll see you soon, make sure my future wife gets home safe and that you do not touch her" the two shake hands and Jack leaves, and then closes the door.

"What's really going on Mike, that's bullshit?" said Red, to add "How often do I bring someone in, besides when I talked with Jim, he told me if I brought Jack in, he would pay me a quarter of a million dollars, so where is my money"

The commander pulls up a green bag, to set it on the desk to say

"Listen Red, I'll watch over your friend, but I can't promise you anything, besides the guy looks strong mentally and with emotions in tact, I don't think it will be a problem, besides I got Washington breathing down my neck, especially, with this whole International Super spy fiasco.

"Besides Red , this is best for all parties concerned, this should be fun, If he ever gets wind that you're the one who set him up, I'd find a place to hid for the rest of your life, as for his girl, is it true she will be his wife?"

"Yes, that's what he wants" said Red, taking the bag in hand.

"Then, from this day forward, she will be protected, you drive her home, don't worry we will have an agent on her, to keep her safe, then we will see you on graduation day."

"Yep, If he will make it by then"

"Your right he will be on the fast track program'

"Well, I'll be there for Jack"

"Great I'll see you later, I gotta go and now, I'm late" the two, shook hands, as the Commander leaves the room.

Jack opens the door to the assembly Hall.

Jack slowly moves to, from behind a curtain and takes a seat in the back; in front of him must be at least fifty people of all types, shapes and sizes, the Commander hit's the floor running literally.

"And now Ladies and Gentlemen please give a round of applause to our President and head Commander of this Academy for International Fugitive Recovery Person's School, please welcome Commander Michael Johnson, they all clapped, Jack rose as did the majority of applicants.

"Please sit down, and thank you for the applause and welcome applicant to a new class and from the look of it, looks mighty strong, in a moment we will get started, let me tell you how it works here, there are two classes of twenty, one the marshal's and the other is made up of those wanting to be International Bounty Hunters, but this class will have a few surprises along the way, first off I want you to pair up in groups of five, you can do this after I'm through here, and then pick a team captain, then I need you to file out single file in your groups of five, we will exit through the door that says start, good luck and I hope each and everyone of you finds what you are looking for."

Jack stood up and looked around to see a young black kid who was coming his way and off to his left stood a tall brunette, who spoke with a broken English accent, as she said "Hey you, wanna be with me"

Jack turns to see a very tall skinny brunette, who stood by Jack now; it was if he was drawing them to him.

"My name is Raphael, I'm from Croatia"

"Hi, my name is Jack"

"Jack your our team leader, my name is Bennie "the blades" Carter, I'm at your service." The two tried to touch each other with Jack offering his hand for a shake and Blades just tapped it on the knuckle and said "That's how we do it in the hood, bro", to add "Like your necklace."

A squeaky voice spoke up "I'm Teresa; I'd like to be on your team.

Jack looked behind him to see this young girl with long flowing hair and a very tight and petite body. An older man came up to the group and said, "My name is Larry, I guess you're the last group and I want to be the leader, I know"

Each person passed by Larry led by Jack followed by Bennie, Raphael, and Teresa and behind them was Larry.

Jack hit the door first, and saw a line and came behind a whole group when he heard "Group number nine"

The group in front of Jack all went into a room. A guy with a clipboard came up to Jack and said

"Who's your team leader?"

"I am" spoke a Larry in a weak voice.

"It's Jack," said Bennie and ads "Don't listen to that fool."

"Your Jack Cash, so the rest of your team makes up of you Bennie Carter, I see Raphael from Croatia, Teresa from Honduras and lastly you have Larry O'Connor, alright I need you to go to room number five, last door on the left. Jack led as the group followed; Jack came to the door, turned the knob and opened the door to see. The room was a big warehouse on the right was the end of the line, which was their beginning. Then on the left was the finished product; a lean mean fighting machine. Jack saw others starting at different parts of the warehouse, as he assembled at the line, he could see the person in front of him was asked to strip down to his underwear a tailor quickly took some measurements, entered it in the computer and the guy stepped forward.

"Please wait behind the line sir" said the operator.

Jack watched the guy hit every station and make a left hand turn, when a bigger man with a clipboard said "This is our last group, your group Leader is Jack Cash from Germany, your team colors are Red, now lets go, I'm your groups liaison chief, my name is Carl

Lewis, first off I will tell Jack everything and as a group you must follow what he does, does everyone understand this?"

"Yes" they all said

"Jack I want you to strip down, to your underwear and on your left is a bin". "Place that bag and all your possessions in then use your left hand place your I D card, Driver's License and or Passport in. That's all you will need, lets get started"

Jack began to undress and placed everything into a bin that was marked Jack Cash, Jack was told to hold his arms out as he held on to his documents, as the tailor took the truest measurement and was told; "Step forward"

Jack went to the next individual, who handed Jack a large duffle bag, which he was told to keep in his right hand.

Next, he saw underwear, t-shirts in red, he was seeing red everything was red.

"Step forward"

Jack went forward to see a pair of red pants and a red shirt which he put on, then stood and two more sets of pants and shirts was given.

"Step forward"

Jack noticed off to the left his bin went through a big wrapping machine to seal his contents and then drop out of sight, on this station all of his tactical equipment, then he noticed a large board on the right that read the following "This station contains all tactical equipment when you receive it move forward on your own."

"Step"

Jack was already moving as he carried his now heavy bag around a large corner, where he received his flax Jacket and his choice of holsters, he chose under the arms, which hung on a rack then above it read "this holster is for U S Marshal special agents only.

Jack let go of that one and ended up with a single hard cased holster, which was placed, in his bag.

He was finished as he was where he had started, fully redressed upon receiving his boots and running shoes; he was walking and now dragging his heavy duffle bag, which was full into a room with three large counters, with a high desk.

"Next please"

Jack went to the voice in the middle who said "Let me have your passport and I D's. Jack placed them on the edge of the counter.

"Step back, please" said the voice.

Jack did so with his heavy bag and noticed a little girl at the desk, as she said "Smile"

Poof, off went a light, nearly blinding Jack, a few moments later on the left of him was Bennie and on the right was Raphael, he smiled at her, she smiled back.

"Jack Cash, here you go"

Jack went up to the counter, retrieved his documents on the left on the right was a small box and a freshly laminated I D card Jack pulled it towards him to look at it; on it read his fake name, Jack Cash, the word official, professional and diplomatic immunity, then in big letters it read" "International, Fugitive, Recovery Agent with a raised stamp, then he noticed a serial number that read 001-24-1962 also stuck to that card was a official social security card with the number printed on it. Jack placed all the documents into his front pocket, and moved out of that room, dragging that duffle bag, into the next room, which opened into a small classroom.

"Come in and please take a seat "barked a voice.

A man dressed in a military outfit, was seating everyone.

Jack was asked to walk down a open aisle way to the last seat, and sat down on the end of his row, he was in the very back, in front of him looked like at least four rows of five on his side and that same amount on the other, next to him was Bennie, then Raphael, Teresa and finally the whiney Larry they all took their seats.

A big man came to the podium and began to speak and he said;

" Welcome people, to a new class for the U S marshal program and Bounty Hunters, oh I'm sorry you guys changed your name to Fugitive, Recovery, Agents, lets start with my name, I'm Doctor Greg Williams and I'm the classes clinical psychologist and one of the judges on the panel, at the door was your class handler, Sergeant Snyder, off to my right is Martial expert Souza, and lastly the two trainers are first your liaison officer and a fellow student who is stationed at the end of each row and your Captain, please get on your feet and give him a warm welcome; his name is Captain Jonathan Knight".

The class hooped and hallowed, even some whistling occurred as Jack watched the man sashay up to the podium and say "Thank you Doctor Williams" and ads to the class, "Thank you newly classified agents, I know this is a big honor and only the top one percent is chosen for this honor." "As your captain I will see to it that each and everyone will have the ability to succeed."

A guy in front of Jack said "Who is this guy, what a load of crap, just get him off the stage and let's get going already".

"Now I will tell you that, this is my first time with all of you so make sure you have your names on all of your clothes, your handler and liaison officer will assist you with that, now some of you in this room will make it, while other will fail, for this part of the training you will not be paid, although after those who are selected, your pay will, be the standard one thousand a week, paid at the end of the week, enough of that, after the next three days, we will talk with those who made it, now lets begin, over the next four days you will be tested in the following areas;

"Your ability to withstand physical endurance, mental toughness, emotional pain and the will to succeed by a spiritual drive, each of you has been assigned into a group, there are ten groups of five, during this week of training we are looking for those who stand out or make a personal sacrifice for themselves or others, that's how we can determine if your Marshal material". "Let me tell you, what your playing for, if you happen to make it to further training you will receive a lifetime tax exemption, in addition to that you will receive a salary of over fifty thousand dollars a year, for the rest of your lives, then there is the issue of protection, you will receive a arsenal of weapons you need to maintain and have on your person."

"And lastly you will be given a title, which gives you the right to be protected by our government in the case of any incident involving assassinations, murder or simply an innocent killing."

"I will tell you this that you will be a licensed killer, abductor and mediator for first the U S Marshal service and then from any agency that needs you, your service will be based on, the years you have left to age 55, then you will be placed on active reserve until your 60 and then finally declassified and your status retired."

"Therefore, with that I need you to single file and exit out and go with your Liaison Officers to your assigned dwellings, put your stuff away and change into your running gear and meet me at the flagpole in 30 minutes. Thank you" said the Captain.

Jack watched as some who were in the aisle had their duffle bag on their back and it was a growing trend, so that's what Jack did as did his team, one by one they filed out, Jack was behind another until the cool night hit his face and the bugs were out in force, Bennie was swatting them away, much to no avail,

"Come group, over here" said a voice

Jack's group assembled around their officer as he says " My name is Devlin Cates, and I was just like you four month's ago, I'm over halfway through this and I can tell you it was fun, behind me is your groups room five beds and a shared head, go in and get changed, I'll see you in twenty minutes".

Bennie was first in, and found his area and said "This is my bunk" and slung a curtain around him.

Jack placed his stuff on the rack near the door as the two girls took the beds in the middle and the left side, across from Jack was Larry, Jack laid his bag on the rack.

Jack looked around his room, to see his desk a light, a chair with arm rests on wheels and a dresser a sliding curtain on a track was a fixed to the ceiling, he saw everyone else pull theirs closed, even though Teresa had hers part way opened, he could see everything and watched her pull off her top and pull on a t-shirt and then step out of her pants to hear "Guys we only have ten minutes" yelled Larry behind his curtain.

Jack quickly changed and sat on his bunk thinking of his last place of confinement, thinking how nice this was and how much nicer they were treating him. Bennie slid his curtain back to see Teresa and Raphael talking in the middle and Jack sitting on his bunk and Larry all decked out in his body armor and saying "Jack you look down, never fear Larry is here to led the group, come guys" Larry opened the door and led the two girls out.

"Jack are you coming" said Bennie giving Jack a hand.

Bennie and Jack emerged in a now lighted courtyard.

Where at least fifty or so people stood, Jack thought to himself, and we are going to get down to ten, "Wow"

"Men and women can I have your attention, I want you to assemble in a line facing me, at arms length apart, I want your team leader in the middle and the two physically strong on the ends and now move." said Sgt. Snyder

Jack stayed where he was at as both girls flanked him with Raphael on his left and next to her was Bennie and on the other side was Teresa and Larry.

"Now when I blow my whistle we will begin the training session and we will first start with some stretching exercises. Watch your Liaison Officers"

Jack and his team went through a series of stretching exercises, and then they heard the whistle.

"Now our next exercise is Jumping Jacks on my count lets go"

The physical exercises were beginning, Jack and his team kept up with the easy exercises and the total body workout ended with a whistle.

"Now that we are all warmed up, we are going to do our first test a three mile run, your team has to complete the course faster than the bottom five, which will automatically will be eliminated from this program, also you will be given 100 points for each member of the team that finish within the time, of Thirty one minutes"

"In addition, will will award points along the way for performance, strength and endurance. On my whistle group, one and two will start the course, then five minutes later group three and four and so on until everyone has gone."

"Remember we are timing you, so give us your best overall time for your group."

The whistle blew and Jack and his team watched as Larry said;

"Listen team, I've trained for this, so if you want to follow me"

"Shut up" said Bennie, and ads "Take off that body armor you look silly"

The team watched as their Liaison officer came over to them and said;   "Listen up team, if you follow me we should go through the course in around thirty one minutes, which averages out a ten minute mile and also along the way they are gonna stop you and have you do a series of strength tests, so when that occurs, I would like you to pair up with a buddy, I'll take your team leader, also along the way will be water stations, only drink small amounts, not the whole bottle and lastly we are a team, in order for you guys to get maximize points you all need to finish, if one of you wants to quit just let me know, any questions?"

Bennie moved away from Larry when they all heard Teresa speak up and say "Raphael will you be my partner."

Raphael said "Yes Teresa I'll work with you"

Bennie resolved himself to face Larry as to know he would have to work with him made the first move to say "I guess it's you and I"

"You're not my first choice either" said Larry

"Listen up we are going to start slow, with a slow cadence and work up to a fast count, some of us like to sing if you know a song and like to sing it, and then just go for it"

"Groups nine and ten ready the start line"

Jack and the team walked over to the lighted start line, and heard the whistle, off they went, they all started in a pack with Jack next to the Liaison officer, and Bennie, behind them was the two girls and then it was Larry as the other team was in a single file line, easily passing them they heard them begin to sing" Hey, hey, here we are, we are group nine and were coming to getcha"

Group 9 took off and went ahead, Devlin led Jack's group. While Jack fell in behind him, then it was Bennie holding his own, followed by the two girls and Larry who was lagging a bit.

Then Larry announced "You guys are going way to slow"

With that Larry passed them and said "See yea"

"What's up with him" asked Jack

"I don't know, but he won't last "said Devlin

The first quarter of the mile was flat then it started to go up a hill. For the second mile, they were unrelenting not more than fifty paces up the hills, enough to feel them in your legs but not enough to wind you except Larry, who was a bit out of breath, and at the rest stop, slamming down water cups in the well lighted area, Group nine had just left as Jack's team arrived.

"Stay running at a slow place, now stop" and ads "Team up with your partner and do 100 sit-ups, in one minute of time".
Jack was first and laid on his back, bent his knees, Devlin held them for Jack; it was the same for Bennie and Teresa.

"Ready go" said Devlin
Jack interlocked his hands behind his head and began the exercise, much to his surprise, how quickly one minute went by, when Devlin said " Stop the count" and ads "Switch partners, Jack you can sit out this one, you just did 79 sit-ups, what did you others get?"

"Teresa did 46" said Raphael waiting to go.

"Bennie did 52" said Larry on his back still breathing hard.

"Are you guys ready?"
They both answered, by saying ready.

"Then lets go" said Devlin
Jack went to the two doing the sit-ups only to begin to root for Larry and say " Come on Larry, you can do it " Jack did a silent count for Larry's repetitions only to discover, his slow rate led him to do only 19.

"Stop, what was the totals" asked Devlin

"Raphael did 48" said Teresa, helping her new friend up off the ground.

"Larry did 29" said Bennie, getting up to help Larry up as well.

"Let's go" said Devlin
This time it was Devlin leading out as Teresa followed him, then it was Raphael, followed by Larry then Bennie and Jack took up the rear, the pace was slow, much to Jack's dislike, so Jack spoke up and said;   "Team ten are we ready to pick up the pace, come follow me"

"Yeah" was said in unisons
Jack sped up and past Devlin who seemed to be struggling a little bit, Jack increased the tempo and Bennie was on his feet, Bennie began to sing, with the steps of the beat and it began an echo as he would sing a bar of words; Jack, Raphael and Teresa would return the words, Bennie became more creative and began to Rap a word or two and they would Rap it back.

Devlin and Larry brought up the rear as they came to the second stop point. A young Chinese lady emerged from inside a tent to say;

" Where's your Liaison Officer? No matter, drop on my count and start doing pushups on my go, ready set go"
Devlin and Larry made it just before the team started.

"Now stop, Devlin get their totals"

"Alright, in the following order"

"Can we give you our total's on the road" said Bennie already moving, Jack led the team, followed by Raphael, then Teresa and Bennie.
Devlin turned to say to Larry "how many did you do?"

"12" said Larry whose slow pace was now down to a walk as he sees his team disappear over a hill.
Devlin caught up with Teresa and the group to say "O Kay what are your totals"

Teresa said 42, and Raphael said 40 and then Jack said 60.

"Excellent, guys but you're losing Larry on the back end"

"I'll go back and help him up here, if you guys want to keep the pace going" said Jack.
Who turned and went back only to hear Bennie say "This pace is too slow, can we speed it up?"

"Sure go as fast as you can, I'll catch up with you guys" said Jack.
Bennie took over the pace setting on the front, and began to increase his lead over the two girls who had slowed a bit to wait for Jack, much to Devlin surprise.

"Why are you girls slowing down? If anything you may want to sped up, to get within the time limit or get eliminated"

"Were waiting for Jack our team leader" said Raphael.

"Listen, I'd more worry about yourselves then worry about a lard bag Larry, besides if Jack helps him and they come in after 31 minutes then they and you will both be eliminated"
The two girls looked at each other then decided to go, and kick it up a notch, they ran for a while, whereas Teresa led the way, followed by Raphael, in the upcoming mile they caught up with Bennie who was

at the third check point, stopped and was talking with Dr Williams, as the two girls arrived, he told them that their time is recorded at each stop and deducted at the end of the run, so they calmed down and sat and waited for Jack, until five minutes passed when Devlin said;

"Let's do pull-up, up on the bar on my count, go"

The three were hanging on the bar and began to lift themselves up, slowly, in the background, they could here Jack yelling at Larry, motivating him to the next check point, they arrived as Devlin said;

"Stop and drop" and ads Jack and Larry, get up on the bar"

13, 9, 7 said Bennie, Raphael and Teresa respectfully as Bennie began to take off when Raphael spoke up "Bennie are you waiting for Jack"

"Sure" said Bennie standing on the paved street watching Jack and Larry pump out some pull-ups.

"Stop, what did you get Jack?"

"36" said Jack walking past Devlin, "3" said Larry.

"Listen this is the stretch run, your more than three quarters of the way there, and most of it is down hill, this is where you will pass other teams, as some will have given up, just think we are going to do this all three days" said Devlin.

Larry scooted past them and nearly colliding with Bennie, who jumped out of his way.

Devlin took off and said I'm at 12 minutes, so some are you are faster, some of you are slower, so lets pick up the pace" said Devlin.

Jack and Bennie took off together as the two girls fell in behind, it was a quick pace as Devlin's backpack was all that Jack could see. The semi-lit night was cool and refreshing but had it been in the middle of the day everyone would be dead. The first half mile was still flat and no sign of Larry as they made their way over a hill the first member of the team nine was walking, they passed him and up the ways was two girls who Devlin said they were with team number 7, which means they were out, the road became tilted more and the run was easier, their tempo had increased, only to see more people on the side of the road. Devlin turned his head a said "It's always the two mile mark that hurts everyone, we will see much more up to the finish."

On the right was what they called the walking wounded said Teresa from behind Jack.

"In our country, you will see rebels with their arms on the side of the road left for others to pickup"

"That is true, there is a vehicle behind us, collecting up each station and then they will pickup the last 5 people and send them home regardless of their position, only tonight"

The group continue the descent down and began to pickup speed only to see Larry at the bottom and on the side of the road, at a drink station, they caught up with him as Jack says " Come on Larry lets go their coming to pickup people behind us"

"Go on all be with you in a minute"

The group continued down to the bottom, where Devlin said "Were a half mile away, let's charge home, does anyone want to race me to the finish line"

"What are you saying" asked Bennie

"Do you want to bet something "asked Raphael?

"How about the winner treats everyone else to a dinner at the post's dinner house" said Devlin

"No, how bout you versus us and whoever wins picks what the loser has to do?" said a confident Raphael.

"Are you saying you could beat me, a girl, sure I'm in" said Devlin.

Whereas he sped up, Raphael came up close to Devlin and said;

"Bye bye"

It was as if a track team was unleashed, Bennie led the pace at a full trollop with Teresa close by then Raphael, who was proud of herself for baiting their officer. Jack was behind them, but was closing fast, he caught up with Devlin and said "You're losing the bet"

"I know, who knew"

"You got anything else in that tank, then lets go, I know you can beat our team, follow me, I'll take you there" said Jack.

Devlin hooked in behind Jack who summoned up his reserves to catch up with the group and in a sling shot move, Devlin won the race, followed by Jack who cut off his team, barely but not enough to cry foul.

Jack turned around and went back on the course, while Bennie, Teresa and Raphael caught their breath and watched Jack go. Devlin recorded their times and minutes off.
Jack caught back up with Larry who was walking in.

"Let's go Larry, get moving, lets pickup the pace" said Jack who was running in place as you could hear times being called out on a loud speaker, last call was 26 minutes.

"Look we gotta go were at 26 minutes and you need to get going"

"I'm fine, I've passed at least five people" said Larry.

"Twenty seven minutes"

"You don't get it do you, they said at the beginning you needed to finish the race less than thirty one minutes, and its coming up on that time, do you want to go home and not be the leader of our team or what?" said Jack "So come on already now"
Jack pulled at his arm only to hear

"Twenty eight minutes'

"Come on lets go" said Jack

"Alright, I'm coming" said Larry and began to run, Jack set the pace as time was counting down for both of them to hear "thirty minutes", Larry crossed the line and collapsed as Jack, tried to pick him up and assisted by others, they helped Larry up and into a tent.
An announcement was spoken over the intercom.

"Thank you for your participation, every one that now finishing is eliminated, the rest of you are dismissed we will reassemble here at 0600 O'clock. A M"

"Jack can you tell the others we will meet back at your room in thirty minutes" said Devlin

"Sure" said Jack, as he took off towards the room.
Bennie came up to him and put his arm around Jack and said;

"I saw you, helping that ole dog out"

"You know I only help out those who are weak, besides we made it in as a team, I didn't see you going back after him."

"Oh don't worry from now on if you want me to help say the girls you can count on me to go back and pick them up"
They both laughed.

Doctor Kim Hodges

B oth girls were in the shower, as Jack and Bennie lay on their racks when a knock on the door was heard. Jack rose, and opened the door to see the Liaison Officer, Devlin.

"Hi Jack, is everyone here?"

"Yeah, the two girls are in the bathroom and there is Bennie, who came out from behind his curtain. And took a spot at the table in the center of the room.

"Jack can you get the girls?" asked Devlin

Jack goes to the bathroom door and knocks loudly; the door opens to see Teresa topless and says, "Yes Jack"

He looks at her from up to down, smiles and says, "Devlin's here and he wants to talk, could you hurry up"

"Do you want to come in and watch" said Teresa, holding the door open for Jack to see Raphael, just stepped out of the shower, she watched him, for a moment then just went to drying herself off.

Jack turned his head and said, "No, just hurry up"

Teresa left the door open, grabbed a towel and wrapped it around herself as she and Raphael came out with a towel around herself, as the three guys were caught off guard, they just stared at the two girls especially Raphael, this gorgeous bombshell was tall, with flowing hair, large supple breasts, and long legs. The two girls took a seat at the table.

"What, I need you guys to do, is on these cards, is an evaluation on what you think of each person in your group, or someone outside of your group. Please, fill out each line, there should be four for each member of your group and the best way to do this is to interview them individually and get to know them, then you can comprise a summary of what you think of them and so forth, any questions?".

"If anyone is hungry the chow hall is open till midnight, it's in the main building, if any one is interested I could come by and pick you up say in 15 minutes?" said Devlin.

"Yeah, I'd like to go," said Raphael

"Good then it's a date," said Devlin, getting up and he left. While Bennie looked at Jack and Jack looked back at Bennie. Bennie said "Hmm" and ads "So Jack, you wanna hit the chow hall with me or do you want to wait for Devlin"

"Nah, we can go together" said Jack, watching Raphael get up, the two stared at one another and for her to say "Don't worry Jack, you'll have me long before that guy will" then laughs, and ads "He's cute, but harmless, besides I go after bad boys, which he is not".

Raphael moves behind Teresa then goes back into the bathroom.

"You gotta watch that one she may have the looks Jack but she is deadly," said Bennie

"I'll go with you guys," said Teresa

"Alright let's go "said Jack

"Aren't you going to take a shower?" asked Teresa, with a smile at him.

"Why do I need to clean up"

"But I will help you" she said as she let her fingers glide off of his front, turn and walk back to the bathroom, open the door, then turned to smile at him, then closed the door.

Bennie was nudging at Jack's ribs and said, "Are you kidding, go on boy, you got two girls ready for you"

"Yeah, then let me go get my shaving kit"

Then the door opened and in walked Larry, who said, "Hi guys, thanks Jack for helping me out"

"What wrong with you" asked Bennie

"The commander told me it would be a matter of time before I was eliminated or I could simply just quit, save everyone some time money and energy.

Jack went over to Larry, standing by his rack and said "You knew coming in, it would be hard, why give up now, you have it in your heart to succeed, all you have to do is try, and all of us will help you" said Jack looking over at both girls peeking out from the half open door and to Bennie holding his shave bag and clothes in hand.

"Really you would do that for me" said Larry a little more excited.

"Sure didn't I show you that during the run?"

"Well, yes I guess, I wasn't thinking"

"Stop thinking of being defeated and start letting yourself go, really its not that hard, all you have to do is give it your best effort, and if you do that you will find out if your cut out for this line of work or you simple can't do this then you'll know its time to quit.

"Then, by doing it on your terms, will make you a winner, either way."

"Maybe your right, Jack, I need to go out on my own terms, thanks Jack," said Larry

He passed Jack by and left out the door.

"Where's he going in such a hurry?" asked Bennie

"I imagine he is going back to the officials and telling them he wants to stay"

"Why would you tell him to stay, he is in competition with us for the top twenty place for this next class"

"It's not my decision who stays or goes, if I told you to quit, would you," asked Jack now seeing both girls were fully dressed and had moved over to their bunks.

"Hell no, I'm here for the long haul" said Bennie.

"Yeah, you have a different mindset then Larry, Larry needs, some sort of help, look I'm going to lie down," said Jack walking over to his bunk and pulled the curtain closed. He sat down, removed his clothes aside lay back on his bunk and went fast to sleep.

Several hours passed as Jack was still in the same position, when all of a sudden, the Liaison Officer came in and yelled " Get up , Get up Get out of your racks and you have five minutes to be outside, Devlin swung back Jack's curtain to see Jack standing and looking at him.

"You ready to go"

"Yep, let's go," said Jack, who followed Devlin out in to the darkness of the morning. He stood by the door, watching other people gathering around the flagpole and realized something, this isn't a team competition, it was all about how to test those around you, to see that their was at least ten new people, come to find out, they had the first week off. Thinks Jack, as the last two days has been a cakewalk.

"Hi Jack" said Raphael, standing by him and ads;

"Do you have a plan for this morning's run?"

"Everyone for themselves, if you want to keep up with me, I'm fine with that, but I'm going out strong" said Jack, as the others came out; Bennie flanked Jack and said, "We missed you at the mess hall last night, you must be hungry"

"Nah, really not much, but I want to get to the front of this run and lead it, you can either be with me or just run on your own." said Jack and ads "Lets go and assemble."

Jack took a spot as several whistles blew, then the sergeant yelled, "A-Ten hut.

Everyone stood still as a guy came up onto the platform.

Then he spoke " At ease, candidates, good morning this is the first day of grill week, you can expect this to be your most physical day of training, we will start with a quick stretching exercise then were going on a ten mile run, the top thirty remaining will start the training cycle, we lost ten people last night, if you want to be here you need to be upfront and with me on the line, so lets get this underway", Jack looked over at Bennie who threw up his hands, to say "I guess they really wanted to separate those from who can and those who cannot"

Several whistle blew, the company started some stretching exercises, then on to aerobics.

Behind Jack, Larry said, "I hope we are done here, I didn't sign up for all this exercise stuff"

"Let's go," said the sergeant, waving his arm, Jack was off followed by his team, and Bennie was on Jack's heels.

Jack moved up next to the Captain who was sporting a t-shirt that read U S Marshal, Captain. The run started, slow to get everyone together, the forty plus came together as the sergeant held a pole in his arm and in tight with a banner that read; Class 2054 U S Marshal Training Class.

Jack fell in behind him as the group started up a hill and the pace was picked up, there was five lines of people of anywhere from seven to eight per line, behind Jack was Bennie, then Raphael, then Teresa, then behind her was another group of people, with no sight of Larry. The hills were easy to go down and half pace going up, which kept everyone together, the Captain picked up the pace, Jack watched the Captain out of the corner of his left eye. Jack felt good, and was feeling like this is something he may want to do for the rest of his life.

As the pace picked up, people were dropping off the back, and were walking, trying to catch back up until they saw the main group hit the water, and the run began a swim, into a lake, the sergeant holding the flag, tripped and went down, as the flag went down Jack was there to pick up the pole and placed in on his back and spun the pole. Jack kept up with the Captain who was criss-crossing in the shallow lake, which was thigh deep and waist deep in places, Jack was step for step, then finally the captain realized, it was no use and then made a bee line to the shore where the Sergeant and the Liaison Officers waited, Jack hit the ground first then the Captain, who gave Jack a dirty look and said "Nice try"

The sergeant falls in and takes the pole from Jack, who gives it up freely and falls in behind the sergeant as a loud horn sounded.

"Everyone stop" yelled the Captain, who slowed to a halt.

Jack looked around to see Bennie behind him as well as both girls Raphael and Teresa. Barely winded, and looking fresh.

"Everyone the run is over, go back to your rooms and we will meet in the courtyard at 0900.

The group broke up, with Bennie walked with Jack and said;

"How was that for you, do you want to run back?"

"Nah, I'm good"

"Suit yourself," said Bennie, picking up the pace and he left out of sight. Jack took his time and followed the road, from his position he could see the light breaking out from the east. Down in the valley, the walk down was steep, he could see how the compound was laid out, and it had a nice view.

"Jack Cash" spoke a voice behind him

Jack turned to see the sergeant approach him.

"What you did took guts, and I like that, it defines who you are as a person, I will keep an eye on you and if there is at some point where I can help you, believe me I will, thank you."

The sergeant pats Jack on the shoulder and takes off. Jack resumes his walk, his feet were soaked and squishy, he just continued, down to where the courtyard opened up, Jack could smell the mess hall and stood by the door as a voice from a woman said " Go on in if you want, all you need is your I D card and your meal card"

Jack looked at her and watched as she walked by and ads "My name is Daphne, I saw you this morning what you did will have a lasting affect, good job".

Jack walked off to his room, opened the door to see Larry, who saw him and said "Jack I'm out".

Jack walked past Larry to his bunk and grabbed his shaving kit and a change of clothes, Jack went into the shower as Bennie was coming out.

Jack was finishing when he heard a voice, Jack paused behind the curtain.

Jack peered out to see Raphael shedding her clothes, to stand naked, then steps into the other shower. Jack finished up and turned off the shower; pull the curtain back to see a naked Teresa, ready to step in as she said, "Do you mind washing my back", as she looked down to see rather large member, to say "That thing is huge"

"Sure" said Jack as she stepped in much to Jack's surprise, he stepped back and watched her wet herself down, she was hairy all over even her arm pits, her long flowing jet black hair glistened with the shampoo, Jack picked up the soap and rubbed it together and waited for the invitation, Teresa turned to face Jack, and say "Looks like you want to wash my front as well, go ahead".

That was all Jack needed, he spread his hands all over her small petite breasts, spending a good amount of time making sure they were well cleaned, he worked his way down to her stomach, she placed her hands on his shoulders while he reached her privates, that hairy forest was well conditioned by Jack's hand and fingers as he made sure she didn't have anymore foul water inside of herself, Jack knelt down, and washed each leg individually and her legs how hairy they were, when he was done she turned as Jack stood up and spread his hands on her chiseled back and massaged it for a while, enough for Jack to get his manhood upright and ready, although he stood taller he kept hitting her in the middle of the back, he was trying to force her over while she stood firm, so Jack gave up and knelt down and washed her butt cheek individually, he even slid his hand inside of her which she allowed him to do so, by opening up her legs, then Jack finished her up by doing both legs and then the bottom of her feet, she turned around to see the curtain close.

Jack toweled off and dressed in underwear and t-shirt only to see both girls step out at the same time as Jack closed the door shut.

Jack was on the move to his bunk he dressed in pants and a shirt, he grabbed his I D and important papers and slipped on his boots and went out.

The mess hall had a line, long around the corner; Jack contemplated if he was hungry enough to eat or go back and sleep a bit or maybe go back into the bathroom and have some fun.

Jack turned to go back, when he saw the Sergeant, who saw him leaving the line to say, "Jack Cash come with me were going to the front of the line" said the sergeant.

Who led Jack in and up to the cashier and ads "Show your I D and Mess Card?"

On Jack's turn, he hands the cashier his I D card as she says;

"Finally Mr. Jack Cash, here is your Mess card" and ads;
"This ones on me, Mister" Jack proceeded next to the Sergeant who said, "Is this your first visit here?"

"Yeah, I guess," said Jack retrieving a platter.

With that, Jack put on one plate, a knife, spoon, fork, and a napkin.
The Sergeant then said "That's why your skin and bones, man you need to eat, don't worry I will help you out"

The sergeant took a big scoop of diced potatoes and said,
"This will give you a lot of extra energy"
"Then load me up" said Jack

The sergeant was way ahead of Jack and began to load up his plate, he even ordered four eggs over easy, and took his plate and traded it with Jack who had half the plate size, the Sergeant just looked at him in disbelief and said, "You have to eat, like it is your last meal"

Jack looked at him as if he was crazy and kept his mouth shut, while he watched the sergeant take a seat, Jack found another seat by himself and sat down long enough to see the sergeant found him and sat by him and said, "Sorry I did not see you, where's your milk?"

Jack looked at him dumbfound and sat in silence.

"Hold on a minute," said the sergeant, getting up and going over to the drink machine and he came back with eight glasses of dark liquid. On a platter, to say "Here is chocolate milk, this is the drink of champions, its better than soda, so here is your four eight ounce glasses, enjoy"

Jack picked it up and drank it down slowly, enjoying it and realizing how good it really was. "And yes, it will be a regular part of each meal now". Said Jack to himself. He quickly consumed his great meal, he picked up his platter and deposited in the wash tray and stepped out to still see a long line and smiled when he saw Teresa, and Raphael, as they waved back at him, when a girl in front of them to say;

"Who is that Guy?"

"Quite a remarkable man"

"What is his name? "

"Jack Cash"

"Sounds like a guy I want to meet" said the girl.

Jack went back to his room.

Jack pulled his curtain closed an dumped out the remainder of his clothes and placed them in a stand up wall locker, he carefully folded the rest of his under garments, on the wall was a fan, which Jack turned on, to rotate, he sat down at his desk and lifted up the screen of the computer and looked at the blank screen, instantly Samantha's name came to his mind as he folded the screen down.

"Jack are you in there," said Bennie

"Yeah, come on in"

"Hey I'm sorry are you on the computer?" said Bennie starting to back out.

"No, what do you mean?" asked Jack

"Do you know what I'm talking about" asked Bennie

"No" said Jack

"Here let me show you what you have there" said Bennie, as Jack stood to let Bennie in to sit. And ads "First off Jack, this computer is for you to communicate with your family and friends, you log on and put in your password, only you can create it, look" Jack looked over Bennie's shoulder to see a collage of pictures from his family as Bennie typed and said" You have a web cam, see this camera, it shows you to the person, you have e-mail with you can see the person on the other end, look at this folder is all my wife's home video" Bennie showed Jack his wife undressing all the way. Bennie says, "Do you see how much fun you can have and I know how you are so if you need help I will help you communicate with your family and friends" Bennie looks down at Jack's card is all filled out, to say;

"Your right on for me, and you didn't even ask me a thing, you know what they call that?"

"No what?"

"Instincts, your dead on with all these assessment, you really think I could be supervisor material, as well as Teresa and Raphael, wow, Jack that is nice of you, as Bennie finished going through his families pictures, to say"

"So where are you from, Jack?"

"Mobile, Alabama" said Jack

"Really, your close, I'm from North Carolina" and ads;

"Were going to use "Mobile" as your password but after we log off, I want you to change your password and make sure you put in some numbers as well, so your name is Jack Cash, okay lets write this down, this is your E-mail address for everyone who wants to communicate with you, do you have a book full of addresses.

"E-mail and phone numbers"

"Nah", it was in my phone"

"You know you could have kept it, see here is mine", Bennie shows Jack.

"Listen from this day forward you need a hard copy of your phone and contact list, and two phones, one strictly for business and the other use for personal but you need only to have ten numbers on speed dial which are fake and encrypt the others, you need to keep your information a secret from everyone including your wife and or girlfriends, every Bounty Hunter has at least a couple of girls on the side and if you can get your wife to like them and even invite them in your bedroom then you'll have it made"

Bennie pulled up the white pages for Mobile and said," What's your girls' name?"

Jack thought of a name off the top of his head and said "Samantha Smith"

Bennie did a quick search and said, "Here it is her phone number and she has an E-mail listed".

Bennie said "Do you want me to save it to your favorites"

"Sure" said Jack

"Team you have ten minutes to reassemble, and have your comment cards ready." said the Liaison Officer Devlin.

"Do you want me to send her an E-mail from you?" asked Bennie.

"Sure, what do you think I should say?"

"You can say anything you want, just start talking and I will type it, afterwards we can edit it, so go for it"

"Well, first off I will say, hi, how are you doing are you still in the hospital, did your surgery go well? I'm thinking of you and I hope to see you soon, with love Jack."

"That sounded good, do you want me to send it"

"Nah just erase it, she doesn't want to hear from me," said Jack

Bennie went to delete it and accidentally hit the enter and it was gone and ads "It's gone, now what"

"How about James Combs"

"Here it is, what do you want to tell him

"Tell him, I'm fine and let Sara know how to get hold of me and will talk with you later, out"

Bennie sent that and said "If you click on this icon you will be attached to the world wide web and you can search for any topic, thing, place or anything just have fun and you'll be surprised, and as a Bounty hunter this will be a indispensable tool, you know just like this school, its tools to help you with your business."

"This school has prestige and class and when you graduate you'll have a title."

"Alright let's go team," said Devlin and ads "Jack are you there", Devlin opened the curtain to see them and says, "What are you guys watching"

"And with this web site you can watch video" said Bennie

"We are going to take the remainder of the group to basic classes, put on by the U S Marshal's service designed to get you familiarized with the service, it will be supervised by the brass from Washington D C, so listen up they may call upon you to answer some questions"

"Just me" asked Jack

"No, just the remaining teams, so come with me, and let me have those comment cards I need to turn them in" asked Devlin, the group handed them to Devlin.

Devlin led the team out into the courtyard and into a group of buildings, to a large room; there were several long tables with chairs.

"Do you guys want to sit up front?" asked Devlin.

"Nah, I'd like the back row " said Jack his team agreed, so they all took seats along the back row starting with Devlin then Jack followed by Bennie, then Raphael and lastly Teresa.

A few moments pasted and then people came in one by one, as if they were programmed they marched in starting with the first row, they stopped, as they filled the remaining rows, still at attention they stood.

"At ease class" yelled a drill sergeant

"Take a seat", he looked around then noticed Jack and said,   "Who are you, doing in my class?"

Devlin spoke up first and said," Were with the U S Marshal's".

"Well Devlin, looks like your lost, this is the Marine Corps do you wanna join?"

A laugh was heard.

Devlin looked down at his paper and realized he made the mistake and said, "Lets go" to Jack quietly.

"Have you maggots decided what you are going to do, your stinking up my class"

Jack and the team rose, and they began to exit when the sergeant spoke " You maggots aren't moving fast enough, Devlin you ought to move their asses" as the sergeant came close to Jack and Devlin and said "Devlin you're a fuck up, your group was suppose to muster in the courtyard"

"Leave him alone" spoke up Jack who was now in the sergeant's face.

"What are you gonna do sissy boy"
Jack leaned in and Devlin said "Back off, Jack."
The sergeant spoke to say "Your Jack, Jack Cash" he said in a startled manner.

"Enough" spoke a command voice and ads "Sergeant get your Marines out of here, you're the one who is mistaken, although if you want to sit in and learn a thing about what it takes to be a U S Marshal you sure could stay"

"Class A-ten-hut, on my go you file out into the opposite classroom past the Marshal's." "Right face forward March"
Jack stood by the door, watching each man file past and then lastly the sergeant said, "Sorry I didn't know it was you Jack Cash.

"Come on in and have a seat, Devlin you can go", the group came up to the front and sat next to each other as the man in front of them leaned against a desk, with his arms crossed and said;

"My name is Captain Jonathan Knight, I'm your commander for the next ten weeks, I'm sure by now you probably know that your all safe, each of you has an exemption and from this time forward, your going to do what Devlin is doing, being a Liaison Officer.

"Lets talk, most of the comment cards that come back, is usually bull shit, but for some reason, the four of you had over ten comments each, and then there is Jack who received over forty, and some have come from some who have dropped out of the program, which is un heard of, so with some recommendation, from Commander Michael Johnson, each of you is promoted to Liaison Officer".

"Each of you will have a remaining five team members each, this class is totally different than all the other classes in the past, it is being supervised by several watch groups out of Washington, every day from now on, your going to report to me and keep track of your charges, from each of the people you have you can only select one to go into the actually training with, here is your new teams.

In addition, you will stay together as team leaders and help each other out, here is your folders." said Jon, as he hands them out to the four.

Jack quickly looked through his to see a huge person, a former football player, said he played middle linebacker, his arms were huge, tattoos all over his body and goes by the name of Ham, his first name was Rodney.

"So in a moment were going out to the courtyard where you will meet your new teams, then were off to the log course and from now on work with the person you think will make it to training"
Everyone stood, then began to file out.

"Jack hold up" and ads "Your special, I want you on the platform with me, you have that something extra special that makes you pretty unique, your also getting a reputation around here which makes you a very popular person, its also has some draw backs but I can tell you can handle yourself."

"I also have been informed your not eating properly, so I've asked Doctor Hodges to meet with you this morning, after we meet the teams. Are you ready to go?"

"Yes"-said Jack trying to look at everyone in his group.
They entered into the courtyard; together on the platform was his former team mates, as they made their way up.

"Listen up, from this time forward you have all been divided into groups of five, each of you will meet with your team leader, let me introduce them to you," The Captain turned to the team and said in a low voice" As I call your name please stand."
Jack ready himself, by placing his folders on the chair by Bennie and stands.

"First off I like to introduce from Germany, Mr. Jack Cash"
Jack moves to the rail, so that everyone could see him, a lot of whooping and Hallowering went on even a few whistles, while that was happening Bennie began to look over Jack's folders, picking and choosing what he wanted, leaving Jack with four women and one big black guy.

"Bennie "the Blades" Carter from the Bronx's of New York. He is also known as the Rapper"

Bennie went up to the railing and began to rap out a tune much to the surprise around him.

Bennie finishes and sits down to hand Jack the remaining folders.

"Next is a former rebel, and now an envoy to the president of Honduras, Teresa"

Teresa made her way over by Jack and waved.

"Lastly is a Former spy and now the leader of the cabinet for the Croatian government Raphael", which she stood, her long flowing hair blew in the wind as she waved.

"Now Candidates were going to the log course, there will be no more elimination till Thursday and it will be up to the team leaders to decide, let's meet your new teams"

"Jack this is where Dr Hodges is at, I'd like for you to meet with her, you go do that and I'll have one of your other teammates handle your charges"

The Captain pointed to the building where she was.

Jack nodded his head in agreement and added "Alright" he stepped off the platform and trotted behind the platform down a path to the building, inside he found her name and went up to the third floor, a receptionist was waiting and said "Do you have an appointment?"

"I was sent by Captain Knight," said Jack

"Take a seat; I'll let her know you're here."

Jack sat in a chair along a wall he closed his eyes, several minutes pasted.

"Mister, you can go in now".

Jack got up and opened the door, a quick glance at the wall showed a clock that read ten O'clock, and stepped in, a lady turned around in her high back chair to see him, the two's eyes met, her infectious smile and large saucer eyes, Jack stopped in his tracks.

Jack stared at her, she returned the favor, and she paused and licked her lips, and said "Please have a seat"

Jack moved slowly still staring at her thinking, she sure looks like Sara, only a little larger, especially in those arms, Jack took a seat across from her, and sat down he looked down through the glass table and saw between her legs a pair of white underwear, Jack moved his head, back and forth to get a better look.

"What are you looking at?" she said

"Oh nothing, your eyes" said Jack knowing he got caught.

"You know it's not nice for a guy to stare at a girl"

Jack closed his eyes and said, "Is this O Kay", with a smile

"You can open your eyes; just don't look at me that way".

Jack opened his eyes, and stared at her.

"Why are you staring at me?"

"You're so pretty, you remind me of a girl I know, but you're far prettier than she is."

"Really" she said

"Yeah, totally"

"Does that make you happy?" said Kim

"You bet it does, you're just like looking at a realistic painting, and you mesmerize me"

"Then go ahead and stare at me, I kind of like that" she said with a laugh, now how can I help you?"

Jack thought to himself and said now stand up pull off that dress as he could feel himself rising to the occasion. He actually said "Well I'm not one to stand in long lines for some food that makes me tired anyway"

"Well I can tell you this, your right the food, especially the potatoes, have salt peter in them"

"What does that do" asked Jack

"Its design is to suppress all sexual urges"

"Really, it makes me feel like not eating"

"Jack" she said, "You have to eat, and the key is to avoid anything creamy"

"Yes, alright, I'll stay away from that, but now that I know what they are doing I may skip, eating all together"

"Don't do that" knowing she had caught him again and ads;

"What is your obsession, with staring at me? "

"I'm bad do you want to spank me?" he said mocking her.

"No, do you know why you here?" she said.

Doctor Hodges shifted her body and spread her legs a bit wider. Jack noticed that right off and looked down to get a better look.

"Are you enjoying the view" she said to him, she still had her legs apart, Jack could feel the tension, she was teasing him, he knew, he reached out from under the table to try to touch her, as she inched closer to him and said "I don't usually get involved with the candidates, but I can tell you're an exception."

Jack finally found what he was looking for, he touched her thigh, the white creamy soft, skin felt nice as he slowly stroked towards her, she moved as close as she could, Jack's long arm was at the end as the desk was stopping his progress, his fingers were touching her panties, he began to flick the front of them.

A knock on the door, stopped everything. Jack pulled back

"Your beat red, are you doing something you shouldn't be doing" she said to him and then louder she says "Margaret how I can help you" the door opened to see the receptionist holding some documents and said "The commander sent this over and wants to know if you'll have lunch with him?"

"Is it at his office?"

"Yeah I think so," said the receptionist who was looking over at Jack on her way out.

"Give me an hour of privacy and tell the commander I'll see him around noon"

Jack looked over at Dr Hodges with a smile; she saw him and said, "What are you smiling about."

"Oh I think we both know," said Jack smiling as he got up and went over and locked her door, then faced her, as she smiled back.

"Now where were we, oh yes, why I'm here?"

"I'm a Doctor of Diabetes care and nutrition for this base and it has been expressed that your not eating right and for the nutrition, I'd like to give you a physical, have you ever had one?"

Not that I can think of," said Jack and ads "What does that entail?"

"First you need to get undressed, so take off your clothes and stand with your arms out"

Jack moved to the center of the room, and began to undress slowly as the Doctor sat and watched, Jack pulled his pants down, then his underwear, he was hard as he held his hands out to the sides, the Doctor slowly walked towards him, she touched his chest, and felt his rock solid stomach and then ran both of her hands down his legs as he almost hit her forehead.

"I'll get to this last" she said as she grabbed the shaft and pulled it towards her, teasing him, then she released it and went around to the back, feeling his back, down to his buttocks; she said; "Bend over at the waist. All Jack could hear was a snap.

"This might feel weird at first but I'm sure you'll like it"
She inserted a finger in his anus and pressed, instantly he was deflated as she said " That was a good boy, your prostate feels fine" and ads "What's wrong, big boy can't get it up, you know if you get it up you can have sex with me, she whispered in his ear, I'll give you five minutes to get hard again, if not, then were done here, your actions show a big game, I like you so I will help you out, Jack looked at her as she pulled up her skirt, to reveal her panties and said "I know you admired these earlier" and in one motion pulled them off and stepped out of them and handed them to him.
Jack was still feeling the exam and the last thing he needed was this girl teasing him, as he tried to work on it, he felt nothing, even with her teasing him, he abandoned the idea and said "Why don't you stimulate me and take off your clothes, from my count I still have three minutes, I may not be hard, but let me see what you have to offer and then will see if I can get hard or not."
She was caught of guard with Jack's comment; she was game and said "Alright, but no touching,"
Jack looked at her and walked over to where she was sitting at as she stood and he took her seat, she pasted him, as Jack got a whiff of her smell, that was enough for him, his manhood felt a new supply of blood, it was growing as Jack watched, she slowly and complexly began to unbuttons her lab coat, she was watching him as he was watching her, next was her button down blouse, which she did one button at a time, off it fell.
To show Jack her large white bra, she left her skirt on and began to turn when Jack said "I want the skirt next"

"You have my panties already"

"So, let's see what you got"
She did not hesitate, and unzipped the skirt and let it fall, to show a nice hairy brown bush.

"That doesn't match your hair," said Jack motioning her to come closer as she did.

She looked down to see Jack was ready again, he was hard, as she popped of her bra to let her huge breasts out, she knelt down and began to work him over, he continued to sit there and enjoy it, he lifted her head up and led her to him as she said "I don't usually do this, let me put a condom on you, she pulled something out of a drawer and slid it on his pole.

She climbed aboard and lowered herself onto him, Jack played with her breasts as she did all the work, she grabbed him around the neck and continued to ride him out until she came first and then Jack followed afterwards.

Doctor Hodges, rested her head on his shoulders and said;

"You're the first guy who has ever did that to me, its something you have, that made me so wet"

Jack felt down between his legs and it was dry, he then parted her lips with his finger, to feel a little bit, she stepped off him to show her he was still hard. She pulled off the condom and said, "Is that for me"

"Sure, I'm ready to go again"

This time it was Jack's turn; he grabbed her from behind and bent her over the glass table and was ready to insert when she said,

" Please use a condom, I don't want to get pregnant, you can fuck me all you like".

Jack looked at this object and opened up the package and rolled it on, it was a snug fit and then inserted it into her, it made the intensity even greater, with each stroke, then Jack got an idea, to do what she did to him, and pulled out and it was difficult at first but it went in as the Doctor began to really heat up and began to cry in passion and let loose a wave of fluid soaked Jacks bare feet as he unloaded and then pulled out as she collapsed to the floor, she was still shaking and crying and she made her way over to Jack's still hard member and began to stroke it again, Jack was way ahead of her as he pulled out other condom and rolled it on.

Jack knelt down between her legs and inserted it and began to drill her again this time he took he time as he brought her to another orgasm, this time she began to scream as Jack took his hand and covered her mouth, finally she erupted again as did Jack, she held him in her arms and began to kiss him on the neck and stayed there for a while enough to bite him. Jack got off of her still erect as she said "You got to be kidding, my boyfriend may last once but look at you, your like a young stallion I'm just wore out, as she continued to stroke it some more, and ads "How about I call a few of my girlfriends over, to help me take care of you, I'm tired can we stop."

Jack looked at his victim and said "How about one more time" she nodded her head in agreement and began to stroke him off as he pulled out another condom, she put it on, as he helped her up and turn her around bent her over and slid it in.

This time he took his time a good half of an hour, till she finally pass out from multiple orgasms and exhaustion.

She lay in a heap, he got dressed and picked up a handful of condoms and put them in his pocket, then turned his attention on helping her get dressed, by sliding on her skirt and putting on her bra, then buttoned her blouse and finally helped her with her lab coat, then, helped her to a sofa, which he laid her down and he went out the door.

Jack walked back to the room to actually see a line forming for chow, he passed the mess hall.

Jack got to the room only to see that it was empty, he realized he was a little hungry, so he went back to the mess hall, as the line was down, he stepped in to hear a familiar voice.

"Hey Jack we missed you"

Jack turned to see a group of people with Bennie in the lead, Jack steps in shows his card and swipes it then grabs a tray and looks at all of his options.

"Can't decide on what to get" said a person behind the counter

Jack shakes his head to form a no.

"A good rule of thumb is to choose any fish, chicken or meat minus the bread, then a couple of pasta dishes like Mac and cheese, several vegetables, and mashed potatoes, especially cabbage soup, and lastly some fresh fruits, drink plenty of milk and stay away from sodas"

"Thanks for the info" said Jack, with so many choices.

Jack followed his new rule of thumb, but in smaller portions, and stay away from mashed potatoes. He had enough to cover a 12 inch plate, a couple of glasses of this chocolate milk, and began to eat when his former team came up to him and sat down, Jack looked over at each of their plates to see a lot of different combinations, but none like his.

"What's in the bowl?" asked Bennie

"They said it was cabbage soup"

"Ooh we" said Raphael, "Only poor people eat that"

"So what, I actually kind of like it, in addition to the cabbage, it said it had a creamy vegetable broth and Brussels sprouts, I might go back for seconds." said Jack going back up and getting a new bowl, off to his left he watched another person, crumble up some crackers into it, so Jack tried that, and went back to sit down. Jack overheard the team talk about the early day's events.

"It wasn't that hard at least I tried it," said Teresa

"Yeah Bennie, you didn't even attempt it" said Raphael

"Look black men don't climb well, and besides with this exemption, I'm taking it easy

Jack listen to them go back and forth.

"Hey Jack, your team is the only one to complete the course" said Bennie

"Yeah, some of them in record times," said Raphael

What is the plan, after lunch?" said Jack

"I guess were going back out to the course to finish the qualifier then it's on to tactical training and then and exercise in locating and tracking someone" said Raphael

"Yeah Jack you get to spend the night with your team" said Bennie

"You make it sound like it is a bad thing." said Jack.

To add, "I looked at my team, and they seem fine"

"Well actually, while you were gone, the commander said we could switch around our teams, so between Ralph and I we divided our group and left you with probably the best team, much to our mistake." said Bennie

Jack looked over at Raphael and Bennie to see dejection in there eyes and said "So what your saying, is that while I was gone to see the Doctor.

"You two so called friends, took the strongest players and left me with what a group of Larry's, I don't care who they are, I'm here to go to this Academy and if I'm stuck with all the outcasts I'm fine with that, we will still kick your butt's."
They both nodded in agreement.
Jack continued to eat, finding that eating vegetables, really filled him up quicker, and he tried this thing called Mango, which was really quite tasty, he was nearing completion when, a familiar face showed up and said" I didn't give you your papers" said Doctor Hodges, taking a seat next to Jack as the others got up, as Bennie said "We will be outside, there mustering up at one p.m."
Jack looked over at her and that pretty smile.

"Jack I'm sorry I couldn't keep up with you, you wore me out, I even missed my luncheon with the Commander" she whispered in his ear and ads "Will I see you tonight?"

"I don't know Doctor," said Jack finishing off the Mango.

"It looks like your eating healthily, especially with that cabbage soup". "I can't get most people to eat, the best stuff for you, how about, I see you for dinner tonight and we will go over your meal plan?"

"Sure, I know I need help and that would be great"

"From now on Jack call me Kim" she whispered then gave him a kiss on the cheek

"Next time, I hope you have several friends available if you so need them".

CH 11

Spanish fly

" **M** uster call" spoke the sergeant.

The sergeant went over the list of the remaining people and then said "Lets back to the course, follow me".

Jack walked with Bennie and Raphael, they walked a small distance to a hill side and Jack saw huge poles laid out on a course, in amazement Jack was excited, to see this course.

"Listen up, lets divide back into your teams, and the group with the best score, will receive a commissary card to buy whatever they want at the exchange, I think the cards have something like one thousand dollar limit, so I want Teresa's team first, then Bennies, then Raphael's and because Jack wasn't with us earlier, his team will go last."

Jack stood off by himself when a huge black guy came up to him and said,   " Hi my name is Rodney Hamilton, but you can call me Ham." The two shook hands as Jack said "Nice to meet you, I heard you made it over the course in pretty good time"

"Oh not me, I sat this out my knees are messed up"
Jack looked at him strangely.

"It was them" said Ham pointing to a set of four girls walking towards them"

Jack looked over to see a collection of probably the prettiest looking girls, he had ever seen, each had long flowing hair and a very happy smile on their faces.

Jack simply stared as did Ham, until they made it to there position, as the tallest of the four spoke first and extending her hand out and said;

"My name is Angelique, but please call me Angel, you must be Jack, come here handsome man she gave him a hug and then a quick kiss on the cheek and ads, "That's the way we do it from where I'm from"

"Where's that, "spoke Jack still a bit overwhelmed, by what he was liking Jack looked over at Bennie who had all guys on his team.

"I'm from Florida, I'm part Cuban and part Hispanic, here are my friends, first is Erica," a lovely blonde blue eyed girl, a little shorter than Angel and probably the sheer prettiest of them all.

"They call me Cinderella" as she shakes Jack's hand.

"Over her is our friend from Texas, her name is Bridgett. She is a bit shy." and ads, "Lastly the brunette is Tabby," who came over and gave Jack a kiss on the cheek. The four girls huddled up. Jack could hear some screams and giggles and then they broke their huddle as Angel spoke "So Jack, were you going to run the course with us, because we are short a member?"
Jack was enamored by how they all looked he was having trouble talking when he said" Yes", even thought he had already planned to do it.

"So what is our plan?" asked Angel, pressing Jack for an answer.
Jack closed his eyes for a moment then refocused on the task at hand and opened his eyes to say, "Why don't you lead us out Angel, followed by Erica and Bridgett, I'll bring up the rear with Ham and Tabby."

"I thought he said he had a Doctor's note for which he couldn't participate" said Angel, clearly in charge.

"If you all are doing it, then you should count on both of us" said Jack, walking towards Ham who said to Jack "What's up bro."

"Your gonna have to do it" said Jack.

"I'm not gonna do that course, what did those girls put you up to this?" said Ham.

"No, no one puts me up to anything, Doctor's note or not, if your on my team we all participate, now this may not be your event, if you want to be with us later, you need to do this now, nobody rides for free, just because you're a big guy doesn't mean a thing to me, so what's it going to be Ham yes or no"

"I guess I could try" said Ham

"That's what I like to hear, well, and then stick with me in the back and I will help you over every step of the way"

"Thanks man" said Ham

"Don't thank me yet, lets do this thing" said Jack walking over to the girls and saying "Ham's in"

All the girls surrounded ham and gave him hugs as Angel said;

"I'm going to let Erica and Bridgett takes the lead, I'll be in the back helping you guys out".

The new teamed watched as each team went before them, realizing it was theirs to win, that their time was the fastest. As they were ready, Angel said "This run should put us in first place, and with Ham running the time won't matter, all of it will count towards the prize and one low score will be thrown out."

Finally it was Jack's team turn, Jack was up on the line to start, when the sergeant said "You don't have to run the course, either do you"

"It's our choice right" said Jack

"Yes, but"

"Then lets go" said Jack

"Alright on my whistle, ready set go" said the sergeant

The whistle blew, first off was Erica and Bridgett, who took off, then it was Tabby, followed by Jack, Jack shot out like a cannon, forgetting to help Ham.

Jack easily leaped over the front horizontal poles, thinking it was just like, his prison escape, he was in a zone, up a cargo net to the high part of the course, either choosing a rope to go up or straddle a pole Jack choose the rope, he followed closely by both girls, both athletic in their own right, Jack swung to the next course quickly and to the cheering of those down below. The next set was to walk over some logs and lastly a cargo net to a rope swing over a mud pool.

Jack finished the fastest overall, next to finish was Erica, then Bridgett, followed by Tabby and in true drill sergeant form Angel was coaching Ham through the course to finish in front of her and all came in, missing the mud pool, which had already claimed some people.

Jack waited at the finish line to see Ham give Jack a big hug, and say;   "I was afraid of this course man, thank you for having me do this."

"Listen up teams, the best time was that of Jack's team, followed by Raphael's and so forth. Here are your cards, Jack your team is dismissed for the day, while everyone else will continue on this course till everyone finishes." spoke the sergeant.

Jack and the girls walked over to a large building that read Commissary, the girls were talking with Ham, and Jack followed them when all of a sudden Jack stopped and stared a beautiful striking blonde who got out of a car, and walked past them and into the store.

Jack resumed walking as Ham said "That's the Commander's daughter, don't worry Jack you'll meet her soon enough, she is in the program, she has the exemption, you know being the Commander's daughter and all of that"

"How do you know that?"

"During orientation, they told us a lot about the post and what we could do and what we can't do and she is off limits to us common folks, but your different, your with her you have exemption, I'd love to be with you guys"

"You keep doing what I ask of you, you may have a shot"

"Highly unlikely, you're probably going to choose Angel, I know I would, she's tough, smart and boy does she look good"

"Looks aren't everything, later why don't you and I sit down and tell me why you want to be a Bounty Hunter"

"O Kay that sounds good Jack" said Ham

Jack entered the largest store, he has ever seen in his life, similar to the mall, in Mobile, with one exception, he was limited on what he could spend, but his mind was preoccupied with, what was he missing, I never went to orientation, let alone had never ever seen this people, something is going on, this is weird"

Jack walked alone up and down each aisle when he noticed a backpack, pulled it down, put it on and decided to keep it.

Jack continued past electronics, where Ham was at. Jack walked the whole store, with only the backpack in hand, he saw Ham with a basket full of music c d's and a portable radio player.

Jack entered the Line, as it shortened he saw the girl again, this gorgeous blonde was the cashier. He looked down when he spoke to her as she did the same.

Jack placed the backpack on the conveyor belt; he looked up at her, as she said "Will this be all sir?" with a very pretty smile.

"Yes" said Jack

"How will you pay for this today, cash or charge?"

Jack handed her the credit card, she swiped it and said "Do you want a bag for this?"

"No" said Jack, picking up the backpack.

She handed Jack his card back as the two touched hands, she lingered a bit and then Jack broke free, when he saw another familiar face, he walked to the open door that led into the perishable foods, he stood at the door to see Doctor Hodges hanging out with a tall guy, Jack couldn't see his face.

"Try not to stare to long," said Ham, still pushing his cart, Man I'm going to the barracks do you want to come with me and check out some of this music?"

"Sure, O Kay" said Jack still watching the Doctor, with that guy.

"That's Doctor Hodges, she is a licensed Dietician and with her is the Commander of the Bounty Hunters, they say their an item" said Ham, "If your coming, lets go"

Jack followed Rodney back to his Barracks, an open squad bay with double bunks on both sides and a footlocker at the base.

"The head is on the end, on the other side are the girls' rooms, have a seat on my bunk as you can see there is only about fifteen of us left, and I don't know when I'll be leaving as well, there is really only about four spaces left and this is my last time I can try"

How so?' asked Jack, sitting down on a bunk, watching Ham pour the C D's into his nearly full footlocker.

"Well this is how it works, when you don't have exemption, your put into a mass pool of over fifty people, and you go through what they call hell week, which was last week, where as only ten are selected to move on, you can try up to four weeks, then your sent packing, this is my fourth and last week, however this week, they came and announced to us that there was only two male spots and two female spots available, because they had several hi-profile people in the program and only the top, would be allowed to participate."

"How is it this is the first time I've ever saw you or the girls, I know I would have remembered them if I saw them before".
Asked Jack.

"You have been isolated, your what they call, is a floater, and have been working out with the marshal program, your running in the mornings and classes in the afternoon or in your case, you will oversee who gets in with you on your cycle., that's why everyone is delicate with you, you probably skipped the first two weeks, anyway, I hope you chose me."

"Also you may be chosen to be a International Bounty Hunter, which means you can go anywhere in the world. " "You will probably be assigned a partner, listen, lets keep this a secret, but there is something a lot bigger going on here, also there is one other step above both of them, and that is an International Super Agent." said Ham

"I imagine that's what I will be doing; the Bounty Hunters program "said Jack.

"That's what I would like to do as well, but that in itself is all what they want, to be paid a base salary like over one hundred thousands of dollars for the rest of your life and of that, you'll get two more generations, worth of exemptions, that means, your wife and her children or until two hundred years, after you are gone"

"Isn't that what you're doing here?"

"Sure, but you see, only the top five American's qualify for that honor, if I get into the cycle the best I can hope for is just being a U S Bounty Hunter, which means I can travel state to state and get Bail jumpers, not fugitives, those are left up to the chosen class, only a select few are chosen and your one of them" Ham hands Jack a portable C D player and ads " Put on the headphones", Jack placed them on his ears and listened to the music, then slipped off his shoes and laid onto the bare mattress and closed his eyes and fell fast asleep.
Jack awoke to someone shaking his arm; a familiar face he was looking at, it was that of the sergeant's.

"Get up Jack it is time to clean"
Jack rolled out of the bed and pulled his earphones off, and set them and the C D player on Ham's rack.

"You can either stay or help them clean or go" said the sergeant.

"I'll stay and help out "said Jack

"Fine, grab a broom" said the sergeant.
Jack walked down the middle of the squad bay to the open closet door, which he opened it up, and out of the corner of his eye, he saw a girl half dressed, he continued to stare at her, the door swung open, only to see Angel standing in the door way.

"It's funny to see you here and to help out the guys"
Jack just looked at her.

"You could come over here and help us out," she said sarcastically.
Jack takes his long broom and starts to push it along, away from her.

"Did you hear what I said" she said demanding.
Jack continued away from her, pushing the broom.
She came up behind him and said "Why won't you answer me?"

"I didn't know, I had too" he stopped what he was doing to look at her. And ads "What is it do you want"

"I couldn't help seeing you spying on one of our girls in the shower, do you like to watch?" asked Angel sincerely.

"Sure, who wouldn't like to spy on some girl, hey the door was open, all I did was watch"

"Interesting, most guys could care less, but listen we could use a guy to help us, do you think you might be interested?"

"What do you want me to do?" asked Jack, dropping the broom and began to follow Angel through the men's shower area, she opens the door and yells "Straight man on deck"
Girls appeared, from behind their curtains, some dressed some topless, one was even nude, who had a smile on her face, Jack smiled back, even paused to stop and stare.

"Do you want to come in and"

"Jack lets get a focus" said Angel grabbing Jack's arm.

"Maybe later" said Jack to one of them.

"I'll be here" said the girl.

Jack followed Angel down to the last curtain, he stepped in to see three other girls, sitting on their racks, as Jack took a seat by a locker and said "Where's the show"

"Jack likes to watch girls take off their clothes."

Jack just shook his head in disbelief, to listen to this brash, outgoing over opinionated Angel.

"What's he doing here?"

"You know we need some help tonight" said Angel.

"Ooh yes, you're right, oh that's a good idea" said Bridgett.

"Yes, but what is his cover" asked Erica.

"He is gonna distract the Daughter."

"Yes, that is a great idea" said Erica.

All the girls look at Jack who was still sitting there, then looks up.

"Alright Jack, what we need you to do, is to play a game with a girl, your gonna create a distraction so that we may catch someone in the act of some compromising position.

"Alright, who's the girl and what's the angle."

"For our class project we need to spy on someone"

"Are you girls going to the Academy?"

"Yes, well its difficult to say, we are here to get training on the cutting edge spy techniques, but we heard you're a bounty hunter and that means your tough and we need a guy who is a little tougher than we are, yet you're a guy, and for this distraction we need a professional, so Jack are you in?"

"How is it that you are training with us and not going to the Academy?"

"Let me see, how I can explain this to you, half of the Academy is fake, because of the Academy's shake up from Washington, they needed to show Washington, that the Academy is thriving, but in all actuality it is dying, there recruiting from all over the world and charging over 50k for the training and the certificate, so every other week, all of us girls, in this bay comes out and participate in the field activities, we all live in Montgomery, and get paid for the three days of training, our day jobs are we work as private investigators"

"Alright you convinced me, what I need to do"

"First we need to get you out of those clothes, why don't you try on these clothes as Angel handed Jack a pair of slacks and a matching shirt. The girl's watched Jack strip down to his red underwear, it was their time to stare at him, and everything fit.

"Looks good" said Jack

Erica went in to adjust Jack's clothes and said "This isn't going to work he needs a bath"

"So take him into the shower room and get him cleaned up" said Angel.

Both Erica and Bridgett escorted Jack down the hall to the women's side of the shower, they helped him out of his clothes, he watched as they stripped down naked as well, easily Jack was ready, with his manhood in his hands.

"Don't kid yourself, Erica I have a boyfriend.

Were doing what Angel wants us to do, they said with a smile, they both help Jack take a quick shower, washing him from head to toe. They both lingered in the middle, giving Jack a unsurprised smile.

"Not a word of this to no one" said Erica, helping Jack to dry off and then Bridgett began to spray a fluid around Jack's hot spots.

"What's that stuff?"

"Its called Spanish fly, when mixed with your scent, it will make you virtually irresistible to any woman, hurry up and get dressed"

"Honestly Bridgett, he doesn't need that stuff he is hotter than hell now" said Erica helping Jack on with a wire and a concealed battery pack," and said " I was happy to help you out maybe later you can help me out, if you know what I mean?" said Erica.

"Sure lets see how this goes, this sounds fun so far"

Jack watched Bridgett disappear, for him to say, to Erica;

"Thanks for helping me out."

Said Jack and the two met up with Tabby and Angel.

"Alright Jack, let me tell you how this will go down, I arranged for a meeting (a blind date) with this girl we know, who is extremely beautiful, but can't seem to get a date, so we told her a older gentleman was interested in her and would like to go out with her, your going to drive my car and pick her up, take her out for two hours or so, here is her number I will get her on the line and you sell her yourself. Jack watched as Angel dialed the phone number and handed the phone to Jack and said "It's ringing."

Jack listened to the other side pick up and say "Hi, this is Allison, please leave me a message" beep

"Hi this is Jack, Angel refered me to you and asked me to see if you would like to go out on a date, say dinner and dancing, call me as he read what Angel quickly wrote down 321-4250."

Jack closed the phone up.

"That was better than expected, oh she will call, and she is desperate to go out with someone" said Angel and ads "Trust me, that girl asked me to hook her up"

The phone began to buzz

"That's probably her now, answer it" said Angel looking on with excitement.

"Hi you got Jack"

"Hi Jack, my name is Allison are you a friend of Angel's?"

"Yeah, she and I went out a few times, so do you want to go get something to eat"

"You sound much older than I expectected"

"Does that matter to you" said Jack to the other girls who were holding back their laughter and giggles.

"No not really, when can you come by and pick me up?"

"Where are you at I'll be there as fast as I can go and we can make a night of this"

"I'm at my dad's house on Main Street, it's the big white house in the middle of the lower east side field, just pull up front and I will come out"

"Alright I will see you soon, bye" said Jack

"That was great, you're a natural pro, here is fifty dollars and tell her you're an extra for the Academy's training, as a Bounty Hunter, she will dig that, just be nice to her and win her over, the most important thing for you to know about her is that she likes spontenanaty"

"Alright where do I go?"

"I'll lend you my car"

"So I will drive her around?"

"What you will do, is all of us will drive to her house, then a block away you will drop me off and you can take it from there" said Angel.

Angel led the way, followed by the rest of the girls, then Jack, they entered into the night, Tabby got into a van, as did Erica and Bridgett, enter a side door to look at Jack.

"Here are my keys, you drive" as Angel tosses them to Jack.

Jack slides into a candy apple red, Grand Prix, he adjusted the seat and felt the contour of the steering wheel, and he put the key in and fired the 500 cubic inch engine up, the 750 horsepower, roared under the throttle of his foot.

"I had this souped up, she can really fly, so if you get stopped by the cops just, tell them your with, show them your I D and you get out of the ticket also were on base so you won't have much trouble everyone knows this car."

Jack backed up then dropped it into gear and stepped on the gas pedal, throwing up rocks and debres as he sped out, Angel gave him directions on where to go.

A block away he slowed to let her out.

"Remember you can hear us, but don't talk to us back, we will be listening to you and help you out all the way" Angel closed the door.

Jack sped up and then slowed down as he coasted to a stop at a modest white three story house with arched columned front, out in the middle of no where, when someone moved a curtain on the front top window, in a instant the front door opened to see a girl with a cap on, come close to the car.

"Jack goes out and opens the door for her you need to be a gentleman"

Jack got up and went out and opened the car door for her and waited.

"Hi you must be Jack, I'm Allison" as she extended her hand out.

Jack looked at her "Pull her hand up and kiss her knuckles"

Jack did that as Allison said "Jack you are a gentleman, thank you" Allison sat in the car.

"Close the door for her, think of her as a precious baby, you need to care for all of her needs, honestly after this we are gonna teach you some manners".

Jack got in to hear "So Jack what you do?"

"Oh I'm an extra in trying to get into the Bounty Hunters Academy"

"That's nice" she said with a smile.

Jack looked at her, she looked familiar, but said "Where too"

"There is a place on the lake".

Jack took off as she did all the talking, or was it angel in his ear.

"This place serves the best oysters, do you like oysters Jack."

"Can't recall ever having them, are they good?"

"Yeah, they say it's an aphrodisiac" said Allison.

Allison keeps looking at Jack, as Angel is in his ear, telling him where to go, Jack continues to watch the road as Allison moves her hand to Jack's leg, and begins to rub the thigh and says " Do you like that Jack?'

"Yeah, it feels good"

"When you said you were older, I didn't expect you to look so young, how old are you?"

"Don't tell her, just be coy, lead her on."

"Is my age a matter to you, were here lets have a good time and lets see how it goes" said Jack trying not to look at her.

"That sounds fair; do you want to know how old I am?"

"No not really" said Jack "Jack watch it" said Angel.

"Why not, I'm going to tell you anyway, I'm nineteen"

"You look good for nineteen" Jack repeated what he heard.

"On your left is a place you can park, park under the tree and then look in her eyes and give her a kiss"

"Where are you going the place is on the right?"

"Ssh, I have a surprise" Jack repeated what Angel said.

Jack came to a clearing then up a hill and parked on a hill overlooking the lake, her hand was still on his thigh as he turned to look at her, he pulled off the cap to see the pretty commissary girl next to him, as he used his left hand and pulled her head close to his and gave her a unexpected kiss.

He let her head go and she said

"Wow that was romantic and unexpected, I like you Jack, what's your last name?"

"Tell her' It's Cash" said Bridgett, "No, No, no not your real name, oh Jack, I'm sorry"

"Its Jack Cash," said Jack to her.

"Really, if its not real, will you tell me someday" said Allison moving in for another Kiss this time she was the one lingering, biting his lip and sucking on his tongue, Jack went with it and made out with her as Jack's hands went to touch her breasts., for her to say;

"Yes touch my breasts."

"Stop don't touch her breasts" said Angel

They both froze as Allison said "Did you hear that"

Jack looked at her and said "I thought it was you alter ego speaking"

'Maybe it was my Dad speaking telling me not to have sex, but honestly, I can't controll myself, you hot and I'm really heating up, you won't tell my dad will you."

Allison begins to unbutton her shirt when Jack says "I thought we were going to get something to eat"

"We can after you fuck me"

"Listen Jack, lets slow down here, as Jack fires up the car, and speds out, throwing her back against the seat, she was laughing and still unbuttoning her shirt to expose her white bra.

"At all costs don't have sex with her" said Angel

Jack was trying to button her shirt while he drove all the while; he ended up fondling her breasts,

He stopped and just parked and said "Look, how about after dinner we come back up here and I will give it to you, besides I don't have any condoms.

"Good Jack, yes that's it"

"You promise, you know, when you get a girl hot and bothered, there is no stopping us from having sex and Jack you have pushed me far over the edge, and if I don't get it, I may explode"

"I know what that like is, and we can't have that, of course I will take care of you."

"Good, cause look what I have; showing Jack a strip of condoms. And ads "How many will you need?"

"Oh atleast three" said Jack with a smile.

They got to the obscure restaurant, which was on the base but close to the town, a few cars in the parking lot and a couple of motorcycles out front. Jack parked the car, got out and raced around to open the door for Allison, who had rebuttoned her top; he helped her out of the car.

"Thank you Jack"

Jack closed the door and went ahead of her to open the restaurant door, which she just walked in, with a smile on her face. Inside the bar was smoky and filled with undesirables and harden men and women, Jack took the lead and took her hand to pass the bar and into the main dining room, where a girl stood to say "How many tonight?"

"Just the two of us" said Jack

"Do you want private or with company?"

"With company is fine" said Jack, as Allison spoke up;

"Private please."

"Let me seat you" said the hostess.

Jack still held her sweaty hand, but she continued to try to kiss his ear.

They were seated in a booth overlooking the lake, all by themselves, Jack took a seat across from her, she had a smile on her face, as a waiter handed Jack a menu and said several dinner specials.

A voice in his head said "Order for her, I heard the chicken is good here, and get her a glass of chardonnay, which is wine, Jack."

"Do you want me to order for you",

"No Jack, I know you didn't just say that to her" said Angel.

"No, that's O Kay, I know what I want" said Allison.

"Well tell me and when the waiter gets back, I'll tell him for you, remember, I'm your gentleman tonight"

"O Kay I'll have the chicken and pasta" said Allison

Jack folded his menu closed as the waiter came close, Jack ordered two chicken and pasta's and a bottle of chardonnay.

"So Jack tell me why you want to go to the Bounty hunter's Academy, or be a Marshal?"

"Because it was a lifelong, dream" Jack stopped repeating what Angel was telling him to say" After being a commercial fisherman for so many years I felt it was necessary to find a new line of work and being a Bounty hunter seemed like a nice way to meet people and make some money at it as well."

"Fair enough, I can talk to my dad and see if he can get you aboard."

"Sounds good, how about you, what do you do" said Jack following it word by word.

"Currently I work at the commissary as cashier, but I too want to become a Marshal and participate in the Academy"

"Good, for you, you'll make a fine Marshal" said Jack getting more use to the ear piece.

"You really think so?" and ads "That's so nice for you to say"

The food arrived; the two began to eat as Allison said "Can you bring us twelve oysters on a half shell please"

Jack ate slowly as Allison played with her food, each bite she took, was slow and dilibert, Jack had his head down for most of the time, as the food was marvelous, and very tasty.

Jack actually liked it when out of the corner of his eye, he noticed a flyer on the bulletin board, he looks up as Allison sees what he is looking at and says "That is the new velodrome"

"What is that" asked Jack as both Allison and Angel are telling him what it is.

"Enough" said Jack as the two stop, with Allison looking at him.

"Sorry, my mind is on a bit of overload, as you were saying" said Jack

Allison went ahead and continued, to tell Jack what it was how it worked and then out of the blue said "I can get you inside, do you want to see it?"

"Sure, that sounds fun"

"Only if you let me drive your car?"

"Sure, it's all yours", "No, No, No Jack you're not going to let her drive my car"

Jack finished his plate and two glasses of wine.

Jack looked up to say and said "Check please"

"You hardly touched your food,"

"I wasn't really hungry, I liked the oysters they were great". "You know I kinda feeling horny now, and you know you promised you would fuck me, so let's get out of here and I'll take you to the velodrome and we will do it in there." said Allison.

Jack paid with the fifty and was pulled out the door with Allison by the driver's door waiting for the keys, which Jack threw to her, she caught them and in a flash, Jack was holding on as Allison was doing a couple of burnouts on the dirt road, then she began to shift gears on the steering wheel. To say "Cool you have electronic shifting, six gear transmission"

Jack was sliding back and forth left and right as she guided the car around a corner, and red lining it and then kicking on the speed as she got onto the main road, and picked up speed, a car began to follow, when the next thing you knew Jack's head was against the seat, as they both held on, in a flash as that nitro oxide kicked in, that car took off, in a flash they were coming up to that building, and she slowed it down, and killed the lights as she drove past several large working machines and parked in the back.

"Your car is cool, every time you take me out I want to drive this car, can I" she leaned over and begin to get frisky with Jack, who was trying to defend himself from her advances as she climbed over to sit down on him and face him, she was unbuttoning her top, which she flung off, then it was her bra, she pulled it off, to say "Jack your getting me so hot."

Jack tried to hold back, but it was no use, as he was rock hard solid and ready for action, she pulled it out and in a instant it was in her hand and was stroking it, as she slid on the condom. She lifted up her skirt to show Jack that she wore no underwear, she climbed up onto him and lowered herself down on him, she did all the work as Jack sat and absorbed her fury.

"Sorry Jack" said Angel in his ear piece.

Several orgasms later from her, Jack released into her, as she fell into his arms and held onto him.

She was shaking and crying with delight, he pulled back to see her naked body, she was taunt tight and firm. And as she said;

"Jack I like you, your like no other guy I've ever been with, your so, so big, come on lets go inside" she said opening up the door and getting out.

Jack zipped up, and re-buttoned his shirt to see her naked except for her skirt and her shoes, opening up a door and turning on the lights.

Jack came through the door to see a huge indoor track, with raised corners; Allison had a bike in hand and was pedaling it.

Jack found one and caught up with her, she hit the track, in stride, with Jack closely behind, she slowed, to let Jack catch up then said;

"Stay here and I will go to the other side and when I yell;

"Go," you will pedal as fast as you can to catch me , if you pass me we will do it in here, if I catch you, we will do it in your barracks, you have ten laps to do this"

Jack waited for her to get over to the other side, and then she yelled; "Go"

Jack took off slowly, this single low geared bike, took some time to gain speed, but it wasn't long, as he was up to full speed, as the laps kicked off, he was neither gaining or losing ground to her for each pass, even the faster he pedaled she was still a ways away. Ten laps had come and gone as Jack was still trying to catch her when, a siren was heard, Jack slowed, as Allison caught up with him and passed him, she slowed her bike to a stop and said "Lets go, follow me."

Jack slowly pedaled his bike to where he found it, he could see her seat was saturated with fluid, he got off and followed her to the door, she opened it as the two watch the firetruck leave its house next to them, as she said " It gets them, every time."

Jack pushed her through the door.

Jack got in the car as Allison turned out the lights and locked the door.

She got in and said "Take me to your barracks; I want to fuck you in your rack."

Jack hestated then looked at her, his ear piece, he checked his ear was gone, he said to himself "Oh shit."

"Come on lets go, I'm horny and I want to fuck you, like you promised"

Jack drove slowly and carefully, occasionally looking over at her and her partial naked body, she was playing with herself in anticipation. Jack parked the car, by the mess hall, not a soul was around, Jack got out, Allison carried her clothes in hand as Jack made it to his door. Jack opened it up, and led her to his rack, Jack carefully closed the door, and saw she was on his bed, she pulled his covers down. and pulled off her shoes, Jack pulled his curtain closed, then stripped down and joined her, he was inside of her as she laid on her back Jack did all the work, orgasm after orgasm, she tried to keep quiet by putting his hand on her mouth, but she still let out a scream or two, finally they both fell fast asleep together.

"Get up Jack" yelled Bennie and ads "We got Physical training" as Bennie came through Jack's curtain to see Jack, lying on his side and Allison next to him, he looks over at her trying to get a glimpse of anything, as he pulls Jack's arm to get him up, Jack pulls the covers back to expose himself and Allison naked body, for his full viewing pleasure.

"That's not what I wanted to see, we have a three mile run, it's the final run and they said they would have final cuts today, so get dressed"

Bennie tried to cover up Allison when she turned and said;

"Who are you, are you my next guy"

"Nah, I'm married"

"Oh, that's a shame, why don't you invite her over" said Allison with a smile

Jack dressed, quickly, and went out the door, with Bennie, only to see Raphael and Teresa and half of the teams, although Tabby was there, she came up to Jack and said " Where is she at?"

"In my bed, wanting to take on my friend here" said Jack

"Were sorry Jack, she was a total innocent girl, wow what is that smell as Tabby gets closer and says "How about we do it right here"as she begins to lift up he top to show Jack her two firm breasts, Jack Whisks her into the room, fast enough to see her, pull down her shorts, to see her naked and says "Come Jack fuck me too. Allison flung open his curtain to see Tabby.

Jack pushed Tabby in and closes the door.

He met with Ham and the rest of the group as they assembled, Raphael was close to him when she said "Jack is that you, what is that smell, here let me smell you" she said in a sexual way, as they assembled to stretch and exercise, Raphael was smiling at Jack.

They started the run, this time it was, only the sergeant leading the group, about twenty was left, the road was familiar up the hill to the reservoir and beyond the first chance Jack had He dove in, and then like a reaction, everyone followed him, a wave of euphoria, had engulfed the runners as his scent was on the whole field, especially the woman who were horny as ever, some out of control, as Jack bailed from the run.

Women were taking off there clothes as men were also excited, Jack was being chased by Raphael, Teresa and two other girls, he kept a strong pace, finally they gave up as he ended up by the girls barracks, inside he went, to see Angel and Erica, both had towels on to say; "Something is wrong, you got to help me out, girls are after me and"

Both girls dropped their towels as they got a good whif of his scent.

"This is different than what it said on the package." said Erica, barely able to contain herself, who was touching Jack as Angel was the more logical one and said" Let me climb onto of you, wow, whatever you gave him is totally turning me on, I've got to control myself" and ads "Let me hold him down while you search for a andiote. Nude Erica ran around their room searching for a substance she that was used to spray on him, she found it and said "I got it."

Erica read the bottle, it says, caution extremely toxic when combined with the opposite sex, use one drop per application in the event of a orgy breakout, and use a bath of ammonion to vinegar to ten parts of water"

"How much did you spray on Jack, Erica?"

"It was Bridgett, and she sprayed it on all his hot spots, she wanted to make sure it would work" as Angel was trying to get Jack's shorts off, she felt the heat, and it was becoming intoxicating to her and said "Go mix it up and bring it in here, I'm trying my best to hold back, as she finally found what she was looking for, as eager as

Angel was she tried her hardest to hold Jack back, but when she pulled his shirt off, that was it, she had to have him, and inserted him into her as she was along for the ride, she rode him out for a good orgasm and then Erica arrived, she too was horny, as Angel kept pushing her away, think about yourself first.

Erica, finally knocked off Angel, to lower herself onto Jack and began to grind him while Angel took a sponge bath in vinegar, as Erica came, she said "I told you you were going to satisfy my needs Jack."

Angel began to bathe her friend, but it still didn't calm her temptations, whereas she still was riding Jack, till she was done, as was Jack, who dumped a load into Erica. Several condoms down, the two girls bathed Jack, and neutralize the poison on his body, after a half hour of washing, they finally found him to be just slightly sexy, but one whiff, is all it took for Erica, to grab at Jack and away she went again, Jack was naked helpless as Erica overpowered him and he gave her another orgasm as he let go himself again, the girls gave Jack new clothes to wear and said "Overall you did a good job of destracting Allison, we got the info we needed, were sorry for what she did to you"

"That was great at first, then scary, as every girl I knew came after me, even Tabby."

"She did, where is she at" asked Angel

"She likes to run, so she was with the Marshal's this morning" said Erica, smilling at Jack

"Honestly Jack, I didn't know this was going to happen" said Angel with a smile.

"Great now, I'm hard, how will I disguise that?"

"Just take cold showers and wash with ammonion and vinegar"

"I'll wash your shorts and those clothes from last night and bring them to your room, do you have keys to my car and where is that ear piece?"

"I don't know, I think I lost it at the Velodrome"

"That's alright Jack, we have done enough damage to you for a while" as Angel touches Jack's manhood.

Jack jumps back and says "Awe that hurts, I'll be resting that for awhile" he turns to see Bridgett at the doorway who says "What did I miss, you know the base is on a Emergency shut down, and everyone is asked to go to the clinic, there is a outbreak of some foreign substance"

"I wonder what that could be" said Angel.

Jack leaves, and begins to walk back, as trucks and cars race past him, even an ambulance.

Jack gets back to his room to see men in suits.

The large orange space suits with helmets and face guards,

"Come with me" said one, as Jack is lead to a room, they strip off his clothes and though a decomp process he goes first to wash his body, then a rinse and then a desensitized station and finally a dry rub solution, "This one checks out, clean, Jack puts on a robe, and walks into the last tent, to see Rapheal and Teresa.

"I'm sorry Jack, for coming on to you, I was so horny, you know they think it was Allison, who was taken to the hospital, she had it all over her body, as did a girl named Tabby, who authorites believe gave it to Allison, the whole base is on lockdown"

'How are you feeling Jack" said Teresa, who her and Raphael came and gave him a hug.

"Oh, I'm fine now, they waited until the last of the people were decamped and a announcement was made," At this time we need you to go to the clinic, to get a shot and for further vaccines"

"What does that mean" asked Jack

"That means for those who had unprotected sex, may be at risk for STD's" said a girl who was eyeballing Jack.

They walked in force as a group with Raphael and Jack together, they got to the clinic, to see it was overran, they divided girls and boys, Jack was given a shot and some blood work taken a set of new clothing was given to him as he went into a isolated room, a few moments later a Doctor came in followed by a Military Policeman, " We have your results back, and no you don't have any STD's or are HIV positive, how many women did you come in contact with?"

Jack thinks to himself and honestly answers "Three"

"Wow, that's a lot, said the policeman, writing something down.

"Alright open you robe, I need to take a few scrapings, and then you can get dressed."

"I have a couple of more questions for you" said the policeman

"First off, were you, in the group that ran today?"

"Yes"

"Do you know who might have started this?"

"What do you mean?"

"When did you first notice everyone attacking, everyone."

"When they hit the water, it was like a frenzy occurred."

"That's because water is used to react to that particulate poison and the wetness caused a mass explosion of mental thoughts, whoever did this sure knew what they were doing, it put twelve people in the hospital to include the Commander's daughter" and ads "Lastly your name is Jack Cash, where were you last night and this morning?"

Jack thought about it and said "I was sleeping in the candidates barracks." Jack paused to add more when the Policeman said Can anyone collabolate on that story?"

"Sergeant Snyder, saw me there" said Jack

"That will be all for now, your free to go"

Jack got dressed, and then went out into the lobby to see Raphael and went to see her when a cotinguicy of armed troops. Followed by a leader who was calling out his name "Jack Cash, are you in here?"

"I'm Jack Cash" said Jack

"Come with me sir" said the officer.

Jack was led to a vehicle, as Jack was lead inside, he sat quiet confident and oblivious to what was going on as those around him were chuckling and holding back the chance to laugh, the ride was short, Jack exited and into a very large building that was empty, the officer escorted Jack up to the second floor and through a glass door that read "Commander Michael Johnson, Base Commander. Jack waited while the officer knocked on the door.

"Come in"

Jack was lead in, as Jack stood, in front of the Commander.

"That will be all sergeant" said the Commander and looks over at Jack and says "Take a seat" and ads "You probably know by now why I've called you in to see me, it has come to my attention that my daughter Allison, went out with you last night, and the two of you had a wild night together, it may come to no surprise to you, but my daughter is a whore, she has probably screwed half the men on this base and you happened to be the next victim, however, my daughter likes you and I can't tell you how many times have I tried to control her, until now, she has asked, for you to be put into the program, which we already know your enrolled.

Besides if you're anything like Red Combs, your considered to be tame compared to him, I have to admit it, that whole Spanish fly scare is quite hilarious, but what it has exposed is a plot against me, thanks to you, you exposed the threat, all four girls have been apprehended, and all thanks to you. Your what some call a enigma, your what this Academy is here for, graduating men and women who takes chances, which simply means, your going to probably be the best in your class."

"Listen, I got an idea, will you help, me out, and agree to watch over my Daughter and keep her safe, I'll put the two of you together for all the training and if she can calm down and get some discipline then, what the two of you do together is up to you, Listen Jack, you're a guy I think I can trust, lets keep the Spanish fly away, and I promise you, we will get along just fine, and from now on, your hell week is over, here is your fifty thousand dollars you paid to get in."

"You keep it, the more I see the more I like, consider it a donation"

"Thanks, you can go and come back on Friday for orientation; in the mean time I'll have the sergeant, take you to your new quarters along with some new clothing.

"Welcome your in and a unlimited commissary pass.

"Good luck" and ads "One more thing Jack Cash, I need your help with a small problem, but I want to know if you can help me out"

"Sure, whenever you're ready"

"It will be on Friday, I'll meet with you after orientation."

"Sounds good" said Jack as he exited the room and the awaiting men while the sergeant spent time with the Commander, he came out and led everyone down stairs, into the vehicle they went, they drove a short distance to a group of individual houses and stopped.

"Get out Jack, this is your stop, your house is the corner one"

Jack got out and walked a short ways to the front door, tried the door knob and it opened, he walked in and closed the door he turns to see a stunning black girl with piercing eyes and a magnificent physique. To say "Hi, my name is Jack Cash."

CH 12

Becoming a Spy

S everal days had past, he felt like a shut in, everyday was the same, and revelry was sounded at zero six a.m that meant for Jack to roll out of the rack. Then at zero eight o clock a plate was sent over, he read some fascinating books on becoming a Bounty Hunter as well as being a Marshal, he even read a book on manners and proper etiquette. The library was across the street from his quarters, more importantly he read a book on how to treat a woman properly and with respect.

Most importantly, Jack learned about the internet. He had been corresponding with Samantha, who was out of the hospital and decided to help. Samantha decided how Jack should run the charter business and met and is working with Sara, and with Guy and doing the marketing and the business side of it all.

Every day she would send him an E-mail and even make the calls as a personal assistant and making sure the boat was still on time and on progress, which will be in four weeks from now, he also had his phone back, along with all of his belongings.

He had called Sara, his real true love, who by all measures is the best thing to have happen to him, she was driving up with Leslie on Friday to pick him up and spend the weekend with him, it was Friday morning he was notified by messenger that orientation begins at 0900 am at the main hall across from the practice grounds, dress in anything appropriately, as prescribed by the Commander.

Jack carefully laid out his clothes and pack some others into a new suitcase, along with a Music recorder system that holds up to 20,000 songs, which he listens to, he is more refined in how he walks, talks and acts, not looking at every woman he sees as a potential bed partner, he even says hello, to people he doesn't even know, the great thing about this place is all the camera's and the hourly patrols by the Military Police, he even has a title Mister, Jack Cash.

Then while on the internet, he went searching for his past, but have come up with dead ends, so he abandoned the search, he used the iron last night to press out his khaki slacks and a nice dress shirt, he had his hair cut, but kept his goatee and thin mustache his hair was combed straight, he went out the door at zero eight thirty AM and walked over the grass to the sidewalk and across the street to the huge administrative office for the Bounty Hunters and walked in. Behind the desk was a receptionist who motioned for him to go down the hall, Jack followed the hallway down to a counter.

"How may I help you?"

"I'm here for the Bounty Hunters school"

"State your name, please"

"Jack Cash"

"Mister Jack Cash from Germany?"

"Yes"

The guy handed Jack a package from behind the counter and said, "Here you go" the guy lifted the side counter and said,

"Come back here and it's in the main room".

Jack followed back into a room that had big comfortable looking chairs with a number embroidered on them, Jack looked at his paperwork to see the number in large black letters TEN, he found his seat, in the third row, next to a girl who had short blonde hair and a cute face, he took his seat as others filed in, when he saw Allison, who took a seat next to him, she smiled and quickly went through her package, at a glance to his right past Allison, he saw Raphael take a seat, she waved to him, in came the sergeant who said;

"Welcome to the U S Marshal's Bounty Hunter's Academy". Each of you have been chosen from over hundreds of potential candidates, each of you possess that something special, so for those who don't know me, I'm Senior Sergeant Sam Snyder, and I've been with the Marshal Service for over twenty years."

"Now before I introduce your Captain, I want to say, when an officer is present please rise, until told to do otherwise, this is roughly a nine week intensified course in learning all fundamentals of Hunting of Humans, this course is like no other, I will tell you the top two will go on to become U S Marshal's, International Bounty Hunters, which is only open to U S citizens, which is fourteen of you, the other six are nationals, sent by other countries to receive this training, look around your classmates their the ones who will protect you and work missions with you, each of you should be a entity in their own right, in your package is ten fugitives loose around the United States of America, each of you will work your own cases, you can however work with others in apprehending them, and as a team you'll receive points, everything you do from now till graduation, you'll receive points, and it become combinative, meaning if your leading by the half way mark, you may elect to sit out an event".

"But you must follow the schedule, you will be in each class together, and take tests together and work as a team together, if one man goes down". "I hope you will find away to carry them along", "There are over one hundred written tests and over twenty physical tests, later we will go do our Physical test, any questions?"

The room was silent; Jack was looking down at his package wondering what was inside his. When a hand came across and placed it on his thigh, she moved it quickly to reveal a wrapped up note, which Jack put in his pocket.

"Please rise and welcome your group's Captain."

Sergeant Snyder composed himself to say "Captain Jonathan Knight".

Everyone applauded a few whoops and whistles. A smile appeared on his face, as he said

"Sit down" much to everyone laughing, even Jack, as he saw Allison not smiling.

"Ladies and Gentleman, welcome your class number is 2054, you're the 54th class since the year 2000, our Marshal service has seen its fair share of violence over the years, and our branch alone has had its fair share of senseless killings, your class makes up another group of hopefuls that we hope to graduate intact, however with our current record, 2052, only graduated five and in 2053 we are predestining, seven and as it goes back in history, we only have two hundred International Bounty Hunters now, so lets talk about why you're here. We chose twenty, because it is an easy number to handle, each of you has a type a personality, each of you is aggressive in some form or another, however, all we ask is that you come together and be one team, for the next nine weeks and try to pull everyone together, to up our graduation percentage.

"As some of you went through Hell Week to qualify for this program, I will tell you this, only the top two will qualify for the International status, and as you had classes before, the classes you receive at this level, will be, unlike the other classes before you, where it only lasted one week, the longer, you work as a team the stronger you will become as Hunters, I' d like to go around the room and ask If you will stand up and state your name, where your from and how long you have been a fugitive catcher or a Spy."

The first person gets up and turns around and says "my name is Vladimir, I'm from Russia, I'm a Policeman." he sits down, while his brother gets up, and says his name as Jack decides to pull out the note and unfold it and began to read the letter.

That said" Dear Jack, I'm pissed off at you for using that drug on me, I want you to leave me alone, you don't know the humiliation I went through and being expose to all those people, your going to pay for that, I know about my dad is assigning us together, but I want out, so leave me alone, remember I'm the one who got you in this program and I'm the one who will take you out of this program", as he looked over at her, to smile, she frowned back.

Jack folded up the note to hear a raspy voice say his name was OX or OXEN who knows, who cares, then another giant appears and says his name is Johnny "the pit bull" Henderson.

He is from Las Vegas, Jack held onto his package as the number nine was called "Hi my name is Allison, and I'm studying to be a Bounty Hunter" she sits down as Jack Rises and says "My name is Jack Cash and I'm from Germany."

Jack sits down to hear someone say, "How long have you been a Bounty Hunter"

"Who cares?" said Jack to silence everyone.

Next to stand was the Ice Princess, was what Jack wrote, next was Raphael, then behind her was Teresa and then Ham followed by a jersey Girl and another giant, Jack thought about what Allison wrote then shrugged it off, and his only thoughts was on Sara as the Sergeant said "At ease"

"Alright, lets begin with the Oath, please stand and raise your right hand, do you promise to honor and abide by this Oath, so help your God?"

"Yes" in unisons

"We pledge as a group to uphold the Academy's view on being professional, ethical and supportive to our fellow classmate, we will act, talk, walk and be a solider in the fight against those who harm us and furthermore to protect the Academy and those here and abroad against those enemies, here in the United States and beyond, with this oath I do solemn swear to god, this Academy and to ourselves"

"Please be seated, at our Academy our mission is to lead, inspire and challenge you to excel by actually doing the actions, that's why each week for the next nine weeks you will receive over one hundred dossiers containing well known fugitives, some may be close, others far away, points will be given as follows for someone close up to 100 miles is 100 points so if you flew to Hawaii and back you would get 4250 and several of you, have a couple of fugitives. Now most of you are practicing hunters now and for you go ahead and work your files, for those who have never, captured or arrested someone after this class, we will instruct you on the finer points on what to do, next I want to talk about behavior, each class here is designed to involve behavior of yours that of the fugitive and that of the law, currently Bounty hunters worked under a special legal rule, in the past you needed a court-certified copy of the bail bond, a letter of affidavit from the bail bondsman and a authority to arrest signed by the bail bondsman, well guess what, all you need is you I D and the form in your dossier.

That will give you full rights, to bring to justice that fugitive dead or alive, that's right I said dead, you are authorized to use deadly force, as you see fit, the U S Government, will grant you legal immunity once you graduate from this Academy, while you are a student, your in what we call a limited liability standard, as you capture each individual you will develop a pattern, on how you capture, arrest and use deadly force, that's why this is in place, if you shoot first and then drag the body in you will quickly gain a reputation, or if you escort them in unharmed, it will show a pattern."

"Whereas most agencies will call upon you to help them in there search for a killer or a nationwide manhunt, as you progress each of you will gain a reputation, it will be this reputation that will carry you for the rest of your lives, it is my job and my staff to help you accomplishing your dreams and aspirations and utilize your classmates, at this time please rise to welcome our Commander Michael Johnson"

Jack rose to look around then at the Commander.

"Please sit down, welcome class 2054, the next nine weeks, will be the most demanding training you'll ever receive in addition to your class here at the Academy we also train and re-train U S Marshal's which after you graduate, may come back for training, retirement and final resting place from those you have caused great pain to there immediate families." They all laughed.

"Then there will be those friends, who will seek you out, and try to kill you, this is by far the most dangerous job in the world, especially those from other countries, and for your service you will be given a weapon issued to you, as you will each year qualify with here, replacement weapons as you see fit, tactical equipment a vehicle of your choice and a salary, here in the United States, you will receive 5000 a month on the first of the month."

"In Addition to that, any fugitive you capture, plus their Bounty money, as you know and for those who don't know each fugitive carries a cash reward with them, an average fugitive carries the price tag of at least 10,000 dollars and as high as one million, depending on local authorities and what the government deems necessary to capture that person, in addition to the fugitives you capture a pattern will occur and their pattern will determine how effective you will become, from time to time you may seek additional assistance or rest and may come here for that protection and safety and lastly, once you graduate you will be the enforcement tool for the government to use as they see fit, so be prepared to travel, for your first ten years or so once you hit the age of 55."

"Then you will retire from service, internationally and work specifically with a designated state, a state may even request you, through these classes it will help to define you, but the greatest tool at your disposal is the library, a place I hope each of you takes the time to study, this is your time to rest, relax and indulge in this experience."   "Lets try not to indulge to much, as we did have a situation earlier this week from one of your classmates, it was actually quite clever in its concept and its reward, although some people got hurt the overall concept was genius, although it was not the right context, it does however, show who that individual is and at what lengths he will go to expose a known fugitive, attempting to kill me."

"that's right I said kill me, there was a plot to expose me and hurt my family fatally, this person who was instrumental in their exposure and outlandish behavior opened a clear path to a alarming security breech, for this action, a reward of 12 thousand five hundred is awarded to Jack Cash, please rise"
Jack looked around then stood up, to hear the applauded.

"He was able to put the scent on the target, so when she left the base she was detained and discovered, arrested and awaits trial, along with her is three other accomplishes, all having large amounts of this scent on them, this goes to show you outside people can not be trusted, only ones you can trust is yourself, now in closing, my door is always open to you and I hope you try to make this the best experience you can, and now if you will all rise, I'd like for you to give a nice welcome to Linda Jackson special liaisons to the President."
Jack rose again this time with a smile on his face.

"Thank you, please sit down, I'd like to first tell you why I'm here, and second what I want to do, I was asked to come here from our President, to oversee the training and development of this branch, and it was my intention to close this down".

"But after seeing some of the classes and going through that museum it has occurred to me that you save more lives than you take and for this I'm going to suggest he earmark more money and resources to you, I've been working with the Commander Johnson, to try to strengthen your all's longevity and try to graduate more, with the limited resources now, I'm working on a plan I hope to include each and everyone of you, it is my goal to graduate all twenty of you, try to keep you safe and in doing so create a new branch, aside from being a professional Bounty Hunter myself, I am a professional Liaison officer to all the other agencies".

"With that said, I'd like to pair you up with some of the prior class mates, will the following, as I call your name come up, number 012 Raphael, and 010 Jack, you two come on up. Please."
For the rest of you, good luck on your training and from time to time I will be checking on you, Thanks"
Jack rose, only to feel Allison's arm on his, he looked at her as she said   "I'm sorry Jack, I didn't know" Jack smiled back at her, with his package in hand, he walked up to the front and out the door, he followed Raphael, as they were led to a bigger room, it was Linda and her two men who wore black suits, mirrored eye glasses, and ear pieces,   "So that is what a Secret Service agents look like" and the Commander says "Have a seat"
Jack sits next to Raphael as Linda stands in front of them and says;

"The Commander has made it known to me that you two display yourself in the manner of that best suits me".
Jack looked a t Raphael to look back at him.

"What I'm trying to say is that you're the best hope to become International Agents, so it is my duty to inform both of you as this point forward, your training will be different than everyone else's, I want both of you to participate with your class, but in addition to that class you will also attend the U S Marshal program, which is normally eighteen weeks to include a tour overseas and a week at the Pentagon, from this day forward you are both known as the president's own Secret Agents."

"You both have scored far superior on your entrance exams and have shown great ability to handle yourselves, in addition to this title I have bestowed to you, both of you will participate in all classes and workshops together, with our group there is only ten such agents in the world now, upon this day's exit, you will be known to all, here as Special Agent's in training, do either of you have any questions? "
Raphael raised her hand, "yes "what is it"

"You said Special Agent what does that mean?"

"It means, you're recruited to serve us here in the US and abroad"

Jack just spoke to say "what I think Raphael wanted to know was are we International Bounty Hunters or what?" asked Jack

"Good question, hear me out, this will be a little history lesson, The US has not an official Spy program in place, we do however have smaller agencies that run around putting out little fires, what were looking for is a person to who can put out the really big fires, and compete with the British, the Chinese and the Russians, and to be in their league takes a special person, as of today we have ten agents doing that, however, it isn't enough, to be honest with you were losing the spy battle, and there is no end in sight, we just cannot go out and find a Super Spy, their one in one million, actually that's not right, try one in one hundred million, so in front of me are two superb candidates, who both have been there and that is why we choose you"

"Any more questions?" she looked at Jack then at Raphael.

Jack looked over at Raphael, who smiled back at him

"Good, well be in touch" said Linda.

The commander sits in front of them on a desk and waits till the group leaves before speaking and says " Alright you two, I know it is a whirl-wind of events but trust me, you're the only two qualified enough for this position, both of you have a history of being in a Spy Program, Jack we know who you are and it was good of Red to bring you in to us, your going to be safe now and your real name protected, as for Raphael, your just like Jack your home country of Croatia won't know of your being our Super Spy, since your defection and married to a local national, from this day forward you both have immunity".

"Raphael you can leave now, and return to the classroom, I need to talk to Jack".

Raphael gets up and smiles at Jack and leaves, there was a pause then the Commander said;

"Jack we know about your past, and we of the U S want to sincerely apologize for you being incarnated for those last twenty years, first off it was told to me, it was for your own good, and what we would like to do is put you through a battery of tests to see how much you remember and then, we will set you free, if you decide you want to be our spy.

You will be given all the tools to protect yourself, if you choose to walk away, we will let you go, but you will be on your own"

Jack spoke up " I'd like to stay, I know I'm some what not right, but if your going to help me, then I'm all in, besides I like this idea of being a International Bounty Hunter"

"No Jack that isn't what your title will be, if you choose to stay, your title will be way above that, to a rank of General, and the title of Super Spy, but your cover title will be I F R P, In addition, you will be given special privileges others would never see"

"Sound interesting like what "said Jack

"first off lots of help, a team of professionals assign to your every need, and then there are those you want protected, they will be assigned and protected as well, lastly whatever you see or want you can have."

"Meaning like if I wanted a island"

"Then the Government would find a way for you to have it."

"Well this sounds really good for me, count me in"

"Good, that's what I have hope to hear, I'm going to assign a another student to help you with some behaviors, she is and excellent student and will bring another perspective for you to develop and also there is the incarceration package, the government has set up a fund for you, which that 50,000 dollars you gave to me was added, this fund is where your money will be deposited into on the first of each month, for security purposes each month you will receive a new card, destroy the old one, if your in the field, you will receive a special mission card, and with this card" The commander presents it to Jack, Jack takes it and looks it over.

"it is your new I D Card, which is U S Government issue and states your top secret clearance and status, for civilian action your known as Chief Commander, the highest civilian rank directly under the President, and under the Military side your known as a Special General in Command, over the next few month's were going to train you to become a better spy, we discovered, that regardless of all the training out there, it still doesn't specifically train you to be a spy."

"Linda and I and the director of the CIA has agreed to allow you this privilege, for this, and every situation in the future, you will be helped, learn as much as you can, then when you're needed, you will be sent out, so do you have any questions?"

"Well what about the life, I had left behind before I came here"

"What do you mean, the life in Mobile, tell me about it"

"Well I have a boat and I met a girl"

"Okay Jack you can continue your cover working with Red, we can use him to be your sponsor, when do you want to go back?"

"Oh I don't know say on the weekends or a break in training"

"O Kay, you're free to travel down to Mobile and we will work out the details later, but for now let's focus on becoming a spy and in the meantime become a Bounty Hunter"

The two-shook hands as the Commander said, "Inside that package is you newest assignment, with classified information for your eyes only."

"Come on let's go back to a new classroom and meet your new partner"

Jack walked with the Commander back to the empty classroom as Jack saw very tall shorthaired ebony looking lady, with a notebook in hand, she looked very familiar.

"Jack this is Daphne, she is the highest point gainer in her class which is 2053,"

Jack extended his hand, she touched his and said "Hi", he looks at her and smiles.

"Let me show you the way" she said, walking past Jack and placed her hand onto a 12 x12 glass surface, a door clicked open, Jack followed, something wasn't the same, maybe it was the air conditioning the hallway was darker, yet lit, she was in the lead and turned a corner as did he into a room, that looked like a small conference room, with one exception, a oversized chair, was in the center, with a small desk and chair, Jack walked into the room.

"Have a seat in the chair and relax," said Daphne.

Jack took a seat in the comfortable lazy boy, a key pad was lying on the arm pad, on it was a wheel, he turned it and it adjusted the pitch of the chair, he hit a button, and it lifted the chair up ward another button extended the chairs leg rest, while Daphne was gone.

Jack quickly went through all the buttons, he even discovered a hidden television hidden behind a panel, he closed his eyes briefly until Daphne and Captain Jonathan appeared.

Jack opens his eyes to see the Captain, who stood by the door, and uses a key pad a pocket door slides close as Daphne takes a seat by him with a folder.

"Jack, welcome, let me first, say how nice it is to meet you and to see that you're a team player, you took all of our challenges with ease and was even able to flush out a assassination team, here to kill our Commander, lets get down to business, for the next nine weeks, you will be here on the base to observe, participate and learn the fine art of apprehension of potential fugitives, upon the nine weeks, you will receive a badge signifying the title of International Fugitive Recovery Person or I F R P, for short, by now I'm sure you know it's a cover, in addition to the school you will participate in missions".

"This is designed to strengthen your ability to be a Super Spy. "That's right Jack, from this day forward It will be me, who is your Liaison Officer, and with the government, it is my job, to assist you as you see fit, I may participate, engage and be your right hand assistance as you see fit, you're my boss, I will inform you of specific missions and the necessary intelligence, in the event you need additional support players, I have a team available to me, to support you at any time." said Daphne.

"Jack from now on and into the future. At any time, I will be there for you, in this folder is a dossier of who you are, as I have updated your current name and measurements, is there any one you want protected?"

"All I can think of is my two good friends, Sara and Samantha".

"From this day forward, they will be protected, anyone else?
"

"I don't know I guess their families too"

"It will be done, now lets talk about this"

Daphne slides a blue phone over to him, to say "Go ahead and pick it up, as you can see it is a touch screen, that phone you have now is dead, all of your information, has been pulled from it, as you will find out, you can set your new phone in a foot's distance and all of the other persons phone info will go on to yours, in case of a virus, your phone has a reverse virus, in addition to all of that, its an x-ray machine, has GPS and a tracking device, its totally indestructible, and can submerge into four miles deep in the water and work, lastly, you have ten phone numbers on the phone, with unlimited songs and ring tones, see this booklet" she slides to him, to say "this small manual goes over all the features, but remember this is your phone only, your current phone is now programmed on their, any questions?"

"Yeah, I'll like two, please"

"No, there is only one phone, and you have it, it's a one of a kind, its so state of the art, it's not even available to the public market. "said Daphne.

"As I was saying, you have the ability to participate as a Bounty Hunter". Jack was looking over his new phone.

Jack turned the wheel, to see his name appear "Welcome Jack Cash".

With five buttons on each side, he saw a USB port.

Daphne was continuing to talk, saying "And capture as many as you like on that list, as for compensation, you'll paid for the Bounty, but if it is a government mission, you'll be paid one million dollars each for each mission, on top of the that unlimited per-diem, you will receive, in your current package you have, your new bank account number, which is encrypted, if you plan on withdrawing money from your retirement account, you need to simply place your pinkie finger on the pad on the back of the card and then insert it into any ATM machine for which ten thousands of dollars will be dispensed to you, for each machine in the U S that is a A T M 's limit, you can also do that with the mission cards."

Captain Jon Knight came back into the room, to say "I'm your handler, so from this point forward, you will see me only in training".

"In the event of a special meeting, from this point forward, you will meet with Daphne, exclusively, in the event of her death". "Another female agent will be assigned to you, thank you Jack, and any questions?" says the Captain. Jack shakes his head "No". The Captain leaves.

All was quite until the door closed shut; Daphne said,

"Do you have any questions for me, Jack?"

"What happen to you after that night?"

"I should have not done that, it was wrong"

"What kind of training did you go through to be selected as my assistant?"

"I will tell you this it has been five long years of grueling, intensified training, I grew up wanting to be a F B I agent and after graduating college with a degree in forensic sciences I was recruited to the F B I special investigation department, where I began to help, solve crimes, then I saw an opening for a Special Agent program".

"I liked what that entailed so five years later, here I am, let me tell you the training was tough, both physically, mentally emotionally, it turned out to be a spiritual belief for me to be here today, when I got the assignment of being your Liaison Officer, I did my own research on you, but kept my distance, I had another agent watching over you, I have been trained to be your sole support system you need to accomplish the missions they assign you and provide you all the resources you need to accomplish them, so lets take a look at your package, open up your package"

Jack flips it over to read "Top Secret Only Open When Told To Do So. "pulls out all the documents, a wallet, he flipped open to show the badge and what looked like his I D card, as he was doing that Daphne said   "Alright your going to start with the wallet, I can see, you see your badge, that's right its all yours"

"its official, you're a International Bounty Hunter, and welcome, to a life long service agreement, next is your I D card, can be pulled out and used as a knife, be careful when pulling it out, see the fine edges, it is a double edge blade hold it on its sides and in the middle is a depression for you two fore fingers to hold onto."

Jack picks it up, gets a good grip, and says, "Yes that is nice" then puts it back into its sleeve.

"If you need to pull it out to show anyone, under it, you will have a diplomatic I D card, to show, don't worry about the I D Card while its in its sleeve, but if you need to pull it out for any reason, it will automatically trigger a remote signal, giving us your position or whoever may have your wallet, above your I D plastic clear case is three credit cards.

The first one is your per diem card, anyone can touch that one, use for gas for a vehicle it has a limit of five hundred per use, with an unlimited limit, used anywhere in the world."

"The one next to it, is the mission card, a universal card that has unlimited funds available, it comes with ten matching checks, if needed inside the wallet, to include, twenty, one thousand dollars in freshly sequenced bills, to use as you see fit. Jack spun the money in his hand.

"The top card is your retirement account access card, you can use this card to transfer money, withdraw money, or use it for local purchases, you can even check balances, look along the rib of the wallet, it is a hook attached to a flash drive, pull that out, it doubles as a zip line hook, pull it out, like this and it will hook on to a one inch line, the other end is a pull off the end U S B hook up and this is a receiver computer, hard drive that has unlimited secret intelligence and support, it also can be used as a small explosive device, simply twist the bottom cap instead of taking it off and wait five seconds and it will blow, lastly behind the badge is a compartment for a single throwing star, you'll get that later"

"That's nice" said Jack.

"We want you to carry it on your left side pocket on your shirt, above and in front of you heart. it is also a titanium Kevlar protection magnet, it will draw the bullets up to 50 cal to this wallet, thus protecting you head, and other body parts, it is effective from point blank range up to two thousand feet away, it will track the bullet and pull it in, it will probably knock you back, but it will bounce off, I know I've tried it, it works, everything works, it has been well tested, next is your watch, this state of the art watch, is a computer, turn the dial and the top comes off to expose the key pad, and the dial can be placed on any digital screen to project to its size, the dial can also be used as a movie camera, or as a still picture."

"the images are sent back to us, at the I T center, it also has a G P S locater, for you, plus up to the moment images via a satellite, the dial needs to be placed upward to the sky and on the digital T V to work, we will go over the uses of the simple watch with a led face, that adjusts automatically to the time changes, in addition if anyone else puts the watch on, that is not five feet from you then a injection will occur and poison that new wearer, this watch is your signature exclusive. "Oh I almost forgot, if you spin the dial, it will kick in and its diamonds will cut through any thing"

Jack slides the watch on and clips it into place, then places the wallet into his breast pocket and buttons it up.

"Also Jack both the wallet and watch are shock and waterproof up to 200 feet under the water., next we have to decide on a vehicle for you, she hands him the up to the date cars of the world, he turns the pages for her to say "Choose anything you would like"

Jack looked it over to see one car in particular he liked, taking a mechanical pencil he circles it and slides it back to her, for her to say   "Alright, it will be made for you"

"Next let's look in that folder it's your dossier on yourself, it's your file"

Jack shut out her speaking as he opened the file to see two pages.

"As I was saying Jack we don't have much information, on your real identity from Germany, all we know is that you were classified as a top Government Agent assigned to Washington, which dates back to 1999 .It says you had information that led to the exposure to those behind the secret East German police and the breakdown and destruction of the Berlin Wall. That is why, we protected you, however, they had connections, the Germans, and every place we put you they found you until we lost you in our prison system and over the years, they forgot you. You killed a few people and you now had a life sentence and ended up on the coast, near Mobile, and your cover was a serial killer, so you were placed in isolation and forgotten, honesty I feel they took advantage of you."

"I am sorry I said that, but listen".

"You are going to be watched for a while, they know they can't hold you now, not with the technology today, and now that

I'm your assistant, I swore I would give my life, to defend yours, that means telling you the truth, I'm your protector from this day forward."

Jack looks up at her.

"You can ask anything of me and I will do it, so that file is yours to keep, keep it somewhere safe, it is your life file."

Jack slide the file back towards her to say "Can you keep it for me".

"Now on to some more business, with what you're doing for us, we would like to do something for you".

"Like what do you mean?" asked Jack.

"The government will pay out to any beneficiary of your choice one million dollars each year for twenty years, or greater, depends on how long I'm your Liaison Officer, if I'm still assigned to you, for me I will live in the city you choose to live in, I can even work in your front business as a Bounty Hunter and may even participate, I'm yours for the rest of your or my life."

"Thank you" said Jack sincerely.

"The rest of the papers are questions about yourself, a record of your new name Jack Cash and your number 013, this number is your I D with the government, when dealing with espionage and International criminals, so Jack now that you have money and are suitably armed ready for you training to begin?"

"Yes, but I thought I would take off this weekend, I've got my girlfriend up in receiving waiting for me."

"O Kay let me show you a few things first and I will let you go around noon"

"Good, thanks"

"I could, meet her and bring her in and get an I D card for her, is she someone special?"

"I may marry her and take her last name."

"Good then I will meet her and get her an I D card, you know she will have around the clock protection and receive a salary as well as yours?"

"Can I get married this weekend?" said Jack kidding

"You can do whatever you like, let's go and get a gun made for you," said Daphne, and ads "How much marksman training do you think you need?'

"All of it, I like this place, I guess for the next ten weeks, and into the future, why do you ask, I thought you were the one training me?"

"I was thinking of asking my mom to visit and spend some time with her"

"Yeah, go ahead"

The two got up, as Daphne led the way, she opened the door, and Jack was right behind her."

Daphne led Jack to a door that said restricted on it, using her hand on a plate glass surface it open the door, they walk into a cool slightly dark room, the door closes and the lights come on.

In front of them was a long cool white counter in pristine clean conditions.

Jack steps forward to the counter as a guy comes out from behind a curtain to say " Welcome Jack Cash to the armory, we have been waiting for you, first off what kind of hand gun do you want to carry", Jack looks at him weirdly but doesn't respond.

"You know like small, medium or a large size, being a Super Agent I imagine, a medium?"

Jack nods his head in acknowledgement,

"What I need you to do is stick your hand in this box, up to your elbow, then rest it on the frame, then hold the medium gun that is in their."

Jack laid his right exposed arm into the clear glass box on a rest and held on to the heavy gun as the guy began to calibrate the machine.

"Now hold you hand steady, you keep tilting the gun down, is it too heavy for you, is that why it is moving around?" said the guy,

Jack began to grimaces, with the weight.

"Alright I was just kidding" he pulls the gun out of Jack's hand and places a sleek lightweight gun in his hand and says;

"Sorry it was a dummy five pound gun."

They all laughed.

"Now Jack I want you to pull the trigger all eleven times, and do it evenly and with consistency, were measuring your exact signature, this computer gun, will adjust the exact weight you can handle for up to twenty four hours of holding it out stretched and shooting it.

This signature gun will be custom made and milled for a standard 9 mm ammo and become a porcelain in its material totally undetected by radar or x-ray machines or wands, your gun will also carry a taser in the butt to be used by you or shock someone picking it up, to it has a automatic locator in the body, as this weapon will never be blown up, fire burned or destroyed, the signal when you away from it is programmed in your watch, this gun will be your for the rest of your life, the serial number will match your number 013., now that is over." "Your gun will be ready in about two hours, come over here and chose a holster, we have three for you, you can have all three styles, first one is the arm sling try it on"

Jack, with Daphne help, slide it on, Jack make the necessary adjustments; the guy comes out from behind the counter with a tape measure and jots down some measurement.

Then says " This one is purely a dinner jacket and tie, holster designed to be concealed under your left arm, as you are right handed, do you want double holsters?"

"Yes"-said jack

"Alright, on the tactical holster I will add an additional, one lets take off that one for this one, the guy places the right side one on when Jack said, "What's your name?"

"My name is Ronald, Ronald White, why do you ask"

"Just curious to know who my gunsmith is?"

"Oh, I'm not your gunsmith, all this information is being sent to a private location, where the gun is being made and then by courier, it will arrive, I'm merely a clerk, who does the fittings, but thanks anyway, great, now, you'll have a belt holster which will be a tactical belt, custom made to fit any weapon of your choice, it won't be the signature gun, because you may lend it out to someone else, here is a catalog of all the known handguns of the world, new and old and even retired, as your looking for that, I'm going to program the dimensions for all of your holsters"

Immediately Jack found his weapon of choice and said with zeal,

"I choose the Colt Combat Commander, 45 cal model."

"I just happen to have one in stock."

After a little searching Ron pulls the freshly oiled gun, sets it on the counter, and says, "This large gun carries fifteen rounds in the magazine, and has accuracy up to 500 feet, pick it up."

Jack lifted it up and tested it felt good and said, "I'll take it"

"Not that one, it is merely a demonstrator, I will have a brand new custom made to fit your hand and several boxes of ammo, next I want you to go through this catalog and choose as many weapons as you would like"

"Do I have to do it right now or can I have a chance to look at all one thousand pages plus, I think that will take some time," said Jack looking at Ron.

For him to say "Right here right now, just kidding, I'm just excited we have a new Super Agent on the base, besides usually some one other that you will order them."

"You can come in and ask me and either Daphne, what you want and It will be made and sent to you.", "But, in the meantime

"Take this copy, from my private stash, and go ahead and circle all of your choices in pencil, I like you Jack Cash, turn it in when you get a chance, and "I will have them ready for you as soon as possible."

"Thank you Ron" said Jack and ads "Where to now Daphne' that was fun"

"Well you can't leave the building, until you get a holster and your gun, lets go to clothing, now and get you fitted, for a custom shirt, pants and shoes and other accessories"

Jack follows Daphne out into the hall, which was quiet; they walked a ways, then paused at an unmarked door, then placed her hand on the wall, the door slid open as the two walked in

A single person stood there, this young woman said, "Come in and strip off your clothes" and ads "You can wait for him outside"

Daphne walked out as the door closed shut, she waited out in the hall when she saw the captain, who saw her, and she turned away.

Captain Jon, approached her to say, "How are you and Jack getting along?"

"Fine, he is getting fitted, right now, and then were off to the firing range".

"If you get over there in about an hour, I'll have the platoon over there."

"Yeah, will try, although he doesn't have his weapon yet"

"You have yours don't you?"

"Yeah, but."

The door opened and Jack stepped out, to see the two of them.

"Hi Jack".

"Hi Captain," said Jack.

"Hey what are you guys up to now?"

"Its up to Daphne, I don't know what she has planned" as Jack looked at her for a response. She was silent.

"So Jack were going out to the shooting circuit for qualification, do you want to go?"

"Sure, if it is alright with Daphne?"

The two men looked at her, waiting for a response.

"You could go I guess all the administration process I could finish, like where you live in Mobile, who is your next of kin, who your beneficiary is?"

"Sounds like you still have some time left to finish processing, I'll see you later" said the Captain. As the two shook hands.

"Ready to go, Jack" said Daphne and ads "Come with me." Daphne went down to the end of the hall to an opening receptionist and then behind her into a room with a large round table.

"Let's sit down and fill out all those forms."

"You mean those two pages, that shouldn't take to long?"

"What about your girlfriend, isn't she waiting for you?"

"She can wait, let me finish those forms, have a seat" said Jack.

Daphne sat beside him and help him fill out the forms, when it came to beneficiary Jack said, "Can I put two down?"

"You can put as many as you want, you can even put my name down"

The two laughed.

Jack wrote half share for Sara Sanders and the other half for Samantha Smith. Completed the documents and gave them to Daphne.

"Is that all, can I go?"

"If you must" said Daphne.

"Sounds like you don't want to go" asked Jack.

"Its not that, I really don't like the Captain."

"Yeah, I can tell something's up, you can tell me if you like"

"Listen Jack, it's personal, between him and me"

"What does that mean?"

"It means none of your business"

"That sounds to me like he either has something on you or he is on you, you know like you and I"

"Shut up, your not suppose to say a word about that, ever" said Daphne as she looks at him and with a smile.

"Listen if he ever touches you, I personally will hurt him, so he will never be able to touch you ever again"
She began to smile, and then spoke "Do you want me to bring your girlfriend out to the range?"

"Sure, if you can"

"Jack, you now have more power than anyone on this whole base, as a representative of the President himself, you don't really know what you have do you? "

"No, that's why I need you"

"That's sweet of you to say" said Daphne.

"Then once you graduate he himself "The President" will probably come and visit you and present you with some accommodation, your whole life will change from now on."

"Will you stop; I'm just like you, just an average guy. Who happens to be in the right place at the right time?"

"Oh, you're much more than that to me," said Daphne with a smile on her face.

"Are we done here, I'll see you soon oh by the way where is the range"

"I'll get a driver for you, hold on a second, and you can't leave the building without a weapon, so if you want lets stop back by the armory and check out a gun, then I'll let you go" said Daphne who went up and dropped off the forms and arranged to have a driver from the motor pool. As she came back to the table, with a package in hand and said,   "Here this is for you" she hands the package to him.

Jack opens it up to see a file, which was named "Carlos Gomez", Private, Property U S Government, and Destroy after Viewing"

"I will take it from you, after you have finished reading it. "

"Look there is your ride; I will meet you out there soon." Let's go to the armory."

They entered as Daphne spoke up to say, "Ron we need for Jack to check out a gun"

"Yes Ma'am, what would you like?"

"I guess any 9mm you might have, with a box of Ammo."

"Yes sir, here is a card", Jack signed his name.

Jack picks up a simple 9mm cocks it back, checks the chamber, as Ron hands him a clip on holster, which he inserted a empty magazine, then locked it down and placed it on safety, and into its holster.

Jack pulls out his phone to see it was someone, he let it go to voice mail, then placed the phone on vibrate and then placed it in his breast pocket. Then out the door, he went while Daphne watched him.

—— CH 13 ——

Rifle Range

The road was dusty, the open ground, broke open to a large up hill travel to the top of a hill, into a valley, to show a large structure and a open field with straight lines as the vehicle made its way down to a parking lot as the Jeep came to a stop. Jack jumped out and into the door he went, the room opened up to show men and women were sitting at some long tables, some had rifles and pistols, Jack was out of place as everyone else wore camouflage outfits. Jack was sitting next to a girl who had a side arm and a rifle, he looked over at her paper that gave the diagram of the kill house and of the rifle range, she noticed him and slid the paper over closer to him, but kept quiet.

Jack notice she and the girl next to her looked the same in the face, the clothing made her look the same. The captain was done speaking, as he passed at least fifty people to see Jack and say;

"Hey, you made it, I was going to leave, but now that you're here, come on get up, and do you have a weapon?'

"Yeah, a 9mm, why what do need".

"Come with me" The Captain said sternly.

Jack got up and followed the Captain into his office.

"Close the door".

Jack closed the door, to face the Captain to hear;

"Where's your assistant?"

Jack looked at the captain, then said, "She's picking up my girlfriend and bringing her out here"

"O Kay, I just wanted to know if she was going to be here, if I need to have a slot open for her, that's it"

And ads "Sergeant" he yells then says "Escort Mr. Jack Cash to the armorer and issue him a weapon for the kill house."

"Thanks Captain Knight" said Jack, getting up and he followed the sergeant down along the hallway to a counter in between the two offices to the armory. Two soldiers stood awaiting for the armorer, as the Sergeant and Jack arrived a armorer said " Welcome Jack Cash, Ronald called to say how nice you were to him and that your gun is here, I'll call Ronald and have him bring it down to you, hold on." Jack stood and waited until the armorer to get off the phone and then the Armorer said "Can I get you a Rifle" as everyone heard a jet take off.

"Wow you near an airport," said Jack

"Nah, most Jets fly in at night and when special V I P's come in for target practice, like you". To add;

"The airfield is on our back side, maybe it was the Jet that landed ten minutes ago, with a important person, like yourself, so Jack do you want a M-16 or a M-4 carbine, or both of them".

"The whole armory is at your disposal, which shall it be?"

"I guess an M-16 will be fine, do you happen to have a Colt Combat Commander 45 cal?"

"Actually I do, it is my private weapon, I could let you use it, it's in a side arm holster, let me go get it, hey Brian, Mr. Cash would like a A R - 15 "

"Does Mr. Cash want the rocket launcher?"

"Nah, just the weapon" said the armorer, as he returns with the holster and weapon and hands them to Jack as Jack pulls out the holster and the 9mm, to hand it back to the armorer, to say "I have this on loan from Ron, can you hold it for me, also this kill house seems interesting, may I check out a weapon for that as well?", Jack then wraps the holster belt on and uses the leather ties to wrap it around his leg, Jack pulled the well oiled weapon and without hesitation, began to disassemble it and said " You got a rag, I can wipe off all this oil," looking at the armorer, Jack began to work on the pistol as he received the rag Jack realized the armorer used the weapon as trophy rather than a practical shooting weapon. Jack cleaned it up quickly, as the armorer placed a cleaning kit, with drying agent next to him.

"Thanks" said Jack, who finished up, reassembled the weapon, and received a loaded magazine he loaded and locked it in place as Brian handed the rifle to Jack, and says, "Can you sign our card".

Jack signs the card and says "What about the pistol?"

"I trust you," said the armorer.

Jack adjusted the sling like he was a pro, and slung it on his shoulder. The the Armorer handed Jack pictures of the kill house pistol, and said choose one and we will have it ready."

Jack holstered the 45 cal pistol under his left arm, and out the door he went to meet up with the Captain, to say, "What's first? "

"Whatever you want to do, I usually leave it up to the Sergeant and his handlers, but now that you're here it is up to you"

"What do I need to do to qualify this rifle?"

"Let's go to the rifle range, and I will get you qualified, follow me"

The Captain leads Jack out to the range as they made it out to the party of people to listen to the Sergeant speak "I need you to form up into groups of four, then decide who will pull and then who will shoot, Jack looked around to see two girls came to him to say "Hey do you want to work with us?"

"Sure "said Jack, looking over at the two girls who were smiling at him

The captain looked over to Jack to see him conversing with the two girls to say, "Jack are you ready".

The Captain looked hard at the two girls with Jack, the two girls followed closely, to the Captain's dislike, then turns to Jack and said,   "Do you want to go first?"

"Nah, I'll pull for these two soldiers," said Jack as he followed the rest of the people down to the targets.

Jack had a instant flashback, he stopped and stood there in the middle of the rifle range and said to himself " Oh yeah, I remember this, I love to shoot target practice" then hurried his step down the steps to see the open target to his right, each target had at least two to a target, except Jack, when they heard on a speaker say " Ready the targets" Jack saw everyone to his right pull the targets close together, so Jack did the same, he was ready, in front of him was a round black on one side and white on the other pins, " Ready on the firing line, targets pull" Jack pulled his up, "

"Ready, Set, Fire."

A crack was heard, Jack pulled his target down and near the bulleye, and he stuck in the black face in the center of the target and pulled it back up.

For the next hour, he pulled the target for the two girls, when he heard the word "Cease fire, clear your weapons and put them on safe, let's leave the line and trade with your partners. Jack was first up the stairs with his rifle slung over his back, he made his way up to the line at 200 meters, and his number was 16. The two girls stopped by Jack to say; "Thank you for pulling our targets" said both Tiffany and Bridgett, both smiling.

"It was a pleasure, both of you did a good job of shooting"

"Thanks, do you want to meet up with us later tonight?" said the Bridgett.

"Get moving soldiers" yelled the Sergeant.

Jack watched as the two girls fell in line to follow the group down to the targets, Jack turned to see two familiar faces, in the observation tower, stood Sara and Nicole with Daphne waving at him, he waved back and smiled.

Behind them a diplomatic car pulled up, Ronald got out, he carried a white wood box with a clear top to show off its contents, with a notice on the top, carefully he carried it into the barn and into the Armorery, to say, "Hey guys, anyone here, he sees his friend step out to say; "Hey Ronald, what do you have?"

"I have the weapon for Jack Cash, he is here?"

"Yeah, he is on the firing line, come on in here and see for yourself"

"I'd like to, but I got to get back, can I get you to sign for him?"

"Yeah sure, leave it on the counter, here is a card, we already printed out a release for Mr Cash."

Brian hands Ronald the card and says, "Here is the 9mm, you lent him, so you need to sign off, were in here watching the action, only to hear;

"Ready on the line, set fire"

Shot after shot, the two girls were stuffing the black round circle in and near the bulleye, quickly approaching a perfect score, as the supervisor, was in their stall making sure the shots were true and not what the girls were making up., as the two Armoreers sat and watched the closed circuit television set only to hear, a loud noise, then "Oh, oh, oche"

Then they heard a thump, both armorers, tore out of their chairs to see the counter, immediately, the Armorer, was searching his area to see that box was gone, the other Armorer, went around to see a fallen solder, still shaking, as the voltage still ran through the former F B I Agent's body, the guy expired right in front of there eyes, off to the guy's right was the pearl white signature hand gun, next to it was the white box, open and broken .

"Oh shit, were in trouble now"

"What do you think we should do?'

"Either call Ronald back down here or I'm afraid we may have to call Jack Cash."

"We can't, and then the Captain will probably come in with him"

"Hey I got an Idea, don't you have an asbestos blanket, and we use the staff of the colors and tap it into the blanket."

"Let's try it."

Jack laid at the 500 feet line with the Captain over him, when a large beeping noise started from his watch, he stopped pulled his weapon off of his shoulder and rested it, and placed it on safety, he turned the dial as it popped up, he stopped and thought to himself, if I hit this center button, will something denate, he reversed the process, and replaced the dial, the beeping sound was evident, Jack slid the watch off his wrist and into his front pocket to muzzle the noise, and went on to finishing to shoot a perfect course record of 150, beating the current record by two.

"Good job, Jack that was some of the best shooting I've ever seen, now lets go to the pistol range and get you qualified", just as they both heard "On the line, prepare to clear your weapon and place on safety, is the line all clear, the line is all clear, all groups need to assemble, for we now have a new range record and record holder, in lane 16, it was Mr Jack Cash, Thank you"

Jack got up off the tarp a solider had laid down for him, Jack slung the rifle over his shoulder and wrapped up the tarp and gave it back to the solider that went without but was happy for Jack to set a course record.

"Attention please on the course will Mister Jack Cash please come to the armory."

"What, does that guy want his 45 cal pistol back already" said Jack in somewhat of a statement, The Captain said "I'll walk back with you, Sergeant make sure they all assemble at the pistol range"

"Yes sir."

Jack saw Sara, he felt like he really did miss her, as he produced a smile when he saw her, she waved back at him as most of the other soliders watched this beauty queen, come down the stairs wearing only a tank top and shorts, much to their delightment, and ran into Jack's awaiting arms, their lips met as the two eagerly kissed each other.

Jack lingered with the perfect kisses of passion to all the soldiers delight as they passed by.

"You smell so good whatever that colonge is I want some of it, your driving me crazy" said Sara, and ads "Did you see I brought our bed friend Nicole for a little threesome tonight, and tomorrow and for as long as you want her, Honey I'm so proud of you".

"You broke the course record, your well on becoming a professional Bounty Hunter"

"Come walk with me, I need to go into the Barn; do you need something to drink?"

"I could use some water," said Sara wrapping her arm around his as the two walked together followed by Nicole and Daphne.

"I will be in my office, catch up with me and we will go to the pistol course together I need to fire my weapon as well," said the Captain.

Jack nods his head, and says "Why don't you wait out here, this is a secure area"

"O kay, just as long as you kiss me good bye" said Sara Jack bent over and kissed her on the lips, she closed her eyes and let it linger, while he was gone.

Jack stepped into the armory door and stepped over the person on the floor to say, "Do you want your 45 cal pistol back?"

"No, actually we have this for you, sorry about the box, it fell on the floor"

The two look at the expired body together and say "I guess you shouldn't touch something that does not belong to you," said Jack and ads "Do you have another side arm holster?"

"No, but we have a side belt holster"

Jack raises the lid on the box, and reaches in and grasps the weapon as it is sucked into his hand with force.

"Now that's a perfect grip," said Jack proudly displaying the new white handgun"

"I took the liberty of loading two magazines with 15 rounds each of 9mm shells, on this particular model you can either have 9mm or 45 cal rounds its up to you, there in the drawer inside the box."

Jack pulls the slide back to check the barrel and then takes a magazine and loads it into the chamber and locks it in place, then pulls the 45 cal pistol out of the side holster with his left hand and inserts the ceramic gun in the holster and pulls his hand free, to say " Now that was a grip"

The Armorer hands Jack a belt holster, which Jack puts clips on his belt, while he was doing that the Armorer said, "I can take that rifle from you and clean it up and restock it."

"Don't you want me to clean it first?"

"Listen, Mister Cash, you're the first Secret Agent here in a long time, that is considerate to us workers and it would be an honor to clean that rifle for you, so go out and score another course record"

Jack unslings his rifle to hear the Captain say, "Who is this guy on the floor sergeant, is he", "All right"

"No sir, he had a heart attack and died from receiving 10,000 volts of electricity" said Brian.

"That's a shame, I really liked him, can you get him out of here, and he is starting to smell"

"Sir we called C I D and there sending out a detective and the coroner"

"Good job then Sergeant carry on" and ads "Are you ready Jack".

"Yes Sir I am, and thanks guys"

"Mister Cash what about your box"

"Keep it" said Jack on his way out with the Captain, as the two walked together.

"Are you going to be running with us every morning?"

"Just during the week I'm off on the weekends" said Jack and ads "Besides I need to take care of my fiancé"

"Absolutely, it should be your first priority, she is sure a doll"

Jack met up with Sara and saw Nicole who had a smile on her face and Daphne, who spoke first;

"I see you have your handgun now"

"Oh yes and it is magnificent, yes?"

"Hi Jack" said Nicole who reached up and gave Jack a kiss on the cheek.

"Hi Nicole, nice to see you're here as well"

"My dad is in the Army and I like to go shooting from time to time," she said in a statement.

The Captain followed by Jack and Sara walked towards the pistol range.

"Now on this course, we have 10, 25, and 50 feet distance, usually the top ten highest scores go into the kill house to compete for the title of top shooter for the day and get a prime rib dinner with me tonight, but in your case, you three will be my invited guests"

"Its up to Sara, I don't know what plans she has"

"We would love to dine with you Captain just as long as my friend Nicole can come"

"Sure, let's make it a date; I'll arrange it after the shoot"

Sara leaned into Jack and whispered something.

Then Jack said "O Kay" and ads "Captain Knight, Sara want's to know if she could qualify with a pistol?"

"Sure, let me get a line supervisor and we can get both of the girl's a weapon to shoot"

"A-ten- shun," yelled the Sergeant

"At ease men and women, Sergeant Can you go into the armorery and get two 9mm pisols for me with two loaded magazines each"

"Now I want to say, were going to do this a little different today, each of my V IP's will get to select a candidate, to be on their team, no scratch play, were all on the up in up."

Several vehicles rolled up and several men got out including Raphael, with Devlin in tow as she walked up to the group,and said;

"Hi Jack, Captain Knight and Ladies"

"Hi Ralph," said Jack and ads "This is my girlfriend Sara and her friend Nicole and my new friend Daphne"

"As I was saying, instead of one lets make it two and I want, the Sergeant and the line supervisor to play", the Captain got a good look at Raphael, but knew she was a Super Spy as well, so he backed off from her and smiled at Nicole, who smiled back innocently.

The Sergeant returned with two pistols, two magazines, and the wooden box.

"So I would like our guests to pick first, Daphne are you going to play along? Asked the Captain, with a smug smile on his face, to her.

"Sure why not"

"Miss Daphne, will pick first, followed by Nicole, Sara, Raphael, Jack, Lieutenant, then the Sergeant all after I make my selection, first, I choose Hernandez and Memphis."

Then Daphne choose two men, as did Sara and Nicole. All four men were eager to help the two girls out, Raphael took a man and a woman and Jack took his two girls from the rifle range, as he called out   "Tiffany and Bridgett" who both got pretty upclose to him as Sara was off with her two strong men, the Line supervisor took his two partners and the Sergeant pulled out the two armorers.

"So we now have the field set, each group of three will stand at the 10 foot line.

We shoot the targets, we will replace them, after each round, and these dog targets have 15 places on them."

"To aim all you have to do is set yourself up and you have one minute to get all fifteen shots off, then we switch."

We will do this for the ten, twenty five and fifty, lets get up to the line, any questions, Ladies?"

"Lieutenant Do you have enough personnel to supervise this event?"

"Yes sir I have five left, one in the tower to call out one on the road two on the line and one in the Armory. The rest are out and will wait in the barn."

"Fine, let me assign the lanes, on one, I want you Lieutenant and your boys, on lane two, I want the Armorers and the Sergeant, lane three, Daphne and her two guys, I'll be in lane five, next to me in lane six is Nicole and her two large guys"

The Captain looked up to them both and said "Wow, they are huge and big" and then continued " Lane seven is Sara and her two guys, next is Raphael and then in the last lane is Jack, in your teams decide who goes first , second ond so forth"

The line supervisors showed up with a box of ammo and several targets for each group.

"Attention please, if you have two weapons you want to qualify do it after everyone shoots this first round " said the guy in the tower and ads " with the targets in place are we ready on the right" Jack raises his hand " 'Are we ready on the left, commense shooting on my count three two one shoot"

Each team quickly went through each shooter, with each team captain firing last.

Jack had Tiffany, then Bridgett go first, both girls were F B I agents here to train in defensive combat and tactical support for FEMA. As they told him, in between firings.

Jack and the group of team leaders with the exception of the girls and the armorers shot additional time, they finished all the targets pulled and replaced, they all moved down to the twenty five foot line a large wire ran the length of the line at knees height.

"Attention shooters on the line for this next test it is the alternate shot where you lie on the pad and shoot then kneal for a shot and vice versa until all fifteen shots are fired at the dog target, on my ready, are we reloaded and ready on the right" said the voice over the loud speaker.

Jack raised his arm "And are we ready on the left, good on my command you have two minutes on my count three two and one, fire"

The roar of gunfire went off as bodies went up and then down on the hard rubber mats, each getting a shot off Tiffany was slow in this event barely finishing when she hit her last shot to hear;

"Cease fire, cease firing, the time is up, clear your weapons." "Step off the line and remove your magazines, reload and the next person to fire step. Up, ready on the right, ready on the left"

Jack watched as both of his girls, laid on their mats as both Sara and Nicole began to fire and move with their weapon, Jack thought to himself maybe I ought to buy both girls a hand gun for protection and to be safe, or share the two I stole, what about those" he thinks..

"Cease fire"

Everyone stopped, knew the routine, and did as they were told.
Jack stepped up to hear;

"Now we get to check out that butt," said Bridgett.

Jack focused on the dog target as he heard the countdown to fire and squeezed off his first round, it hit in the number one spot, as he went to kneal an odd thing occurred a bullet flew directly over his head, he ducked an turned to see, Daphne fallover and still get off a shot, she aimed at the captain who she missed and Jack who took the round at the heart. He shrugged it off and finished out the string, at cease-fire call Daphne was gone.

The Captain looked pissed off, Jack knelt down, picked up the bullet, and shrugged it off, and stayed in his knealling position to pull out his borrowed 45 cal pistol, to hear the call, to shoot and began to shoot the bulky gun and still hit the target he was focused as he put the whole Daphne issue to rest, after the cease fire call, Jack looked around to see where Daphne was, she was gone as well as the one armorer and two of the line supervisors.

As the group Jack was in, he said, "I'd like to go first this time is that alright with you both?"

"Yes go ahead, we don't mind just as long as you come and visit both of us tonight"

"Sorry I can't tonight, but maybe some time later, how long will you be on the base?"

"Were both gonna be here for the next two weeks"

"Sounds fun" said Jack with a smile as they assembled on the fifty-foot line.

"attention shooters, this will be a single standing shot firing on my shot count as, I say one you shoot one I say two and so forth are we ready".

Jack used the hot 45 cal first, and held it out on the new dog target. Jack heard the pre count to Ready, Set "and I say One, two," Jack fired on each count at each number on the count to fifteen, as they finished Jack holstered the weapon.

Jack pulled out his pearl white gun and this time he hit the lower lip of the reciever to the barrel and the gun disappeared or so it seamed, it looked like Jack held nothing as he heard the command to fire, he fire at number one but knew he missed that one.

Jack let his mind off and visualized the shot as he tried to center his hand on the target realizing he has to see the weapon in order to aim the weapon, again he tried to hit each number sequence, he stumbled as each round found another place, so then decided just to keep it in the center and nail the nine center boxes, to hear;

"Cease fire"

Jack released his Magazine to discover what he did he did to get it into stealth mode which he bumped the reciever and the gun reappeared, he quickly reloaded the weapon and left the line, he troted over to the barn, where Daphne was bent over, getting sick into a bucket, beside her was the armorer and two line supervisors.

"Is she alright" asked Jack

She looked up at him with her eyes glazed over and in tears and said;   "It was something I ate"

Jack looked her over to discover a cut on her arm, which he pointed out, to the two supervisors, who went to work immediately, as one got a small wet sponge and the other a first aid kit, as Daphne finished up what she was doing.

"How do you feel now?" said Jack concerned

"Thanks Jack, that means so much for you to care about me, I feel a little bit better now"

Daphne was able to produce a smile as the two supervisors patched her arm after wiping up the blood.

The Armorer picked up the bucket as Daphne said to Jack " I fainted, I'm sorry Jack all those guns going off and the heat, I just don't know what happen, I hope I didn't injure someone"

"Not to worry, you hit me in the heart, has this happen before?"

"Yes" she said slowly and a bit embarrassed.

"It will be alright," said Jack as he held her in his arms, she began to weep, to say "Thank you, Jack".

"It will be fine I'll talk to the Captain and if he don't listen I will go to the Commander"

"What is that smell, your getting me a bit excited?"

"Come on that is the sickness talking". said Jack.
You Agents are all alike, listen Jack you don't need this to get me into your bed"

"Jack, is she alright"
Jack turned to see the Captain and the Sergeant, to say, "Yeah she is fine, just had a touch of the flu I guess" as she broke away from Jack to go with the Armorer back to his cage.

"That was close if I hadn't seen her go down she would have shot me," said the Captain.

"I guess it was you cat-like reflexes, that saved you," said Jack sarcastically.

"Well guess what, I have the results, you are the new owner of the top award as another record fell today as you shot a perfect score on the course for a record of fourty five, the highest since 1986, and on your 45 cal you only missed one shot, which is also a record for the 45 cal pistol, so it will be you, Raphael, and surprisingly your two girlfriends Sara and Nicole which tied eight others and myself."

"Next up is the kill house, so whenever your ready, one by one you'll sit on the bench and await your turn, each course is graded on where you hit them, how you hit them and if they are friendly or not, so do you want to go first?"
Jack nods his head and says "yes"

"Then it will be Jack, followed by Sara, Ralph, Nicole and then myself and the rest" said the Captain.

"Jack do you have a minute" asked Raphael.

Jack stood still while Raphael spoke, as the men and women were cheering him to begin.

"Listen, I really don't have time now, but I think we have an issue with Daphne, can we talk later, oh and I shot this course earlier, all you have to do is think the target and in a split second, it will be over" said Raphael, to Jack as he left her behind and entered the door, off to his left was the Armorer's window.

"Jack you can place your weapons with me except your handgun, if you would like"

"Nah, I hold onto them"

"Here's how the course works you will have fifty targets to shoot at."

"The more you move the easier the target is to hit if you stand there, it will be hard for you to get a good score, here is your three -D visor and choose the lighted up model of gun on the wall you chose earlier."

"Or I can choose this replica Colt Combat Commander, ah yes this will do nicely"

Jack placed the visor on his head by the armorer and said;

"On my count I will turn the lights out and then the game will begin"

Jack turned to fairly see nothing until the lights went out, the whole place lit up in different colors and visible targets appeared as he was in a living version of a computer game, he turned and twisted to each target pulling the trigger , some times holding it down, just as fast as it started it was over as the lights came on, Jack laid on his back, as the soldiers were screaming and laughing at him, Jack pulled the visor off and handed it to the Armorer who was helping him up.

"How was it?"

"Fun, it takes a bit getting use to the trigger, I like the course, and I'd have to practice that one to get it right."

"Sorry it's one and done, the computer has a million or so courses to choose from, it matches you with who you are and at what level, it has thirty levels"

"Which level was I on?"

"Level ten, we have your results, in the barn, also there is some chow available on the other side, the troops are waiting for you and your guests to go through first, so it would be an honor if you would have lunch with us."

"Alright, thanks, do you want your Colt back?"

"No, consider that a gift" said Brian, the two shook hands as Brian held the door open for Jack, who went out, another person handed Jack his result as another person went in.

Jack saw Daphne, resting and went to see her.

"How did you do?" she asked.

"Here is my results" he hands her the paper.

"Oh my god, you scored a 96 percent, that's great, all I could muster was a 51 percent".

Jack just looks at her, to see his handler, who has no backbone, or is something else going on?" Jack says;

"Have you had lunch yet?"

"Lunch, no thanks, I still feel a bit queasy."

"Come on, it will be fun, at least get a plate maybe they have something for your upset stomach."

Jack crumbled up the paper and tossed it into the trash, as he headed into the kitchen, to see a single line of buffet trays.

"Hamburgers or hot dogs, Sir."

"Hot dogs I guess" said Jack

"One, two or three"

"One"

The guy hands Jack one hot dog and bun, Jack serves up a spoon of potatoe salad, to stop, thinking of the salt peter, then a scoop of French fries and a apple, then two cartons of chocolate milk. Then goes to the condiment station and opens a mayo package and spreads that on, then mustard, ketchup and diced onions, then some relish and a mixture of chopped banana and jalepeno's, he sprinkled on top, then he used a dry herb shaker and put some on the potatoe salad and lastly he sprinkled some dried kelp on top of the hot dog and went back to see Daphne still sitting down on the table as Jack came by to sit with her, she took one look at that hot dog and left immediately holding her hand to her mouth and saying " Ooh."

Jack sees Sara who has a smile on her face, as she came over to him. "Jack that was so much fun, according to my sheet I scored a 96 percent at a ten level, is that good?"

"Yeah that's good; there is some food, if you go through that door"

"I thought I would take you out today, but if you want to eat here, I guess I can wait for you to eat, Nicole is in there now, where's Daphne?"

"She's in the bathroom I guess, she had seen something that made her a little sicker."

"I'm going to go check on her, I'll see you soon."

Jack tore into the hot dog, finished the potatoe salad and ate a French fry one at a time dipped in the remnants of the mayo mustard ketscup, and drank down the two carton's of milk, with a good belch out of the way, Jack began to eat the apple, when Nicole and then the Captain came out at the same time, laughing and she was giggling as the two broke apart to receive their scores.

Jack watched the Captain as he went into his office and then came out to see Nicole accompany him to the chow line, Jack finished his apple, picked up his plate and threw it all away, he stood by the trash to see an official car pull up, the Commander got out and came to Jack.

"We have been trying to get in touch with you, do you have your phone on, and oh I see you got your weapon, any causality yet?"

"Yeah, one guy tried to grab it and it got him"

"What the prognosis?"

"He is dead"

"That is a shame, where's Daphne?"

"She is sick and in the bathroom, oh there she is," said Jack.

"You two come with me," said the Commander as he escorted Jack and Daphne into the captain's office and shuts the door.

"Now the whole point of you being his handler is to answer your phone twenty-four-seven. If this ever happens again, do not think I will not replace you even though you are based out of Washington D.C.   "Now that I got that off my chest, Jack I want to thank you for breaking and setting the new range record in rifle and in pistol, we got a situation about twenty miles from herein a town called Wetumpka, there is a hot springs there, exclusive to private society gentleman and ladies, we have a operative in the society world that could be a good match for you Jack, here is her picture.

"She looks nice and smart," said Jack

"How did you determine she was smart?"

"She's working for you"

"No, she's not working for me"   "She's working for the President, to whom she is on loan from, here is your mission, find this guy, his name is Carlos "AKA the killer" Gomez, bring him in."

"Yeah, I saw the paperwork earlier on him"

"And your still here?"

"what do you mean?" asked Jack.

"Well, once you get your orders, your suppose to spring into action"

"Daphne didn't say anything about that, or where I need to go or how to get there"

"Her, whole purpose is to assist you, are you understanding what I'm saying to you, Miss Wilms, you need to send him out immediately"

"Where, when, how, I don't have any of that information"
Said Daphne, trying to defend herself.

"Well where do we go from here, lets resolve this, so what your saying is once I get my orders I go, and I find my own way, is that right"

"Yeah, that's about it, you can use any modes of transportation you want and any resources you need, and lastly don't just count on Daphne to make the decision for you."

"Then lets go, give me the fastest mode of transport to this place" said Jack getting up to move.

"Whoa wait a minute, its not that easy, as Daphne knows, if you want a jet, we will have to call a squadron."

"I'm not saying that, what do we have on this base, at my disposal?"

"Daphne would know best at that, I'm here to get you going on this mission"

"What about Raphael" asks Jack?

"Oh, she's not ready"

"How do you figure that, you gave her a special gun, if she needs experience, and then let her come with us?"

"What's her cover?"

"Who cares what her cover is she is a Super Spy, for the government, it doesn't matter what she is let her find her own way and with some practical experience she will grow to be the agent your looking for, besides I think I could use her, her experience to help me with this":

"O' Kay Jack you got it, I will let you have Raphael, for this mission, but she is still under probation, and you need to keep a watchfull eye out for her."

"She's a big girl; I think she can handle it, said Daphne I will be there to help her out".

"Jack, Daphne has no field experience, she can't even answer her own phone, she is too busy worried about being sick"

"I'm right here sir" said Daphne, looking at him defiantly.

"If I had it my way, you would have been long ago, but the Washington Brass believes in you, so I must put up with you, any more screw ups and your history, I mean that literially, you hear me miss"

"Yes sir"

"I got another issue," said Jack

"You don't have any issues, you solve problems, and what is it?"

"My girlfriend and her friend are here on the base, and is here to see me and'

"How did that happen? Don't you know civilians, are not allowed on this base at no time without written and prior approval from me and a complete investigative background check, who authorized her arrival on this base?"

Daphne raises her hand.

"That's just great, who in the hell do you think you are?"

"I just thought that Jack would want them to be by him"

"You thought, how about ask permission from this point forward, and I suggest for you two attend all of the spy classes and protocolls, then you will realizes your perameters, I'm really watching you from now on, so if this ever happens then you're gone"

"So what you're saying, we should stay, or shall we go, come on leave her alone," said Jack

"What are you gonna do about it"

Jack pulled his weapon and pointed it to the Commanders head and said;   " It has been brought to my attention, that you're a dead man walking, if I find out that your involved into something you can be sure I will be standing over you and make you suffer, more than you can ever think about it, especially, if you think you know me"

The commander changed his tune, by now looking more in fear than defiance, as he spoke slowly, "I'm sorry, I was out of line, I don't think I made a mistake, I realize I had better watch my step". He said in a calm tone, to realize who was really the boss, as he looked at Jack.

Jack moved in and whispered to the commander's ear and said;

" A little birdy told me that you were once involved in a cover up, here on the base, if you try to stop me I will come at you full force and if anything happens to my girls, well you think the whole Spanish fly fiasco was something, wait till you see what I really can do"

"O kay Jack you win, we could play this all night, your girls will be fine, I'll put them up in your quarters, with round the clock protection, good luck to you two."

Jack retracted his weapon and holstered the weapon.

"What do you have there on your belt, is that a Colt Combat Commander"

"Yeah, I got it to remember you by"

"Funny Jack lets go".

Jack led, the Commander and Daphne out of the office, and into the Barn to see The Capatin, Sara and Nicole and Raphael sitting together, next to her was Devlin, Jack goes up to them, they all look up at him.

"Sara can I talk with you for a minute?"

Sara got up and went up to Jack and stood in front of him, putting her hands on his chest and said;

"Yes"

Jack looked down at her and said " I've been called to capture someone close by I don't know how long it will take, so why don't you go home and wait for me either way I will see you as soon as I am done with this job, O' Kay."

"You promise"

"I promise, I need to get going, the car is waiting for me" he reaches down to use both of his hands to pull her face to his and then kisses her on the lips in a long drawn out experience.

Finally, he broke off the kiss, and went to the armory and dropped off all his rental guns and then said, "Goodbye guys, we will see you soon, thanks"

Jack passed by his two girls and the two FBI agents to wave goodbye, to get inside of the car and shut the door.

The strech limo had the Commander, Daphne, Raphael a strange looking man and Jack, Jack was off to this guy left next to Raphael and across from Daphne, the two men sat next to each other when the Commander spoke "Jack I want you to meet your boss while you're out in the field, he is simply called the Colonel"

Jack responds by saying "Hi" not really looking at the silver haired guy.

"Jack, we decided we could use your help in capturing a top ten wanted fugitive, but there are complications, we have an Agent inside, who wants out."

Jack looks over at the Colonel to see he is handing him a picture, he looks at it and hands it back.

"Can you recognizes her if you see her again "

"Yep"

"Next you will meet with your support team and they will go over the logistics of the mission, so good luck"

The car came to a stop, Jack was motioned out, as they all got out except the Colonel who continued on the ride, Jack watched as the vehicle left through a side gate, either perturbed about leaving Sara behind or having to do this, Jack followed the Commander into the Security Guard shack and he and the Commander went into a large room, to see two smoking hot girls, Jack's eyes lit up, the first girl smiled, she was short and of some type of asian background to say

"Hi Jack, my name is Michelle, I will be your Laison Officer with my collegue, her name is Madaglena."

"We are her to escort you to the rendevous point where you will meet your real contact, so let's go"

"What about Raphael, my partner?"

"Sorry Jack she needs to find another way and another cover, this is a solo act"

She led Jack out a side door to a van, where a tough looking girl stood, she opened the door for Jack as Michelle, Jack and Madaglena got in followed by this rough girl, Jack took a seat on a uncomfortable chair, as he was jerked around to see these girls trying to hold on, as the van lurched forward, easily it became apparent that they didn't like each other, Jack just smiled, while he stared at this one tough girl, This girl had a scowl on her face all the time, Madaglena who sat next to Jack said;

"Here is your mission file, the girl you are staring at is a Jamacian DEA agent her name is Candance, and she will accompany you to see Carlos, the two have a history together, we captured her only a couple of days ago, she is tough, she put a very experienced Agent in the hospital, she wants to get back in"

While she was speaking to him, he focused his eyes on her cleavage, her revealing shirt exposed her breasts to the point it drew Jack's interest.

"Jack are you listening to me?"

"That's better, you guy spies, are all alike, don't worry Jack there will be plenty of opportunity for that on this mission, Carlos loves blondes, brunettes and redheads, so you and him should have something in common". " Lets focus on getting back to this, now back to your chosen operative, you should be familiar with her, she is on every newspaper in the world and her face is as recognizable as our own president's, but here she is just two hours ago."

She shows him the picture as Jack's eyes went back to Madaglena large breasts.

"I told you should have reduced them," said Michelle and ads   "Don't worry Jack I can't stop looking at them either, there huge compared to my working set."

"As I was saying, your cover is the newly married Mister Kenneth Biltmore, your took her name to carry on the Biltmore name, even though your keeping your name Winchester."

Jack nods his head to pull out the picture of Barbara, "Wow' he said to himself, this flaming Red headed beauty queen has chosen to work with me" Wow," he said to himself.

"Let me have the picture back, please"

"I was admiring her arms," said Jack refocusing his eyes on Madaglena's breasts.

Then in broken English, she speaks.

"Who is this guy? a pervert, I'm not working with him"

Jack bends his head up to take the stare off of Madaglena to look at Candace and in an instant pulls his weapon and points it at her, as the van goes quiet and then Jack has a scowl on his face.

"No, no ,no, don't kill me I'm sorry" she said pleading to him, while Michelle just froze and Madaglena, tried to lean back as far as she could, Jack's face was nearly resting his chin on her breasts, he could smell her sweet scent as he said " Shut up and keep your mouth shut"

"I will I promise, just don't kill me"

Jack reholstered his black-colored gun and put it away thinking why did it change color.

Madaglena looked at Jack who had not moved since the altercation as she strain to keep from going forward, she arched her back to support her position, Jack eased off of her and sat up to watch Madaglena do the same.

"Can we all get along here" said Michelle

"Now as I was saying Barbara, is famous the world over and has agreed to participate fully with whatever you need her to do, as usuall you will have two credit cards one your personal account and the second the mission card you will be paid one thousand dollars a day`, for your service and reimbursed for all of your expenses, if for some reason you earn more than your allotment for that day you can keep it it will be yours, you can store it in any of the fifty offshore and Switzerland bank accounts we have set up in your real name, your computer flash drive, can access, can you think of anything you need"

Jack went back to staring at her breasts.

"Besides them" said Madaglena, smiling.

"You know Mad, if Jack really wants them, I believe the Colonel said whatever Jack wants we are suppose to give him" said Michelle.

"Shut up Michelle"

Jack smiles and says.to himself "What have I got myself into, please let me go back to the base, please.

CH 14

Barbara Biltmore

The van came to a stop, Michelle slid the door open to help Candace, Madaglena and Jack out, and Jack followed Madaglena and Michelle as he was in some sort of warehouse, in through a door to see a fully bearded man and a cute black-haired woman and a nice complexion.

"Hi Jack my name is Jim, I'm the gadget's guy and this is the Agencies protocol liaison Officer, her name is Isabella, "Jack have a seat, I see your wearing your watch and let me have your wallet, Jack hands Jim the two cards he was given to Jim.

"Thanks, now here is your phone and wallet back, do you need any cash?"

"Nah I don't think so, I still have ten thousand"

"Here is twenty more, put it in your breast pockets, handing him a stack of twenties, divided in half.

"Wait aren't you the one that escorted me out of that prison in Atlanta?"

"Yeah what took you so long, the door was open, and it's been over three month's later"

"I thought it was a trap"

"Yeah, one that almost killed you" said Jim

"Enough you two, what's in the past in forgotten, unless you have a grudge against the Government Jack?"

"Nah, I 'm fine and ready for work"

"Now I need your gun and holster, for this undercover mission, is purely intelligence only to gather and release a deep cover operative and replace her with Candace his true and dedicated lover, so when you see Jodi free her and bring her back."

"What about Carlos" asked Jack?

"He is not the target anymore, besides, we need you to do this as a way to find out how you perform as a agent, anyone could go in there and shoot up the place and get lucky to kill him, I've said enough".

Isabella will give you Jack, all the details just have fun and when the mission is over I will give you your gun and phone back good luck."

Jack places his special gun in a familiar looking box, and takes off his holster and unclips his belt and begins to undress, to put on a new shirt and dress slacks and a tux tie and a jacket.

Jim hands him his wallet back.

"Jack, I will tell you what to do, and it is your Job to execute it, your Job is to accompany Barbara to this spa, you will treat her as a lady should be treated, always ask for anything, remember you need to be a gentleman."

"I have this book I want you to memorize each page and when you are ready let me know. "

"Come on Isabella we don't have time for this non-sense, tell Jack what he needs to know and let him have your precious book" said Jim.

"You need to sign this book out; it is worth a lot of money."

"Where do I sign" said Jack, who signed his name.

"Jack we have a car waiting for you, come with me".

"I will keep the book safe in my breast pocket" said Jack as Jim led him through a door to see a familiar face Michelle, dressed in all black and holding the door open for him.

"Thanks" said Jack getting in to see a nicely dressed Candace, who jumped over to the opposite side of the car to face him, with her trademark scowl look.

Jack looked at her and then went down to her chest.

"Do you mind, gentleman don't stare at women's breast, especially mine, I'm gonna have Carlos kill you, you disgusting pig."

Jack continued to stare and then produced a smile. Candace was now fuming, and said "If you don't stop staring at me I will come over and wipe that smile off your face."

Jack looked down to her legs.

"Stop looking at me you pig, especially between my legs," she closes her legs and puts her hands on her knees.

Jack looks at her chest, her plunging neckline show her breasts off well.

"I knew it the moment they put me in this dress I would hate it, stop looking at me you pig, or I will."

"Do what, "said Jack with a laugh, as he set back.

"This" she led with her right fist as it glanced off Jack's face, as he saw her coming at him, he caught some of the blow, and grabbed her around the waist.

Then moved his hands up to her breasts.

"Get your hands off my breasts you bastard."

Jack wrestled her to the carpet floor, from behind while holding her breasts, she was trying to kick him and yelled "Get off of me you pig, I swear I will kill you, no one touches my breasts and gets away with it."

Jack repositioned himself to slid one hand down between her legs to find the femoral artery and hit the soft silky skin as she forced his other arm up to wrap around her neck as she was screaming and kicking, Jack missed a few times much to Candace's dislike until he found the artery and instantly, she cooled down and he also was choking off her air supply, she held his arm trying to dig into his arm and with her mouth she tried to bite him several times as the car came to a stop.

"Will you stop this, if I release you" said Jack.

"Yes" she said between breathes and sops, he released her when the door was opened by Michelle to say;

"Is everything alright here."

Candace knelt up, adjusted her dress as Jack had one hand under her dress and when she stood up he pulled her panties off of her, to see her say "You bastard" and kicked him in the jaw, Jack slumped down with a smile on his face and thinking what a feisty wild cat she is, he collected himself to see Michelle over him "Do you need help?"

"Nah, it was just playful banter, I'm fine" said Jack climbing out of the Bentley with Michelle's help, Jack stumbled then regained his balance to see Candace off to the right still adjusting herself as Jack had her panties in his hand.

Michelle who was helping him said "Did you two have sex?"

"Nah it was more like a battle" as he throw the panties at Candace as he walks by her and says" The next time will be your last time."

Michelle helps Jack up the stone steps of this Chateau, Michelle rings the bell, the door opens to see a cute red-headed lady tall for her size to say "Hi I'm Lisa, and I'm from the CIA, you must be Jack, you look more handsome in person than in the picture, we will call your bride to come down."

Jack stepped in followed by Michelle and saw two girls.

One who had some surveillance gear and the other in a black suit, Jack couldn't help not to stare, he was only thinking of one thing and he was hoping it would happen soon as his manhood was rising, off to the left and down a flight of stairs was his new bride, Jack turned to see; yes, by far the prettiest woman he had ever seen, wearing a white with some poka dots pattern on a sun dress, wearing gloves and a hat to show off the best features of her face those beautiful full lips and beautiful shaped nose, she stood nearly as tall as him as she stayed on the top step awaiting for Jack to help her down, she extended her hand to allow Jack to help her.

"Looks like your glad to see me. She said with a bit of a laugh.

Jack couldn't, nor wanted to hide his enthusiasm for seeing her. As he touched her extended hand and helped her down, as she brushed up against him and whispered, "I'll take care of that later," and ads;

"It's nice to meet my new husband" she said with glee and stature as she took a seat.

Jack sat on the sofa next to Michelle to see this girl in the dark blue suit say "My name is Devlin, I'm with the DEA, and you too have been placed together to extract a unsuccessful and disturbed agent named Jodi Thomas, who we believe is being held at the famous Pine Acres spa, just out side Montgomery, this oasis is for the very rich and famous." said this perfectly sculptured girl.

"Hence Barbara's participation as she agreed to stage a marriage reception and retreat to get you Jack inside and find out what is going on, while inside you can switch the two agents, Candace who is still cooling off outside, and bring in Jodi, we want you Jack to first find out where she is at and second make the exchange and thirdly find out as much information on Carlos's operation, we will be in the van monitoring your progress, here is a ear piece and a pendant for you to wear so we can hear and speak to you and through the lapel see what you see, now on to you Barbara, remember whatever Jack says you will do without hesitation" said the strong and mighty Devlin.

She nods her head in agreement.

"Great let's go to the spa". said Devlin.

"How long will this take" asked Jack.

"As long as it takes for you to extract Jodi and replace her with Candace, who will travel with us, and gather some information, realistically I'm thinking three weeks."

Jack rolls his eyes and says "Great."

"Cheer up your just been married to the hottest older starlet of this country, believe me she will treat you well, and if she doesn't do it for you I will personally get you someone who will, so take a chance and enjoy this experience, this spa were taking you to is a one million dollar a day, so enjoy it to the fullest."

Jack was escorted out of the house to the car and Madaglena opens the door to the Bentley for Barbara, as Michelle goes to the drivers door, while the three girls all watch from inside the house, Jack settles in next to Barbara, who hands him the book and says;

"I hope this isn't yours."

"Yes it is", said Jack proudly as he opened it up and began to read, while Barbara sat and stewed only to say "Your suppose to be a Super Spy."

"Can't a guy constantly learn, I know I'm not perfect, so I like to read to keep my mind sharp" said Jack.

She looks at the book and says "The book says Etiquette, who reads that, besides chivalry is dead."

"Super Spies do."

"Alright you read that book mister" she said with a smile as she places her hand on his waist only to say "You're not happy to see your wife now."

"Nah were married, you know what they say."

"What do they say Jack. "

"Once you get married then the sex goes down hill to none."

"Well Jack, we have not consummated our marriage yet, so I would say we are in the valley yet to get to the hill."

"Besides if were together for the next three weeks....."

"It won't take three weeks; we will be out in less than a week."

"Really how do you know that?"

"That's why I'm a Super Spy."

Jack went back to his book and then began to turn the pages as his speed reading was coming back to him, in the next thirty minutes he finished the book, and placed it in his breast pocket of his Jacket, also he pulls out his wallet to see it was different and the badge was gone only a picture I D that read Kenneth Winchester the third and a address on it, in Montgomery, as the Bentley slowed to a stop they could hear Michelle saying Mister and Misses, Kenneth and Barbara Biltmore, is here."

The big steel doors opened, and Jack put his wallet away.

Jack lowered the dark window to see a large play field.

"That is the polo grounds, you will have to play a match, that's what we do."

As the car made a turn around a fountain and came to a stop, Jack waited as Barbara, held his arm and said "You just read that book; you need to wait here until she opens your door. secondly, there are cameras all over this place so look at me" Jack turns his head to receive a kiss from her on the lips, quickly Jack pulls away as she say; "What's wrong."

"Your lips stink like a skunk."

"Oh you'll get use to that I smoke cigarettes, do you want one?"

"No thanks", ads Jack, who opens the door, and steps out and closes the door, to meet up with his new wife, and comes to the two glass doors that open up, where ten people stood five women on one side and five men on the other. One steps forward and all says; "Welcome to the Pine Acres spa."

"Our staff have assigned the following for you Miss Biltmore, you have Jimmy the Masseuse." "As for the spa, spa specialist for you Mister Winchester, we have assigned Missy." "For sports activities Mister Winchester, you have Blythe." "For you Miss Biltmore, Pedro has just come off the professional tennis tour having just won at Flushing Hills." Lastly if you need any other special attention Miss Biltmore you have Brian and Miss Biltmore has requested for you Kenneth to Sail in our lake so we have here Caroline who has just come from America's Cup as one of the head skippers, and my name is Robert, I'm the manager, show them to their rooms."

Brian led the way as they reached the first room number 110 and says; "This will be your room Miss Biltmore, as everyone entered a large foyer that led to a huge bedroom and off to the right was a large double bath room and a keypad to open the door as Brian says;

"This will be your room Mister Winchester."

Brian opened the door and Jack went in, to hear; "Now I will leave the girls with you while we help Misses Biltmore get ready for the spa."

Jack stood in the middle of the room to see Missy was the only one left, dressed in a white outfit and a very short skirt, she said;

"What would you like first? A full sensuous massage or go into the spa and receive treatments."

"What kind of treatments?" said Jack teasing her as he moved closer?

"There are over one hundred types of services" she said. She stepped away from his advances.

"What do you suggest?"

"Seen that your old, older I recommend the mud bath first, to soften up your body, then into a hot mineral bath, then for a full body seaweed and salt scrub."

"Alright I'm at you disposal" said Jack.

"Fine let me help you get undressed" she moved in with a smile and began to undress him, as she knelt down on her knees

Jack looked down to see her very large breasts, in the skimpy outfit she wore, she helped him off with everything and said "I will come back later and clean all of your clothes and over here is a safe, only I and you will know the combination, it is open now, Jack puts his cash and wallet and watch inside and spins the wheel shut the combination is your wife's birthdates" she places a terry cloth robe around him and places a set of rubber slippers on him and says "Follow me," she leads him down the hall, Missy says "Mister Winchester, you and only five others are here for the weekend, I guess some whale has purchased the whole rest of the spa for the weekend, your wife and four others, so we will have most of the spa together for ourselves. "Do you have any special requests?"

"Like what?"

"You know you need anything to drink or anything in particular?"

"No, not that I can think of, I'll let you just take care of me."

"In that case, I will have Caroline help me support you, she has shown me, and she has some interest in you, if you know what I mean."

"I guess I can figure it out" said Jack moving closer to Missy as she leads him into the mud room.

"Here let me have your robe."

Jack unties it and removes it slowly to let her hold it while Jack eases into a deep mud the gooeyness spreads in-between his toes and quickly the cool mud surrounds his body.

"The cool mud slows down your pours and lets your body start to heal, I'll be in and check on you in thirty minutes."

Jack found a step to sit on and placed his back against a pillow.

Jack pulled a towel up over his face. And placed his hands into the clay and to his side and closed his eyes.

Thinking finally at peace with myself.

A knock on the door.

Jack says "Come in" still with his eyes closed, the door opens to hear a voice say, "Sorry dude I was scheduled for the next session."

Jack looks up to see a younger guy nude standing in the door way, only to be pushed in further by Missy who said " Now Mister Scott, the two of you can share that large mud pool, while she stood at the door Jack watched the guy get in and position himself across from Jack.

"Hey Missy, why don't you join us and take off that outfit."

"No," she said firmly.

"It is your obligation to please my wishes, or I will tell Robert."

"No, it is a service for you exclusively, if Mister Winchester wishes it then I will."

"What do you say Mister Winchester?"

"No, the lady said no and so do I."

She smiled and then left.

"But dude you can command any one of them to do whatever you wish, you should try her out she has an amazing."

"Enough", spoke a deep voice, as the guy went silent to say; "Yes Mister Gomez."

Jack kept his eyes closed and still resting his head as the guy said; "You guys don't mind if I join you. "

Jack kept quiet as the other guy said "No" as the other guy stepped in to raise the level of the mud to around Jack's throat; his peace and quiet was fast fading as the two other gentlemen began to talk.

"So Mister Scott how do you like the spa?"

"Its fine, except you said I was going to be taken care of."

"You are, aren't you?"

"No I mean, down there."

"Come on Mister Scott, there is a gentleman present."

"I'm sure Mister Winchester, doesn't want to hear about you getting your rocks off."

Jack looked up for the first time to see the man they call the killer.

Jack opened his eyes to, pull off the towel to say, "Your right sir could you both keep quiet."

Jack eased back into his pillow, and covered up his face, with the towel as the killer Carlos stared at Jack for the longest time then began to laugh, out loud and with hardiness to stop to see Jack staring at him to say, "I like a man who has balls, come join me by the pool side a little later, I heard you're a heck of a trap shooter, I have several of your families rifles we can shoot. Jack was silent as Carlos continued,

"Then later, I'm holding a no limit Blackjack tournament and you and your wife is invited, will you come?"
Jack stood up and tossed the towel away to see Missy had returned with some drinks, as Jack received one to say "No, sir, I have a date with my wife" Jack steps out of the mud to see Missy hand Mister Scott and Carlos a drink and then comes over to him, Missy uses a scraper to wipe off the residual mud from Jack, Missy puts a robe onto Jack and the two leave the room.

"What is his problem" said Mister Scott

"He is married to the most famous woman in the world, I think he thinks the whole world's weight is on his shoulders, leave him alone I like this guy" said Carlos.
Jack takes a small drink of lemonade, the flavor is worth remembering.

"you like it, it is freshly squeezed lemons and simple sugar mixed with truffle oil and blended with herbs and spices, it is called a south beach special, and thank you for sticking up for me, back there it is true I did get naked for Mister Scott, but he nearly raped me, so I have to be careful for who I undress for now, but he is right, here at the spa is anything goes policy, and whatever I can do to make you stay the best it can be, I will do it."

"Your fine, I like the rest and relaxation, just try to keep me away from others" asked Jack.

"I will do my best, come in here, this is the hot mud pit, just like that of the dead seas mud, you can literally float on the surface, let me take your robe Mister Biltmore."

"You can call me Kenny", said Jack showing her how much he appreciated her and she looked down at his package to say,

"You're welcome too."
Jack entered the hot mud oil pit and walk slowly to a bench under the water, to sit and relaxed as Missy went around and placed a rolled up towel for his head, Jack lowered his head down in it. Moments later, only to hear that loud and obnoxious voice, just as Missy said;

"Kenny do you want me to join you"
They both looked up to see Carlos.

He was walking in nude and full of the green mud with a huge Cuban cigar hanging out of his mouth and a bottle of rum in the other saying;

"How come, I can't get someone to scrap me off."

"Sir", Caroline said "I was going to be in there in a moment to take care of you and Mister Scott.

""I couldn't wait any longer, now get out, so I can spend time with my new friend Mister Winchester." said Carlos as he entered the hot mud pit to sit across from Jack, who went back to looking at Missy huge cleavage.

Jack and Missy was in a private discussion, to hear.

"Why don't you either lose that dress and join us in the mud or get that tail out of here" said Carlos.

Missy got up and walked to the door to say;

"Sorry Kenny, I won't share, especially with that creep" said Missy, walking out the door.

"So Mister Winchester what do you do, while your not building weapons for mass destruction, I don't know if it is purely a coincidence that you decide to marry the riches woman in the world and decide to spend that huge celebration at the most exclusive spa in the world, or that you knew I was coming to spend a weekend here, a well known weapons dealer in the free world, which is it?" asked Carlos.

"Shut up and be quiet, you talk too much, I came for rest and relaxation, knowing that her and I would be hounded by the free press for a while, so what about you why risk getting caught by the U S government and stay here rather than your free country of Cuba." asks Jack.

"Let me tell you why, Mister Winchester, this spa is my sanctuary from the Governments' Secret Agents, we know who they are and who trains them, currently they are down to eight and everyone of them is out of the country, they have two recruits, one is a woman for the first time and the other is some old German Spy easily in his fifty's so I say to you Mister Winchester, I feel very safe, here, where is my service" yelled Carlos.

"Coming" said Missy carrying another platter of two drinks each.

She hands Carlos the first one and then comes over to Jack and sets the platter down and kneels down to whisper in Jack's ear to say;

"Your wife asked if you would come down to the pool for lunch."

"Sure, only if you get in the mud with me now."

"Yeah, that's what I am talking about" said an excited Carlos

"What's all that racket going on" said Caroline and sees Jack to say "I have been looking for you; Missy, Hi, didn't you say you wanted my for Mister Winchester? "

"Sure, just wanted to know when you were going to join us and his friends" said Missy.

"Well how about right now" said Caroline ready to walk into the mud pond when Missy said;

"Not with that bathing suit on, you have to take that off to be allowed in that pool" said Missy.

"Fine I get Mister Winchester then, while you can keep Mister Gomez Company."

With that Caroline popped off her bra to reveal a firm set of breasts, and she stood over by Miss and Jack.

Caroline slowly pulled down her small bikini briefs to exposes a bit of delicate blonde hairs before she stepped in, meanwhile not to be left out Missy said;

"Oh what the heck". said Missy.

She pulls off her white top and white big bra to reveal two very big breasts, with big areolas and two large nipples, then in one quick motion she pulls down her skirt and panties to expose a dark bush of hairs and slipped into the mud to position her next to Carlos.

A half hour went by as both Carlos and Jack was being rubbed by both girls as they were rubbing them, till Missy said "How about we all go into the mineral pool and then Caroline and I will give you both a seaweed salt scrub and hydrating mask, then we will top it off with a full body massage."

Caroline nods her head in agreement as Jack has his hands all over her body as the two of them kissed, both Carlos and Jack are led out and both girls scrap off the remaining mud, then both men take their turns and scrap off the girls, then all four of them climb into a already made up mineral pools one for Carlos and the other for Jack.

"I want to switch with you, for Kenny" said Missy.

"Nah, sorry, you asked me to help you, so I'm sticking with Kenny, he is mine" said Caroline.

"Hey buddy, how are you doing" said Carlos.

"Fine, I guess" said Jack.

"Hey, my offer still stands, why you don't join me and my girl's for lunch down by the pool, around noon" asked Carlos.

"Do I have any choice?"

"No, you will be my guest; we shall have steak and lobster."

Just as Caroline lowered herself down onto Jack and pushed her breasts in his face.

"Don't worry, you need not to answer, I know I can count on you, to being there" said Carlos as Missy sat next to him and stroke him off.

The mineral pool was short lived as Missy announced its time to move on to the seaweed salt scrub, come on boys, as Missy helped Carlos out of the pool he saw Jack's manhood still hard and Caroline whispers to Missy " Oh my god, he has been hard ever since I got on top of him, how about yours ."

"Five minutes, tops"

"Oh my god, I'm sorry".

Carlos looks back at Jack and gives him a stare, then holds him up and says" I want to know something."

"Yeah what? "

"How do you keep it up so long?"

"What do you mean?"

"You know that?" pointing down to his manhood, then they looked at his.

"Oh yes, I see, well, actually its all about the mind control, and you need to be aware of what stimulates it. "

Jack was led into the big room first, to say, "Then focus on that and wham-o you'll be hard for hours".

"That is a secret, Jack" said Caroline, with a smile on her face as she led him by his shaft.

Jack was swatting away the smoke and said, "Maybe its time you stop smoking those nasty smelling cigarettes."

"These nasty smelling cigars is what they are called Mister Winchester."

"Call me Kenny, I'd say were friends now." said Jack.

"Good call me Carlos, lets go" the two walked together, naked as buddies with Carlos's arm around Jack's neck the two walked together.

Carlos started to sing a song and just like that Jack picked it up, he had heard a similar song while in prison, ever cementing their newly founded friendship.

"Alright boys this is where we need to break you up" said Missy.

"Aw why that is "said Carlos.

"Look only one bed".

Jack looks in and says "I think we both can fit on that", as Jack and Carlos both get on the double bed together.

"Kenny let me take you down to Cuba we could have some pretty fun nights together, you'd have to talk the misses into that, I'd be game to anything you have to offer.

Missy closed the door and said "Who gets who?"

Caroline stood by Jack side and said "Kenny and I have unfinished business together."

"Let them have their fun, and I will try again this time" said Carlos.

"Alright, Caroline help me out, you start at Kenny's feet and rub that seaweed mixture all over his front"

"Can I do it while I'm on top of him?"

"If you like" said Missy who was haphazardly wiping it on Carlos who was watching Caroline slowly and sensually put it on with her body and he watched as Jack's flagpole was at full mast, while he was flaccid, Missy tried with Carlos and with no success, Carlos watched as Jack worked over Caroline, till she exploded, literally soaking the bed, which Carlos had never seen before, he got up and left the room.

"Finally he is gone, share him with me" pleads Missy.

Caroline stands up and repositions herself at Jack's mouth, for him to continue to please her while Missy climbs aboard to ride the Jack's train till, she had her own climax, after a while, both girls together successfully got Jack off.

Both of them rolled him over and both of them gave him a good seaweed salt scrub.

Afterwards, they led him to the shower for him to wash off, which they helped him, as he helped both girls, while they both went down on him. Jack said "Please don't tell my wife."

"Don't worry, what your getting is nothing compared to what she is receiving she has five hung boys at her disposal, and from the looks of it we could call in our own set of reinforcements, Hey Kenny have you ever had a orgy?"

"What's that?" asked Jack.

"It's where I invite twenty of my closets friends and we all fuck, how does that sound?"

"Sounds like a fun time, can I invite my wife?"

"If you want, it may be a little weird, as the purpose for an orgy is to experience as many bodies as you can at once, what has happen here is a threesome, most men don't get that chance, but from the looks of it, I think you are ready, it will be a wedding gift from the staff at the spa."

"When will that occur?"

"How about tonight I will set it up, both myself and Caroline will be there."

Missy led Jack over to dry, his smooth silky skin off, and then led him to a table where she and Caroline began to apply body butter, allover his body including his still hung pole."

"Does that thing ever go down, your like a twenty five year old man", they let Jack lie on his stomach as they finished the rub down and then the massage as Jack was fast asleep.

Jack awoke to see it a quarter to noon, so he got up and saw a yellow swimsuit, he put on, and a new clean robe and those rubber slippers, and walked out of the spa area to see a older woman with big breasts and red hair says "Hi, I'll see you later."

Jack looks at her and shrugs his shoulder and walks down the hallway passing the front desk to see a very young looker, her blonde with dark roots shyly said "Hi, how can I help you Mr. Winchester, my name is Tami, and I'm your concierge?"

"Just looking for the pool, but maybe later."

"Ah yes maybe, your party is out on the deck, waiting for you," said Tami with a smile.

"Nice fingernails, I like the color red" said Jack as he made his way out to the deck area at the pool to see Barbara and Carlos. Jack steps out into the hot sun, and sees two blondes, flanking Carlos.

Jack pulls out a chair as he looks over to see a cute bartender licking her lips and simulates something with her hand and mouth together; he shakes it off, thinking maybe he was in a dream.

Jack sits down to hear Carlos say, Kenny, I've been talking with your wife and she says that you have not decided where and what you want to do for a honeymoon.

So I suggested, that you both be my guest on my yacht off the coast of Cuba, we can go down to Jamaica, I have a friend down there I'm looking for, and one I can't seem to get rid of"

"Maybe you ought to practice more of what we talked about earlier" said Jack.

"Maybe you're on to something; I could sure use your help. I like you Kenny" said Carlos.

"I like you too honey" said Barbara who put her hand on his chest.

She was shaking; Jack leans into her and says "Is everything alright, your shaking".

"Its nicotine withdrawals since we kissed this morning I haven't had one cigarette."

"That's your decision, honey, don't worry about it, we just won't kiss" said Jack.

"But I want to kiss you" said Barbara and ads "Also want to do other things to you."

"Will see, now it looks like were off to the Caribbean" said Jack.

"It wasn't my idea it was Carlos's, she whispered, then spoke out loud, Carlos can you tell my husband that it was your suggestion, that we be your guests."

"That's right Kenny, it was my choice to invite your wife and you to Cuba with me and my friends we will fly down there tomorrow morning, but lets party now and enjoy our meal, waitress, over here."

"Yes" said Nadia a fiery brunette, who kept looking at Jack and smiling, she took everyone's order and came over to Jack bent over, to show Jack her breasts and whispered in his ear.

"Yes" said Jack and ads "That will be fine"
The well known starlet, felt a little left out as all the attention was directed to Jack, even the famous Drug dealer was making her man more popular than her, as she leaned in to him and says;

"What is going on, it seems everyone likes you way too much".

"Carlos and I bonded earlier, in the mud baths."
"You had a mud bath, I want that."
"What have you been doing?"
Oh, you know, mostly by myself in my room"
"My massage therapist said you were getting down with five guys."

"What, I would never cheat on you" as she hit him and got up and left.

"What's wrong with your wife" asked Carlos.
"I told her that I really like that girl over there."
Carlos looks over his shoulder, then turned his chair around to see what Jack was looking at, then Carlos says "You want that psycho bitch, that bitch is going in the ocean, I'm going to throw that bitch out over the ocean and hopes she dies, that's why I got her handcuffed, she is a wild one, I even ducted tape her mouth, because she is so dangerous." Jack himself thinks about how nasty she is and fully agrees with Carlos.
Jack sees Jodi walk back to the table, as Carlos watched Jack look at his number one girl, and ads "Ah, for that one I'll trade you your wife for her" he said jokingly.
Jack thought about it and said "Can I have a chance to think about it."

"Are you serious, I was just kidding, hell you can have her if you want, and she isn't that great?"

"Screw you Carlos, come with me Kenny, I'll service you, I'll give you what Carlos can't deliver."
Jack got up and slowly passed the bitch who seemed to be pleading with him with her eyes, as Jack just laughed at her, Jack followed Jodi inside and past the front desk to see no one and saw the room she went into, Jack stepped in, only to see Jodi began to undress, with her back to him, she turned topless to him and say" Aren't you going to get undressed?"

"No, I never said I wanted to screw you, I just wanted to talk with you."

"Its just that Carlos uses me for everyone's pleasure, so when you said you had some interest in me, well I ".

"I'm here to get you out of here, do you want to go?"

"No, sorry I can't, I'm stuck here with Carlos, for the rest of my life, you know he has other girls as well, so yeah, I'd love to come with you, come here and let me service you."

"What do you know of the girl that's tied up out there?" asked Jack.

"He thinks she is a DEA agent."

"How did he come up with that conclusion?"

"I told him".

"Why would you do that" asked Jack knowing her ID', as the agent who wants out.

"Why do you care" asked Jack.

"That chick is a psycho bitch, one minute she is here, and the next police arrive and she is missing and the first time I was with Carlos that bitch came in and nearly killed me, I say that bitch should die, she won't be good for you or anyone, she would as soon be happy just with Carlos himself, but he likes lots of women."

"What about you, do you want out? Or not."

"Want out, hell I'm the happiest I've ever been, is that what Carlos said to you?"

"Excuse me" said Jack getting up and went to the door, when Jodi went to him and said" Listen I'm sorry, let me make it up to you, she went around to his front side and dug it out and put it in her mouth and began to work on him when Carlos tried to enter the room. Jack held his hand up to block the opening, for him to say,

"Ah Kenny didn't think it would take you that long, you're only on the first step still, forgive me, I'll leave you guys alone for say several hours".

"Yeah, that should be long enough" said Jack as Jack pulls away from her and zips up his swim trunks and closes his robe to say;   "Listen to me, I'll put Carlos down and get you out of here, get dressed, and give me an hour, you hear me say that I'm a US Marshal and place him under arrest".

"No you can't your going to get us both killed; besides he has diplomatic immunity."

"Really, not from where I'm at, I have International arrest powers"

"So you're the one, who is getting me out."

"Yeah, so sit tight, and wait for my signal", and then Jack leaves her room, to walk into the hallway and down the hall into and unto the deck to see his plate and the prostitute wearing a skimpy outfit with her breasts literally sticking out, her hair was all messed up, as Jack took his seat as his food was all alone.

"I was thinking about eating it"
Jack looked her over, and he could see her dress was hiked up, as she was scratching herself between her legs which she held wide open.

"Got an itch"

"Nah, I still feel a bit unsatisfied, because Carlos began to work on me, when all of a sudden, he got up, after I had a orgasm and said where is Jodi, so he left."

"That's a shame, is there anything I could do for you?"

"Sorry, I'm a property of Carlos, he is the only one who gets this, as she shows Jack, which was nasty wet, Jack ate half his steak and a little on his lobster tail, gets up and simply leaves, to walk over to the wild cat, Candace and said "Bitch your gonna die" and walked away as two body guards was forced to hold her still.
Jack made his way over to the other side where a ten foot platform was and took off his Robe to show his swimming trunks, he climbed up the stairs, and turned to see the street and one girl stood outside, looking at him, then all Jack could think about is the ear piece and

the camera, so he ran off the end and pulled his knees together and did a cannonball with a splash that didn't do anything.

Jack swam out to the edge to see Jodi and the other blonde was together eating the rest of Jack's plate.

Jack went up to the bar and got a towel, to dry himself off and realized he better get his robe, Which he went back and put it on and went inside passing the front desk to see that young hot girl who smiled at him, to knock on Barbara's room, the door opens to see that she was crying, Jack closed the door and said to her "What are you doing, you agreed to be part of this, when are you going to start acting like a wife, then some girl, who always wants her way".

"I don't know, I called my mom and she says the same as you do, we need to spend more time together and she suggests that we go to a church and talk with our father to work out our problems".

Jack noticed a lamp shade was titled when he went to adjust it; he looked up to the bulb and saw a miniature microphone, then says;

"I forgot, but can you come close to me" as she got up and went to him, he motioned for her to sit on the glass table, as he opened his robe and pulled his hard manhood out.

"Ha, what do you want me to do with that?

She laughed as she tried to hold it, and began to laugh?

"Just what I thought, so what is your birthday?"

In a serious voice she said "it is January 10th 1974, why do you ask"

Jack puts it away and closes his robe, and walks into his room and closes and locks the door, he went to his safe and tried the combination several times till he unlocked it, it was 1-10-74, it opened to see the lapel camera and a note, that said;

" I know what your doing here and me and my friends will help you in any way possible, also we know your not married to that prude, I talked with the guys and said she is old and broken down, so watch out my friend, I can give you much more than she could ever dream, I arranged it to have ten girls for you after nine tonight, we will be in the building across the street in the apartment complex, A-332 and so bring yourself and a friend if you want, here is my key to get into the building see you soon love Missy."

Jack placed everything in the safe and locked it closed.

Jack went out to the pool. Only this time it was different, first off there was a girl, sitting in her stand and a girl on the platform, then one by one, little children, one by one jumped off the platform.

"Hey you, did you get my note?"

Jack turned to see her, it was Missy, who he was getting to like more and more, even more than his wife, as she put her arms around Jack and said "I got it all set up for later, she let go, when she saw the manager come towards them.

"I was looking all over for you, Carlos said he was looking for you, he is waiting for you in room 3, when can you get there." Asked the manager.

Jack turns and says "I've had enough of this, wait here for me" said Jack as he walks out the front door, and down the driveway as the girls scramble to move towards him as he walks past the beams to open the gate, the small single gate opens up as the girls dive in, they start the van, and begin to take off, Jack holds onto the side of the van as it made its way up to the roundabout and says " Can I get a pair of handcuffs, I've had enough, your agent is being held against her will and she is by the pool, in a room, she is your leak, I'll have Carlos for you in a minute."

The van came to a stop, as Jack jumped off and went back into the spa, and said "Now Missy show me room 3, Missy picked up the pace as she showed him the room, Jack went in and found a waste bag and in an instant handcuffed one arm and then the other. As Jack placed the waste bag over Carlos's head.

"Come on Missy I told you I didn't want to do that with you" said Carlos.

Jack held onto the trash bag and cinched it closed, then pulled him off the bed and dragged him to the hallway, then Jack lifted him up and said your under arrest, I'm a U S International Bounty Hunter, and took him out to the hallway and escorted him to the lobby only to see the Colonel, Isabella, Daphne and the other Agent girls.

"Jack its over."

They pulled the bag off the other agents head, and uncuffed him

"So what this was a set up" said Jack, "You wasted my time for this bull-shit."

"Yeah it was, and everyone was in on it, were going to let you go and bring you back to the base, it was a good job, we will debrief you on Monday, go back to Mobile and we will talk about it later."
Jack went back to his room and unlocked the safe and pulled out the cash and his wallet and went out to the hallway to see that bitch, Candace who said "I hope you have no hard feeling."
Jack swung and connected with her jaw, and down she went, out cold.
Jack went past the Colonel and said "If I ever see that bitch again, I will kill her, I know it was a training exercise, do you know how I know, it was something Ronald told me, never leave home without your gun, and the cigar your Carlos was smoking was no Cuban, it has a sweet smell, not a skunk smell."

"Listen if you want me to be your agent, and then send me to him."

"Right now he is in Cuba" said the Colonel.

"So send me down to Cuba, they got to have some resorts down there, send me down there with the pop star and we will do this again, this time I will bring you this fugitive."

"Alright Jack I will set it up."
Jim stood outside to hand Jack a plane ticket, his wallet, his gun and watch.
To say "How did it go?"

"You don't want to know".

CH 15

Gold Mine

Jack laid in the center of the bed, while Leslie was on one side and Sara on the other after a night of wild and passionate sex, his phone   was ringing, Jack got up, and went to his phone, he answered it by saying "This is Jack Cash How may I help you", then ads "yes, really tonight, I'll be there, you said Hanger C as in cat, alright, out."

"Who was that, can you come back to bed," asked Sara.
"Jack, are you out there," as she gets up to investigate his where a bouts, she hears the shower going, peaks her head in the bathroom to see her man taking a shower as she surprises him" Boo". Sara says as she opens the glass door, Jack turns to show her his excitement which she then steps into the shower and joins him, the two kissed as Jack placed his arms around her head. She held on to him as he said " Sara, your going to have to go home and take Leslie with you the next few weeks are going to be pretty rough, I'm going on a special mission, with a few famous people, so whatever you do don't try to call me, I'll contact you, "

"Jack there is something I want to ask of you, will you let me join whatever your doing? "

"What about medical school, and follow in you father's footsteps".

"That's not my goal any more; I want to work with you, see more of you and be with you more."

"Well I don't know Sara, once your parents knew it was me who had convinced you to go back to school they loved me, now you want to work with me as a Bounty Hunter and catch criminals, I don't know, Sara, but if you want you can help me out part time until I finish this school in ten weeks or so."

"Alright what can I do for you? She said in a seductive voice and using her hands to get him very excited.

"How have you and Samantha been getting along? "

"Great, I just love her; she and I are getting to become better friends"

"That's what I like to hear, so I need you to drive back home, and help her with the charter business, heck; get your brother involved I don't care"

"Alright Jack I will" she said while she was playing with him.

"Listen when you get back to Mobile, I need for you and her to use a list I provide to you and contact everyone on that list and invite them down for a free fish charter in the gulf, even set them up with a first class ticket to fly into Mobile, ask Leslie to help out by being a escort for them to their hotel, and allow for ten to twelve per trip."

Jack washes her front side to say, "Next I want you to check in with Guy and see where the progress of the boat is and have it moved to the Public docks, will you do that for me."

"Yes I will Jack "she said.

They continued to spend some more time in the shower using up all the hot water in the building, and finished it off by shutting off the water, to see Sara was perfectly clean and Jack was content with a smile on his face, both were going in two opposite directions, as Jack dressed in his slick teal slacks and a white buttoned down shirt and a brand new sports tie with a camera lapel pin, he snapped into place, he inserted a ear piece into his right ear, next he swung on his custom made under-the-arm holster and his porcelain gun was in place with the single magazine with fifteen rounds secured inside.

Next he put his badge in his custom heart pocket and buttoned it into place, lastly he put on his sport's jacket and slid into his slip on custom black shoes, freshly shaven to leave that thin mustache and goatee in place, he was ready to go.

Jack was on the phone calling a cab, he paused and to look at his girl, who was dressing as he watched, until she was done, she came to him with a smile on her face and says;

"Do you happen to have Guy's phone number?"

Jack checked his phone and said "Here it is", he gives it to her and says "I'll be leaving soon, I want you and Leslie go home and jump into this with both of your feet, running, especially if the boat is done, I will call you from time to time on this phone" which he hands it to her."

"Thanks, this is cute color, to hand him his phone back."

"Sara, that is a secured Phone, you will only use it for our phone calls, do not call anyone of your family with it".

"Alright Darling, we will wait till you leave then we will go."

"No wait till four hours at least, and then go."

"Yes sir."

Jacks phone rings, he answered it to say "the cabs outside, I gotta go".

Sara kisses Jack goodbye, a nude Leslie who was carrying the top sheet, but not covering much as she held onto Jack and kissed him on the lips, as well...

Jack breaks away from her leaving her standing there when he opened the door, and slammed the door shut, stepped into the cab, the two girls watched from the window, to see the cab speed off.

Jack eased back in the seat to watch the city come and go and then the sign to Montgomery Airport, departures on the right, the cab came to a stop as Jack handed the guy the money plus a tip, out-the-door he went to the United Gate, in through the door he went, up the escalator to the ticket counter, where a girl said "What is your name, Sir."

"Jack Cash".

"Yes, I have you here, I need you to come with me," she said as she led him, through a door and into a room.

"Please wait here" she leaves and a door opens, to see Isabella, who stepped out and said;

"Alright Jack, I guess your ready now, and now it's for real, let me see your wallet."

Jack pulls it out and hands it to her and says, "Do you have any information on where I'm going."

"Yeah, but its your responsibility to know about where your going and what you need to accomplish, If I were you I would go to some store and pick up a book on wherever you go, just to give you a little bit of extra knowledge." Jack stood with his face to the wall when Isabella said, "Jack I want you to meet, your wife," Jack turned to see a vision of beauty, with a very pretty mark able face this lady was that a very fit and stunning girl for which Jack offered his hand and she came in and gave him a kiss on the cheek and said, "Don't worry I stopped smoking a couple of days ago, just for you."

"So she was real?" asked Jack.

"Yes Jack, she and all the members of the Spa."

"What about Candace, was she. "

"Fraid so" said Isabella.

"So she will be on this flight as well."

"She is your bargaining chip."

"You mean dead agent, don't you know, if he even suspects she is an agent she will be killed."

'Were the one's taking that risk, not you."

Jack couldn't keep his eyes off of her of Barbara, as Isabella said;

" Jack you are Kenneth Winchester, the now new husband of Barbara Biltmore, and you two have decided to spend your honeymoon in Cuba, where you Jack will enter in a high game stakes of Black- Jack, with a twenty million dollar buy in, for which the DEA has set up for you, you will have two DEA agents and two CIA agents there on site, the same cast and characters you have come to know, Kelly, and Lisa, then Devlin and of course your close contact will be Devlin" and ads " any questions, here is your wallet and twenty thousand in twenties, you two come with me, I'll get you on this flight."

Jack holds the door open for the two girls, as Barbara smiles at him, Jack brings up the rear or decides to watch Barbara's rear in her tight mini dress, they came to a door which opens to the outside as Jack tries to keep up, they go down to come back up, and led into the plane.

Isabella stops and says "Good luck Jack and Barbara."

Standing at the door then steward guides them to their seat, through a curtain in the front section of first class, Barbara takes the window seat, as Jack took the aisle, then the steward pulls a curtain closed. Jack hears "Open up the door, the package is secure."
Jack looks over at Barbara who smiles back at him; he closes his eyes and relaxes, until he hears.

"All passengers aboard flight 73 from Montgomery Alabama, to Santiago de Cuba, our flight time is roughly four hours and we will serve you a snack so buckle up and be prepared for a safe and easy flight."
The steward pulled the curtain back to reveal no one else in the First Class section, except the two of them as she said, "You two can get up and move around and sit wherever you like."

"That's alright, I will sit with my husband" said Barbara, taking a hold of Jack's hand and holding it, Jack still kept his eyes closed, until a steward said, "Sir can I get you something to drink."
Jack opened his eyes to see a familiar face it was Devlin, the DEA agent, dressed in the steward's outfit.

"No, I'm fine however do you have a book on Cuba?"

"Why yes Sir, I need to go in the back and get you that book, hold on sir."
Jack opened his eyes, looked around to realize his hand was getting sweaty, or not his, but it was hers he was holding onto .

"This is your Captain speaking we are about to take off, steward's prepare for take off."
A book popped into Jack's lap as Devlin made her way to her seat. Jack peered down to see the book said "The traveler's guide to Cuba." Jack picked up the book, it slipped, Jack broke his hand away from Barbara's and took the book in both hands and opened it up, as the plane took off, it went up climbing slowly, then leveling off, the seat sign went off only to see Barbara get up and say to Jack;

"I'm going to the restroom, do you want to come?"

"Nah, I'm fine"
Jack tore into the book and put his speed reading to good use, only slowing on pertinent places, this 954 page book was easy reading as Devlin showed up to say, "Where's your bride?"

"She's in the bathroom, even though she acted a bit weird."

"Why's that" asked Devlin.

"She asked me to go with her."

"Wow, she's better than your last go-around, this girl wants to have sex with you, it's called the mile high club, the next time you have an offer like that you may not want to turn it down" said Devlin.

"I'm not worried."

"Worried about what", said Barbara.

Devlin passed her and left, while Barbara stood besides Jack admiring his book, she leans into him and says" You and those books, do all Super Spies read, "

"Only the ones that want to be successful" said Jack.

"I told Kenneth I would be away for three weeks and during that time, I hope you can take care of my needs," she said, as she sat back down.

"You caught me off guard" said Jack.

"Listen, you're the Super Spy, I know that, but I have needs too, so I want you to follow me to the bathroom and give it to me, you got that."

Jack pulls her arm towards him.

Jack says "I'll do this for you now, but that means whenever I want it and with whom I want to join us are you O Kay with that."

She pulls her arm back and says "Yes, now let's go".

She pulls Jack out of his chair, and he drop kicks his book, as he tries to catch up with her as she opens up the small door and goes in, Jack hesitates, only long enough for her to pull him in, he lands on her and in the sitting position and the door closes, with barely any room, Jack is standing with his hands on her exposed butt, as she is bent over.

"Come on, do I have to tell you what to do."

"Enough, shut up," said Jack as he, pulled her panties down and undid his slacks and he was ready, so he stuck it into her, the beginning was now and for Barbara, she thought it would soon be over, but much to her surprise. Jack held on during the turbulent times and the calm stretches to the continual occasional banging on the door to the Captain's warning that were one hour away, as Jack had pumped her through five standing orgasm's and him coming twice to him still being hard, till Barbara said," Enough, you win, I've had enough."

Jack pulled out and she literally collapsed, Jack stood up and used her panties to clean up, then zipped up, he then helped her up and opened the door to see a long line. Jack got some serious looks and some mean looks as he helped Barbara back into First class and into her seat, she was tired part of her dress was wet as she sat down, she fell fast asleep, meanwhile Jack found his book and went back to reading it.

The plane started the decent downward, fasten their seat belt sign came on, Jack had pulled Barbara close to him and laid her head on his shoulder, she placed her hand on his stomach and whisper into his ear and she said " I love you darling, I love to fuck, made men but your something else, I have never been in a position like that ever, and with my current husband, we never do it, he has a impotency problem, so he invites others over and allows me to fuck them while he watches.

"That's a shame, Barbara, well for as long as I'm your husband, it will be just you and I."

"You mean that Ken".

"You can call me Kenny or Mister Biltmore"

"You would take my Daddy's name."

"Sure why not, it has a good ring to it."

Barbara turned around in her seat and gave him a big hug and then a kiss on the neck.

"Please sit down Miss, we are about to land" said Devlin, looking at Jack with a smile.

The plane did a right hand turn and off to the right was a mountain range, then another right hand turn, Jack eased into Barbara's seat to see the landing field and just like that, they were down and on the ground, taxi-ing, finally the plane came to a stop, the door opened and Devlin was escorting Jack and Barbara down the flight stairs and onto the tarmac, the air was musky and filled with the smell of tobacco, Devlin led Jack and Barbara to a hanger door, which she opened it up and they all went inside, as the other passengers exited the plane, while the three watched.

"Jack" said a voice behind him; he turned to see it was Jim.

"Hi" said Jack

"Alright you two, I'm your ground liaison for you both, and I was able to find you some transportation, as he pulls off the black cover to expose a marquee car and says;

"this is a 2005 Mercedes-Benz SLR McLaren, with a top speed of over two hundred miles per hour, it has the latest of innovations, from a remote control where you can control the car to underwater turbo system, fully bullet proof, and you have two forward missiles and a pair of twenty millimeter guns, also run flats and a oil squirter, to a side guns and lastly a homing pigeon, with a high powered camera, so in the event of a crash this pigeon will be released and fly back to me, any questions?"

"Where's the keys?"

"Right here, but you must go through customs first and I will have it and your luggage waiting for you."

"Guys are you ready to go" asked Devlin.

Jack nods his head, and follows the two ladies out of the door and into the terminal where Cuban officials await, with batons in the hands, when all of a sudden a huge crowd broke free and began to call out Barbara's name and her husband Kenneth.

Over the noise the custom official said "State you business and why you have come to Cuba."

"My name is Barbara Biltmore, and my husband Kenneth Winchester, were here to spend our honeymoon, we will be staying at the Castillo des Cuba, and we will be her for next three weeks."

Jack looked around for that bitch Candace, but knew she wasn't there. They used a wand for the pair of them, as another waved them on.

The security guy looked over Barbara and looked down to see a picture of her and her husband's wedding on the national paper and said;

"Go ahead, oh wait sir"

The guy held the wand up and down Jack finding nothing he said "go ahead and walk through."

Jack walked through the metal detector, and didn't look back as Barbara finished with the autograph signing to make it out the door as the crowd dispelled to the police actions. Jack held onto Barbara's hand walked out to see their new car, Jack opened the car door for her, and let her in, then closed it, then got in and turned on the car, it roared to life, they put their seat belt on and Jack took off. It took him a moment to familiarize himself with driving, as he had the car in drive and on the steering wheel was a large clear cover for a specific letter K and around it was A thru J all under a clear cover, with a fingerprint sign on the depression.

The ride was smooth and fast, as he followed the signs up to the castle on the hill over looking the bay, Jack put his thumb on the print and thought of black it went black as he came to a stop, in front of the entrance, got out and gave the guy a twenty dollar bill as Barbara was being helped out, the car sped off and Jack and Barbara went inside.

The hotel manager was their to personally greet them by saying;

"Welcome Miss Biltmore, and Mister Winchester, to the Castillo de Cuban hotel. We have given you the presidential suite, can you come with me, your bags have been sent in advance, up a flight of stairs, to a single landing with only one door, he opened it up, to show the spectacular view of the harbor, glass windows all around the main room and off the left was the bedroom with a huge sky light that a set of stairs went to, where another bed was then he shows them, the master bathroom, a small size pool with nozzles all over the place.

"Wow," said Jack as he pulls a single one thousand dollar bill out and hands it to him, as the manager nods in gratitude and said; "Order whenever you want room service, and the Prince of the Magnes region would like for you to be his guests tonight in our casino, where he has authorized a ten million dollar initial line of credit, for both of you, and thanks for the hospitality and enjoy."

He leaves and closes the door.

The pair of suitcases was together on the floor as Barbara begins to open her cases and began to unpack, in an instant; she pulled off her dress as Jack watched."

"So you like to watch, I'll be slow for you."

Jack took a seat on the stair up to the loft, while she stood naked in front of him and said, "Now what?"

Jack just looked at her near flawless body, as she came to him and said, "Now make love to me like I know you can".

She attacked him and pulled his pants off and was eager to have him inside of her when his phone rang, while she did all the work, he answered it and said, "Alright we will meet , give me thirty minutes as he looked at her and replied make that an hour."

Two hours had passed and Jack found the suite's safe, where he placed his weapon inside and Barbara gave him some jewelry to put away.

Both were redressed into something new and had showered they were off to a night that was filled with celebration and carnival, dropping down two levels to the casino, it was near packed, everything under the sun was being played, while Barbara went to the bar, Jack stood off to the side and watched people cheer and win as they lost every four or so, he watched as they placed their bets and threw two dice, off to his right was a table, empty. With a large chair and two chairs. Then a man came and pulled a curtain around to close this off, then they closed off the craps table, Jack went, to be by Barbara, who was into her second drink when the Casino shut down, as the lights went down, over the intercom, it said,

"Ladies and Gentlemen, the casino is closed, so please exit and come back later, by order of the Prince of the Manges, as the remaining people were escorted out only Jack and Barbara were permitted to stay as the door closed, out came a woman dressed in red and of jewels, wearing a headdress made of silk, the hotel manager motioned for them to come, as Jack led while holding Barbara's hand, to the lady, who bowed in front of them, Jack was to busy looking at her, through her see through revealing outfit and she said;

"My name is, Princess Maria of Manges, and the future wife of Prince Carlos Gomez, please come and sit at our table and we will have a traditional feast.
Princess Maria sat first, then it was Barbara, then Jack, who occasionally looked at the magnificent looking Princess, who was staring at Jack, who stared back at her equally, as the two played a quick game, only to have the Princess look down, when the Prince came in.
Jack saw Carlos for the very first time, and watched as the Prince took his seat, Jack followed his every move, off to his left was Maria, who continued to smile at Jack.

"Let me introduce myself, I'm the Prince of Manges.
This is my soon to be new wife her name is Maria, and my name is Carlos."
Jack continued to stare at Maria, while Barbara took aim and connected with a kick to his chin as she said "Pardon my husband's manners, he seems to be rude around pretty women, my name is Barbara and this is my husband Kenny."

"Yes I know of Kenny, he is my arms dealer, and would like to say this is a pleasure and an honor to finally meet you after all this time, as it took for you to marry the most popular girl in the world, I told you before, Kenny your always welcome down here and from the looks of it, you like what you see, she is yours, you can have Maria as a wedding gift."
Her eyes lit up as did Jack's.

"Then it shall be done, looks like she approves of this deal, so she will be yours to do with whatever you see fit, so Kenneth, while you are here, do you want to tour the areas your guns have been put to use, and I will show you my plantation, lets say in a couple of days, lets now eat."
He claps his hands and servants brought out, the first course, a freshly baked soup, with a pastry crust and a bottle of wine, Jack watched as Barbara ate and he followed her lead, much to her surprise.

"Listen up, we shall have a royal ceremony, to marry Kenneth to Maria, as he has but only one wife now, and in this country you can have as many as you like, he shall have two and possibly more, a ,ha, ha, " as Kenneth laughed, looking over at Barbara who was not amused. The next course was the, salad course, then it was a meat course, then a fish course and finally a dessert course a decant-ant chocolate raspberry cake, served with a cordial. Afterwards the Prince got up and said "Tonight, we will have a celebration and tomorrow you and Maria will be married, my good friend from the United States, let us party.

Jack and Carlos strengthened their bond overnight, as the two ended up in a suite together and Barbara and Maria in the other as Barbara awoke to see Maria standing beside her bed, Barbara jumped back and said "What are you doing here?"

"The Prince ordered that, I now live with Mister Winchester and his Bride."

"He can't do that to you, you're a grown woman."

"He can do it, and he made it public, which means it will be so."

"Besides, it was meant to happen, that's what Kenneth told me, before he came down here."

"What do you mean by that?" asked Barbara, curling up on a pillow.

"My master told me that when Mister Winchester would come to Cuba, that he was going to present him with me as a gratitude for all the weapons, he had sent to Carlos and to keep our providence safe."   "Don't worry I know my place, I will only service Mister Winchester only when you don't want to please him, for I am ready to have a child" said Maria.

"Have you ever seen Mister Winchester before?" asked Barbara.

"Yes he come to our village say six months ago, he was wearing a full beard on his face and smoked a lot of cigarettes" said Maria.

"That's my Kenneth" she said quietly under her breath. To ad "We may have a problem".

Maria pulls out a necklace, made of gold and says, "This is a gold flake necklace I have made for him, to give to him as a present for accepting to be my husband, don't worry here in Cuba, Mister

Winchester, can have many wives as he wishes, besides he fancy's several other women of my village"

"That two timing son of a bitch, she announced, "You can have him" she said in a huff getting up realizing she was losing her composure, over her other husband, not Jack Cash, as she pulled it together to say "You know I had Kenny, shave his beard off and quite smoking, so that he would marry me (in truth she actually did)," said Barbara.

"Will we all sleep in the same bed?"

"Yes, we will" said Barbara realizing that Maria didn't believe a word she said, she sat with her hands to her face and began to cry, whereas, Maria came to comfort her and say "That's alright Miss Biltmore, I like this Mister Winchester better, for he carries the scent of the gods" as she pats her back and leans over and gives her a kiss on the cheek.

Princess Maria, says "That doesn't mean a thing, either way I still get to go to America" and ads "We as girls could have fun together."

"What" said Barbara, looking up at her as she began to undress.

****

Jack awoke, in a make shift bed, looking at a half dozen children looking down at him, he slid around in the bunk, to sit down, the room was primitive, he rose to realize he still had his wallet but his Jacket was missing, he moved suddenly.

The children dispersed, opening the door to see the light of the day, a young man appeared in the door way to say in English;

"The Prince, asked me to be your translator, for the community, my name Hopi".

"Where am I at, Hopi?"

"You are in the village of the Manges family."

"The family has a village, is that like a small town" asked Jack.

"Yes, the family is made up of Grand parents called Elders, and then our Father, the Chief.

He has many wives as he can take care of, which are called the women and of them there are mothers and workers, and of course the children, in this village alone, there are over seventy children."

Jack looked up at the boy, being blinded by the morning light, to hear;

"And you my friend, are going to marry one or two or so" said Carlos as he busts his way in to see Jack.

Jack looks up at him with a glaze.

"Cheer up, tonight you will be in heaven, not only will you marry the leaders main daughter, and unite yours and theirs family, but you will be marrying their entire family which means you can have the run of the liter, by choosing as many as you want, for more wives, that's what I did, several years ago, when I uncovered this wealth source, and then we all became brothers, in arms."

As Carlos hugged Jack and said "Now you need to make a donation to the men of the village, in the form of plants, animals or wisdom, you need to give them something that they don't already have, like the arms you have provided us over the years, but this time you need to make a special one time donation, so I will leave you here".

"I hope that you may win over them, and that they approve of the wedding, so get up and come join me, with the morning feast and I have asked Hopi, Maria's brother to help with the translations so come on out." Carlos places his arm around Jack's neck and leads him out into the street to a large table, which sits under a open fixed roof, a single space was open on both sides of the leader, who sat at the end of the table.

Jack sat on the end and Hopi across from him while Carlos, went down to the other side and sat with the mothers.

A plate was already prepared for Jack, Jack looked over at Hopi who said in English "Eat everything on your plate, if you want more, they will bring you another. The more you eat, and the more they will like you"

As usual Jack watched others eat, and he did the same using a fork and knife and a spoon, he ate a sample of different things some salty some sweet, another thing was sour and lastly something bland, he was near full as he was eating slowly to keep up with the chief.

The Chief got up and yelled something, everyone disbursed, leaving only Hopi and Jack and the Chief.

The Chief said something as Hopi translated it and said;

"My father says he wants to show you around and wants you to see the house he had built for you and Maria."

"Fine let's go" said Jack.

The three began to walk down hill to a lagoon, where Hopi said;

"This is our fresh water fish farm, some times we get other fish in here when it really rains."

Jack followed the chief and Hopi behind them, then the chief stopped and made some loud noises as Hopi said "Our father is offering you a chance to see our wealth, he wants me to show you inside our mine, come follow me"

Jack passed the Chief, and followed Hopi, up a worn path to a entrance that was large, a huge generator sat on one side as Hopi handed Jack a pair of ear plugs, that sat on his ears as Hopi fired up the loud, generator, and the lights came on, shining brightly, Jack followed Hopi in, above him was support beams, as the noise died down, the passageway took a turn up, using a ladder of sorts Jack climbed, to a big cavern that opened up and on one side was a fresh ocean breeze, large beams made up the inner framework.

They continued upward, as rocks that have come loose was evident to Jack seeing them being supported, as Hopi pulls off his headphones as does Jack, he says " This is our gold chamber, look above do you see that ore line, see that vein, Jack tried but couldn't see a thing and said;   "You need some water up here."

"Why do you say that?" asked Hopi.

"It would get rid of the dust so that you can see the vein better" said Jack looking at the wall, touching the wall to feel the thick dust or soot that has formed to protect the gold, Hopi returned with a bucket of water and hands it to Jack who took it and in one swing threw it up on the wall, the water splashed and dripped off the wall as Jack turned to Hopi to say," Do you happen to have a hose?"

"No, we use water we collect from the lagoon."

"Listen I got an idea, how about, instead of you digging the wall out by hand, use water to dig it out, then let the remains flow down a chute to a drain box."

"I don't know, what you are saying to me, you're going to have to convince my father to accept this."

"Fine let's talk with him".

Jack put his headphones back on and followed Hopi back out, to see him turn off the generator, Jack looked down to see particles of dust with gold in it, and picked up a bucket and filled it with water, and scooped up a handful of powder and placed it in the water, the gold was very visible at the bottom.

"Hopi, come here and look", Hopi comes to Jack and looks inside the bucket and says "Yes I know, we do this all the time, let me show you", and leads Jack to a pond.

"Look its all over, we call this the dead pond, nothing grows here, and it is hot at times."

Jack began to laugh, and says "Hopi, you can save all that gold dust powder and sell it as dust, for like 1000 dollars a ounce, and you probably have several pounds in that pond."

"What I recommend is to place a drain box in there then, drain that pond and build it up with bricks and you have a hot spring to soak your aching bodies and lastly we get a hose and start excavating the ground out with water, and use several catch boxes to collect the gold dust along the way."

Jack looked at Hopi who looked back at him, clearly not understanding what Jack was saying, for Jack to say;

"Go ask the chief if I can do this for him, tell him it will save him time, energy and make him a very rich man."

Hopi nodded in acknowledgement and went to his father and the two talked while Jack stood off in the distance, he could here the Chief yelling and swearing and even swinging his fists in the air, finally he calmed down just as Jack was feeling ill, he made a run to the outhouse, and just made it, as he let loose it was painful, he lingered in the smelly room a local paper was next to him, with Carlos's picture on it, stating he was putting on a huge poker and blackjack tournament at the castle scheduled for this weekend and that the pot would be worth 100 million for the player and 100 million for Cuba, invitation only, Jack was feeling better, he got up and went out to see Hopi all alone and said "What did the chief say?"

"I convinced him that you bring change, If he accept you, as his son, then he needs to allow you to bring what you offer, so he finally agreed, and will allow you to build your boxes and I will help you, as will my brothers" said Hopi.
Jack felt for his phone and pulled out his satellite phone and found Jim number and made a call;

"Hey, Jim this is Jack, he said quietly, I need some supplies put together and sent out to me, O Kay, first is a chop saw, on a stand and a extension cord, a portable generator, a big box of screws".

" Next I need a portable drill, then I need, as a base, a plywood surface of say eight by eight feet, with sides, using plywood sides reinforced and inside fill it with some pine planks, say l/2 inch by 10 inches by 8 foot long. I'd say I needed 60 or so pieces, and 20, inch strips by 8 foot". "Next, I need, 20, 2 by 4s. Lastly, I need a sump pump to drive a hose that must shoot at least one hundred feet. And all this as soon as possible, you'll bring out the generator yourself, alright I will see you soon."
Jack closes up the phone and sees Hopi with a broken shovel and two hand held diggers, for Jack to say " No, no no," and picks up his phone and gets Jim on the phone and says "in addition to all that, I need at least ten new long handled shovels, pickaxes and any type of hand tools you can come up with to include some hammers" said Jack as he closed up his phone, and put it away, then Jack began to survey, the entrance.
Jack then walked around the side to see a pile of dust, looks up to see a hole, then decides to go inside as Hopi comes to him and says;

"How can we help you?"

"Hold back now, I've got reinforcements coming."

"All you did, was make a call, who will help us, we barely have enough food to feed us let alone anyone helping us."

"What about the Prince, he is your brother isn't he."

"Yeah, he gave us one hundred head of cattle, when he married our sister Rose, but when they drank from the dead pool they all died and he comes to visit, to take our gemstones and gold, in return he brings us a shipment of some food and takes my sisters, and then they return to have babies" said Hopi.

Jack then walks up the hill to see houses on the left and some on the right, up to the top of the road, to see the ocean and he could feel a constant breeze of wind as Jack gets another idea, then looks over to the left and sees a path, narrow in width and follows it down to a small valley that has huge mango trees with some type of black fruit trees.

"They call them avocado's, we pick them green and they ripen up." said Hopi.

Jack feels how spongy the ground is and walks over to the wall to see the sulfur water is flowing in, filtering, in giving Jack another good idea, and says "Come on, lets go I have an idea".

Jack leads Hopi out , onto the landing behind the mountain and walked to the pile of gold dust, they both looked up for Jack said;

"That is where I will tap, the wall and set up the boxes and over there is where we will drain it to the bottom, whoa we need some bags to bag up the dust"

"We make some waterproof jute bags"

"Why don't you get one for me, so I can see what it looks like."

Hopi leaves as Jack survey's the rest of the land and gets one final idea as he notices a large truck coming down the road towards him.

Jack made his way to the road to see the truck come to a stop as Jim jumps out and says "You're the first spy in all my years that has asked for timber and hand tools to build something, usually all you guys want is cars, cash or weapons, Jack your one odd guy, so lets see what I can do for you"

"Just leave everything, I will do it, it is my gift to the leaders.

In return, I get to have the hand of a fair maiden"

"You're already married, to one of the riches ladies in the world".

"Yeah, so what, she was a gift from Carlos, so I need to fulfill my obligation to the family of the girl and if I need something else I will call you, thanks."

"Jack , it doesn't work like that, it is my job to support you, and if you need something built, I'll do it."

"Sorry not this time, but from now on, I'll just stand back and let you go."

"Then help me off load it" said Jim.

Jack looked around and saw Hopi, to say "Hopi can you get your brothers to help unload this truck and set everything by the cave."

"Yes sir"

Jack watched as the ten brothers off loaded the truck and the big box, which Jack had them carry it to the pasture on the back side, while Jack and Jim turned the truck around, and backed the new generator, into place, it was abit hidden, then unhitch the generator, as Jim sets up the chop saw and both pull out the electric drill and tools, planks of boards are stacked up, while Jack hands out brand new shovels.

Jim looks at Jack, who waves him off, and he gets into the truck and says to Jack "Call Lisa or Kelly, they have some information for you."

The truck takes off and leaves, while Jack gets to work as Hopi says; "My brothers and I want to thank you for the new tools, they will help us out."

Jack fires up the somewhat quiet generator, and plugged in the saw and began to building the sluice box, he counted his wood it measured enough for ten boxes, three planks each, using the thin strips spaced out across the bottom which Jack cut to fit and screwed down, he cut the two by four for the top to use as a upper support, quickly he made all seven, having carried one inside the cave to place along the wall, where Jack had the brothers dig out a trench, and enlarge, the hole out which Jack pushes the newly made sluice box out and then modifying the other box as Jack fasten the two together leaving about a foot short on the inside box, to continue the downward motion.

Then outside Jack uses the two by fours to build a ladder.

Jack stands on it as the boys above dig a hole big enough, Jack installs the next one outside to inside, under existing box and just a little lower, as he goes back inside and screws them together. Then the next one he positions at an angle, he uses 2 by 4 to build a support frame, Hopi was right beside him, learning to see what he could do for Jack. The next box, sat under the existing box and turned in to parallel the pond, on a built up dirt base, then Jack, uses two together, screwing them together. As he turns the last two towards the pond. Jack begins to work on the drain box, which, Hopi and his brothers, worked in the mushy field to dig, about half way down, till they hit water and stopped. Jack had the boys carry the newly made box, to the orchard field next to the last completed chute.

Jack stood back to look at his work, as the brothers were undoing the hose and attaching it together, they hand it to Jack.

Jack pulls out the pump and hooks on the hose, with a adjustable nozzle, and throws the pump into the hole the boys dug, inside the dead pond and then plugs into the extension cord, into the generator, that was off while the battery power was being used.

Jack, had the extension cord plugged into the light system in the cave and hooked up to the pump and then went inside the mine, with the hose in hand, up to the Gold wall and began to turn on the water, easily cutting in the wall, as the hot water began to flow into the trench the brothers dug, down to the first box, as Jack took out a section then stopped. Hopi and his brothers watched, with excitement.

Jack went down along to see it was working, as good size nuggets was trapped along the strips as he then set the hose a bit ways to allow the water to run in the box, the dust thinned out and all that remained was gold as Jack held a waterproof bag, he began to collect off the strips, up to the wall, then went outside to see a mess. The water was everywhere, but it was doing its job of catching the gold dust and all the way down to the final box, as Jack held the bag, Jack looked into the final box, to see, as the brothers did as well, the box held the glimmer of the gold.

Jack went back inside to talk with Hopi and tapped him on the shoulder and said, "Can you get the Chief, and let's make this official."

All the boys were on the wall one even using Jack's hose, so Jack and Hopi walked out towards the leaders' household. Whereas Jack waited till the Elders and the Chief came out as Jack handed the half full bag to the father, who took it and looked inside and spoke as

Hopi translated, he says many thanks for this will buy much clothing and needed food".

"No, that much Gold, is worth much more than that" said Jack.

Everyone looked at him, even Hopi, who didn't know what to say.

"How much in peso's five thousand or so" asked Jack.

"No not that much, maybe one thousand peso's" said Hopi, and ads "Usually the Prince pays us what he feels it is worth and for all that he will pay us sometimes around five hundred peso's.

"That's not right, this is worth much more than that, what I would like you to do is to smelt this into blocks of gold, that way I can exchange them for cash in the United States and exchange them for pesos.

"My father says he will allow it, if you will show us how to smelt it, he says you can transport it back to, to the U S and he trusts you to do this in exchange for the hand of Maria and he approves of the marriage of you and her." And ads "Tonight we will celebrate the union of you two."

"What about him going to see what I did for him."

"Don't have too, the mine is our boys business, he will accept what ever I tell him, so you're welcome Kenneth, is that your real name?"

"Yes, why do you question that?"

"Because the Kenneth that came before, had his way with two of my sister, who are now pregnant, and he suggested that we all leave this place and that he would build us a place up on that hill, but your not like him, you show compassion, and respect, and would be honored to have you as one of our brothers and we would like that portable generator"

"You can have it all, come with me and I will show you, how to cook the gold, and smelt it" said Jack, "by the way my name is Jack, Jack Cash, International Bounty Hunter, I'm here to rescue someone, and along the way help those that need help, will you keep my secret?"

"Yes Jack I will, it will be our secret, my new brother, the two walked together; till they came to a big fire pit and Jack lifted the big cast iron pot.

"What are you going to do with that?"

"Were going to use this to smelt the gold."

Jack carried to an area by the generator, using a shovel, Jack dug out a pit in the sand then, using two by fours he built a frame and hung the pot, and then Jack tilted the pot, then let it go, he cut a board for it and retilted the pot and then, set the cut board underneath it. He then cut a couple of two by fours, and place them in the sand, then he knelt down, and dug out in the sand what looked like big dog bones, there were four of them, then Jack said, "Hopi go get some fire wood, and we will make a fire."

While Hopi went to gather firewood, Jack, poured in all the gold flakes and nuggets into the pot. Then Jack went back into the cave to see the boys at work, it was like a fine-tuned machine as two boys held onto the fire hose, one was sweeping it to the wall while others dug a deeper hole to catch the water as the water went over the edge, it took some of the gold, they were making huge progress enough so that two more boxes needed to be made, while Jack was collect it at each rung and put it into his bag, he collected the ten rungs inside, then went outside and collected it from the remaining thirty five or so, rungs, down in the box was filling up with water, and realized he needed to put a spigot on the bottom and filter the water out into a cloth of some type, and catch the rest, then with his bag heavy, Jack went back up to the pot, and dumped it in, then Jack arranged the wood for the most effective fire stance, as Hopi, brought over a log that was still somewhat burning and placed it in the center, and then the fire was lit, easily getting very hot quickly, thus melting the gold, and burning off the ore, as it popped, you can smell it and seeing it was ready.

Jack titled it over and using a new shovel he broke up the globs and tried to pour it into the sand, realizing it was not hot enough , Jack stopped, and placed the fire back under it, as Hopi took it over, and allowed him to do it. Jack stepped back to watch, he must of seen this before, because he easily got it to a melting point and then, poured it into the four molds that filled up, quickly, as it cooled. He wrote his name in all of them with a fire poker that read "HOPI 1 through HOPI 4, then let it cool, the remainder sat in the bottom, which as it cooled was scraped out and set aside.

"You should build a shack around this operation, to keep it secret, heck I would even build a wall around this front part, to keep people out" said Jack, as the sun was going down, Jack knew it was time, for Jack to get back to civilization and take a shower.

Jack pulled out his Phone and made the call, Devlin answered it and said she was actually watching what we were doing and thought it was a nice gesture, she said she will be down shortly.

Jack put the phone away, and thought it would be nice, to build them a new house with modern, plumbing and electricity, heck there is even a pole along the highway for electricity.

Jack stood watching Hopi still work, a car came up and Jack got inside as it turned around and left.

Candace, the devil herself.

J ack stepped out of the shower, and dried off, after the long hot shower, reminded him how grateful he was of him living in the civilization, whereas while he helped Hopi with the gold mining experience was nice but it was dirty, grimy. Especially, seeing that there was not one good source of fresh water to drink, that will all change thought Jack, as he remembered talking with Devlin about building a new home for that family in the size that could house all seventy five family members, comfortable in the house, complete with a filtered water system, tap a well, to a septic tank and field, building a support for the hot springs.

Jack finished toweling off and to put on some underwear and a t-shirt, went out into his new room, to him to find a newly tailored suit and tie, which Carlos gave to him. He put on a brand new shirt, unbuttoned his left side pocket and placed his wallet and phone inside, he looked in the mirror as a stack of cash, was in front of him, whereas he put it in his breast coat pocket, as he finished dressing, then he noticed a box off to his left, which he opened it upto see the box was full of freshly rolled Cuban cigars, it was his new passion, and he liked it, he was beginning to think more about Carlos than for what he is accused of doing, to learning about the Magnes family, to going on these trips to impersonating other people to uncovering a major weapons trafficking operation, to them holding Kenneth Winchester, to Barbara, finding out who her actual husband is, and for her to flip out, in her hysterics she wants a divorce, but for the moment she must pretend to be married to Jack, now she will be the bridesmaid to Maria for her wedding that Carlos, set up and paid for. Jack checked the mirror one more time, then he went out to his foyer, looked around to see if there is anything else he needs, he stepped out into the hallway, he looks at his watch, to see he has about two hours to go, for the celebration to begin, as he walked he sees Lisa, who was dressed very sheik, as she pulls Jack into a cubby hole to say" We got some bad news for you."

"What's that?" as Jack pulls himself closer to her enough to smell her perfume.

"Kenneth Winchester is free and heading down here."

"How did that happen?" asked Jack.

"He gave us the slip, and he also let Candance out, so the two of them are together."

"How are they together/, I thought we were exchanging her for this Thomas girl?"

"Not anymore, ever since you got involved, as how you have, we decided to keep her and see what you could do".

"Great, so what are my orders now?"

"You'll still continue with the marriage, and from there we hope you spend more time with Carlos".

"And as far as Kenneth and Candace."

"Well that's up to you."

"I will try to get this whole thing under control" said Jack as he pulls away from Lisa and into the ballroom he went, he looked around and sees Barbara at the bar, drinking a drink as Jack came up from behind her and says," How about you and I go into the room and get wild and crazy."

"Nah that's alright," she turns to see Jack, and ads, "Oh its you, if you want."

"What's wrong darling?" asked Jack.

"You know, my husband is a gun running trafficer, where do I go from here?"

"Cheer up; you have me, ain't I better than him?"

"Yes, but what can I do, the public is going to blast me."

"Who cares what the public says, it is your life and you can do what ever you want to, and honestly you probably could get it annulled, you didn't consummate it "

"Only with you, we were married only a couple of days ago, who knew what his secret was" said Barbara.

"Well, I got even more bad news for you, he has impregnated two of Maria's sisters, so look, cheer up, put your game face on and lets rock this place and have a good time, its my wedding so were going to have fun, oh and by the way how has Maria been in your care?"

"You don't want to know."

"Actually I do want to know, this sounds interesting".

"Maybe later you'll find out for yourself what I mean".

"I look forward to that", said Jack as he peeled off from her and went into the casino, where a big bouncer stood at the door, saw Jack and let him in as he saw a picture of Jack and Maria on the door. Jack went in to a casino where only the well dressed were, and in the middle was Carlos holding court.

Jack moved over to Carlos.

Carlos said, "Hey you sure did make a good impression on the family; they said they would open their arms up to you and accept you as one of their own sons".

"Yeah, it was nothing, I was glad to help."

"I got a special, thing for us to do tonight, we are going to drive into town and see a fight, my number one fighter is taking on the number one challenger, and we are gonna have front row seats, do you want to gamble, its on me.

Jack sits down, adjust himself, as others move down to let him in, as a dealer slid one million in chips to him.

"I have another gift, for you, my sister, her hand in marriage, if you will have her?" said Carlos.

Jack looked over at Carlos to say," Sure, why not, that should cement our bond as brothers, when will I meet her?", said Jack as he saw Barbara was at the table, quickly a chair was open, next to him, so she sat down.

Jack watched as the cards were being dealt, and began to count cards, when the dealer said "Sir are you in?"

"Nah one more round" said Jack now starting to get the hang of the cards, Blackjack was easy thought Jack, count the cards, to see what people have, then determine the remaining cards, it can't be that hard, now the betting, I need to place a teaser bet, then I'm dealt another card, that's where I can stand or fold and or double my bet." thought Jack.

Jack watched Barbara cleanup with a nineteen, each color represented a dollar amount, and Jack placed out some chips, as the dealer dealt in Jack.

He had one hundred thousand, and slid a pre-stack towards the pot, two colors, purple and black, there were double that of purple than black , much to a hush over the rest of the players, as Barbara looked at him and slid two purples, as did everyone else, Jack's first card was a Ace, he slid another black chip ontop of the other, as did everyone else,on his right was a gentleman who had different colors, and a huge stack of chips as Jack received his last card a king, which he looked at it and slid his whole stack in, several folded, and two stayed in as the dealer was now sweating as he turned over his first card that read a four of hearts, then his next card was a ten of spades, then he turned over the next card which was a four of clubs, Jack knew he was solid, but two other players, took cards, one let out a scream and turned over his cards as the other had a huge smile on his face, Jack held firm as the dealer turned over his last card, it was a four of hearts, a sigh of relief as the dealer went over, the other man showed twenty one, with three cards and Jack had a perfect twenty one, so the dealer, counted out, double the amount of his chips, plus two silver chips.

The Dealer pushed the whole entire players pot towards Jack, and the other guy he got doubled his bet, Jack began to stack up, all his new chips and placed the two silver chips in his pocket as Barbara leaned in and said, "You just won over four million dollars on that one hand, those silver pieces are worth over one million each, you started with one million in chips, as did the rest of us."

"I know," said Jack as he stuck to the black, he won more than he lost.

Carlos and Jack were going at each other, but as the night wore on Jack had acculumulated, ten silver pieces, and as stack of other chips, he was strong as black was his favorite color, which meant it was a one hundred thousand dollar bet.

Carlos spoke up to say" Enough of this kids, game time is over, were changing the game and a new shoe, and dealer, bring Bennie over here and sit with the big boys."

Carlos helps Jack by saying; we will play this shoe out and then leave".

"What will you have sir" said the girl as Jack looked at Kelli, with a smile.

"A lemonaide with a shot of vodka, rum and tequila, please."

"Nice choice, I'll have one of them too" said Carlos, and
ads   "That girl is fine huh."

"Yeah sure," said Jack as he counted his chips, some six million in chips, he was moving around, with six more silver chips, which he promptly put into his pocket, then got down to business, and slid out his black chip, causing a bit of a roar as to the others.

"Don't mind them, they are pussies, go ahead and bet that chip" said Carlos.

Two cards were dealt, they were both fours, as he had them laid down, he decided to split them and follow up his bet as the dealer recognized it and dealt him two more cards, a five and a king, Jack placed the same suits together and as then his play came around to him he raised it on both with two more black chips each, and two more cards each, everyone looked at Carlos and he nodded they stayed into the game and the played on, when Jack looked at his cards, to hold with one and asked for another, as the field was done with the bets it was up to the dealer, on the table was over twelve million in bets. The first card for the dealer to turn over was a three, Jack raised the pot by one million, everyone was in, all ten guys, and Barbara, the next card was a six of the same suit, Jack raised it to be another million, without blinking an eye.

The last card was a seven of the same suit, the pot was at 14 million as it all came down to the dealer, he took another card, he turned it over to show a queen, he busted...

Carlos turned his hand over to show a he had twenty, some one down on the other side said "I have twenty one, does that mean I win" he announced.

Jack stood up, turned over his two piles of cards, to show he the two blackjack's, as the dealer rounded up the chips divided them three ways and pushed them towards Jack to say, you have just won over 19 million., how would you like it sir?"

"Cash me out, I'm a bit hungry."

"Cash me out too" said Carlos.

"How about we go into town and have some authentic Cuban food."

"Sounds good, how about the ladies."

The dealer slids eighteen silver chips to Jack and six black chips, Jack puts the silver chips away and hands the dealer a black chip and says; "Thank you for that hand."

"Your welcome sir", the guy said excitedly, then stands up and leaves.

"Where is he going?" asked Carlos, to his bodyguard.

"He said he is quiting, he has enough to live on for the next twenty years."

Carlos begins to laugh, as he hugs Jack and says "You are something and soon you will be my brother, come lets celebrate."

Jack looks at Barbara and says, "I'm going out with Carlos into the streets, can you go up and let me in so that I can get my gun?"

"Carlos, I will meet you out front, say I will take my car" said Jack.

"If you like," said Carlos at the bar.

Jack led Barbara up the set of chairs to the top floor and to their room, which had the door was part open, Jack pushed it all the way open, to see the safe was open and a man was lying on the floor dead, Jack reached in and pulled out his gun and holster, he took off his jacket to hear.

"Is that man dead?" said Barbara.

"Nah he is just knocked out, but help me, get him up, as the two of them carried the dead guy under their arms, Jack stopped in the hall, and propped him up long enough to pull his wallet, turn him around and push him down the laundry chute and said,

"When he wakes up at least he will have a nice resting bed."

"We better call room service and have that urine stain cleaned up" said Barbara.

"Good idea, can you take care of that, while I'm gone" said Jack.

"Yes I will that stinks, he sure did suffer some kind of shock."

"I'll say, I wonder what happen to him," said Jack putting his jacket on to disguise the gun, and he buttoned it up, and went to Barbara, as the two kissed each other for Jack to say "take care of this, and I'll see you later at the wedding."
Jack left her and was down the stairs , Jack choose to dial up Lisa and let her deal with the guy, she got on the other line as Jack told her what had happen and she said she would take care of it and of Barbara. Jack put his phone away, to step outside and asked the valet to pull up his car, which they promptly did, the slick car, had a nice new wax job, as Jack admired it under the lights.

"That's what happens when you tip huge amounts, your treated like a king", said Carlos, as he fires up another cigar and hands one to Jack, who eagerly lits it up and pulls off along drag, savoring the moment and says, "Get in, lets go" as Jack gave the vallet a twenty dollar bill, as the two men got into the car.

"I thought you would have had a brand new SLR McLaren, do you go to the grand prix."

"Nah, I just like the fact that it is a reliable year of this vehicle and that it goes fast".

"Yeah look at the steering wheel shifters, like in the Formula One cars, you shift the six gears on the right up and down shift the gears on the left," said Carlos.
Jack put it in gear, and tried it out as he took off in first, took the right and down the hill he gained momentum and shitfted it smoothly, gained speed and shifted, got onto the highway and let it out, in a flash they were on main street going slow, as Carlos told Jack to park, he instructed him to back in under a carport, they got out and Carlos pulled a door down to hid the car.

"There, the car won't get stolen, lets go inside, lets use the side door".

Carlos lead Jack in, to a locals hangout, and took a seat in the rear, Jack sat across from him with his back to the front, here is a menu, order whatever you like, I suggest you drink beer from the bottle, you won't get sick," said Carlos, with a smile, as he gets up and goes into the bathroom.

In broken English an older lady says, "What will you have?"

Jack scanned the menu and said "Beer, two please."

It was clearly an ethic menu and it had every kind of seafood.

"Order the fish taco's, there the best, with some hot sauce" said Carlos. He came back looking refreshed.

The server brought out two beers and saw Carlos and freaked out and began to scream, then all of a sudden they were rushed, guys were hanging on Jack, getting in some punches, Jack returned with punches of his own, he heard shots, Carlos stood on top of the table and began to throw, as someone pulled out a another gun and took several shots at Carlos, Jack subdued, his two attackers, pulled his weapon and shot the attacker right between the eyes, he droopped to the ground, as the place went silent, Jack put his gun away, sat back down and looked at the menu to see Carlos take his seat next to him, to say "Your not Kenneth Winchester."

"Why do you say that?" asked Jack.

"From what I've been told he is a lousy shot."

"Had you ever thought he might have been faking it to allow others to win?"

Jack looked at Carlos to see his cover was fading fast, to ad "Besides my dad is the founder of the durable and super straight low impact pistol, why wouldn't I be a solid and straight shooter, so what will you have?" asked Jack.

As Carlos, looks at him, and says "Alright, Ken we must go out shooting sometime."

"How about tomorrow, don't we need to go out and get us a pig or something for the feast?"

"Yes we do, your right, why don't you come to my palace tonight after the fights and tomorrow, before the wedding we will go on a game hunt" and ads "So what will you have?"

"The fish tacos" said Jack.

****

The flight was long and cramped as the two stowaway, laid together in the cargo hold of the plane, as Kenneth, constantly tried to hold onto Candace, she fought back and the two were constantly throwing punches, as Ken said "Alright enough bitch, you hit me again, I swear I will tie you up and torture you to death."

"You and what army, you stay over there, and away from me, and I will leave you alone, besides my new target is Jack Cash, the Spy."

"Then once I tell Carlos who he is, then Jack is a dead man."

"Come on honey, from what I heard he manhandled you pretty good."

"You think a Super Spy knows your out there, now that you escaped, if I were you I'd get as far as away from him as possible, from what I heard he is likely to kill you"

"Super Spy or not, I'm telling Carlos everything, even about you, you scum bag, how you double crossed Carlos and stoled one hundred million of our money, so you stay away from me."

As Ken lunged for her, wrapping his arms around her and began to kiss the back of her neck, and said "I like a wild cat, especially as ugly as you."

He released her as she had driven her foot into his crotch, which he held, then when she got up she kicked him in the mouth putting him out, as the aircraft was in its landing position, she waited as the landing gear came down, and positioned herself, above the front landing wheels, and jumped out, rolling and was on the move, running across the field and into the brush, she held her positon, while the plane came to a stop, the baggage cart, stopped and the ramp was raised, the cargo door opened, and the luggage was placed on the moving ramp, Ken stood up and waved to her, then sat down on one of the larger pieces, and rode it down, and at the bottom, jumped off, then walked over and got into the line.

Disgusted with herself, for not waiting, she watched as Ken made his way through customs and out onto the street where she saw him talking to a police officer and pointed her way.

Ken stood there laughing and yelled "There you go bitch, have fun."

He watched the police with siren's blasting moving within the tarmac and watched as Candace was flushed and on the move, but for only a moment as the police tackled her, and handcuffed her, as she screamed, he watched them put duct tape on her mouth, as he got into a waiting taxi cab.

****

Carlos and Jack walked the rowdy streets to the forum, which showed two fights on the marquee, as the two walk in, the place was filled with Cuban cigar smoke, and lots of loaded people, some from the place they ate, they found a spot on a bench, in the second row, when a young beautiful girl sat next to Jack and said in broken English;

"How much you pay me."

"Nothing," said Jack as he pushed her away, as she moved closer and said with her hand out, "How much you pay me."

"No Ken, she doesn't want that, she is here to collect the wager. Said Carlos.
Jack pulls out a black chip and sets it into her hands."

"Now you need to tell her who you want to place it on."

"Who is the underdog?"

"It's the younger brother" said Carlos and ads "I'll go for the older fighter" as he hands her a black chip as well.
Jack sees across the room a familiar face, hanging with an older guy, it was Lisa.

"You fancy her, she is with that heavy industrialist, from Montana, they are looking to buy into Cuba and convert, some acreage into a new market, Just like when you set up shop four years ago and set up that plant, on my north fourty, supplying weapons, to the terrorist, each and every day someone new comes along, to make a name for their selves and steal what we have, if it weren't for me, American Captalism would have taken over Santiago and commercialize it with hotels and fast food shops."

"That's why the President appointed me Prince of the Southern valley of Cuba, and that is why I pick and choose who comes and who goes, Ken I like you."

The two fighters came in together, as one was smaller than the other.

"That one is yours, and if he does win you'll make a cool two million dollars, he is twenty to one, whereas my guy is the favorite, he is ten to one, which I will put that million to work."

Jack was getting a feel a good feel for Carlos, it was getting close to come clean, and end this game for good."

He began to think about this whole spy business, and what if he just went in there and grabbed him, everyone has a story, and a reason why they do something" thinks Jack as he watches the younger man, get pummeled, in the head, so Jack gets up and heads towards the restroom and Lisa gets up, as Carlos watches, Jack who goes in as Lisa waits in the hall, Jack reappears to see her, as she says;

"Candace has been caught by police and she is saying you're a impostor and asked for Carlos."

"Why can't you go in and silence her."

"That is not our job title."

"Oh but hanging off a industrialist arm is".

"How did you know?" asked Lisa.

"Who cares," said Jack as he passed her to come to his fighters' corner.

Jack says " Hit him in the ribs, he'll go down", then walked over and took a seat, while he watched the fight progress it looked like the battle of wills, as each round passed Jack continued to look at his watch.

An hour had passed since the start of the fight, and as the smaller boxer hit the big one in the ribs on the right side, he winced, then he hit him on the left side and the older guy went down, as the place erupted.

"You're a rich man, who are you anyway, I know your not Kenneth Winchester, you're a Spy aren't you, there is no way you are married to Miss Biltmore, your too tough a guy for that broad, tell me now, so I can stop calling you Ken, if that is your real name but I know different."

Jack looks at Carlos to see he is genuine and realizes it that, his cover is no longer.so Jack decides to come clean, turns to see several men, armed with assault rifles, storm the place and begin to fire, standing at the door was a familiar face dressed in camoflauge gear, but Jack knew who he was, and pulled out his gun and aimed at his lower leg, and fired, the guy was hit and immediately, went down in pain and agony, as the others looked around as Jack yelled " I'm a U S Agent, now drop your weapons or I will shoot all you one by one, as Jack held his pearl white gun out stretched as Carlos crouched below Jack, as Jack's support team moved and was set into position to help.

"Now one by one bring over your weapons and place them on the bench and you can go freely."
Carlos slowly got up and said "Thank you, I was assured to be killed tonight".

"I doubt that, I was the only target" said Jack.

"Was I your target," asked Carlos.

"You were, but now I have a more pressing target, in one Kenneth Winchester."
The police storm in as the men surrendered their weapons.
As the crowd calmed, a greater force came in, to subdue and help arrest those men.
Jack reholstered his weapon as he saw some pretty familiar faces lead by Lisa, who joined in with the capture, was Devlin and Kelli.
Carlos watched as some of his friends were on the ground and was being hauled off.

"Sit down my friend, I like you, and on this day, the day before my wedding, we are friends" said Jack.

"So the wedding is for real and still on?" said Carlos.

"Yep, I'm still going on with it, I like the idea of becoming your brother-in-law and welcome all that it means"

"What about all this and what about us?"

"First off lets draw a line in the sand, lets say you get a second chance to a new life, you're a Prince of a country which is ninety percent a dictatorship, we can't change that, but we can change who we are and what we stand for, so Carlos I ask of you which side of the line do you want to be on, there side, which means they are all going to Guantonomo bay, or on my side."

"To be free, to continue life of being watched, and being free to spend with all those wifes, and to have control of all those women.

said Jack to add" Now lets see what choice I would of made, what I like are all those women, I envy you, cause if I had all those women, it would be a baby factory, like the Manges family, unit, I like that, and if in Cuba, I can do that, then you can count me in, so I say to you Carlos, which is it going to be for you, surrender and go with your friends, or be free and move forward with your enterprise and forget those men ever existed."

"Its like you have put my head over a barrel and your holding my head under water, while still holding a gun to my head and asking me to betray my fellow countryman, for what, you who pretended to be someone you are not, I knew the moment I saw you with her, she wasn't your type, but I offer up a girl who is one hundred times richer and ten times more cultured as a lady and you fall flat on how incredible beautiful she really is, I knew then your not who you said you were, and then I take you out in those woods and yes I was going to kill you, when, I noticed your hands are not of those of a privileged person, but those hands are of someone who works like I do and decided to test you and from out of know where you help solve a mystery with the Manges to create a mining operation, that has been going at break-neck speed and re-energized that whole community, no Ken, if that is your name, I knew then, you were either a Agent or some type of Policeman, so yes I drugged you and yes I didn't kill you, and yes I did have your Jacket and yes I did test for a DNA match to really see who you were, and you know you came back a mystery."

"So who ever you are, you one untraceable guy."

"I guess, were done here, Officer, you can take this one too."

"Hold on I didn't say that" said Carlos holding onto Jack's arm, and ads "Lets make a deal".
Devlin, held her gun out on Carlos, eager to take Carlos in, but Jack said   "Here's how it goes, Mister Gomez, we want Mister Scott and Miss Thomas, released to us."

"Done, what else,"

As Jack said, "We will give you immunity from prosecution, in exchange for information, from where all those guns went and its entire operation" said Devlin.

"Done, what else?" asked Carlos, with his hands out and pleading.

"We want unlimited access to the casino records and of your three illegal operations out of Havana, I'm sure Jack will assist us on this one".

"You know that, I'm the one behind those operations?"

"We have had you under surveillance for over the last three years, and in each time we have found it out that your name keeps resurfacing, so I ask you one more time, are you on our side or are you on theirs?" asked Devlin.

"Yes, I will give up and come clean, only to him, I like him, I don't know if you knew that and had him planted in to be this person, I commend you for that, you got me,. but like Jack said maybe its time to reevaluate my life and recaputure afocus, so yes I would like to try, if you will help me, I will tell Jack everything, you can count on me, and." As Carlos rose, fully up, to see Devlin lowered her weapon, and the sounds of the ambulance leaving he said "For the first time I feel safe and with Jack's help maybe I can become an honest person and a good husband and confide in a faithful friend".

"For now, your free, where can I find those two that I seek?" asked Devlin.

"There at the Palace, I'll call my staff to open up the gates and you may be allowed to go inside and get those you seek, I'll have them waiting in the living room."

"Thanks that's the cooperation we are asking for" said Devlin.

"What about the casino and the other stuff" asked Carlos.

"Lets take things one at a time, tomorrow while you two are at the wedding we will take a look at the Casino", she then turns to say   "Jack, are you still planning on marrying Maria?"

"Heck yes, if she will have me, this will be an Honor and a pleasure, I like this rules down in Cuba of having more than one wife, and I may make this a permanet place of residency."

"If you do that I'd give you, say two hundred acres."
Jack looked over at his new friend to shake his hand to say;

"You got a deal, just as long as it is, along this beautiful coast line and on a hillside" adds Jack.

"I'm gonna leave the two of you together, but remember this Carlos, from now on you will answer your phone when we call and we expect your full cooperation in the future or this deal is off the table."
Said Devlin.

"Devlin, were ready, what about Jack, is he staying or going?" asked Lisa.

"I guess Jack and his new found friend Carlos, will be staying and Jack is gonna get married tomorrow" said Devlin with a smug look on her face.

"Really, get married to a local, why you say" asked Lisa.

"I guess if you're a Super Agent you can do whatever you want, yeah, what about us, aren't we pretty enough for him?"
Asked Devlin and Lisa together.

"Nah, he likes girls that are easy and not rough, besides were the type of girls who are having the time of their lives, why turn that in to be one of his own?"

"I guess your right, who needs that" said Lisa.
Both girls turned and left without saying a word, as Jack thought;

"Good, get those biches out of my hair."

"So Jack, that is your name right, what does this mean now?" asked Carlos.

"Yeah, its Jack Cash, International Bounty Hunter, have a seat, lets talk about that land you said you wanted to give to me."

"How about I say partner, I give you half of what we draw as a profit at the Casino and cut you in on some other types of businesses."

"I'm not greedy, how about a quarter and I'd say where good".

"No, listen, I'll make you a half partner, my draw right now is ten million a month."

"I'd give you, half of that, but I need additional help."

"Like what?"

"For one muscle, the ability to come down here on a moment's notice and help me out and for that, I'll give you half of the casino and from now on everything will be legitamate and legal, that is to the American's way, if you will help me out."

Jack reaches into his pocket to pull out twenty silver chips and hands them to Carlos.

Carlos pushes Jack's arm away and says "No, keep that consider it a gift, and yes you did win that fair and square, in times we have cheated and got away with it. But from this point forward, it will all be legitimate and fair.

"One more thing, stay away from the Manges family. "

"But they are my family", pleads Carlos.

"Sure you can visit the elders, you know what I mean, the mining operation".

"Why are you taking over that, to have the money for yourselves. "

"No, it is not my intention of screwing their family of hard worked money."

"Do you know what you are saying, that money could build you a compound like my palace and stock it with help and provide some security" pleaded Carlos.

"That's enough, my rules, my way, take it or leave it".

"Fine, I'll do what you say" said a sulking Carlos.

"Alright, when's the next fight?" said Jack.

"Let me make a quick call".

Jack nods his head and watches as Carlos leaves to go into the office and leaves the door open as Jack puts his chips back into his pocket and his badge away, only to see Carlos reemerge from the office, only to see Carlos stop and annouce "Don't worry folks, the last two fighters will be out shortly so place your bets, the winner closest to predicting who gets knocked out and when, will take the entire pot, bet"

Aloud cheer went off as people, mostly men scambled, Jack sat calmly, looking over a fallen flyer of the two warriors as Carlos came up to him and then took a seat, next to him and said;

"Who do you like in this fight"?

"Who are you betting on?"

"Well my fighter is my cousin Jonny Gomez, and that is who I'm going with".

"Then I'll go for this other guy, Henandez, Rico, that seems like a bad ass name." said Jack.

"What do you wager?"

"What I made on the first fight, and he will knock out your cousin in the seventh."

"Sorry I can't cover that bet, if you win, you'll make over forty million dollars. Said Carlos to say, that will include the house take."

"Wow, really you can't cover that, alright pay me out the one point nine and I will bet another one hundred thousand" said Jack, getting up to go to the restroom.

Jack came back to see that the fighters were in the ring, as Jack came close to his man, in his corner, Jack said;

"I'll give your man one million dollars, if he knocks him out in the seventh, in less than the first minute, after that all money is off the table". Jack then took his seat to see Carlos holding a brief case.

"Here you go two million dollars" as he hands Jack the case.

Jack sits down pops it open to see all the cash.

Jack began to divide the money in half and counts out one hundred thousand and folds it up and closes the case, to see the runner, a charming young girl, who held a slip of paper and said, in good English "What will it be Sir?"

"One hundred thousand dollars on Rico Henandez in the seventh in under the first minute, please."

Jack watched her write it down, and then give him the carbon copy as a receipt".

"I guess its official now" said Carlos.

As the introduction were announced, Jack counted out one million dollars, in higher denomination bills, and set them aside, and the rest he put in his jacket pockets, then got up, as the fight started to show the trainer, the money and said "This is yours, if he puts him down in the seventh before one minute"

The trainer shakes his head with zeal and excitement, as he yelled out something in Spanish or something like that, as Jack made his way back to his seat.

"What did you do that for, are you trying to bribe your guy," said Carlos.

"Nah, just insuring he will win, in the seventh," said Jack calmly.

"I have to tell you that my cousin is the Cuban champion and your guy is a cream puff, we just threw in there."

"Just in Cuba Huh, lets see what happen when you give the cream puff some incentive, I guess, we will just see" said Jack.

The fight started, as all was cheering, everyone against Jack, as the crowd went wild as Henandez hit the canvas, woosy, and wobbling, Rico just made it up, before the ten counts, by the judge, who kept looking at Carlos, who relayed a thumb up signal.

"I hope your playing it fair, I don't want our relationship to get off to a bad start" said Jack loudly to Carlos.

The fight continued to the first bell, seconds out was sounded, as the fighters took it back up in the center ring as Jack watched, each of them duck and weave, using one hand for a jab or to keep one away from an immediate attack, then Hernandez hit Gomez with a crunching body shot as Gomez doubled over as the corner was yelling at Hernandez, the standing aid count lasted a long time as Carlos stood and yelled to his cousin, for his fighter to continue, as the fight continued, to the bell, round three, four and five, looked like a dance card, only short jabs and no big punches as the round ended.

The start of round six was a nightmare for Hernandez as Gomez, put him down, in the first minute and he got up, then in the second minute and then got up and lastly in the final minute, Hernandez, laid face first planted on the ring canvas floor.

With his corner sceaming at him to move, Jack was on his feet as was Carlos and all the other some one hundred plus, to see Hernandez rise up, pulling on the ring rope, to get to his feet as the bell sounded, Hernandez stumbled and fell into his corner.

"Was that your round" asked Jack.

"No, I have the eighth, so I'm glad he got up too" said Carlos.

Hernandez's corner were all screaming at him as Carlos said;

"You have given that boy hope, as they are telling him, its now or never, give it all you got, now."

"Thanks for the translation, that remides me, I'll have Maria, by my side from now on, at least then I'll know what your saying."
Round seven started in the oddest way, Rico, staggered to the middle of the ring.
The two men came together, Rico stumbled, and fell as Gomez looked at him as Rico hit Gomez's knee, with his head, sendig Gomez to hop around a bit as Hernandez regained his balance, enough to catch Gomez off guard, to land a over the hand right to Gomez's ribs in such a way you could hear the scream that Gomez made while going down, he hit with such force.
Rico stood over him as he was quickly counted out and signaled it was over, as both corners filled the ring and they were screaming at each other as Carlos says "I don't know how you do it, but it looks like you won again, to me and everyone else it looked like a foul, but it happen so quickly, the ref and the judges, didn't indicate it so I guess, you win," said Carlos just shaking his head and ads "Lets go collect our money."
"What do you mean, you bet against your cousin" asked Jack
"Yeah, I did, when you offered Hernandez one million dollars, I realized I better switch my bet, so lets go split that four million plus, as Jack hands the brief case to the manager for Hernandez and follows Carlos to the window, where two cases were, they both carried one out into the street, to see the police force was still present and the two,
C I A agents were waiting by their car, talking to each other. Jack made it to the garage where his vehicle was at. Carlos lifted the door as Jack opened the trunk, Jack found a brief case and an empty gym bag, where he opened up the case and dumped the cash in, and tossed the briefcase aside and closed the trunk, got in, pulled forward, and waited for Carlos to get in, then drove off.

****

She paced back and forth in her small cell, as the shift changed, another new guard came in to check on her, only this time it was a young boy, maybe 13 at the most and in his pretty good English he said "Hey lady, do you need anything?"

"Just to get out of here, I need to see Carlos Gomez."

"You know, Mister Gomez, are you one of his ladies?"

"Yes I am, now let me out, and I won't tell him that you kept me in this jail."

"Prove it" said the young boy.

She looked at him a bit weird, like this was just a test, but she knew she wouldn't fall for this kids trick and said "How, do you want me to prove it."

"That's easy, any woman who is of Mister Gomez, puts a scratch on their back, or other areas, show me your back, and I will see if your telling the truth" said the boy, now moving up to get a closer look at this woman.

Looking around and seeing no one, thought maybe there might be a scratch.

But it might of healed since their last encounter, the boy might be right, Carlos is sure rough, well O Kay, she thinks and moves her back towards the bars, and raises her shirt, to show off her back,

"Do you see anything?"

"No, not yet, your shirt is blocking the light, can you take it off?"

She thinks about it and then just does it and ads "How about now?"

"I don't know, I think there might be something under your bra, that is one of the places I've seen it" said the boy.

She thinks a moment, then unhooks it in the front and pulls it off, and says "What about now? "

"No, It was just a red mark, but your back is catching a lot of good light, another place is on the back of the legs, as I guess he likes to hold onto that area" said the boy, with a huge smile on his face, as others had heard the boy and were in on it as they watched from the doorway.

She thought about which way would be best to show the kid her legs, so without hestiation, she, un-buckled her pants and pulled them down in a flash as she caught her thin panties at the same time to her ankles, and said "Do you see anything now?"

"Yes I do, can you bend over, forward, and I"

The guards were behind the boy now as Candace bent forward as the kid stuck his finger inside of her. She lunged forward and turned around, to see the boy and the guards were laughing at her, as she pulled up her pants and put her bra back on while the guards watched, one guard stayed behind to watch as the others and the young kid left and watched her get dressed.

"Sorry ma'am, that little bugger, gets half the women to do that, before I have to come and break it up."

"When I get out of here I'm gonna kill that kid and the rest of you, I want to see Carlos, will you let me out" she said.

"Only if you allow me to fuck you" said the guard.

"Sure, let me out and I'll let you do me".

"Nah, why don't you strip off your clothes, then back your butt up against the bars and I will stick it to you, and if I feel satisfied I will let you out and drive you myself to see Mister Gomez..
She thought about it for a moment, and then decided what she was going to do and said;

"If we are going to do this, I want you to wear a condom, dim the lights and a bottle of water, and I will be here, waiting in the nude."

"No, you will strip as to when I can see it "said the guard.

"fine, go get the condom and the water bottle, then" said Candace as she stood watching him, leave and then come back and turn off the lights along the pathway, but kept her lights on, and stood in front of her with a new water bottle.

"Can I have it" asked Candace.

"Sure, here you go" as he passed it to her, she placed it on the floor and said "I'll save that for when I'm done, that is pretty cold?"

"Yeah, we keep it in the freezer, but not cold enough to severly freeze it, are you gonna begin"

"After you get undressed, I want to see what I'm working with, then I will slowly get undressed" said Candace as she watched him remove his belt and set it down behind him and then un-did his pants and let them drop, he pulled it out, to show her as she said;

"Why don't you pull them down so I can see how much space I need to back into you?"

He did as he was told and dropped them to his ankles, he held it in one hand as it normally grew a bit, and the condom in the other and said;   "Now I'm ready lets go, he said anxiously.

She started by pulling off her shirt to show her bra off, then in a instant popped off her bra, to reveal a nice set of medium sized tits, with large nipples, she placed her bra on top of her shirt, next she unbuttoned her pants, and pulled them down, with her panties, and pulled them off to show the guard everything, as she had her legs apart, she watched him become fully erect and ready as he slipped on the condom as he said "I'm ready, hurry."

   "What's the rush, I like it a long time" she said.

She turned her back to him and moved back slowly, she felt the cold bars on her butt and waited, she was wet with excitement as the guard pierced her slowly, she felt him inside her, it was tight, and after a couple of good strokes, the pain was over and she began to heat up and actually starting to enjoy it, when she went forward, turned around with demon eyes she grabbed his dick and picked up the bottle and whacked his dick, she grabbed him by the arm, then slid up to his neck and held him against the bars.

She was choking the life out of him and said with her softest voice, get the keys and open this door or I will suffacate you and cut off your dick and stuff it into your mouth.

He nodded as he reached out for his belt while still holding onto his dick, which was bleeding, he lifted the belt to her, she yanked it out of his hand, found the key, unlocked the door, and went out to see the guard slumped over, crying in pain, and helped him up, and took him to her cell, and laid him on the bed, then pulled out his gun, and checked the rounds, then took the handcuffs and cuffed his hands behind his back and then rolled him over and sat on him to hid his dick and yelled" Guards, guards, come quick, something is wrong here I think he is hurt."

One by one the guards came in as Candace shot each one, in the head; she got up and shot the guard on the bed in the groin.

She got re-dressed, collected the weapons magazines and chose a 9mm she liked and a pair of cuffs and went out into the office to see it was empty, then opened the door and saw the young kid across the street, then decided to slip away quietly, and around the back to find the cars, the only one open, with a key in it was the Jeep, she got in and started it, had some difficulty with the clutch, then got it to work, and swung around to get onto main street, she paused long enough at the light, then charged the kid and crashing into the street vendor, she got out, pointing the gun at the kid and said "Alright you little bastard, get in the Jeep and drive, as she picked up a piece of chicken on a stick, and kept the gun on the kid as he waited for her to get in.

He was visably scared as she said "Now drive me to Carlos's house now".

——— CH 17 ———
Princess Maria Manges

J ack sat by the well lighted pool, drinking a margarita, at the table side, with two hotties, the first one was, a secondary gift to Jack as when they got there, was a line up of girls to choose from. It was Jack's bachelor party, he choose, a hot young girl named Margarita, and a bleached blonde, tall Hispanic girl with big breasts in Raecine, while two brunettes ran around in just panties and a bra, they were, the tall Angela, with her French manicure, and big lips. Then there was what Carlos called, the sophisticated sex kitten, named Alexandra, or Alex for short.

Then sitting on the bar by herself, sat a small nude girl who liked to show off everything and her name was Elvariste, sitting across from Jack was two of Carlos's most beloved ladies, first across from Jack was the oldest and mother of his seven children and the school teacher, a white/ Cuban woman named Frieda, her natural blonde highlights, could be seen up and down as she wore no underwear as Jack had a full view as she only wore a small teddy, it was see through, next to her was Rose, Maria sister, and her closet allied, yet she wore even less, as her huge breasts were barely contained in that small outfit, and she also wore no underwear, as a huge jet black mound could be seen, with a cigarette hanging out of her mouth, and one lit in the ashtray, then over on a chaise lounger was the youngest of Carlos harem, a young, barely seventeen year old, long haired, with big breasts, barely covering them with a black bathing suit, arching her back as she too was sucking on a cigarette, while Carlos played with her. He looked back once in a while at Jack, as the two continued with their card play.

He would show Jack he was having a fun time, as Carlos was loud and boisterous and Alba was carrying a huge smile on her face, Jack got up, he too was nude showing off his hardware for all the girls to see. Jack walked over to the bar to stand in front of Elvariste and watched her play with herself, with her legs spread apart wide as Jack says;

"I'd like lemonade."

She closed up her legs and got down to stir up the picture, and served him up a glass on crushed ice, Jack sipped it as he watched Alba stand above Carlos, to use hand jesters signaling Alba beat him, while Jack watched, then sees Alex, walk up the stairs to the top platform, then stands at the rail of the fifteen foot platform, and began to take off her top and then her bottoms and yelled "Jack come up here, and fuck me."

With that invitation he couldn't refuse, as he was swinging free.

Jack was inches away from Alba's face, as she reached out to touch him. Jack pulled away, thinking how nice this would be if only he could have what Carlos has and all those pretty women.

Earlier, he had a choice from the women and girls who were the friends and out of respect to Carlos, he chose not to take any of his women which was actually a insult, until Rose spoke up and volunteered, as did Frieda, then Alba who was left out, spoke up that she wanted to be a part of it, as she was fairly new to all of this and actually loved it. Jack came up from behind of Alex; he put it to her and drove her against the railing, her tight firm body quivering against his touch, which drove her to scream, as he worked her over.

Jack noticed a Jeep pull upon the side down on the lower valley road, along the access road, along a fence line while he continued to drill Alexandra, until she erupted, but stayed inside of her, till the end.

Jack had her by the hair, and held her down, to see what he needed to see, he let her go, and pulled out of her, to still be swinging, and then he jumped from the platform, doing a modified cannonball as he hit the water, he resurfaced in the warm water to see both of his playmates had joined him, both nude now, the little Margarita, and the heavy breasted Raecine, as Jack tried to make his way to the other side, it was too late, as the two of them tackled him, for the first time he was vulnerable as he knew what was coming and he couldn't do a damn thing about it, the more he thrashed around the worse it got.

Jack let in and let the two girls have there way with him.

In the distance, shots rang out, his paradise, was thrown in panic mode, in his mind, as he went with it, only to see Carlos, get up and slip on some shorts, and instructed his ladies to go inside, both of Jack's girls stopped what they were doing, and finally let Jack go, as he made his way to the edge of the pool and he stepped out, found his swim wear and slid it on, only to see Carlos with a gun, who then tosses it at Jack and says, "Do what you do best."

Jack caught the Beretta, took it off safety and held it in a defensive position, knowing full well who it was and it was time to get rid of her ass.

Carlos was behind the bar, when he emerged with a shotgun, in the ready to fire position.

Jack turned to the south as Carlos went to the north, Jack made his way to fence, the iron rod enabled Jack to view into the lower field where the security breach took place and he could see why; it was Candace with a gun taking down Carlos's security team.

One by one they fell, as she was like Custer at the battle of little big horn, Jack watched as she was confronted by a small army of Carlos's men only to put them down, in a way Jack felt sorry for this miss-understood woman.

On the other hand, he remembers her up close and knows what she is capable of. Jack watched as she would take each man's weapon after she put him down, to continue the fight, for she was on a mission, she was getting closer to the fence.

Jack anticipated the move, as he held his back against the stucco wall, just behind a solid wood fence, and the gate that open up, slowly as Jack held the gun out, to the brown hair flowing in the wind, he said; "Drop the weapon," as he placed the gun, on the side of her head, while letting her come in to the courtyard. Jack closed the door as she dropped the weapon.

"Put your hands up" said Jack, moving in behind her.

She did as she was told and lifted her hands above her head.
Jack knew she was very dangerous, and kept her a little ahead of himself and said;

"Keep moving," said Jack.

She made it to the table, now abandoned; only to see Carlos with a shotgun in his hand raised it up.

"Take a seat," said Jack.

She sees Jack and then Carlos and says, "Hi honey it so nice to see you", then looks over at Jack to give him a smug look, when Carlos delivered a single blow to her head with the butt of the shotgun, that instantly put her out.

Jack placed the gun down and said, "Do you have any handcuffs."

"Yeah, I'll go get them," said Carlos, meanwhile Jack stayed with her. Her forehead was bleeding where Carlos had struck her, Jack wondered, "How good of a Super Spy she would make if she just wasn't so ornery, and stubborn, she is a wildcat and so reckless, too bad this is where she will be put to rest", finally, getting her out of his mind, he picked up the gun to point it at her, then decided he would finish it now.

"Jack I found a set of cuffs, help me get her up."

"Don't worry, she is coming around," and ads "Get up," says, Jack still holding the gun on her.

She begins to rise and in doing so she kicks out her chair causing it to go into the pool, they both saw her rage was building as she yelled at Carlos, " Why did you do it, I loved you, you made me one of your wives, why?"

"Its simple Miss, you're a wild cat that has no control and then I find out your American DEA agent, feeding all my secrets to the government, that's why" said Carlos as he held onto the handcuffs.

"I came here to warning you about him, he is a Super Spy and had been sent to capture you and bring you in dead or alive."

"I know, he told me all about it, and I'm O Kay with that, I even cut a deal with the Government in keeping me safe."

For that deal places me here, in my country, and with my wives, unlike you who, used me, infiltrated my organization, even killing a few of my associates" said Carlos.

"It was you who sent me to eliminate them."

"Your disillutional, I told you not to kill them."

Carlos stood in front of her looking at her while Jack was behind her.   "What I told you to do was, simply extract what information they had and bring it back to me."

"You're a liar, I did no such thing", as she turned to look at Jack. He saw her trying to play both sides, still holding the gun on her.

"It was you, that betrayed me when you accidentally killed my brother, after he told me what you did, how you made a deal with Edwin to ship those drugs out of Cuba and into the U S via the cargo ships" said Candace.

"Shut up "he yelled at her.

"I was simply confiscating it, and then turning it over to our Government to process it." Said a defiant Candace.

"What about the money for all that drugs" she said. To add "I kept it, but I was planning on giving some of it back to you, after you released my sister."

"Leave her out of this, she lives with me on her own free will, and actually since last month, she has become my wife" said Carlos.

"What about the policy that you cannot marry sisters, which you did when you married me? "to ad" Come on Jack help me out here, is he wrong or what?"

"Nah, Carlos is right; he can have as many wives as he wants, I don't know about marrying your sister."

"So you two are in this together?" she tries to spit at Carlos and Jack.

"Listen Candace, I can't do anything for you, the authorities are on their way, why did you kill seven of my men, and they were my friends.

"Well, I just wanted to see you and the main gate was locked, and I wanted to get your attention".

Carlos sees the rest of his force surrounding them, as he has his hands up to say "Open up the gates and allow the police chief in. "

His force disbands as Jack was firmly holding the wildcat, by the arm. "You know as soon as the police chief comes here, they will kill you themselves," said Carlos.

"You're not going to help me," pleads Candace.

"No I'm not, actually, turned around" says Carlos applies pressure to the handcuffs and whispers in her ear, "You did this yourself, I have a girl in the CIA who was helping you out, her name is Lisa.

She has assured me you were going to get out, but for you to go off and kill my security force for no reason, is inexcusable and for that I'm sentencing you to see you swim for your life", as he pushed her, she propelled forward, trying to hold back but went into the water.

Carlos stood at the edge of the pool to say "Your going have to pay for what you have done, your nothing but evil and out of control."

"Carlos," said Jack

"What" snapped back Carlos?

"Look who is here" surrounding them was all kinds of law officials, some military personnel, a helicopter, with a big beam of light shone down on them, as police yelled;

"Drop your weapon."

Jack laid it on the table and stepped back and raised his hands in the air, as did Carlos.

Then the police officer said "Handcuff both of them, lets take them in for questioning", just as three young woman came out, one he recognized immediately as his daughter to say, "Alba, is that you, oh how you have kept yourself and you worried your mother, handcuff, that one too." as the other women tried to make a break, but were caught.

Carlos was looking at Jack, motioning for him to make a move, as his hands were behind his back and handcuffs, were placed on him as he shrugs back to Carlos.

"Let's get some one in the water and save that one, then round up all of his wife's and charge them with prostitution and explorations of the law."

"You're not going to get away with this Hector."

"As I see it Carlos, you're the one in handcuffs, and your white friend there, will make for a good slave, it has been a while, but now I have you".

The police commissioner stepped around then said, "Lets round everyone up, collect any weapons and contraband and line up his women, were gonna have a party,

Escort those who are not his wives out, we don't want any unforeseen trouble."

"Sir, seven of the wives escaped into the hills, we found a door open and saw the last one leave."

"Lets round up the rest and bring them out here, we will let the boys have their choice."

Jack stood by the Commander, and was getting a little uncomfortable, he knew a bigger force was overcoming them and the best thing for him was to get Candace free and let her have at them, as he was feeling a bit helpless at the moment.

Then, when another guard appeared, he was confused, crying and said something in Spanish "Mando, manar, magico, hombre, difunto."

Jack watched, as the men scurried about, as Alba and Rose were together, as Rose gets close to Jack and says "Here" and kisses him on the cheek, as she hands him a key, as Jack folds it up in his hands.

"Bring him with me" said the Commander. Leading Jack inside was a guard, and into the room Carlos gave to him.

On the bed laid two girls nude, both dead, and a body of a commando laid face down, next to his body was the pearl white gun and holster.

"No," yelled Jack as he tried to break free as the Commander tried to touch it, and did, as they let Jack alone, while they watched their beloved Commander short circuit and fell to his death, a panic ensued as the next in line tried to grab it to show he could do it and he to died, Jack undid his hands and realized he was here to stop all of this and be the Super Spy, he will be trained to be, and then sprang into action, by saying "No' no' no," and no one didn't do a thing, so it was Jack turn to dive for the weapon, Jack took it with authority, knocking another man to the ground, and just like that he got off three shots, all hit their targets and the room cleared.

Jack began to speak "Arma, arma, arma," said Jack, as he remember Hopi, say something about that, slowly men started dropping there weapons as Jack slid on his holster, then his watch, and motioned them out, and herded them out, while keeping an eye on them and said; "Rose can you translate for me" said Jack. Jack still was holding his weapon out and said, "Tell them to put down there weapons and leave and no one else will get killed."

She spoke twice as fast as long until she was done.

"Tell them that the Commander is dead as with him is his two or second in command and for them to take them as well and go home," said Jack.

Carlos was released, by Alba, who didn't appear to look to good.

Rose spoke freely and easy, as they all replied, "Si" acknowledging they knew. The ruckus was averted and Jack watched as they were escorted down the drive, to their cars, meanwhile a couple of their guards, picked up the dead security guards and carried them to the driveway, awaiting, the coroner and the city police, who arrived just before the Commander's troops left, to see that the Commander was dead, the police chief said "It will be a relief to know he is dead, how did it happen?"

"Electrical shock" said Jack.

"That's too bad, who are you?"

"Name is Jack Cash; I'm an International Bounty Hunter, from the US."

Jack turned and went back in.

The police seemed happy to once again see the one who wiped out half her force, however these men looked oddly different, like the men in purple suit, it was now quiet as the police took Candace into custody, and led her out as she was screaming something to Carlos. "Carlos please take me back I'll show you that I'm loyal and faithful."

Carlos just waved to her to say "I believe the police will find something useful for you to do from now on."

"I second that; watch out for that one, she's a wildcat, "said Jack wishing he had a chance to beat the living shit out of her.

The police carried out the dead bodies, as Jack watched.

Frieda came up to Jack to whisk him to their rooms, a series of rooms that were all interconnected, they came to a lounge area, where a huge flat bed stood, all in red, where she allowed Jack to undress. Jack laid on the bed as each woman came to him to offer what she felt was repayment for what he did, to have Frieda whisper, "Jack there is only one way for a woman to repay a man, and that is for her to let that man inside of her, you saved my life and that of my husbands, for that you shall have me."

She said that as she lowered herself onto Jack's manhood, thinking Carlos was coming through that door at any time, knowing that his gun was right beside him, as other wives were snuggling up and hands were all over his body.

Frieda finished with Jack, it was Rose who was next, and she was tiny in the hips as she had a hard time with Jack's manhood, but continued till it was satisfying.

For Jack, he was looking like the purple monster was back, as Rose's ugly face had turned Jack off till he saw his final prize, there standing above him, she was naked, she knelt down, to spread her legs, she inserted that purple stick inside and took the whole thing, he touched her big titts, and played with them to say, "Carlos was the one who protected me from my father, but it was you that killed him, for that I am grateful, I know of no other way to repay you except this, although this is not near the gratitude I have for you, I asked Carlos if he would allow me to be one of your wives and to serve you as I have served Carlos, to grant you any wish that I may give to you, and to wait on you hand and foot, for this will you accept me as one of you own," she bent over to kiss Jack who smelled her breath, to smell the same old stinky breath, to say "Only if you quite smoking, and then I will think about it".

Jack stayed in his position as required by Frieda who supervised the session, a necessity as she explained, when Alba finally let loose, she fell to her exhaustion.

However when she rolled off of Jack he was still hard, as it bobbed in the air, the other wives all looked at it, for Frieda say "Alright one at a time, Margarita, you go next,"

Her petite body has had the feel of Jack's huge man sausage, as she eased down on it, her hip action was greater that Jack's mind control, and just like that Jack warned them as she got off of it, to use her hand to watch it erupt.

Jack felt relieved, as he relaxed, he went soft, enough for Frieda to place a blanket over Jack, and turn out the light.

The next morning Jack awoke, to the sounds of giggles, Jack opened his eyes to see, ten little faces poking fun at him, till Frieda came over to sweep them away.

She stood before Jack to say, "Today is your big wedding day, to Maria, what we would like to do, is take you to our bathing room, and get you cleaned up, so come with me."

She led Jack along the hallway, to a room that said Bathing, she held the door open for him, and he walked in nude to see over twenty women naked, in four separate bathing pools.

"These are our quarters, only those truly honored are allowed, here you again, can sample any one of us, including me."

"Well it looks like its you and I again, but between you and I, you can you keep Margarita away from me."

"I know Carlos says the same thing."

Jack also noticed something else, to say "I don't remember them last night, as Jack's eyes lit up to see the sophicated sex kitten, to say;

"How about her, and her and her"

"Yes, you may, " said Frieda, as she led Jack into an empty pool, then says, "Girls, listen up, Jack would like, Tina, Angela, and Sara, to come join us and for you Alex as well", she saw Jack and smiled, to say," Here I come" she made her way over, to enter before the other girls, as she saw Jack was ready, but Frieda said "No, no, no, that was over last night, now it is time for pleasure, allow them to bathe you, with our scented soaps, then they will wash your whole entire body clean, as will I, then we will dress you in traditional Cuban attire, to lastly, feed you the fruits and vegetables, then we will take you to the ceremony, and hand deliver you to the Elders".

"You will have the ceremony, then consummate the vows, for next three day, you will be in ceremony, then you will be let loose, to go do what you do." said Frieda.

Jack was resting, with his eyes closed, as he felt all the hands on him as did his pole, to think, "So this is what pleasure feels like".

Isabella looked over at her group to say "Now what?"

"Well all we know is that Jack has now sided with Carlos."

"So do you think he has deserted us" said Ronnie.

"Ronnie we need you to get into that wedding, break it up and kill Jack."

"I second that" says a fierce looking man."

"Davio, you didn't need to get involved."

"Well I am involved, when you let Kenneth and Candace escape, what am I suppose to do, let this whole thing get out of hand, this is such a mess, that the director of the CIA, Walter Breem, wants to get involved, tell me what I'm suppose to do?"

"Well for starters give us some room to do what we do best, besides we still have control over Jack, as long as he has no wind of this we should be fine, now we have El Sanchez."

"He will get us in the wedding party, if all else fails we will send in the Navy Seals, go in and extract him."

"Well now that sounds like a better plan, send the Seals in and extract him bring him here and we should be good" said Davio, then ads "What about Preston Scott and Jodi Thomas?"

"Well, we have Mister Scott is on a flight back now, and Devlin has Miss Thomas, keeping an eye on Jack.

"Interesting, they release her and she will turn around and capture him how nice" said Davio.

"Once we get the information from Mister Scott about Carlos's accounts, we should be good, and then honey you and I shall go off to Breem's palace in Miami."

"Is he on board with all of this," asked Isabella.

"No if he gets wind of this we could all be in trouble" said Davio.

Jack sat by himself with a bag of his regular clothes and his weapon inside, on the luxurious sofa, in front of him was a assortment of dried fruits and assorted pastries, meats and cheeses, he was thinking of, that big boar he shot with that rifle, he borrowed from Carlos, it was only rifle they had, as Carlos flushed them boar out.

In front of him stood, the very young Alba, she was wearing what Jack fancied, a tank top and shorts, she was refreshing his drink.

Jack felt like a big swollen up geisha girl, he wore a thick outer layer of sewn textiles, that were spectacular in the colors of bright blue with authentic gold trim, for his outer coat, underneath that was the finest silks the has ever felt, to under that, of some of the finest smells available, from oils to gold leaf flake, his skin was rubbed down by all twenty six women, and pampered in the very best olive and safflower oils and fused with fragrant rose pedals.

The women worked a bit lower to his member, they covered it in a antiseptic, which numbed it up, and coated it with a bee's wax solution that has harden up to his right thigh, the Lenin on top of that is pure silk and over that was a stiff woven textile, down to his traditional hand made boots, with small jewels, all hand stitched to match each foot, it was a gift from the Manges Elders, lastly was the head turban, consisting of a hard woven textile, which has flaps and a visor that can fold down in case of sever weather, other that that he was fine except for that itch, he couldn't get to, he was all wrapped up in a bundle.

"Master is there anything else you need, I must get ready for the wedding, from this point forward I will serve you for the rest of my life, and if you agree, then will you take me back to America, and allow me to be your servant?"

"If that is what you wish, or would you rather be free?"

"I do, I will serve you far better than any other girl, as you can see from the plate I place before you, and I can see that, that was what you ate the most of you liked."

"Yeah, especially that meat on a cracker, what was that?"

"It was braised pork from that wild boar, you shot, yesterday, I had a portion of the inners cooking, before the bachelor party, I was the one who prepared the meat, and now its at the Manges village, on a slow spit, being basted as we speak, that was the scraping from the insides, you know its quite a delicacy down here, but I can also cook American food, as well as Traditional, in addition to that I will bathe you daily, and take care of all your special needs."

"Are you sure, you want to do that? "

"Where would I go, end up in some poverty stricken situation here, or be with a strong and powerful man"

"Alright, then I will take you with me, under one condition, you stop smoking those awful cigarettes."

"You're cleaning up here" said Carlos, looking at Jack to add;

"This is the first time all the ladies of the household have united, and your walking away from here with two of the best pleasure seekers, both Alexandra and Alba are two of the finest, not to mention, Alba is probably the best cook we have here, so your one lucky man, on top of that getting Maria you stand to inherit over a billion dollars of wealth, I estimate that mine to be one of the largest gold veins ever discovered in the world, and the Elders gave it to you, how is it so many people like you, especially Alba, my half-sister hasn't been that excited in years."

"Wait, did you say she was your half-sister?"

"Yeah, you know from one of my many wives, or I guess you would say she is a in-law, as she came from the same father as I, but a different mother".

"Really, so her father, has many wives such as you"

"Oh, yes, he did, but now he is dead, you have power now, the police commissioner is dead, my father, that bastard., than you will have young women, who will seek you out, you know on a daily bases, girls from, especially Havana, will come down here, wanting to find the very rich, and latch themselves onto men like us, especially Alexandra, she is special."

"She is from the Dominican Republic, where I found her, she was from a rich family, instantly she wanted to be one of my wives, so I agreed, we returned, to discover her cousin was Margarita, which killed that deal, which forbidden me to marry her, just like Maria, yes she was in my possession and I may impregnate her, but I was not allowed to marry the same sister, so that is why I must allow her to go, but you know Alex likes you as well".

"You know Jack; you are allowed to have more than one wife in your own country."

"What are you saying?"

"What I'm saying, is that its not uncommon for you spies to be married to more than one wife, did you know in the earlier days of the US, the spies were the peace makers, and would go into a country, marry the daughter of a king of that particular country, take for instance the land deal from France, and thus have its allegiance for the future, and you have that same privilege, the other Super Spy, I believe his name is Ben Hiltz, has 12 wives, but they are from all over, like the emperor's maiden number two, Keiko, who if her sister were to fail, she would and he would assume command over the southern provinces of Kyoto."

"So Jack see, even a colleague of yours, has multiple wives, do you know the real secret as to why the Super Spies are allowed as many as they like?"

"I still don't know what you talking about."

"Because, they are the trusted ones, they live and die on being loyal, just like Alba, you won't find any other woman like her out there that will live to serve you, one moment she will be up to her knees in the rice patty, or on your back walking on it with that petite body she possess, or just simply bend over so that you may feel pleasure, yeah Jack she will honor you for the rest of her life, as well as produce as many younger Jack's to fill your household, I'd say you made it."

"Now let me help you up, were going to a family wedding."
Jack just looked at him, strangely, for what he just said, his walk was short, everything was stiff on him, as he stood, for the car that await him, in the garage, only to see the wives all started to make their presence known, all wore the similar outfits, or as Frieda called it our colors, in the form of the old knighthood.

Their emblem stood proud on the front and back of their tunics, they were dressed in all red, with gold trim, except Alexandra and Alba, who wore elegant gowns.

Jack realized now what family wedding meant, he looked over at Alexandra and Alba to see that they were all happy, he was trying to think of when he said he wanted to marry them, all he remembers is to agreeing to allow them to come to the US, now after today he will have three wives, and two girls waiting at home, yes about Sara, she did say, if I did choose other women, that she would accept the third or fourth position, I may be screwing this all up or she may accept it.

"Carlos could be right, I remember reading a book on the etiquette of Spies, their allotments and privileges, the two famous Utah spies were actually instrumental in stopping the civil war, and thus were granted numerous wives, so they moved from Ohio to Utah to have a better life."

Jack waddled into the massive garage, to continue his train of thought,   "So hey, if it don't work out with Sara and Sam I'll just come down here and live with Maria, wow, thinks Jack think of her to say;

"Is she pretty or what, and young, she has to be just eighteen, those dark seductive eyes, Carlos told me she is a true virgin, meaning she had no contact with any man, and lived under the roof of the Elders, she has been well protected."

Jack and the others to include Carlos got into the largest limo Jack had ever seen, holding his bag was Alba, as it was a surprise, when she first picked it up, the gun and holster was inside, and nothing happened.

The ride was extremely short, they hit the bumpy road of the dirt, all the way up to the village, the car stopped, first out was Jack, he was helped out by a dressed up Hopi, who helped him to a shack to rest, while Hopi said "It is only moments away, this is your day, let me tell you how all of this go down, first The Prince of the Manges Valley will present you with his gifts, then you will receive our gifts, then it will be the Elders pledges, and then lastly you will have Maria hand, and body, we will put you into a specially designed and built house, for you two overlooking the ocean, and you shall have three days to consume the ceremony, afterwards you shall be set free, to go back to the US, then if you so choose, you may bring them back with you or allow them to stay here."

Hopi leaves as Jack ponders his next move, when a tap at the door, Jack says "come in"

Standing before him was a well fit Devlin, who said "Look we don't have much time, I just got wind of a plan that they are trying to capture you and bring you in on some questioning."

'What are you talking about?"

"My bosses have informed me that Mister Scott has told them that it was you and Carlos are together with the weapons and all the drugs being smuggled out."

'Well that's not true." said Jack, feeling confined up.

"I know that, which means it's a cover up, so after the ceremony, we will have multiple agents all over the grounds to help you, all in all call Kelli, her and my team will extract you, understand?"

'Yes" said Jack looking at her.

"Good luck" she said and left.

Another knock on the door and Jim steps in to say "Do you want your car here?"

"Sure, I don't know, it's your call".

"Alright good luck" said Jim as he shakes Jack arm.

Jack was wondering where his bag was, his gun, his watch and wallet.

The music started, it was loud and the beating of the drums was like he was awaiting his sentence.

Then straight out of a movie, the Witch doctor, rips open the door, and out into the night, Jack is taken, escorted by two burly brothers of Maria, their grip was tight, up the hill they went past the feast area, to a newly built platform, he was hoisted up on it, where the Witch doctor, whose decorative head dress was a bit intimidating, he was singing, chanting and swearing.

Jack stood looking out at the crowd, waiting for the bullets to penetrate his coat of arms, as he searched, he saw some familiar faces, and some not to memorable, some was a in a hurry, others just stared back, then the music stopped.

All was quiet as Carlos, stepped from out of a shack on stage to say, in his native tongue, "Welcome Ladies and Gentlemen, to this celebration, to unite this distinguished gentleman, of wealth and prestige, into our home, village and community, I accept him as my brother in arms and for diplomatic relations, I ask of the same, for he now has the title of The Prince of the Loomis Valley, the parcel of land north of Santiago Bay, also known as the coconut province, you will honor him as your own and with that I would like to present him with the first gift, from me, my sister Alba".

A loud cheer went up, as she appeared, wearing a veil, the Witch doctor said a few things, he brought together Jack's and Alba's hands, and made a blessing, in turn everyone cheered, moments later the doctor broke the bond, and led her to her seat.

Carlos went back to speaking" Next is a present from the dictator himself, a token of his love for his people, he has asked that the Princess of Dominguez Republic, be his possession, to strengthen the ties to our sister county, here she is Alexandra, she too is brought to Jack as he holds her gloved hands, facing her.

Jack sees a huge smile on her face, through the veil, as the Witch doctor is doing a crazy dance with jumps and summersaults, it was an intense work out, he then holds their hand to make a blessing, and then she was yanked from his grasp and was escorted off.

The drums began to beat, as the wedding percussion was coming, a clear out has taken place by all the brothers, as next to Jack stood Hopi, who whispered "I'll explain what just happened, its more than a prediction, than anything".

Jack waited to see Maria dressed in this magnificent red with jeweled outfit, instantly Jack saw how great her beauty was, her face rivaled all others in clarity and distinct features, it looked like she was walking, in all actuality she was being carried on a platform, where she stood, it four of the largest men, and all the rest of the men of the village walking towards him, till she was hoisted up to the level of the platform, as the drum beats increase, till the Chief, stood and waved off his hands, while the Witch doctor, danced around them.

The Chief, pulled off his jeweled crown, as Hopi said "Bow in front of him."

Jack did that, as the Chief placed the crown on Jack's head, to raise his head and hands up to begin the chant, while Jack got with the program and raised himself up, he held her hands in his, as their gifts were being presented, she received a gold necklace, and Jack also received a gold flake necklace, from Hopi, as he placed it over the crown, the Chief lowered his hands onto both Maria's and Jack's shoulders, as the Witch doctor clapped his hands three times, as Maria moved in awaiting the kiss.

"Go ahead and kiss Maria yelled Hopi."

Jack moved in and kiss her on those soft pouty lips, she parted his and their tongues met, for a game of who can catch who, Jack pined her down easily, as that instant she broke away and raised her hand and smiled, and said something.

The all cheered, as Carlos led Jack into the shack, to say, "Now its over, you may rest, it is her time to receive gifts, as Alex and Alba will receive them for her."

Hopi came in to say "That was most excellent".

'Why's that?"

"She accepted you."

"I thought that was what we were here for."

"No it doesn't work like that, you were a prophecy, that was coming true, as a young girl she dreamt that a strong man would come and change all of our lives, he comes with compassion and with honor, thus that man is you, wearing that crown signifies you're the new leader of this tribe, we are your servants, all the women are now yours." said Hopi.

"What does that mean," asked Jack.

"It means the chief has retired" said Carlos, to add, "From this day forward, the whole village is yours to do with as you see fit, just like a king, you now have over 20 thousand acres of forest and mango trees, not to mention the gold mine, and the jute trees. But your most important crop is your tobacco."

"Did you know that the Chief was going to do this?" asked Jack.

"No, it is a complete surprise to all of us, we had no idea, I thought he would give it to me, but you are getting to have the hand, of his most beloved treasure, and you marrying her is a secret, and thus the Chief has given his kingdom to you as well."

Jack just sat down, to drink some bottled water, provided by his support team, to listen to Carlos, say "In addition to Maria, you got Alexandra, which is pretty revered around these areas just for her sheer beauty, and those incredible hips."

"you can expect lots of children, then there is my sister, also known as the worker, she will be your servant to the day you die, as well as being Maria's house helper, your off to a good family start, and then you have the choice of some 200 plus, other girls, who are all over the island and in other countries, not to mention all the resources from all the men 75 plus, what do you have to say now?"

"Let's get started on building a new housing conditions and better food supply."

"What do you mean?"

"Why can't I have them do farming?"

"Because they are a fishing community."

"How's that?"

"Yeah, they are all fishermen, every day they go out and catch fish, then return with some money and fresh fish."

Jack gets up to say, "What you're telling me is that the entire community is fisherman."

"Yes, why?"

"Where are all their boats?"

'Oh, well they use dinghies and nets". Said Carlos.

"I got cha now, so nothing modern is that what you're saying?"

"That's right, they like the old paddle boats."

"Really" Jack had another idea."

"Alright its time for the feast lets go."

Carlos leads Jack out slowly, to the platform that has a huge table on it well as a make shift tent above the table but high enough to feel the cool breeze, a head chair in the middle, on one side was a secondary chair, that sat Maria, next to her was Alexandra.

On her right was Alba, for a place on the end for Carlos.

Jack pulled out his chair, to take a seat, next to the departing Chief, Hopi helped Jack push in his chair, as Jack looked next to the Chief to see another man, but from his arms looked like the Witch Doctor, then on the end Hopi took the seat, each plate was different, Jack took a sampling of each, Jack waited till everyone all had equal portions, on their plates, and the empty platters were stacked up and removed, everyone held hands as the Witch doctor began to chant, then it was concluded, they ate, Jack was his old self, slow, enjoying the different kinds of fishes, octopus, shark and lobster, melted fresh goat's butter, and cheese, a fruit salad, and coconuts were all over, in butter, milk, and chunk form, not to mention shredded.

Maria still had her veil on, and ate as slow as Jack, as other caught on, they too began to slow, down below others held plates and sat on mats, to eat as slowly as Jack ate, he finally finished.

Jack got up, with Hopi's help, not feeling very well.

It was Hopi and Carlos, moving, to help get Jack, to the other side of the platform they went, to a door, for Carlos to say "This is your house they had built, as they went in, to a foyer, Carlos said "Off to your left is the out house they dug."

Jack went inside and closed the door, as the girls came in, as Hopi and Carlos stepped out, it was Alba that closed the door. Hopi took a folding chair and took a seat outside the door.

Inside Jack was getting rid of that very rich meal, from both ends. It took him like eternity to pull off those pants, which left indentations in his skin, he got up feeling a bit light headed, as he took two steps then collapsed in front of the door, the girls too were not feeling well, and fell where they stood.

Hopi stood guard, as he saw guns came out and the shooting begun, he dove out of the way, as a friend to the family began to shout out, to Hopi he was El Sanchez a farmer, he had two handguns and shooting them in the air, Hopi watched as he engaged with the pretty girls he saw, he stayed crotched beside the two houses, laying in the mud, watching this all unfold, he saw Carlos with a gun, shooting back at El Sanchez, who had his men searching for Jack as he yelled out, most of his Elders, were safe, in the mine. Hopi could see his moms and children were running wild, he saw a brother go down, as he clichéd his fist. To hear "Hopi help us" from below window.

Hopi scrambles down to see Alba, to say "What is wrong?"

"We have all been poisoned, its for hemlock poison, get the shell fish powder from your Mom, hurry please" she pleaded, Hopi was on the move, down the backsides of the houses along the beach front, to his mom's house, he went inside to say "Mama, Mama, Maria and Alba, are poisoned, she said she needs shell fish powder."

Maria's, Mama, pulls out some bottles of water, unscrews the tops and pours in some shell fish powder, to shake it up, to say "Hopi go find your father and your sister, here are four bottles, Hopi placed them in a bag he swung around his neck, and was away.

Jack crawled up to his knees, he opened the door, to close it, and finish what he earlier started, he knew he was poisoned, as gunfire could still be heard, but as the adrenalin coursed through his body, he pulled himself up off the stool and fell into the door, he opened it, to see Alba, in the foyer, waiting for him, she helped him down a flight of steps.

Jack saw his bag, he fell at it, he was helped by Alba, who began to undress Jack, while the others were out, down to his underwear and t-shirt, he unzip the bag, in a sock was his watch, he put on, he was feeling better, when Hopi called out to Alba, she went to the window, to receive the first bottle, and one for herself, which she went to Jack and gave it to him , she shook it, as Jack took some sips, , he was feeling better, his eyes were still blurry, he knew the drink mix was the antidote, he finished all of it, he threw the bottle aside. Jack found his shorts, he pulled them up, he had help from Alba, Jack he threw on his holster, and Alba helped him up with his shoes, he pulled his gun out, long enough to reach down to get his badge, as Alba was buttoning up his dress shirt, which he slid it in his front pocket, his strength was gaining, as he said "See if the others are alright."

Jack heard screaming outside, as Jack made it up the steps, he opened his front door, to she the man with two hand guns, as another man was running, Jack shot at the guy who saw Jack first, he took a minute and then aimed at the fleeing man and shot him. The guy fell flat forward.

Jack shot at the hands of the man, who was screaming and shooting, as each gun flew out of his hands, he knelt in pain, crying as his two hands looked mangled, Jack saw Carlos and yelled Hopi over here, check on Carlos." yelled Jack.

Hopi responded and took the antidote to him, as Jack held his black handled pistol at the ugly hombre to hear" He is ours now, said Kelli, as a team of helpers secured the angry man.

Jack looked around as he could feel his body need to pass more poison, and went back into the his house, to have it come out both ends.

Moments later a knock on his door, Jack answered it to see Jim holding a vial, to say "Here is your antidote, to hemlock poison."

Jack unscrewed the top and drank it down, instantly he felt better, in a couple of days you should be fine."

Jack closed the door for a moment, and then re-opened it to say;

"Jim come walk with me."

Jack and Jim walked out onto the street, the two walked, and stopped to say "Alright I need you to build me a twenty five foot fence from the ocean to the tree line, then I want a fence before the hot springs, next I need the hot springs dug out, say about three feet deep and pour concrete, for a pool, next I want a guard shack on one side, and the other a long family style rooms to house all three hundred people, can you do all of this for me?"

"Yes who will pay for it?"

"I will, how much do you think all of this will take"

"I don't know, but I do know this, the Army Corps of Engineers, is always looking for a job to do, I could give their regional director a call, there is your man power, as for the supplies"

Jack hands him his retirement card, to say "Use that."

Jim looked at the card, to hesitate taking it.

"Well take it, what's wrong."

Jim took a deep breath, to carefully say "I can't."

"What is wrong it's only a card?"

"No its not, that is your card."

"Well let's go together and I will swipe it at a home improvement center".

"No, it doesn't work like that, actually I don't know how it works, hold on let me call my boss, to find out the correct procedure, as he went to his phone, a car drove up it stopped, and Lisa got out,

Jim went up to her and used his hands to explain as Jack watched from a distance.

Lisa looked around, and then got back in, and the car turned around and left.

"Who was that?".

"My boss, she said whatever you want you get, I will stay here and get this started, and make some calls to get the necessary supplies down here to get what you want done."

"Great do you need my card?"

"No, It doesn't work like that, our supplies come from a secret place and will be flown in either by plane or helicopter, usually with some agents in the past, they usually want things for themselves, until you, you want things to benefit other peoples lives, and for that we really don't have a operation plan for, but as you grow and we work with you, on a moments notice I'll have a completely stocked plane that will fly to wherever you want it to go, what your doing here is being a good will ambassador, some what un-heard of for spies." "Most spies, all they care about is themselves, but your different, you see the good in people, you try to save lives, rather than kill people, heck this village made you their Chief, things don't happen to everyday people."

"They happen to the extraordinary who go out of their way to help others".

"Just like this poison, you could have been laid out, but you pulled yourself up and came out to the streets and stopped the problem, listen why don't you go back to your shack, and rest up, while I will get started on solving this problem, take a mandatory three days with your wives and we will see you later."

Alright will do" said Jack, as he walked back to where Carlos was at to see he was still alive, as Hopi helped him into the car, it sped away, Hopi came to Jack and hugged him to say "Two of my brothers are slayed".

"Who was this silvered hair man "said Jack.

"He was a farmer named El Sanchez, but I don't know who that American was, good shot you hit him in the back of the head."

"Not my intention, some time, if I forget to aim it down, it goes, aw forget it" said Jack, on his way back to the shack, to hear it was all quiet, as he made his way in, and closed the door.
The other women were up and recuperating. Jack went downstairs, to take off his holster and gun, to his bag; he unbuttoned his shirt and slipped out of his shorts.
Jack laid down in the middle of the bed, to see both Maria and Alex, standing at the edge of the bed, each one slipped out of their dress, come in to rest on each side of Jack, he placed his arm around the two of them, while Alba picked up the dresses, and cleaned up, then sat down in her chair, watching over them with a gun of her own at the ready.

——— CH 18 ———

Prince of the Loomis Valley

T hree days has since passed, the multi leveled house, in the village, was quite large, aside from the bed on the first floor, a lower level, was the kitchen, and dining and washing area, and below that was the other two beds for the other two girls.

Jack had hours and days with Maria, whose perfect body was amazing to touch and stroke, she was not the least bashful, as Jack freely touched every part of her, the two lay naked together, by themselves.

Outside was a line of roving patrols of Marines, guarding the shoreline, the US corps of Army engineers, landed, and began work as to what Jack wanted.

Alba took the lead and prepared all the meals, fresh, from produce she received daily from Hopi and his brothers, as their was no communication between Jack and Maria during this time, it was coming to an end, as a loud horn sounded, Maria leaped off the bed, and began to dress, as Jack watched, only to say in amazement,

" Where are you going, stay here in bed with me."

"Sorry, I can't," she said, as she dresses, then leaves.

Jack lays back, with his head in the pillows, only to feel two sets of hands, touching him, Jack looks up to see the sophisticated sex kitten, then out of the corner of his eye was Alba, picking up some clothes and then leaving, as she closed the door, Jack saw candles were lit, as Alex stood up on the bed, and began to undress, slowly, her near perfect body glistened in the light. She looked down to see Jack was ready for her; she had a smile on her face, as the last piece of clothing fell away, and she stood above him naked. She bent down, to spread her legs, to sit on his flat stomach, she bent

over and kissed him on the lips to say,   "Maria is first I'm second and Alba will be third."
Jack looked up at her to say, "You mean three more days?"
     "Yep and have I got some things planned for you."
Jack held on for the ride, the first day or night was fun, his mind control was fading, as the sophisticated sex kitten, was live, and more willing than even Sara, thought Jack, but at the second day was coming to a close, he had enough, and she was still wanting more, so by the end of the third day, the horn sounded, she leapt up from the bed, Jack watched her leave.
Next to enter was Alba, as sweet as ever, she brought food in, and lots of it, Jack was up, and over to sample the delights, while Alba changed the sheets and blankets, he ate till his belly was full, and drank bottled pop, even though a fully stocked bar was at his disposal.
Jack turned to see new sheets and a different smell in the air, incenses were burning, as he took a seat on a chair, to see she brought in a tub, with the help of Alex, and all three women filled the tub.
Bucket upon bucket of warm water, as Alex led Jack to the bath, Jack got in.
The two left, leaving Alba, who undressed in front of Jack, stepped into the bath, she was behind him, and began to wash his back, then his neck. She was the most sensual of his new companions; her touch was soft and delicate, thought Jack. He continued that train of thought as he felt her arms slid down his, it was interesting to feel something totally different with each woman, Maria, was reserved, private and instructional, whereas Alex was the total opposite, anything and everything went on, she was the aggressor, and come to find out her reputation was greater than her actual escapades, so she confide in him, that she hooked up with a well known Cuban, that led her to the myth and explorations of a torrid past, where in all actuality she was a novice, till Jack came in her life, now there is Alba, she too was a little miss-understood, having made her way to Carlos, through the network of slave traders, she escaped her father's abuse, both mental and emotional, to find her way to a public auction, in which Carlos bid on her, she was a mental

wreck, just month's ago she was raped, beat up, and humiliated in from of all the other slaves, Carlos took her under his wing, and the two developed a closeness, that led to a relationship, only for him to discover she was his half-sister, then it became one of a brother and sister friendship.

Enter Jack, when Carlos realized his strength, he offered her up to him as a gift, then he asked her, she was unsure at first, that was until the bachelor party, where she decided, Jack was her love choice, yet she knows her role as the number three, even after the morning talk they had.

Where as, Jack told her that there was two American girls, and that her role and was that they were all equals, each has something to offer equally, and that after the nine-day love fest is over, he was taking a break.

But later recanted that idea, to say, "Make a list on the calendar, and alternate who sleeps in my bed".

Jack felt Alba getting up, and stepped around him to face him, she knelt down, as Jack eased back, she washed his front to say, "And, what do you like best about me?"

"That you're mine for the rest of my life."

"Yes, I will only be yours, that is true, but is there a certain feature, or thing about me?"

"I'd have to say, you stop smoking, those awful cigarettes."

"That was my sister's thing."

"'you have a sister."

"No, what I meant was Rose, who is Maria's sister, but when we all live under one roof, we call each other a sister, and we call you our master."

Jack looked at her, her big beautiful breasts.

She leaned forward, to run her hands up his legs, to his stomach, her smile was infectious, she showed off her white teeth.

Jack says, "I like every little thing about you, matter of fact I Love You".

Alba, eyes grew big to say, "Really, I'm a bit over whelmed, I don't know what to say."

"Say whatever you want."

"What I mean is that, for most of my life I've been a servant girl, and now I'm royalty, all of my life others have told me what to do, what to say and let alone love, and now that I met you, you have changed my life forever, how can I serve you oh Master?"

"First off, stop calling me master, my name is Jack, or Honey, or whatever, except Master, next your all equals, you Maria, and Alex, what I'm looking for in a wife, is an extension of me, I like to help others, and hope you'll do the same."

"I can try what do you mean?" she asked honestly.

"Well I was thinking of bringing you along to accompany me when I travel, and meet with my suppose workers and the villagers."

"Yes, I can do that."

"I need someone to translate, what they are saying". to add,

"Then I will need you to tell them what I'm saying, can you do that, or are you willing to do that?"

"Yes, I think so, it will be like, I'm your assistant in speech, rather than household chores."

"Yes, exactly", said Jack, looking at her weirdly, as the two talked in the tub, then over to the bed, all for the three days, he knew she wasn't ready, and she sensed he needed a break, but told him, that at some point the would have to do it to her, and he agreed, as day was turning into night, she was bent over along a desk, nude, and Jack was rising, as he went for it, he spread her cheeks and began to lick her with delight, she became overwhelmed, with a flood of emotions which she showered him with, he got up and inserted into her, from behind, thinking she would be tight, she was firm, yet receptive, and stroke to stroke, long and lasting, his mind was shut down just enjoying the action, he was about to erupt, when the horn blew, he let go as did she, with such force, it saturated him.

It was like a starter's gun went off, machinery could be heard, as generators roared to life, the sounds reverberated throughout their thin walled structure, Jack went back into the tub to wash up, as Alba joined him, when they finished, she dressed him, as he gave Alba a shirt and pants to wear, she left to get them hemmed up, Jack slid on his holster, and gun, his watch and lastly in went his badge.

Jack went up the stairs, to pull open the door, the sun was setting behind him, as he saw the chair in front of the door, he moved it away, then went out into the street, to see the heavy machinery.

Jack looked in all directions, from his advantage on the hill, he saw the massive trench they were digging, and then there was all those stacks of blocks and timber, then Jack looked at the setting sun, to see the port, and another idea came over him, thinking; "What a nice spot to put in a pier, with individual slips."

Jack sensed someone behind him, to turn to see it was Alba, dressed in his back up outfit, smiling to say, "I'm ready for work."

He saw she held onto a tablet of paper and a pen, she seemed happy as she followed his walk towards all the work, on the right was the goldmine, that was once open, now has a newly installed door, as they continued downward, there was a privacy fence put up around the generators, one quiet and the other one was noisy, past another big gate shut and locked.

The two walked together, they rounded the corner to see the once open field pasture, was now a sea of materials, many workers were among them, easily 500 or so, doing everything, from digging a huge trench, to digging out the basement, a high table, was in the middle of the make shift road, in the middle of all of it was Jim, who saw Jack, to immediately come up to him, to say; "What do you think?"

Jack looked all over, to say, "This looks nice, what are your plans?"

"It's not my choices, I am doing what you want, Jack I want you to meet Commander Johnson, Jim began to yell, to say, "Commander Johnson, over here please."

The man comes over to salute, to say, "Reporting as ordered, how can I help you sir?"

"Can you give me a report?" asked Jack.

"Well sir, we are doing what was asked, it was mentioned you want a fence, instead of a safety fence, were installing a solid eighteen foot wall, along the north face, then along the east side, along the trees, down south to the hot springs, then were going to dig out the spring to let it run clean, but first, as we speak, were digging out the run off pond first, then building a wall, and a top so that you may go in there and rest or bathe, whatever sir."

"Then the water will be filtered, and pumped into the house were building, look here is the plans that were drawn, per your request, as you can see there is four stories up and one down, were about four feet above water line, in the basement is a safe room, for 100, also a weapons room, all there storages, steam heaters, and water tanks, a power generator, is coming by ship, will replace the two portable ones, for the mine, and house and guard shack".

"From the main house to the guard shack, we will have a tunnel under the road, in addition, where the supplies are now, will be a ten acre field, where a irrigation system will water, the soon to be planted clover and alfalfa field, behind the guard shack will be a barn built, 50 head of the finest Texas longhorn."

Jack looked at the Commander, to realize, there doing what they want, so he just went along with it, as he continued to ramble on.

"Courtesy of the President of our US, as a personal gift from one of his ranches, in addition, 25 Guernsey cows from New Jersey, in addition, a professional chef, who also is a gardener, and also a team of additional support personnel". "If we have your permission, may we house them in the old houses that will be refurbished?"

Jack looked over the officer, to say," Perhaps".

Jack looks the guy over to say, "Maybe once the house is finished and the elders move in, now I will change your train of thought, can you and your group put in a pier, along the beach front, and a fish processing plant."

The officer looked at Jack to say "Yes, whatever you want, we can do that and much more, can we walk together," as he leads Jack into the open field to the beach, to say, "Sir, I must say, when I received the call from the President himself, I picked up the entire base, we are what you would call a mission ready team, devoted to support you in every action or as you see fit, in addition, we have a small situation, we discovered a small cell of unknown parties, while you were recovering, we called in special forces, to go in and eradicate them, well, we have them at Guantanamo Bay, held under lock and key, as we speak, professional interrogators are coming down here." he stopped for a moment, then continued;

"In addition, I want to let you know, that same group has four platoons, and they will be here for as long as you are present here, but the support personnel will stay here for up to 6 months, or until, there is sufficient enough management of the crops, fields, animals and water, anything you need?"

"Yeah, after you put in that pier, I want ten 100 foot fishing boats, bought, and delivered here, with some captains, in place." Jack stops to look around to say, "Where are all the villagers?"

"As I know, everyone except you and your wife Maria, and her two attendants, have been up in the Loomis valley, to provide you some help to, well that is all I can really say."

"Alright, I'm going back in for the night, will I be able to get out tomorrow?"

"Yes Sir, you will," said Commander Johnson.
Jack calls for Alba, who runs over to him, as they leave Jim's sight, to see his old friend, to say, to Commander Ted Johnson, "Hey did you let Jack know about his car in that make shift garage."

"No not really, I told him about that terrorist cell."

"What did he say?"

"He didn't seem too concerned; didn't you say he was a super spy?"

"It doesn't matter what I say, we all work for one guy."

Yeah, sorry, him" said Ted.

"No, I meant the President."

"True, true, I hope I wasn't out of line," said Ted.

"Ted, don't worry, Jack has no idea, how much power he possess." said Jim.

"True, true, you're right Jim. Said Ted.

"Damn it Isabella, your losing control, it seems since your man has been down there, were losing our troops, not to mention now, that special forces are all over that place, what do you plan on doing about that one?"

Sorry Davio, since El Sanchez was put down, I had no idea, they hit us inexpectly, who knew, and we got competition and their getting their act together."

"The American Spy program, is not as sophisticated as our underground network, we have been undermining them for decades, that's why the British is so much more dominating, listen I will get

Breem on board with us, but in the meantime, I'm sending you two of the top British agents, to help out your situation, and once and for all we will get this Jack Cash under control."

"Really Davio, you would do that, you're an ass, we got thing under control, were waiting for Jack to leave that compound, then we will strike, we have Nationals here ready to do what, your planning "

"Yes, but there no super spies."

"That's true; well I guess we will wait for them."

"No, just proceed, and when they get there, we will coordinate the capture" said Davio.

———————

Next morning, Jack awoke, something in his mind, triggered him to get up, he was thinking of Sara, he got dressed, slipped on his watch, slid his wallet into his breast heart pocket, then his holster, and weapon, he pulled on his windbreaker, to leave the confines of his room, down into where all the noise was, there sitting at the head of the table was Carlos, who's eyes lit up when he saw Jack, to say, "Its about time sleepy head, hey they are sure making progress out on the road, the gate is open, the house is taking shape."

"Yeah, I guess, what are you up to today?"

"Just thought you might want to go visit your property in the Loomis valley, you know that's where your whole village is." said Carlos, drinking a cup of coffee.

"What do you mean?" said Jack taking a seat, beside him. Alba placed a cup of coffee next to him.
Jack slid it to his lips, to drink it slowly.

"Usually what happens is when one of the villagers women gets married, the whole group will go to their lands of the person who marries and help them out, and in your case, the Loomis Valley is pristine, coconut plantation in this area, complete with a processing plant, and distribution center."

"Sounds like it's a big thing."

"Well actually it is, the original owner owed me a lot of money, so I settled the debt in exchange for the land and property, on it is a ranch style house, that you and the girls can move into immediately, the view is spectacular, and the housing complex is vast, along with an airfield, and a helio pad, there are some animals, like sheep, pigs, chickens, and rabbits, at least ten acres of vegetables."

Carlos stops to see a plate of food given him and Jack from Maria and Alba, when Alex came back in to announce "It is just so beautiful out there", Jack looked her over to see she was drenched in sweat to realize she went for another run, her body reflected the constant workouts, for Jack to say, "Sure, lets go, that is after we eat this."

Eggs, scrambled, with bits of shrimp and lobster, a thick slice of bacon, shredded potatoes, with peppers, both sweet and hot, mixed with parsnips root, lastly fresh fruit compote of pineapple, breadfruit cream, and mango.

Jack finished before all, to get up, as the others were much slower, he went out onto the patio, the warm breeze felt nice, thinking, "Yes, I could live here for the rest of my life."

"There you are," said Carlos, to ad, "It is tradition, that once the man of the house finishes, so does everyone else, in a moment, the women will be ready to go, come follow me."

Carlos led Jack up to the road, to see a brand new van, for Carlos to say, "Here you go my friend, it is yours, you'll need it with all the kids you're going to get."

"Doubtful, but alright, so you said the whole village is there now?"

"Yeah, everyone, they have taken over the whole operation, and good thing to, the workers were skimming the profits, rest assured, they are gone, as a new work force is in place, they are cleaning up the grounds, especially around the house, I talked with your boss, Jim, and he said he was going up there to install new windows and dig a safe room for your wives."

Jack turns to see all three, Women, ready and in line, as Jack allows them to pass, all three sat in the far back, as Jack took the nearest back seat, and Carlos sat in passenger's seat, for the driver turned to say, "My name is Ramon, I am your driver."

"That great Ramon, my name is Jack Cash, and behind me are my three wives, Maria, Alba, and Alexandra."

They all waved.

The van took off, past the generators, to the newly raised guard shack, next to a massive wall, already about half up, then Jack slid to the left side window to see the long house, and in its frame construction, the van came to a stop, as Jim slid the side door open, to say," Before you leave, can you authorize a few changes?"

Jack hopped out, to see the guard shack, then he went in, where Ted stood, he slid the papers over to say, "We have to change, some modifications to the storage rooms," as Jack signed them, "and, in the pastures, it will all be alfalfa, as to what the ground team suggests."

Jack signed, as he knew it was useless to argue over signing or not, all in all over fifty changes.

"Are we done now?" asked Jack.

"Yes, you can go now," said Commander Ted.

Jack pasted Jim, to get back in to say, "Alright let's go!"

The van got up to the top of the hill, to turn left onto the highway, past the airport, and through the city, the road opened to see open road, on the right was a huge hillside on the left was the calm ocean, they went around a bend, and lines of coconut trees could be seen, in a symmetrical pattern, they crossed over a bridge, for Carlos to say,

" Under this bridge leads to the ocean", as the van slowed at the turnoff, a sign said Loomis Valley", Carlos said "All in all ten more miles down, and two miles in, covers your plantation."

The van slowed, to a stop, for Jack to see, that they could either go straight back on, or underneath the bridge, and back to Santiago, then off to the right a sign said, "Loomis Valley", the van went right, up a newly paved road, under coconut palms, past a pond and waterfall system.

"That's how they irrigate the palms, by gate valves" said Carlos.

Jack saw the water flow over the waterfall down to each pond.

The van rounded around the front of the hill, going up, it was several switchbacks, to come out onto a flat portion, the van came to a stop, Carlos got out, to slide the rear door open, Jack stepped out, but stayed to help his three wives.

The view from above was spectacular, in addition, water was everywhere, sluice boxes in the ground, as they walked over several, to see the two story house, along the hillside, they stepped onto the deck, with a nice rail system, Jack saw huge windows, that allowed the sunlight in, almost every room, had French doors, the open air patio, was much, all this sunlight. He made it to the end, the master bedroom, he could see the ocean, and down by the highway was a dock, whereas sat a small fishing boat, Jack turned, to follow everyone in, to see the king-sized bed, and a lavished bathroom, then down a hallway, where each girl choose a room with a view, as Jack was walking into the living room, to sit in front of a massive fireplace.

All three girls came into the commercial size kitchen and they all took a long look at their man. Jack stood to say ,"What's down below?"

"Storage, some more rooms, and a big game room, come let's go outside," said Carlos.

Carlos opened the front door, to see a cute courtyard, where a big building sat, for Carlos to say; "That is the servants and workers quarters, Ramon will stay there." Carlos was proud of showing Jack the area, to add,

"Now as you can see the raised garden beds house culinary herbs, on the far right are seasonal vegetables, off to the left there is the animal barn, it has two levels, beyond that is the pastures, and north of that is an airfield."

Jack saw the steps leading up, this place was pretty impressive, he thinks as Carlos leads them up a set of stairs, to a gate, where the trees were cut, and the open field, for Carlos say, "Beyond that is a alpine lake, that is crystal clear and that is where your water supply comes from. In addition, it is fully stocked with perch and catfish, so what do you think?"

"I like it, thanks," said Jack.

"Oh one more thing, down the hill and to the north is the workers cabins and food area, do you want to check it out? "

"Sure, I'll leave the girls here, and you and I can tour the grounds."

Carlos went past the van to wait, while Jack said, "Come here for a moment."

Jack had his head inside the door, to see all the girls came to him.

All three girls, had smiles on their faces, to hear, "Go in and make yourselves comfortable, this is our new house, wander around and check out the animals."

All three just looked back at him awaiting an answer from him, realizing he had to tell them what to do he said," Alright, Alba, will you take charge of the animals, see what the need, and report back to me later, Alex can you go harvest any fruits and vegetables and report that status, while Maria, can you take care of the inside of the house?"

In unison they all said "yes, M" they stopped, as Jack looked at them to say "Jack."

They nodded there heads, but waited for him to turn, Jack quickly caught up with Carlos as the two walked down the hill, to the first turn out to go north as Jack said "This is sure some place, that guy must have been crazy, to unload it."

"Well to tell you the truth, I forced him to do it, I have been eyeing this piece for a long time now, but he owed us several million of dollars, you know from the trucking fees, market fees and his gambling debt, oh that reminds me, you know that dealer, you gave one hundred thousand dollars to?"

"Yeah," said Jack.

"His wife told him, he had to give you a gift, so tomorrow, a truck, of pigs, and several laying hens, will be here, in addition, they would like to know what you like?"

"What do you mean, like?"

"You name it and they will give it to you."

I still don't know what you mean?" asked Jack.

"Anything Jack, like girls, whisky, food. "

"I see now, how about cut wood, to burn in the fire place, I noticed the supply running low."

"Your quite something, you know that chip you gave him, completely changed his life, they bought a small ranch, there putting their two eldest daughters into college."

"All that for one hundred thousand?"

"In Cuba that means oh about a million in a half US dollars."

"Good for him." said Jack.

"No good for you, Jack, your kindness, has attracted, many men here, to work the coconut fields, for you. "

On the right side was long house, for Carlos says, "Each room has two beds, and a fire place, on the end is the restrooms, Jack saw row and rows of this long houses, cut into the hillside, they continued down the road, on the left was the coconut trees.

At the end of the road, was the workers, and the villagers.

Jack surveyed, past the open field where they loaded the carts, to take into a large building, Jack followed Carlos, in, to see every aspect of the coconut being used, husks for rope fibers, and some are made into sitting mats, semi-ripe coconut, is made into copra, coconuts are split in half, milk drained, and coconuts roasted, to make a firm maragine, then others are pressed to make cooking oil, and final discards, mixed with lye to make soap.

Jack noticed someone, behind him; he turned to see that they were not there. But Jack, didn't stop there, as he heard Carlos call out his name, as he went outside, to see a man running, Jack sensed something wasn't right, so Jack pulled his weapon to yell, "Stop where your at or I will drop you."

The man ignored him, as Jack shot him in the back of the leg, and the guy fell forward, as bullets began to fly Jack's direction, the building was getting peppered, back inside, Jack went only to hear that the production shut down, only to see, the male workers were heavily armed, and began to open fire at the opposing force. Jack , ducked his head out to see the force coming at them were being chopped up, then all of a sudden, a loud noise was heard, then a rat tat tat, noise and the tree line was getting pelted, as Jack looked up to see Carlos on the heavy machine gun, Jack was on the move, passing the dead as he made his way into the jungle.

Jack was in pursuit, he was hot on the trail of those running away from him, but as they were running from Jack, it was who was with him that was more of a threat, Jack and a force of 40 angry men, well armed. As the last of the running men went down, they all came to a cabin, on the porch stood, a harden dark Italian, looking man, who was stiff in his position, he raised his hands, to say, "Hold on Jack, I'm friendly." he said calmly.

Jack stopped to raise his hands to say, "Hold it".

But it was too late, Davio's body absorbed a multitude of rounds, as his body did a pirouette, and was dead as Davio went down, face up, he was dead, the firing stopped, as Jack went up to him, he knelt, to say,   "Wrong place, wrong time, sorry, but it looks like your trespassing," Jack went inside to see maps and four photos of women, two British agents, and two local nationals, all beautiful women.

Jack pulled down the pictures, to see all the maps, and a clear government cover up scheme,

"But why are they after me? ", as Jack gathered all of that stuff up, to put in a satchel,

Jack heard noises, outside, as he went out to see, the body was gone.   Jack saw some villagers, to see Hopi, Maria's brother to say,

"What happen to the body?"

"Just like the rest of the men, they are all stripped, there belongings are collected up."

"Alright, you need to be aware of two national girls, and two English girls, let me know if you run across them. "

"Are, you in danger? "Asked Hopi.

"I don't think so, nothing I can't handle, but anyway keep your eyes open."

"Well why you're here, you will be protected," said Hopi, as Jack left, down the path, to see a massive pile of bodies, where as Jack was on the phone; he reached Lisa, to say;

"We have a problem, there are counter agents among us all, as Jack pulled up a expensive looking wallet to look inside to say, "We have an agent, who's name is Davio Hernandez, aid to the CIA head chief."

"How did it happen?" exclaimed Lisa.

"He was where he shouldn't have been, and was shot."

"We have your position, we will be there shortly." said Lisa.

Hopi came up running to Jack to say, In and out of breath to say, "A dark looking women shot at me?"

Jack was following Hopi up the path to see it was empty, and all was silent as Lisa said,

"Try to keep her alive."

Jack looks at the phone to pull it up, as he said,

"How did you know?"

"On your phone, has a scent extractor, for which a scent of a women".

"Specifically, she is an agent, and her name is Isabella," said Lisa.

Jack dove out of the way, as the rounds were coming at him and Hopi, who took off, while Jack held his position, although he could not see her, he kept his weapon up, just as helicopters, swooped in.

Jack held his position, know full well, he was missing something, and turned the corner, to see two Helios, one was lifting off, while the three men positioned themselves, Jack ran and holstered his weapon and phone, to leap out and hit the helio's support, and his knees were on the skids, as in a instant it was up, while one guy hung out and fired on Jack. Jack pulled his weapon, he shot the guy head center, as Jack shook the whole helio, as the ocean was all around them, and the turbulence was playing with the helio, not to mention Jack was using his body motion, to disrupt the flight pattern, while the men in the back were shooting at Jack. Jack shot back, however, his rounds, were causing the helio to begin to smoke, stutter, even the pilot, began to shoot at Jack down below, easily going through the glass, Jack absorbed the bullets, as he shot the pilot, as Jack lost his balance, he fell backwards, but realized the helio was going down faster, it hit and sat on the surface as Jack holstered his weapon, and then zipped up his jacket, he realized he might want to pull in his knees and do a cannonball, he hit, and went in, to a huge splash. Jack resurfaced, to see a boat was coming at him, it slowed, for Jack to see weapons were drawn on him, as Jack had his weapon in his hand, and under the water, he pulled it up and four shots later, the men went down. Jack, holstered his weapon, and climbed in. looked around, pulled his gun, and phone to see he missed four calls, he dialed them up to see it was all from Lisa, Jack called her, to hear, "Is there anyway you can help us out."

"Sorry, I just took out a helio, and right now I'm in the ocean, but hold on" said Jack, as he got behind the wheel, and floored the throttle, only to hear gunfire, as he closed up his phone, as he steers his boat to the dock, he tied it off, and was on the move, he reloaded, while on the run, under the highway, along the beach, looked like a blast from the past, men were all over the place fighting, he wished this team was wearing a specific uniform, so he could eliminate the other. Jack pushed on, looking for Lisa, then he saw her, being pulled along, by a soilider, whereas Jack pulled Lisa away from him, with a fist to the stomach, his foot to the knee, to see the guy go down, Jack pulls Lisa away and free, to say, "Go on up the hill."
Jack sees his flashy car pull up, as Jim gets out, exchanges places with Lisa, he closes the door, as Jim comes down to join in the fight, he pulls off a flax jacket to hand to Jack to say,

"This is yours; I filled it with all your clips."

"You wear it, just hand me four clips."
Jim hands Jack his clips, for Jack to say, "Jim can you go up and get my three wives and place them in the car as well."
Jim left, without a response, as Jack was going headhunting, with 70 rounds available, Jack was dropping the stragglers, as men fled, Jack was dropping them, most of the villagers were wounded and down, even Carlos was gone, as Jack went further into the jungle, one by one he was on a mission and to the last man who turned, raised his hands, to say,

"Don't shoot, I'm un-armed."
Jack slowed to see the man had given up, for Jack to say,

"Strip, take off your clothes."

"What are you crazy, out here, what are you gay."

"No, I'm a international Bounty Hunter, prove to me your unarmed, if not I will drill you where you stand, you're my prisoner now, do it or else."

"You can't I surrender.," said the guy adamantly.

"Do you know what country you're in?"

"Yes, were here to get a guy name Jack Cash, a rogue agent gone bad."

"Who do you think I am?"

"I don't know maybe a faggot."

"All of it take it all off."

"Mister, your not going to get away with this."

Jack sees he removes his underwear, to show that he was unarmed, to say, "Now turnaround."

Jack felt around in his windbreaker to a small zipper, to pull out a zip tie, Jack stood behind the guy to say, "Hold out your wrists."

Jack holstered his weapon, to loop up the tie, and zipped up his wrist, to pull him up, as the guy tried to kick Jack, as Jack cracked his knee, to see him topple over, in agony, to scream, you popped my knee you bastard."

Jack used another zip tie, for the guy's mouth, and suppress the tongue, as Jack pushed him down to say, "There is a new law in town, as Jack pulls out his badge to say, "The guy you were running from, is me, my name is Jack Cash", then strikes the man on the temple, with his weapon.

Jack worked his way, back to a road, that he crossed, when his phone rang, it was Lisa, he answered it to say, "Its over, the last man, is hooked up in the jungle, I'm on way out to the road."

"Do you want us to come pick you up?" asked Lisa.

"Yeah, sure, I'll be walking down the road to the airfield" said Jack, as Jack walked the deserted road, he turned to see a car on the side of the road, where, the hood was up.

Jack causouly walked along, and four girls were screaming at each other, as they saw Jack on his approach, Jack finished his call, to put the phone away.

Jack put his gun away, and zip up, to hear, "Try it now."

Jack approached to see how beautiful each of them were, to say, "Having trouble?"

"Yes sir, said the one who was extremely cute, in her broken English, Jack saw the duct tape, wrapped around the radiator hose, to hear the car come alive, for Jack to say,

"I hope you don't have far to go."

"Mister, do you want a ride?"

"Sure" said Jack, as he slid into the back, he adjusted the satchel bag up front. The two of the bigger girls, were on both of his sides, as a blonde was up front and the cute one was driving, as one of the bigger girls flashed her breasts to Jack, Jack felt a needle in his neck, in a poke, Jack instinctly, knew he was going down, he drove his elbow, into her head, snapping her neck back, she slumped forward, as he smashed the pretty English lass in the face, knocking her out, Jack used his boot in a sweeping motion, to kick the blonde in the head, as she went against the window, Jack felt his energy being sapped, he was trying to stay awake, as the car turned onto the airfield, Jack tried the door, but in the meantime, he put his arm around the cute young girl, who was losing her air supply, then Jack let go, and jumped, out, he rolled out of the fast moving car to, only to get up.

The colonel, said to Isabella, "What a fiasco, we lose over a hundred men, not to mention, Davio is dead, break out the tranquizer rifle, have your men flank out and be ready." said a infuriating Colonel, to add;

"What the hell, what are they doing."

"I don't know colonel".

Jack stood, he fumbled for his zipper, his eyes were blurry, nose was running, as he heard "fire."

Jack felt most of the darts, but only one penetrated him, as he slowly let go, to freeze him, while all the other darts hit his badge, and bounced off, as he fell face down.

The colonel yelled, "Get him aboard, lets get out of here, as the colonel saw three girls emerge, from the car, that was off to the right, drowsy, and beaten, for him to say "I think we made a huge mistake."

"Colonel, this man has electrical current running through him, each of our men are getting shocked"

"Ox, your up, go get our man."

Emerged from the cargo plane, a giant stood, 6 foot 9 inches tall and just as strong and wide, turned to say, "Get the plane ready."

Ox went out and to where Jack was, and in one motion, hoisted Jack up and on his broad shoulders, the heat Jack was giving off, was putting a burn along Ox's neck.

Ox trotted to the running plane, got on, as it turned, the ramp went up, and it was off. As it flew over his silver Mercedes.

Lisa stopped the Mercedes, to look out as the huge cargo plane overhead.

Lisa saw her men, swam the area, for her to say, to herself,

"Thank you Mister Jack Cash, Thank you."

Jim showed up to get out to say, "We need to talk."

"I know, Jack needs a support team."

"Yeah, he needs a team of agents that surround around his perimeter"

"I'm way ahead of you, I've been working on it"

Jim looked up at the huge plane, to say, "Did we just miss him?"

"Fraid so, they have him now, can you activate his tracking device, and I'm going to Washington."

"What about the wives?" asked Jim.

"Don't worry; I'll have a whole division of special ops, for them."

Jack lay on the steel flooring to hear arguing, he was still droggy, but was able to pull himself up to a sitting position, only to see the giant, Jack smiled at him, he got up and strikes Jack in the head, as Jack smile faded, as he went un conscious and into a deep sleep.

The End, for now.